CLASSICS OF BRITISH SHORT FICTION
(VOLUME II)

英国短篇小说经典
（下卷）

朱 源　徐华东 / 主编

图书在版编目(CIP)数据

英国短篇小说经典.下卷/朱源，徐华东主编. —北京：北京大学出版社，2019.6
ISBN 978-7-301-30534-8

Ⅰ.①英… Ⅱ.①朱…②徐… Ⅲ.①短篇小说－小说集－英国 Ⅳ.①I561.4

中国版本图书馆CIP数据核字(2019)第096013号

书　　　名	英国短篇小说经典（下卷） YINGGUO DUANPIAN XIAOSHUO JINGDIAN (XIAJUAN)
著作责任者	朱　源　徐华东　主编
责任编辑	李　娜
标准书号	ISBN 978-7-301-30534-8
出版发行	北京大学出版社
地　　　址	北京市海淀区成府路205号　100871
网　　　址	http://www.pup.cn　　新浪微博:@北京大学出版社
电子信箱	345014015@qq.com
电　　　话	邮购部010-62752015　发行部010-62750672　编辑部010-62759634
印　刷　者	天津中印联印务有限公司
经　销　者	新华书店
	720毫米×1020毫米　16开本　20.5印张　376千字 2019年6月第1版　2019年6月第1次印刷
定　　　价	64.00元

未经许可，不得以任何方式复制或抄袭本书之部分或全部内容。
版权所有，侵权必究
举报电话: 010-62752024　电子信箱: fd@pup.pku.edu.cn
图书如有印装质量问题，请与出版部联系，电话: 010-62756370

《英国短篇小说经典》（下卷）

主　编　朱　源　徐华东
副主编　常少华　李春姬　邹德艳
译　者　朱　源　徐华东　常少华　李春姬　邹德艳
　　　　　刘晓晖　张　伟　姚振军　徐　彬　张　雯
　　　　　唐　莹　李雪梅　于　芳　卢晓娟　肖燕洁
　　　　　闫　军

代序

好的短篇小说集就是一座精品博物馆

——呼唤英汉对照版英美短篇小说经典问世

2016年7月,华东师大校园美丽的丽娃湖畔风景宜人,高朋满座,迎来了来自世界近20个国家两百多位知名作家和学者参加的盛会。这是第十四届世界短篇小说大会,也是首次在亚洲召开的、以"短篇小说中的影响与汇合:西方与东方"为主题的大会。这次大会是由世界英语短篇小说研究会组织的,每两年召开一次。中国作家、学者、翻译家更是积极贡献,打破语言障碍,中外交流,其乐融融;华东师大是东道主,上海文化界、文学界做了全面的部署和多方面的配合,会议开得十分成功,也产生了持久的影响。

及至今日,这使我们应然有了一个直接的积极的理由,来谈论一下英美短篇小说在中国的译介。其中由北京大学出版社即将推出的《英国短篇小说经典》和《美国短篇小说经典》,恰好给了我们一个实体文本,让我们有所依凭地讨论一下这个话题。当然啦,这也给了我一点勇气,让我能够借题发挥,不拘一格,坦露一下自己的观点,开启这两部书的序言——犹如拉开一道无形中被遮掩了的序幕。

一

提起短篇小说(short story/fiction, novelette),许多读者可能不以为然,何必小题大做?时下人们都在务长篇,谁还看短篇,写短篇?更何况是外国短篇小说。花花草草、莺莺燕燕,美则美矣,要不是余闲多多,谁还顾得上?其实,短篇小说不像人们所想象的那样"小",更不是小事一桩,不值一提,要是推介一本短篇小说集,也不至于需要特殊的理由吧?

只要说起短篇小说,人们就会以短小精悍作为其审美特征。可篇幅短小也不是短篇小说存在的充足理由,虽然可以说是必要条件。就文学作品的篇幅而言,可以说,长有长的好处,短有短的理由。在中国长篇小说大行其道的今天,许多人只知道长,不知道短,还要说长道短,就不能不令人担忧了。可我既不是击长护短，也不是主张不长不短，而是主张大家了解短，知道长。这就不得不从长说起，从长计议。

其实，长篇小说（novel），在国外往往等同于通俗小说（popular fiction）或消遣小说（light fiction）。走进一家书店或图书馆，最高的一层就是长篇小说的专库，堆满了顶到天花板的书架，排满了大部头的长篇小说。貌似庞然大物，其实光顾者寥寥无几。而靠近底层的短篇小说集、诗集和散文集，当然也有立于经典而不倒的长篇巨著，倒是读者络绎不绝、流连忘返之地。在大饱眼福之后，出来时也要买上一本，免得空手而归。国内的书店正相反，大部分把长篇小说摆在一层显赫的位置，甚至等同于世界名著。其实许多人看也不看，就直接上楼了，寻找他想要的"其他"书籍去了。这难道不发人深思？

这是什么原因呢？

这是因为，在国外许多有识之士看来，短篇小说才是精品，是艺术品，值得仔细挑选和阅读领会。而在国内，则把长篇小说当作文学经典和代表作，作为某一作家成功的象征和试金石，有的甚至作为获奖的必要条件。不错，据说鲁迅先生当年与诺贝尔文学奖失之交臂，就是因为没有长篇。而沈从文因《边城》获得提名，假若他再多活半年，诺贝尔文学奖的桂冠也许就会降临在他的头上。而《边城》，最多是个中篇。其实，许多中篇小说（novelette）和短篇小说可以等同视之，只是容量稍大，情节也不太复杂，写作上并没有太大的差异。英文本身以novelette兼指短篇和中篇，就是这个道理。而fiction，则是所有小说的统称（所谓"虚构性叙事作品"，无论是韵体还是散体），或者狭义地指长篇小说。路遥的代表作诚然是长篇《平凡的世界》，但他的中篇《人生》却是成名作和代表作，较早地拍成电影，在作者生前就获得了承认。至今重读，发现其结构之严谨，人物之生动，主题之深刻，并不逊色于《平凡的世界》。人们也许会说，前者是单一线索，后者则是复线发展，不错，但这不是长篇与中短篇小说区分的关键。

也许按照中国的惯例，对于一个作家而言，短篇只是装饰和点缀——有了长篇而出了名，何愁不能出个人短篇小说集？但这是夹带策略，算不得正途。许多人连短篇也没写好，就写长篇，缺乏训练基础，反倒弄巧成拙。而中篇是成名的敲门砖，进了此门，真正瞄准的目标是长篇。可惜，中篇在中国也不发达，也许在国外也是个另类。几乎很少会有人光顾这个不短不长、"飞短流长"的折中领域。要不就是短篇写长了，长篇写短了。幸而这一"惯例"，并非放之四海而皆准，也非举世所公认。

退一步而言，路遥当年病入膏肓，来日无多，却拒绝治疗，而拼命要一口气写完《平凡的世界》，其理由无非是认为，长篇作品在于贯气，若写作中止，则文气中断,再接续实为不可能。看来,路遥的选择是正确的,他的生命没有白费。相反,被路遥视为导师的柳青,作为关中作家的先辈,却因为"文化大革命",被迫中断了《创业史》的写作。第一部的完成也略显仓促,待到他缓过劲来,重操旧业,全力投入第二部写作,已经晚矣,终于没有完成,留下了千古遗憾。再由此想到,柳青还计划写完互助组写合作社,写完初级社写高级社,再写人民公社,胃口很大,倘若不是好大喜功,也是为长篇所累,终于功败垂成。归根结底,以有限之人生,写无限之长篇,甚至"悠悠万事,唯此为大",悖论一也。

可是话又说回来,古今中外,写长篇小说出名者多,反而是短篇小说,貌似容易,却难出精品,成功者寡。就世界范围而言,从古希腊的奴隶伊索口述的寓言算起,古阿拉伯的《一千零一夜》、意大利的《十日谈》,到了近代,以语言论,唯有英语中的欧·亨利,法语中的莫泊桑,德语中的茨威格,俄语中的契诃夫,独能以短篇名世。此外,斗转星移,虽然名家辈出,集子不断,但若考究起来,在短篇小说领域,至今称为圣手巧匠者,仍然百不一遇,除了天才与时代因素而外,文体、文类自身的因素,民族语言敏感之程度,难道不也应当考虑在内?

本来,语言问题就够复杂的。文体、文类,难道也成为问题?是的。就写作的难度而言,短篇小说不仅不比中长篇小说容易,甚至更难。且听知者言之:

> 短篇小说是一种极具挑战性的文体,不仅需要娴熟高超的叙事技巧、精巧严密的布局,还需要博大的心志和深邃的思想。真正优秀的短篇小说既不允许有叙述上的败笔,更不允许有思想上的平庸,它是技巧与思想完美结合的产物。(《世界上最精彩的小说》,华文出版社,2010年)

诚哉斯言!

这使我想起美国诗人、小说家爱伦·坡的诗论。爱伦·坡认为长诗之不可能,因为诗歌须让人一口气读完,反复回味,才是正品。诗歌之外,散文和短篇,也符合此原理。书画亦然。

我个人觉得,短篇小说犹如美术博物馆里的古典精品,凡·高绘画、罗丹雕塑、青藤花鸟、白石草虫,皆是小幅作品,方寸之间,显示乾坤气象,而一笔之弱败,导致整幅作品成为废品。哪个不是集终生之学养,得一时之观察,苦心经营,心有所悟,形诸笔墨,才能成功?篆刻较之绘画更甚!

长篇之奥妙,或者说其难处,看来首要的在于结构,因为语言与经验的缘故。短篇亦然。短篇之结构,旨在精巧,卒章显志,出人意料,但不宜过于复杂曲折。而长篇之结构,却是要大气浑成,不炫技巧,从头至尾,一气呵成,容不得拖沓、无聊。如此看来,长篇完全符合此原理者,实乃凤毛麟角。就连有些世界名著,例如《战争与和平》,也不是没有缺点,唯其皇皇巨著,山丘起伏,林壑茂盛,能遮丑而已。更有《红楼梦》,总体设计匠心独运,中间难免冗长拖沓,反复修改,年谱错落,细节照应不周,而续书的缘故,更难免有狗尾续貂之嫌。石涛的《搜尽奇峰打草稿》,顾名思义,更是草创之作,观其结构,虽然巨笔浓墨,气势有之,但缺乏小心收拾,不能说是上品。其原因就是,他是从局部起笔绘制全景,这样的画法并不适合长篇,只能用于小品。小说亦然。

观古人之长篇巨著,如《千里江山图》《富春山居图》《清明上河图》,乃是稀世珍品,而有作者如此心胸和丘壑者,如此精道之笔墨者,历代实为罕见。而如今的艺术馆,尤其是现代书画馆,动辄参天巨幅,除了吸引眼球之外,许多技巧未熟,笔墨未精,丘壑未成,却自命出手不凡,巍然高悬厅堂,夺人眼目,让人瞠目,旋即欲逃走。纽约现代艺术馆里,整座墙壁一幅巨画,或整个展示铺地而来,堆满了瓶瓶罐罐,也令人想起我们的长篇小说,一年据说出两千部,有的人几个月就写一部,可观者毕竟少数,多数艺术残缺,思想平庸,如时下的电视剧,摇头摆尾,重复拉长,捉襟见肘,不堪卒读者,不在少数。这不徒是创作态度轻率所致,与作者的艺术观、文学观,想必也有关系。

作为一种体裁,短篇小说古已有之,以中国文学史为例,最早的先秦寓言,可作为它的前身和雏形,只是因主题而设故事,目的在于道德教训或击败论敌,非纯文学之属;而明代冯梦龙书中的短篇,已具有规模和高度,与世俗生活市井文学相表里,有自然主义之风;到了蒲松龄,人鬼莫辨,狐媚成精,精于构思,文笔摇曳,文言短篇遂攀上了高峰。至于民国以降,乃至新文学运动中的白话短篇,也有不少成就,名家虽不为多,也绝非罕有。倒是后来逐渐衰落了,长篇急剧增长了。这二者之间虽无必然联系,但也不是一点关系没有。世风和心态,体制和褒奖,理论和评论,都有关系。

二

回到英美短篇小说的主题上,始觉得也有一些话要说。

英语世界,原是以叙事见长的,别的不论,就连英语诗歌,也是叙事成分较多,精品接连不断。现代长篇小说自笛福始,名家辈出。近世报业发达,狄更斯得以长篇连载;萨克雷之锋利,哈代之老辣,毛姆之博闻,康拉德之深刻,加上爱尔兰、威尔士,便有乔伊斯之意识流,再加上诗人写小说者,便有王尔德、迪伦·托马斯等。长篇小说叙事传统优厚，短篇与散文，也不例外。美国更是后来居上，华盛顿·欧文、霍桑开其端，海明威、莫里森断其后，作家是黑白并举，作品是长短并收，而欧·亨利，乃跻身世界级短篇小说大师之列，与法国之莫泊桑、奥地利之茨威格、俄国之契诃夫，并驾齐驱。不过，相比于英美的经验论和实用主义，法国审美之感观，德国哲思之神秘，在文史方面，尤见其长。近世以来，法国的小说理论，特别是叙事学和符号学，后来居上，独占鳌头，英语小说似乎有点难以招架，至少在理论上给人这种印象。好在西方世界的现代文学理论，从现代主义到后现代主义，乃是一整体现象，作为文学创作和理论批评，甚至艺术观点和潮流，则是交互的整体的影响。

这使得英语小说的选编和出版，独成别致的景观。

既然是英美短篇小说，自然是英美的资料要充足得多，因为那里是原产地。同样，出版的个人选集和综合选集也要多。个人的集子姑且不论，综合性的集子，以《诺顿短篇小说集》为最全，除了《诺顿文学选读》，还有《小说一百篇》，也是重要的选集。还有一些大学文学课教材，也有按国别分类的，基本上是英国短篇小说选，或美国短篇小说选，而一般通识性文学教材，则是按小说、诗歌、散文、戏剧分类，当然也包括短篇小说。其中大部分集子，既有总序也有作者介绍，还有必要的注释，可以说是应有尽有。这为我们国内的选编提供了原材料。另有一部分，是专门供英美学生作教材用的，包括原作欣赏和写作手册，欣赏部分按主题、情节、人物、语言等方面分类，写作部分则有积累资料、选题写作、修改润色等分类，甚至发表推介都有，十分方便。

就我所见，国内的短篇小说选编，大多数直接取材于上述不同的集子，但也有不同的选编目的和方法。一类是原作鉴赏型的，其中多数不分国别，有原文和注释，有的还有思考题。作者介绍，有用英文写的，也有用汉语写的。这类教材，也有按国别分类的，或按写作技巧分类的，例如情节结构、人物性格、象征隐喻、语言风格等。重庆大学出版社出版的《英语短篇小说赏析》，就是这种类型的，全英文的不分国别。南京大学出版社出版的《英美短篇小说》，除了作品本身、阅读资料和思考题是英文的，其他部分都是中文的，这样便于中国学生接受和讨论，除按主题、情节、人物、视角、象征分类之外，还有实验小说，单列一章，附录则有批评术语解释；每一部分，不仅有作者及其创作概况，还有作品赏析与相关评论，是直接针对这篇作品的，甚至还有问题与思考，更有阅读链接，可以说是体制最完备的了。这套书是《英美小说》的修订版，实际上，原先所选内容也全是名副其实的短篇小说，这也可以看出选编者的学术底线。

外研社出版的《英美小说选读》，却是前英后美，长短不分，即有的是短篇小说，有的则是长篇小说的节录，这样混杂的编排，至少在概念上混淆了短篇小说和中长篇小说，应该说是不够严谨的。不过，这个集子除了与选文密切相关的其他内容之外，还有文学术语或文学知识（理论与批评），其中有的是西方文学理论流派观点介绍，有的是对具体作品的分析。可见这个本子的编选的实用目的和学术倾向。

还有一类是英汉双语编撰的英美短篇小说集，例如华文出版社出版的《世界上最精彩的小说》，甚至封面上有"影响一生，感动一生，珍藏一生"的宣传推介语，号称"最美的英文经典"。乍看起来是有点商业化倾向，但实际上却是严格的短篇小说选集，不仅收录的全是小说名家，而且其译文也流畅可读。

本书以中英文对照形式编排，译者均为文学界的知名翻译家和研究专家，不仅原汁原味地呈现了作品的风采，醇美的译文更能帮助我们深刻体会小说的荒诞、诙谐、幽默与真情，感受大师们的艺术功底和写作才华，是广大文学爱好者和英语学习爱好者的必备读物。（《世界上最精彩的小说》，华文出版社，2010年）

阅读这本书的译文，也有这样的感觉，此番说法感觉并不过分。不过，名家并非全是以短篇小说而著名，有的作品长达二三十页，是否仍然算作短篇小说，也值得思考。这好像又回到了何谓短篇小说，它的文体特征和审美特点是什么这样一些根本的问题上来了。

三

该回到我们手头的这两本书上了。

放在读者诸君手头的这两部书，一部是《英国短篇小说经典》，一部是《美国短篇小说经典》，都是英汉对照，而且分为上下卷，可见出编选者的雄心勃勃和内容的丰富全面。两位选编者一位是从事英语语言文学的教授，一位是立足出版界但从未丢弃学问的实业家。他们除了完成自己的本职工作以外，始终在学术研究和出版上谋求发展，而且取得了可喜的成绩。这四卷部头不小的书，就是他们多年心血和努力的见证。大约十二年前，他们就启动了这项浩大的工程，从三千多篇原文中选出一百篇左右，其中大部分是没有翻译的，大约用了三年时间，完成了翻译工作，又继续精选，淘汰掉不满意的，再加上反复的修改，觉得可以出版了，才准备付梓。结果就是现在的七八十篇了。但和同类书籍相比，已经是鸿篇巨制了。

代序　好的短篇小说集就是一座精品博物馆

他们的初衷，是按照《国家英语课程标准》，为大学生和青年人阅读英美文学经典提供食粮，所以这两个本子，只是按照时间顺序选编最好的英语短篇小说，并且提供上佳的译文，并没有其他的条件限制。原文之前有用英文写出的作者介绍和作品提示。原文之后，用英文提供了供讨论和思考的问题，以便于课堂讨论。最后还提供了参考译文。之所以是参考译文，因为短篇小说作家百人百姓，作品面貌各异，语言风格悬殊，是不可能统一的。且不说英国英语和美国英语差异明显，汉语译文也不可能一样。至于如何体现英美语言的差异，并且反映在汉译中，迄今还是一个没有得到充分讨论的问题，也有待于在实践中努力解决。而我在阅读的过程中，看到个别地方还有改动余地的，便不揣冒昧，顺手改了几处，希望能有助于译文质量的提高。

所选的短篇小说，我还是根据个人兴趣抽取看了几篇。英国的短篇小说，看了哈代写英法战争的《1804年的传说》，使我想起哈代的诗剧《列王》，属于重大题材；王尔德写的《没有秘密的斯芬克斯》（讽刺性很强），以及迪伦·托马斯的《真实的故事》（是写一个少女杀人案的，风格凄美）。因为他们三位同时都是诗人，而且代表了英格兰、爱尔兰和威尔士三个区域文化的创作风格和文化底蕴，可以说是有目的地选取。美国的短篇小说，我看了三个不太熟悉的作家，分别是安布罗斯·比尔斯的《枭河桥纪事》（印象深刻，堪称绝唱），斯蒂芬·文森特·波奈特的《巴比伦河畔》（被题材所吸引，但观感比较模糊），还有著名作家梅尔维尔的《小提琴手》，是天才无名声而快乐的主题（结构精巧，寓意深刻）。这几位作家固然是我所感兴趣的，有的是因为熟悉，有的则是因为陌生而感兴趣，多数作品也都是有兴味的，那些随手翻翻而没有阅读或者看了几行就进不去的作品，没有记录下来，也没有留下太深的印象。

我的一个总体印象是，惯于写长篇小说的，要么把短篇作为长篇来写，要么把不能写长篇的资料用来写短篇，而在写法上基本没有什么不同。而不太写长篇的，或者诗人等其他艺术家，他们写的短篇要好看得多，往往有一个特殊的题材和视觉，特别适合写短篇，或者给人以深刻而新颖的印象，令人过目难忘。而专门写短篇的作家，则有自己写短篇的经验和资料，写起来得心应手，令人叫绝，但他们的短篇小说集，也不是篇篇都是精品，写得多了，重复是难免的，所以，真正传世的，值得一看或反复阅读的，还是那几个短篇作品。这便引出了一个话题，也许最好看的短篇小说集子，是集最佳短篇作家的最佳作品的集子。

以下仅举这个集子中的一例，来验证一下自己的感觉。

在《美国短篇小说经典》（上卷）中有介绍安布罗斯·比尔斯的一篇《枭河桥纪事》，我以为可作为代表。安布罗斯·比尔斯（1842—1914）是美国记者、专栏作家、小说家,一生充满传奇色彩。他以苦涩辛辣的风格赢得了"辛辣比尔斯"的绰号。他的代表作是《魔鬼词典》,而战争中的骇人事件则是他写作短篇的焦点。南北战争中他参加了北方部队,战后,在旧金山做报刊编辑。1913年,他只身前往革命中的墨西哥,在那里失踪,死因不明。可以说,他的一生就是一段传奇,而他的《枭河桥纪事》,是其代表作。

《枭河桥纪事》被称为安布罗斯·比尔斯短篇小说中的佳作。故事的主人公佩顿·法科尔是一个南方种植园主,他因企图破坏北方部队在枭河桥上修建铁路而被处以绞刑。犯人临死前的心理活动描写堪称大家手笔,逼真细腻的描写背后又流露出事件的过程和起因,对人性的深刻洞察和战争的残酷的描写互为表里。一开头被吊在桥上的汉子,以及整个桥面的军方布置,被写得惊心动魄又真实可感,着实发人深思:

一个汉子站在北亚拉巴马一座铁路桥上,俯视着桥下20英尺处湍急的河水。他双手反扣,手腕上缚着绳子。另一根绳子紧紧地套在他的脖子上,系在他头顶上方一个结实的木头十字架上,绳头下垂及膝。几块松动的木板铺在支撑铁轨的枕木上,成为汉子和行刑人的落脚之处。行刑人是两个北方军列兵,由一位中士指挥。这位中士如果在地方上,很可能会成为一名负责治安的官员。不远处,在临时搭建的平台上,站着一位身着军阶制服、全副武装的军官。他是个上尉。桥两端各有一位哨兵,站立成"放哨"的姿势,也就是步枪位于左肩前方,枪机抵住横过胸前的前臂——这样的姿势迫使人身体笔直挺立,动作规范却很别扭。看来他们两个无须知道在桥中央发生的事情,只要封锁好横贯桥面直抵两端的木板通道就可以了。

这一段精彩的描写使人想起南斯拉夫电影《桥》的一个镜头,但比那个要震撼人心,因为有一个人即将被处死在桥上。这里的文字略有调整,因为翻译还是要语句松弛,描写从容些,才能阅读顺畅,有思考的余地。

结局可想而知,但仍然给人以思考:

佩顿·法科尔死了。他的尸身(脖子已经断掉),吊在枭河桥的横木下方,缓缓地荡来荡去。

最后,就自己的观察,谈几点短篇小说的写作特点或技术要求,以求教于方家:

1. 短篇的容量有限,要尽快进入主题,引起读者的兴趣。即使描述也要引人入胜，平淡中也要有趣味，有悬念，否则读者会丢弃不读。

2. 结尾要出人意料，或者在逼近必然的结局时，要么不可逆转，要么能做出新的或令人信服的解释，否则读者会有上当的感觉，甚至不再读这个作家的作品了。

3. 虽然短篇的结构也可以多姿多彩，但最好的结构，是简单而又引人入胜的，内涵无限丰富和寓意深刻的。不要把长篇的宏大题材用来写短篇。

4. 因为展开和铺垫的时间和篇幅有限，要流露足够的信息作为暗示和启示的线索，揭示和解释进程与结局的合理性和必然性，所以要惜墨如金。

5. 过分精巧的布置和细密的文笔，虽然称为"匠心独运"，但终会有不自然的感觉。这在长篇中是忌讳，在短篇中尚可容忍，但最好不要重复地犯这种错误。

6. 过于晦涩或深奥的短篇，如同绘画缺少鲜明的调子，灰掉了。这在长篇中可以说是隐藏很深的技巧，在短篇中却是缺乏鲜明的色彩和感觉，使人莫名其妙，失之朦胧。

7. 生活经验的局限，或者艺术观念的单一，表现手法的雷同，都可能限制一个人的短篇小说创作水平和成就。没有就不要写，不要变着法儿写，否则也会让人看出来。

8. 太像小说的短篇，终究不是上品。上品应是富于诗意或像散文的短篇小说，太像小说会流于精巧或耽于说教，虽然诗歌和散文也难免，但毕竟要好一些。戏剧性强也是太像小说的一类，有看点就行。

9. 无论何种艺术作品，大凡是过目难忘的，或有价值的，需有趣、细腻、深刻、博大、奇妙，但不必平分秋色，切忌过犹不及；一滑入精巧、烦琐、古奥、混沌、怪诞，就走入魔道了。短篇小说亦然。

无论如何，读短篇小说要有心情，今日之时代迸发，时间紧迫，长篇固然要潜下心来读，才有收获，即便要读短篇小说，也要平心静气，不可过于草率。心不定，则思不宁，难于入定，何谈收获与感受？

至于短篇小说的翻译，只能有一个大概的认识。首先是废除翻译腔和狭义的忠实观，使其在语言和语气上达到翻译文学的程度。其次，深谙作者的意图和文笔，竭力向译文靠近。再下来，就是一口气译完，不要半途而废。实在不行的，也要反复修改，使其气韵贯通，文采内敛，切忌浮躁和花哨。毕肖人物语言和精于描述，长于叙事，乃是常识性的说法了。

坦率地说，本来是短篇序言，却写得很长，实不足观。好在这两部英国和美国的短篇小说经典，都没有各自的绪论，以序言充绪论，固然难当重任，而序言本身杂糅中外，兼谈艺术，近乎东拉西扯，也非正途。倘若有可观处，倒是编译者和广大读者抬爱了。

但愿大家能够喜欢汉英对照版的英美短篇小说经典,也不枉费了我在这里苦口婆心地发了一番议论。

王宏印(朱墨)

2018年12月22日星期六

于古城长安西外专家楼

前　言

现代意义上的英语短篇小说形成于19世纪。美国作家埃德加·爱伦·坡既是该文学体裁的早期实践者也是理论家。他在1842年为霍桑的第一个短篇小说集《重述的故事》所写的书评中表明了对短篇小说的看法。他将短篇小说界定为"须要在半小时至一二个小时内读完的短篇散文体叙事作品",这样才能保证读者在阅读过程中不受任何干扰,以获得总体效果。短篇小说家还必须有意识地安排每一个细节,以取得某种预设的独一无二的突出效果。其实短篇小说发展的实际情况要复杂得多。其篇幅从500个英语单词到20000个英语单词不等;其形式变化多样,可以聚焦于某个场景、一段经历、一次行动、对某个或几个人物内心的揭示,甚至还可以是离奇的幻想。但相对于长篇小说来讲,短篇小说无论在形式和内容上都保持了其简洁、经济、紧凑、完整的鲜明特征,基本上遵循了"一人一事""一线到底"的情节发展模式,因而才能产生爱伦·坡所谓的强烈的"单一效果"。一篇短篇小说是一件精心构思、精细雕琢的精美艺术品。19世纪前期的英语短篇小说大多还遗留着西方古代传奇故事的痕迹,同时也受当时西方浪漫主义文学思潮的影响,其中的人物、情节类似于中国古代传奇笔记小说中的"志怪""志人",往往是现实生活与鬼怪等超自然力夹杂在一起,强调故事的趣味性与新奇性。19世纪后期至20世纪初的英美文学是以现实主义、自然主义为主流的时代,短篇小说也不例外,注重对人生、社会现实的细致描述与深刻揭露。20世纪以降的英美短篇小说侧重于用心理手法描写人物的内心世界,发掘故事内所暗含的对人性、社会以及自然的批判与思考。

早在18世纪,英国作家笛福、艾迪生、斯梯尔、哥尔德斯密斯就已经开始写短篇故事,刊登在当时开始盛行的期刊上,着重描绘环境气氛与刻画人物。1827年发表的《两个牲畜贩子》一般被英美评论界认为是现代英语短篇小说之祖,作者是苏格兰小说家、诗人瓦尔特·司各特。虽然这一时期的英国短篇小说还多与神秘和超自然元素纠葛在一起,但已经开始注意人物性格刻画和对人性与社会的揭示。狄更斯和哈代皆属于维多利亚时代老派的讲故事高手,前者诙谐幽默,后者阴郁悲怆。自史蒂文森开始,英国短篇小说的风格焕然一新,化陈腐平常为神奇新鲜,充分体现了奇妙构思与文字表述的功效。继而有吉卜林将传统叙事技巧推向了一个新的高度,显示出其故事的复杂性与多样性。威尔斯的短篇小说同他的长篇小说一样,同样显示出他的科幻色彩和对社会问题的忧虑。萨基的短篇小说擅长以别出心裁的情节和气氛讽刺社会的虚伪、冷酷和愚蠢。毛姆的短篇以简洁而富有悬念著称，描述了欧洲人在异域的冲突，也体现了他对人性的洞察。德·拉·梅尔的短篇充满了唯美、理想化的诗意幻象，其复杂程度与阅读难度极具挑战性。康拉德、乔伊斯、伍尔夫、劳伦斯皆为现代主义小说大师。康拉德突显了异域的叙事文体风格，从语言表述到叙事结构都有创新，同时反映了在英国殖民统治背景下人性、种族的冲突。伍尔夫的短篇小说创作于长篇小说写作的间歇，她探寻的是意识的心理本质，认为在生活表象之下才是超越时间的现实，描写当下的精神活动比描写外在行为更加重要。劳伦斯以精炼的措辞、微妙的节奏感，表现了对现代复杂人际关系的困惑。乔伊斯在短篇小说领域同样开一代新风，在独创的印象与象征的框架下，突出了"顿悟"这一现代小说的关键要素。凯瑟琳·曼斯菲尔德专注于短篇，她以敏锐的观察力和对人物心理冲突的描写见长，在内容和形式上对短篇小说作为独立的文学叙事体裁的发展做出了突出贡献。

现代短篇小说在美国的发展尤为迅猛，成绩斐然。其中早期华盛顿·欧文和霍桑的作品充满浪漫、神秘色彩。爱伦·坡只写短篇，其作品结构严谨、恐怖怪异。梅尔维尔的作品已经初显现代人的精神困惑。马克·吐温和布雷特·哈特展现出西部的幽默与写实风格。安布罗斯·比尔斯在其短篇中尝试了现实与梦幻的结合以及意识流叙事手法的运用。亨利·詹姆斯突出心理现实主义，其晦涩、繁复的文体同样体现在其短篇之中。欧·亨利也只写短篇小说，特点是通俗化、程式化、大众化。史蒂芬·克莱恩、西奥多·德莱赛、杰克·伦敦呈现出对现实更逼真、更无奈、不加道德评价的新闻报道式的自然主义风格。薇拉·凯瑟返回到更朴实、传统的叙事风格。司各特·菲茨杰拉德以浪漫理想化的视角观察浮夸、颓废的现实生活。舍伍德·安德森虽然非一流作家，但他对极端闭关狭隘的地方人物的描写影响了福克纳对于美国南方乡土生活的详尽描述，其简明的语言叙事风格也影响了海明威的写作风格。福克纳以揭示美国南方传统的解体与人类命运的主题而闻名，他常以创作短篇开始，继而将其拓展为长篇小说。他认为短篇小说集中的内在形式同长篇小说中的一样，都必须具有内容与结构上的统一性。海明威的经历极富传奇性，他以短篇与长篇小说创作并重，以描写"硬汉"形象与运用简洁、凝练的"冰山"写作原则而著名。以上三位作家虽然风格迥异，对英语现代叙述艺术形式多有创新，但在描述与揭示现代人面对快速发展的现代工业、商品社会所遭遇的困惑与异化感方面多有契合之处。凯瑟琳·波特的南方题材与福克纳相近，但在叙事风格上却保持了经典的传统英语小说形式。另一个美国南方女作家弗兰纳里·奥康纳既凸显了哥特式、怪异的描述风格又揭示出现代人道德沦丧、精神异化的主题。

前言

短篇小说作为现代叙事艺术形式具有很强的国际性,欧美的长篇小说家几乎都涉足此领域,除了英美之外,成就最突出的还包括俄国的果戈理、屠格涅夫、契诃夫、托尔斯泰,法国的梅里美、福楼拜、都德、莫泊桑,德国的霍夫曼,奥地利的卡夫卡等。

本套英国经典短篇小说选编和翻译共分上下两卷,精选了从18世纪至20世纪中叶英国主要短篇小说家的重要作品。体例上包括四个部分:作家作品简介及所选作品简评、正文、思考问题、对正文及简介简评的全译。我们选编和翻译本套书的主要目的有四。其一,为英国短篇小说课以及英国文学课提供一种适宜的教材。短篇小说的完整性和凝练性有利于学生在有限的时间内有效掌握文学的基本特征,也便于教师的授课安排与要求。其二,本套书是严格意义上的全译,这有助于学生透彻理解原文,借鉴译文,进行文学翻译本身的练习。其三,通过阅读完整的原文,使学生亲历英语语言的历时与共时特点,不同的文体特征,丰富独特的表现力,帮助学生提高自己的英语表达能力。其四,帮助学生深层次地了解英美人士的生活习惯、思维方式、情感表现,以及民族心理特征。本套书适用于高年级英语专业本科生与研究生以及较高级阶段的英语学习者。

编选名家作品常留有遗憾。由于版权或是篇幅限制,我们只能割舍少数名家或名作。同时我们也尽量避免重复翻译,努力保证选材的代表性和译文的文学性。文学翻译往往是"费力不讨好"之事,但有志于文学翻译的人却乐在其中。我们虽然在选编与翻译过程中尽心尽力,但其中仍会存在各种问题,希望有关专家与读者批评指正,不吝赐教。

我们要衷心地感谢南开大学外语学院英语系博士生导师、中国文化典籍翻译研究会会长王宏印教授。先生学贯中西、博古通今、治学严谨、著作等身。能够在繁忙的教学和学术研究中,抽出时间为小书作序,令学生后辈感激之至。他的序言引文如小溪流水、娓娓道来、内涵丰富、沁人心脾……同时要特别感谢北京大学出版社的领导和外语编辑部的编辑对本书出版所给予的大力支持和帮助。

主编

2019年2月

目 录

Joseph Conrad (1857—1924) ··· 1
The Lagoon ·· 1
约瑟夫·康拉德（1857—1924）·· 14
潟湖逸事 ·· 14
Il Conde: "Vedi Napoli e poi mori." ·· 25
艾尔伯爵："看到那不勒斯，死而无憾。" ···························· 39

Arthur Conan Doyle (1859—1930) ·· 50
The New Catacomb ·· 50
阿瑟·柯南·道尔（1859—1930）·· 64
新地下墓穴 ·· 64

H. G. Wells (1866—1946) ·· 75
The Stolen Bacillus ··· 75
赫·乔·威尔斯（1866—1946）·· 82
被盗的细菌 ·· 82

James Joyce (1882—1941) ·· 88
Araby ·· 88
詹姆斯·乔伊斯（1882—1941）·· 95
阿拉比 ··· 95
The Boarding House ··· 100
寄宿旅馆 ··· 107
Ivy Day in the Committee Room ··· 112
委员会办公室里的常春藤日 ·· 127

Virginia Woolf (1882—1941)	140
The Mark on the Wall	140
弗吉尼亚·伍尔夫（1882—1941）	148
墙上的斑点	148
The Duchess and the Jeweller	154
公爵夫人与珠宝商	160
Kew Gardens	165
邱园	172
D. H. Lawrence (1885—1930)	177
Rawdon's Roof	178
戴·赫·劳伦斯（1885—1930）	189
罗登的屋顶	190
The Rocking-Horse Winner	199
木马赢家	214
The Shadow in the Rose Garden	227
玫瑰园中的影子	240
Katherine Mansfield (1888—1923)	251
Her First Ball	251
凯瑟琳·曼斯菲尔德（1888—1923）	258
第一次舞会	258
Bliss	264
至 福	277
Joyce Cary (1888—1957)	288
New Women	288
乔伊斯·卡里（1888—1957）	295
新女性	295
Dylan Thomas (1914—1953)	301
The True Story	301
迪伦·托马斯（1914—1953）	305
真实的故事	305

Joseph Conrad
(1857—1924)

Joseph Conrad was born in Poland. His parents were fervent patriots and were exiled by the Czar-Russian government. At the age of ten he was adopted by his kind-hearted uncle after the death of his parents. He went to Marseilles in 1874 and worked on a French merchant ship. In 1878 Conrad joined the English merchant marine and began to learn English. He received promotions and became a British subject in 1886. During his voyages for 20 years, he traveled all over the world and accumulated a rich life experience. Conrad was good at writing sea novels and was called "master of sea novels". Conrad died of a heart attack at the age of 67 at Bishopsbourne near Canterbury.

Throughout the twentieth century *Heart of Darkness* (1902) is famous not only as one of Conrad's greatest achievements but also as a highly symbolic story—the story about Marlow's adventures in the Congo. *Lord Jim* (1900) is about a young English sea man named Jim who breaches his duty because of temporary meanness and cowardness. He is condemned by the public and his own conscience but he finally regains his lost honor upon death. Conrad also wrote many other novels such as *The Nigger of the "Narcissus"* (1897), *Nostromo* (1904), *The Secret Agent* (1907) and *Victory* (1914). Conrad is a master prose stylist. Some of his works have a strain of romanticism, but more importantly he is recognized as an important forerunner of modernist literature. His narrative style and anti-heroic characters have a profound impact on the Modernist movement.

The Lagoon

In the following short story, Conrad allows the hero Arsat to tell his romance on his own. Based on his narration, the readers may know how he and Diamelen fall in love, how they escape and settle on the lagoon, and how much the hero owes to his brother. By using some elements of horror, mystery and prophesy, Conrad fantastically presents the hero's inner truth to us.

The white man, leaning with both arms over the roof of the little house in the stern of the boat, said to the steersmen—

"We will pass the night in Arsat's clearing. It is late."

The Malay only grunted, and went on looking fixedly at the river. The white man rested his chin on his crossed arms and gazed at the wake of the boat. At the end of the straight avenue of forests cut by the intense glitter of the river, the sun appeared unclouded and dazzling, poised low over the water that shone smoothly like a band of metal. The forests, somber and dull, stood motionless and silent on each side of the broad stream. At the foot of big, towering trees, trunkless nipa palms rose from the mud of the bank, in bunches of leaves enormous and heavy, that hung unstirring over the brown swirl of eddies. In the stillness of the air every tree, every leaf, every bough, every tendril of creeper and every petal of minute blossoms seemed to have been bewitched into an immobility perfect and final. Nothing moved on the river but the eight paddles that rose flashing regularly, dipped together with a single splash; while the steersman swept right and left with a periodic and sudden flourish of his blade describing a glinting semicircle above his head. The churned-up water frothed alongside with a confused murmur. And the white man's canoe, advancing upstream in the short-lived disturbance of its own making, seemed to enter the portals of a land from which the very memory of motion had for ever departed.

The white man, turning his back upon the setting sun, looked along the empty and broad expanse of the sea-reach. For the last three miles of its course the wandering, hesitating river, as if enticed irresistibly by the freedom of an open horizon, flows straight into the sea, flows straight to the east—to the east that harbours both light and darkness. Astern of the boat the repeated call of some bird, a cry discordant and feeble, skipped along over the smooth water and lost itself, before it could reach the other shore, in the breathless silence of the world.

The steersman dug his paddle into the stream, and held hard with stiffened arms, his body thrown forward. The water gurgled aloud; and suddenly the long straight reach seemed to pivot on its centre, the forest swung in a semicircle, and the slanting beams of sunset touched the broadside of the canoe with a fiery glow, throwing the slender and distorted shadows of its crew upon the streaked glitter of the river. The white man turned to look ahead. The course of the boat had been altered at right-angles to the stream, and the carved dragon-head of its prow was pointing now at a gap in the fringing bushes of the bank. It glided through, brushing the overhanging twigs, and disappeared from the river like some slim and amphibious creature leaving the water for its lair in the forests.

The narrow creek was like a ditch: tortuous, fabulously deep; filled with gloom under the thin strip of pure and shining blue of the heaven. Immense trees soared up, invisible behind the festooned draperies of creepers. Here and there, near the glistening blackness of the water, a twisted root of some tall tree showed amongst the tracery of small ferns, black and dull, writhing and motionless, like an arrested snake. The short words of the paddlers reverberated loudly between the thick and sombre walls of vegetation. Darkness oozed out from between the trees, through the tangled maze of the creepers, from behind the great fantastic and unstirring leaves; the darkness, mysterious and invincible; the darkness scented and poisonous of impenetrable forests.

The men poled in the shoaling water. The creek broadened, opening out into a wide sweep of a stagnant lagoon. The forests receded from the marshy bank, leaving a level strip of bright green, reedy grass to frame the reflected blueness of the sky. A fleecy pink cloud drifted high above, trailing the delicate colouring of its image under the floating leaves and the silvery blossoms of the lotus. A little house, perched on high piles, appeared black in the distance. Near it, two tall nibong palms, that seemed to have come out of the forests in the background, leaned slightly over the ragged roof, with a suggestion of sad tenderness and care in the droop of their leafy and soaring heads.

The steersman, pointing with his paddle, said, "Arsat is there. I see his canoe fast between the piles."

The polers ran along the sides of the boat glancing over their shoulders at the end of the day's journey. They would have preferred to spend the night somewhere else than on this lagoon of weird aspect and ghostly reputation. Moreover, they disliked Arsat, first as a stranger, and also because he who repairs a ruined house, and dwells in it, proclaims that he is not afraid to live amongst the spirits that haunt the places abandoned by mankind. Such a man can disturb the course of fate by glances or words; while his familiar ghosts are not easy to propitiate by casual wayfarers upon whom they long to wreak the malice of their human master. White men care not for such things, being unbelievers and in league with the Father of Evil, who leads them unharmed through the invisible dangers of this world. To the warnings of the righteous they oppose an offensive pretence of disbelief. What is there to be done?

So they thought, throwing their weight on the end of their long poles. The big canoe glided on swiftly, noiselessly, and smoothly, towards Arsat's clearing, till, in a great rattling of poles thrown down, and the loud murmurs of "Allah be praised!" it came with a gentle knock against the crooked piles below the house.

The boatmen with uplifted faces shouted discordantly, "Arsat! O Arsat!" Nobody came. The white man began to climb the rude ladder giving access to the bamboo platform before the house. The juragan of the boat said sulkily, "We will cook in the sampan, and sleep on the water."

"Pass my blankets and basket," said the white man curtly.

He knelt on the edge of the platform to receive the bundle. Then the boat shoved off, and the white man, standing up, confronted Arsat, who had come out through the low door of his hut. He was a man young, powerful, with a broad chest and muscular arms. He had nothing on but his sarong. His head was bare. His big, soft eyes stared eagerly at the white man, but his voice and demeanour were composed as he asked, without any words of greeting—

"Have you medicine, Tuan?"

"No," said the visitor in a startled tone. "No. Why? Is there sickness in the house?"

"Enter and see," replied Arsat, in the same calm manner, and turning short round, passed again through the small doorway. The white man, dropping his bundles, followed.

In the dim light of the dwelling he made out on a couch of bamboos a woman stretched on her back under a broad sheet of red cotton cloth. She lay still, as if dead; but her big eyes, wide open, glittered in the gloom, staring upwards at the slender rafters, motionless and unseeing. She was in a high fever, and evidently unconscious. Her cheeks were sunk slightly, her lips were partly open, and on the young face there was the ominous and fixed expression—the absorbed, contemplating expression of the unconscious who are going to die. The two men stood looking down at her in silence.

"Has she been long ill?" asked the traveler.

"I have not slept for five nights," answered the Malay, in a deliberate tone. "At first she heard voices calling her from the water and struggled against me who held her. But since the sun of today rose she hears nothing—she hears not me. She sees nothing. She sees not me—me!"

He remained silent for a minute, then asked softly—

"Tuan, will she die?"

"I fear so," said the white man sorrowfully. He had known Arsat years ago, in a far country in times of trouble and danger, when no friendship is to be despised. And since his Malay friend had come unexpectedly to dwell in the hut on the lagoon with a strange woman, he had slept many times there, in his journeys up and down the river. He liked the man who knew how to keep faith in council and how to fight without fear by the side of his white friend. He liked him—not so much perhaps as a man likes his favourite dog—but still he liked him well enough to help and ask no questions, to think sometimes vaguely and hazily in the midst of his own pursuits, about the lonely man and the long-haired woman with audacious face and triumphant eyes, who lived together hidden by the forests—alone and feared.

The white man came out of the hut in time to see the enormous conflagration of sunset put out by the swift and stealthy shadows that, rising like a black and impalpable vapour above the tree-tops, spread over the heaven, extinguishing the crimson glow of floating clouds and the red brilliance of departing daylight. In a few moments all the stars came out above the intense blackness of the earth, and the great lagoon gleaming suddenly with reflected lights resembled an oval batch of night sky flung down into the hopeless and abysmal night of the wilderness. The white man had some supper out of the basket, then collecting a few sticks that lay about the platform, made up a small fire, not for warmth, but for the sake of the smoke, which would keep off the mosquitoes. He wrapped himself in his blankets and sat with his back against the reed wall of the house, smoking thoughtfully.

Arsat came through the doorway with noiseless steps and squatted down by the fire. The white man moved his outstretched legs a little.

"She breathes," said Arsat in a low voice, anticipating the expected question. "She breathes and burns as if with a great fire. She speaks not; she hears not—and burns!"

He paused for a moment, then asked in a quiet, incurious tone—"Tuan…will she die?"

The white man moved his shoulders uneasily, and muttered in a hesitating manner—

"If such is her fate."

"No, Tuan," said Arsat calmly. "If such is my fate. I hear, I see, I wait. I remember…Tuan, do you remember the old days? Do you remember my brother?"

"Yes," said the white man. The Malay rose suddenly and went in. The other, sitting still outside, could hear the voice in the hut. Arsat said: "Hear me! Speak!" His words were succeeded by a complete silence. "O Diamelen!" he cried suddenly. After

5

that cry there was a deep sigh. Arsat came out and sank down again in his old place.

They sat in silence before the fire. There was no sound within the house, there was no sound near them; but far away on the lagoon they could hear the voices of the boatmen ringing fitful and distinct on the calm water. The fire in the bows of the sampan shone faintly in the distance with a hazy red glow. Then it died out. The voices ceased. The land and the water slept invisible, unstirring and mute. It was as though there had been nothing left in the world but the glitter of stars streaming, ceaseless and vain, through the black stillness of the night.

The white man gazed straight before him into the darkness with wide-open eyes. The fear and fascination, the inspiration and the wonder of death—of death near, unavoidable, and unseen, soothed the unrest of his race and stirred the most indistinct, the most intimate of his thoughts. The ever-ready suspicion of evil, the gnawing suspicion that lurks in our hearts, flowed out into the stillness round him—into the stillness profound and dumb, and made it appear untrustworthy and infamous like the placid and impenetrable mask of an unjustifiable violence. In that fleeting and powerful disturbance of his being the earth enfolded in the starlight peace became a shadowy country of inhuman strife, a battle-field of phantoms terrible and charming, august or ignoble, struggling ardently for the possession of our helpless hearts. An unquiet and mysterious country of inextinguishable desires and fears.

A plaintive murmur rose in the night; a murmur saddening and startling, as if the great solitudes of surrounding woods had tried to whisper into his ear the wisdom of their immense and lofty indifference. Sounds hesitating and vague floated in the air round him, shaped themselves slowly into words; and at last flowed on gently in a murmuring stream of soft and monotonous sentences. He stirred like a man waking up and changed his position slightly. Arsat, motionless and shadowy, sitting with bowed head under the stars, was speaking in a low and dreamy tone—

"…for where can we lay down the heaviness of our trouble but in a friend's heart? A man must speak of war and of love. You, Tuan, know what war is, and you have seen me in time of danger seek death as other men seek life! A writing may be lost; a lie may be written; but what the eye has seen is truth and remains in the mind!"

"I remember," said the white man quietly. Arsat went on with mournful composure—

"Therefore I shall speak to you of love. Speak in the night. Speak before both night and love are gone—and the eye of day looks upon my sorrow and my shame;

upon my blackened face; upon my burnt-up heart."

A sigh, short and faint, marked an almost imperceptible pause, and then his words flowed on, without a stir, without a gesture.

"After the time of trouble and war was over and you went away from my country in the pursuit of your desires, which we, men of the islands, cannot understand, I and my brother became again, as we had been before, the sword-bearers of the Ruler. You know we were men of family, belonging to a ruling race, and more fit than any to carry on our right shoulder the emblem of power. And in the time of prosperity Si Dendring showed us favour, as we, in time of sorrow, had showed to him the faithfulness of our courage. It was a time of peace. A time of deer-hunts and cock-fights; of idle talks and foolish squabbles between men whose bellies are full and weapons are rusty. But the sower watched the young rice-shoots grow up without fear, and the traders came and went, departed lean and returned fat into the river of peace. They brought news too. Brought lies and truth mixed together, so that no man knew when to rejoice and when to be sorry. We heard from them about you also. They had seen you here and had seen you there. And I was glad to hear, for I remembered the stirring times, and I always remembered you, Tuan, till the time came when my eyes could see nothing in the past, because they had looked upon the one who is dying there—in the house."

He stopped to exclaim in an intense whisper, "O Mara bahia! O Calamity!" then went on speaking a little louder.

"There's no worse enemy and no better friend than a brother, Tuan, for one brother knows another, and in perfect knowledge is strength for good or evil. I loved my brother. I went to him and told him that I could see nothing but one face, hear nothing but one voice. He told me, 'Open your heart so that she can see what is in it—and wait. Patience is wisdom. Inchi Midah may die or our Ruler may throw off his fear of a woman!'…I waited!…You remember the lady with the veiled face, Tuan, and the fear of our Ruler before her cunning and temper. And if she wanted her servant, what could I do? But I fed the hunger of my heart on short glances and stealthy words. I loitered on the path to the bath-houses in the daytime, and when the sun had fallen behind the forest I crept along the jasmine hedges of the women's courtyard. Unseeing, we spoke to one another through the scent of followers, through the veil of leaves, through the blades of long grass that stood still before out lips; so great was our prudence, so faint was the murmur of our great longing. The time passed swiftly… and there were whispers amongst women—and our enemies watched—my brother was gloomy, and I began to think of killing and of a fierce death… We are of a people who take what they want—like you whites. There is a time when a man should forget loyalty and respect. Might and authority are given to rulers, but to all men is given love and strength and courage. My brother said, 'You shall take her from their midst. We are two who are like one.' And I answered, 'Let it be soon, for I find no warmth in sunlight that does not shine upon her.' Our time came when the Ruler and all the great people went to the mouth of the river to fish by torchlight. There were hundreds of boats, and on the white sand, between the water and the forests, dwellings of leaves were built for the households of the Rajahs. The smoke of cooking-fires was like a blue mist of the evening, and many voices rang in it joyfully. While they were making the boats ready to beat up the fish, my brother came to me and said, 'Tonight!' I looked to my weapons, and when the time came our canoe took its place in the circle of boats carrying the torches. The lights blazed on the water, but behind the boats there was darkness. When the shouting began and the excitement made them like mad we dropped out. The water swallowed our fire, and we floated back to the shore that was dark with only here and there the glimmer of embers. We could hear the talk of slave-girls amongst the sheds. Then we found a place deserted and silent. We waited there. She came. She came running along the shore, rapid and leaving no trace, like a leaf driven by the wind into the sea. My brother said gloomily, 'Go and take her; carry her into our boat.' I lifted her in my arms. She panted. Her heart was beating against my breast. I said, 'I take you from those people. You came to the cry of my heart, but my arms take you into my boat against the will of the great!' 'It is right,' said my brother. 'We are men who take what we want and can hold it against many. We should have taken her in daylight.' I said, 'Let us be off;' for since she was in my boat I began to think of our ruler's many men. 'Yes. Let us be off,' said my brother. 'We are cast out and this boat is our country now—and the sea is our refuge.' He lingered with his foot on the shore, and I entreated him to hasten, for I remembered the strokes of her heart against my breast and thought that two men cannot withstand a hundred. We left, paddling downstream close to the bank; and as we passed by the creek where they were fishing, the great shouting had ceased, but the murmur of voices was loud like the humming of insects flying at noonday. The boats floated, clustered together, in the red light of torches, under a black roof of smoke; and men talked of their sport. Men that boasted, and praised, and jeered—men that would have been our friends in the morning, but on that night were already our enemies. We paddled swiftly past. We had no more friends in the country of our birth.

She sat in the middle of the canoe with covered face; silent as she is now; unseeing as she is now—and I had no regret at what I was leaving because I could hear her breathing close to me—as I can hear her now."

He paused, listened with his ear turned to the doorway, then shook his head and went on.

"My brother wanted to shout the cry of challenge—one cry only—to let the people know we were freeborn robbers who trusted our arms and the great sea. And again I begged him in the name of our love to be silent. Could I not hear her breathing close to me? I knew the pursuit would come quick enough. My brother loved me. He dipped his paddle without a splash. He only said, 'There is half a man in you now—the other half is in that woman. I can wait. When you are a whole man again, you will come back with me here to shout defiance. We are sons of the same mother.' I made no answer. All my strength and all my spirit were in my hands that held the paddle—for I longed to be with her in a safe place beyond the reach of men's anger and of women's spite. My love was so great, that I thought it could guide me to a country where death was unknown, if I could only escape from Inchi Midah's fury and from our Ruler's sword. We paddled with haste, breathing through our teeth. The blades bit deep into the smooth water. We passed out of the river; we flew in clear channels amongst the shallows. We skirted the black coast; we skirted the sand beaches where the sea speaks in whispers to the land; and the gleam of whites and flashed back past our boat, so swiftly she ran upon the water. We spoke not. Only once I said, 'Sleep, Diamelen, for soon you may want all your strength.' I heard the sweetness of her voice, but I never turned my head. The sun rose and still we went on. Water fell from my face like rain from a cloud. We flew in the light and heat. I never looked back, but I knew that my brother's eyes, behind me, were looking steadily ahead, for the boat went as straight as a bushman's dart, when it leaves the end of the sumpitan. There was no better paddler, no better steersman than my brother. Many times, together, we had won races in that canoe. But we never had put out our strength as we did then—then, when for the last time we paddled together! There was no braver or stronger man in our country than my brother. I could not spare the strength to turn my head and look at him, but every moment I heard the hiss of his breath getting louder behind me. Still he did not speak. The sun was high. The heat clung to my back like a flame of fire. My ribs were ready to burst, but I could no longer get enough air into my chest. And then I felt I must cry out with my last breath, 'Let us rest!'…'Good!' he answered; and his voice was firm. He was strong. He was brave. He knew not fear and no fatigue . . . My brother!"

A murmur powerful and gentle, a murmur vast and faint; the murmur of trembling leaves, of stirring boughs, ran through the tangled depths of the forests, ran over the starry smoothness of the lagoon, and the water between the piles lapped the slimy timber once with a sudden splash. A breath of warm air touched the two men's faces and passed on with a mournful sound—a breath loud and short like an uneasy sigh of the dreaming earth.

Arsat went on in an even, low voice.

"We ran our canoe on the white beach of a little bay close to a long tongue of land that seemed to bar our road; a long wooded cape going far into the sea. My brother knew that place. Beyond the cape a river has its entrance, and through the jungle of that land there is a narrow path. We made a fire and cooked rice. Then we lay down to sleep on the soft sand in the shade of our canoe, while she watched. No sooner had I closed my eyes than I heard her cry of alarm. We leaped up. The sun was halfway down the sky already, and coming in sight in the opening of the bay we saw a prau manned by many paddlers. We knew it at once; it was one of our Rajah's praus. They were watching the shore, and saw us. They beat the gong, and turned the head of the prau into the bay. I felt my heart become weak within my breast. Diamelen sat on the sand and covered her face. There was no escape by sea. My brother laughed. He had his gun you had given him, Tuan, before you went away, but there was only a handful of powder. He spoke to me quickly: 'Run with her along the path. I shall keep them back, for they have no firearms, and landing in the face of a man with a gun is certain death for some. Run with her. On the other side of that wood there is a fisherman's house— and a canoe. When I have fired all the shots I will follow. I am a great runner, and before they can come up we shall be gone. I will hold out as long as I can, for she is but a woman—that can neither run nor fight, but she has your heart in her weak hands.' He dropped behind the canoe. The prau was coming. She and I ran, and as we rushed along the path I heard shots. My brother fired—once—twice—and the booming of the gong ceased. There was silence behind us. That neck of land is narrow. Before I heard my brother fire the third shot I saw the shelving shore, and I saw the water again: the mouth of a broad river. We crossed a grassy glade. We ran down to the water. I saw a low hut above the black mud, and a small canoe hauled up. I heard another shot behind me. I thought, "That is his last charge." We rushed down to the canoe; a man came running from the hut, but I leaped on him, and we rolled together in the mud. Then I got up, and he lay still at my feet. I don't know whether I had killed him or not. I and Diamelen pushed the canoe afloat. I heard yells behind me, and I saw my brother run across the glade. Many men were bounding after him, I took her in my arms and threw her into the boat, then leaped in myself. When I looked back I saw that my brother had fallen. He fell and was up again, but the men were closing round him. He shouted, 'I am coming!' The men were close to him. I looked. Many men. Then I looked at her. Tuan, I pushed the canoe! I pushed it into deep water. She was kneeling forward looking at me, and I said, 'Take your paddle,' while I struck the water with mine. Tuan, I heard him cry. I heard him cry my name twice; and I heard voices shouting, 'Kill! Strike!' I never turned back. I heard him calling my name again with a great shriek, as when life is going out together with the voice—and I never turned my head. My own name! ... My brother! Three times he called—but I was not afraid of life. Was she not there in that canoe? And could I not with her find a country where death is forgotten—where death is unknown!"

The white man sat up. Arsat rose and stood, an indistinct and silent figure above the dying embers of the fire. Over the lagoon a mist drifting and low had crept, erasing slowly the glittering images of the stars. And now a great expanse of white vapour covered the land: it flowed cold and grey in the darkness, eddied in noiseless whirls round the tree-trunks and about the platform of the house, which seemed to float upon a restless and impalpable illusion of a sea. Only far away the tops of the trees stood outlined on the twinkle of heaven, like a somber and forbidding shore—a coast deceptive, pitiless and black.

Arsat's voice vibrated loudly in the profound peace.

"I had her there! I had her! To get her I would have faced all mankind. But I had her—and—"

His words went out ringing into the empty distances. He paused, and seemed to listen to them dying away very far—beyond help and beyond recall. Then he said quietly—

"Tuan, I loved my brother."

A breath of wind made him shiver. High above his head, high above the silent sea of mist the drooping leaves of the palms rattled together with a mournful and expiring sound. The white man stretched his legs. His chin rested on his chest, and he murmured sadly without lifting his head—

"We all love our brothers."

Arsat burst out with an intense whispering violence—

"What did I care who died? I wanted peace in my own heart."

He seemed to hear a stir in the house—listened—then stepped in noiselessly. The white man stood up. A breeze was coming in fitful puffs. The stars shone paler as if they had retreated into the frozen depths of immense space. After a chill gust of wind there were a few seconds of perfect calm and absolute silence. Then from behind the black and wavy line of the forests a column of golden light shot up into the heavens and spread over the semi-circle of the eastern horizon. The sun had risen. The mist lifted, broke into drifting patches, vanished into thin flying wreaths; and the unveiled lagoon lay, polished and black, in the heavy shadows at the foot of the wall of trees. A white eagle rose over it with a slanting and ponderous flight, reached the clear sunshine and appeared dazzlingly brilliant for a moment, then soaring higher, became a dark and motionless speck before it vanished into the blue as if it had left the earth for ever. The white man, standing gazing upwards before the doorway, heard in the hut a confused and broken murmur of distracted words ending with a loud groan. Suddenly Arsat stumbled out with outstretched hands, shivered, and stood still for some time with fixed eyes. Then he said—"She burns no more."

Before his face the sun showed its edge above the tree-tops, rising steadily. The breeze freshened; a great brilliance burst upon the lagoon, sparkled on the rippling water. The forests came out of the clear shadows of the morning, became distinct, as if they had rushed nearer—to stop short in a great stir of leaves, of nodding boughs, of swaying branches. In the merciless sunshine the whisper of unconscious life grew louder, speaking in an incomprehensible voice round the dumb darkness of that human sorrow. Arsat's eyes wandered slowly, then stared at the rising sun.

"I can see nothing," he said half aloud to himself.

"There is nothing," said the white man, moving to the edge of the platform and waving his hand to his boat. A shout came faintly over the lagoon and the sampan began to glide towards the abode of the friend of ghosts.

"If you want to come with me, I will wait all the morning," said the white man, looking away upon the water.

"No, Tuan," said Arsat softly. "I shall not eat or sleep in this house, but I must first see my road. Now I can see nothing—see nothing! There is no light and no peace in the world; but there is death—death for many. We were sons of the same mother—and I left him in the midst of enemies; but I am going back now."

He drew a long breath and went on in a dreamy tone.

"In a little while I shall see clear enough to strike—to strike. But she has died, and … now… darkness."

He flung his arms wide open, let them fall along his body, then stood still with unmoved face and stony eyes, staring at the sun. The white man got down into his canoe. The polers ran smartly along the sides of the boat, looking over their shoulders at the beginning of a weary journey. High in the stern, his head muffled up in white rags, the juragan sat moody, letting his paddle trail in the water. The white man, leaning with both arms over the grass roof of the little cabin, looked back at the shining ripple of the boat's wake. Before the sampan passed out of the lagoon into the creek he lifted his eyes. Arsat had not moved. He stood lonely in the searching sunshine; and he looked beyond the great light of a cloudless day into the darkness of a world of illusions.

Questions

1. How much do you know about the white man? In what ways are the stories about him told?
2. How is the story about Arsat and Diamelen told? In what sense do both the hero and heroine suffer the consequence of being together?
3. What qualities do Arsat and his brother share? Point out the sentences that vividly reveal Arsat's sense of guilt for leaving his brother in the midst of enemies.
4. In what ways does the environment provide an appropriate setting for revealing the characters' mental state in this story?
5. Does the title give any indication of the story? Discuss its appropriateness.

约瑟夫·康拉德
（1857—1924）

约瑟夫·康拉德出生在波兰。其父母是热血的波兰爱国者，被沙俄政府流放。10岁时，他在父母死后由好心的舅舅抚养。1874年他前往马赛，在一艘法国商船上工作。1878年，康拉德加入了英国的商船队并开始学习英语。在商船队他得到了提升，并于1886年加入英国籍。在其20年的航海生涯中，康拉德曾周游世界，积累了丰富的海上生活经验。他最擅长写海洋小说，有"海洋小说大师"之称。康拉德因心脏病在坎特伯雷附近的毕晓普伯恩辞世，享年67岁。

小说《黑暗的心》（1902）之所以能够在20世纪成为家喻户晓的名篇不仅仅因为它是康拉德的杰作之一，而且还得益于具有高度象征意义的故事情节——马洛在刚果的历险故事。《吉姆老爷》（1900）讲述了一名英国青年海员吉姆由于一时的怯懦而贪生失职，后受到舆论和良心谴责的故事，但他最终以死亡挽回了丧失的荣誉。康拉德的主要作品还有《水仙号上的黑家伙》（1897）、《诺斯特罗莫》（1904）、《间谍》（1907）、《胜利》（1914）等。康拉德是散文文体大家。虽然他的一些作品带有浪漫主义色彩，但是他在现代主义方面的造诣更为突出，是举世公认的现代主义文学的先驱。他的叙事风格和反英雄式人物对现代主义运动有着深远的影响。

潟湖逸事

在下面的短篇中，康拉德将爱情故事的讲述权交由主人公阿萨特。读者可根据他的讲述了解他和黛安米伦如何坠入爱河，如何私奔到潟湖之上定居，以及阿萨特又是如何亏欠他的哥哥。结合恐怖、迷幻以及预言因素，康拉德成功地展现了人物的内在真实。

白人男子将胳膊搭在船尾小甲板屋的屋檐上，对舵手说：

"天色晚了，我们去阿萨特家的空地上过夜吧！"

马来人咕哝了一声，继续盯着河水发呆。白人男子趴在那里，下巴搁在交叉的胳膊上，目不转睛地看着水面上留下的船迹。河水闪着金光，从树林间穿过，如同笔直的林荫大道。在它的尽头，夕阳低悬在上空，四周没有一丝云彩，宛如一个金属光圈，放射出绚丽的光芒。河岸两旁的树林阴森森的，纹丝不动，沉浸在一片寂静之中。参天大树下，无干的聂帕桐从河岸的淤泥中拔地而起，长得枝繁叶茂，垂挂在棕色的涡流之上，默然无语。每一棵树木，每一片叶子，每一根树枝，每一个葡萄植物的卷须，甚至是小花的每一片花瓣似乎都陶醉于这片万籁俱寂的美妙之中。水面似乎也静止了，只有那八只船桨在整齐地划动着，有节奏地溅出耀眼的水花；每隔一段时间，舵手就会将桨叶高举过头，左右挥舞着，在阳光下画出闪亮的半圆。河水伴着翻转的桨叶，泛起泡沫，发出浑然不清的低语声。白人男子的独木舟向上游前行着，仿佛进入了一个全然静止的世界，让你将所有对运动的记忆都抛之脑后。

白人男子背对着夕阳，眺望着浩瀚而又空旷的近海河段。距海三英里处，原先还漫无目的、踌躇不定的河水像是抵制不住自由、浩渺的大海的召唤，向它直奔而去。它奔向东方，那里蕴含着光明也隐藏着黑暗。船后传来鸟儿重复的鸣叫声。那声音并不悦耳，有些微弱无力，在平静的水面上回荡开来，最终还没等抵达对岸就消逝在这令人窒息的寂静之中了。

舵手把桨浸到水里，用力握紧，身体前倾着。河水潺潺作响，突然，又长又直的近海河段似乎发生了自转，只见两岸的森林出现了180度大转弯。夕阳绚烂的光芒倾洒在独木舟上，船员们的影子变得细长而又扭曲起来，倒映在波光粼粼的水面上。白人男子转过身来，凝视着前方。船的方向已经调整完毕，现在船头雕刻的龙头正冲着河岸边灌木丛的一个缺口前进。独木舟从中滑行而入，擦过低垂的嫩枝，转眼间从河面上消失得无影无踪，就像某种细长的两栖动物突然离开了水面奔向林中的巢穴一样。

河的支流变得像水沟般狭窄，曲曲折折，深不可测。这里阴暗无比，抬头望去，碧蓝的天空只看得见细长的一条。参天大树高耸林立，它们被匍匐植物花彩般重重装饰起来。河水泛着幽暗的微光，附近随处可见被蕨类植物缠绕的树根，黑黝黝的，了无生气，盘绕成一团，一动也不动，宛如一条被捕的大蛇。桨手们短促的喊号声在小河两岸浓郁而阴暗的植物墙间发出巨大的回响。黑暗从四面八方慢慢潜入；从树木之间，从匍匐植物缠结的迷宫中，从纹丝不动的巨叶后面弥散开来。黑暗神秘莫测，势不可挡。在这难以探测的森林之中，它无孔不入，暗藏杀机。

到了浅滩区，船员们开始撑篙而行。水面变得宽阔起来，直通前方宽广、平静的潟湖。森林隐退到了湿软的河岸之后，取而代之的是一排狭长碧绿的芦苇丛将倒映水中的那片蔚蓝的天空围入其中。一朵软软的粉云在天空中漂游，似乎在莲叶和白莲花下追寻自己带着淡淡色彩的倩影。一座架在木桩之上的小屋映入了眼帘，从远处看去，它显得黑漆漆的。房子附近耸立着两棵高大的尼邦棕，仿佛从背后的森林之中探出头来。它们茂密而高耸的树冠斜垂在小屋破烂不堪的屋檐上，流露出一丝忧愁的情愫。

舵手用船桨指着前方叫道："阿萨特在那儿。我看到他拴在木桩间的独木舟了！"

撑船手们从船的两边都跑了过来，前呼后拥地眺望着他们今日旅途的目的地。其实，他们更乐意到别的什么地方过夜，这个潟湖看上去既怪异又可怕，而且素有诡异传闻。除此之外，他们不太喜欢阿萨特这个人。首先是因为他对他们来说很陌生；其次是因为这个人把这里一个破房子修好后住了进去，竟然宣称他并不惧怕出没在人类废弃之地的幽灵们。这样的人瞥瞥眼或动动嘴就能扰乱命运的安排；他所熟悉的幽灵们要是被旅行者们碰巧撞上可不那么容易讨好的，因为他们会不幸成为幽灵们施恶的对象。白人们并不在乎这样的事情，因为他们压根就没什么宗教信仰，甚至还与罪恶之父同盟。正因如此，他们才会安然无恙地躲过隐匿于人世间的种种危险。面对好心人的提醒，他们会不识好歹地假装不相信。还能拿他们怎么办呢？

撑船手们就这样挂着船篙在那儿想着。大独木舟静静地、平稳地向阿萨特的林间空地飞速滑行，直到撑船手们哗啦哗啦地放下撑杆高声念叨"感谢安拉！"，独木舟轻轻地靠上了房子下面的斜木桩。

船夫们仰起头你一声我一声地喊着"阿萨特！阿萨特！"。却没人出来回应。那个白人顺着粗制的梯子爬上了房前的竹木平台。船老大愤愤地说："看来今晚我们得在舢板上做饭，在水上睡觉了。"

"把我的毯子和篮子递上来，"白人简短地说了句。

他跪在平台边把东西接了上来，之后船夫们把船撑走了。白人站起身，刚好碰到阿萨特正从小屋的矮门中走出来。阿萨特年纪尚轻，身强力壮，有着宽厚的胸膛和肌肉发达的双臂。他身上只穿着莎笼布裙，头上没戴帽子。他直直地盯着白人，虽然那双大大的、柔和的眼睛里流露出急切的神情，但言谈举止却很是镇定自若。他没有问候白人，而是直接问了句："先生，带药了吗？"

"没带，"那位造访者惊讶道，"没带，要药品干嘛？屋里有病人吗？"

"进来看看吧，"阿萨特回应道，语气依然那么镇定，说罢飞快地转身进了屋。白人放下手里的东西，跟了进去。

借着屋内昏暗的灯光，白人看到一个女人仰面躺在竹椅上，身上盖着一幅宽大的红棉布，纹丝不动，宛如死去了一般，而她那双大眼睛却睁得大大的，在黑暗中闪闪发亮，直勾勾地盯着棚顶细长的椽子。她正在发高烧，显然已经昏迷了。她的双颊略有些凹陷，双唇半张着，年轻的脸上凝固着一种不祥的神态——那是昏迷病人死前特有的那种凝思默想的表情。两个男人站在那里默默地望着她。

"她病了很久吗？"白人旅行者问道。

"我已经五天五夜没合眼了，"马来人不紧不慢地答道，"刚开始她听到水里有声音在召唤她，竭力想从我怀里挣脱出去。但今天日出后她就什么也听不见了——连我的声音也听不见了。她什么也看不见了——连我也看不见了——我呀！"

他沉默了片刻，然后轻声问道："先生，她会死吗？"

"我担心会这样，"那个白人悲哀地说。多年前在一个遥远的国度他和阿萨特相识。当时那里正值动乱，危机四伏，所以任何友谊都显得尤为珍贵。自从他的这位马来朋友出乎意料地和一个陌生女人住进了潟湖上的这座小屋后，每每旅行路过，他都会去他们俩那儿过夜，他已在那里度过了许多个夜晚。他喜欢这个马来人，因为他懂得如何去信任教会，如何毫无畏惧地和他的白人朋友并肩作战。他喜欢他——虽然程度可能不及狗主人对其爱犬的感情那么深厚——但他对他的好感足以让他去帮助他、信任他。有时当他在为梦想四处奔波的时候，脑中也会隐约浮现这个孤独的男人和他那位长发女人——她的脸上总是流露出一种冒险精神，双眸间焕发着一种得意扬扬的神采——想着他们隐居深林，与世隔绝，令人敬畏。

白人男子从小屋中走了出来，黑暗正贪婪地吞噬着天边火红的晚霞。夜幕降临了，来得悄然而又神速，就像一大块黑色的，觉察不出的水气凌驾于树林的上空，铺天盖地，席卷了整个天际，吞没了天边的彩霞，也遮盖了夕阳灿烂的红光。不一会儿，天空便挂满了星星，大地一片漆黑。夜空下的潟湖也顿然泛起了点点星光，就像是一块椭圆形的夜空从天而降，掉入了这了然无望，深无边际的荒芜之中。白人吃了些篮子里自备的晚餐，然后从平台上拣了些木棍生了一小堆火。他这么做并不是为了取暖，而是想用烟驱赶蚊子。他把自己裹在毯子里，背靠着小屋的芦苇墙，坐在那儿若有所思地抽着烟。

阿萨特一声不响地出来，在火堆旁蹲了下来，白人把伸开的腿挪了挪。

"她还有呼吸，"阿萨特低声说道，"她还在呼吸，烧得像团火。她说不出话，也听不见声音，还烧得那么厉害！"

他顿了顿，然后平静地、漫不经心地问了句：

"先生，她会死吗？"

白人忧心忡忡地耸了耸肩，支支吾吾地低语道：

"如果她命该如此，恐怕会这样。"

"不，先生，"阿萨特平静地说，"如果我的命运如此，我会看得见、听得到，我会等待，我不会忘记……先生，还记得过去那些时光吗？还记得我哥哥吗？"

"记得，"白人答道。马来人忽地起身站了起来，进屋去了。白人还在外面坐着，能听见屋内的说话声。阿萨特说道："听我说话！开开口吧！"接下来便是一阵沉寂，突然他又大喊道："哦，黛安米伦！"随后又重重地叹了口气。阿萨特走了出来，在原来的地方又坐了下来。

他们俩坐在火堆前，沉默不语。屋内一片寂静，屋外他们身边也是如此，但在远处潟湖平静的水面上回荡着船夫们的说话声，断断续续的，清晰可辨。舢板前部的火堆远远地发出若隐若现的红光。之后，火光熄灭了，说话声也停止了。大地和湖水都陷入了沉睡之中，四周一片漆黑，悄然无声。世间的万物宛然都销声匿迹了，只有那闪烁的星光滑过寂静的黑夜，不停地、徒劳地将其光芒倾洒下来。

黑暗之中，白人凝视着远方，眼睛睁得大大的。死亡既令人恐惧又让人向往，既给人鼓舞又让人疑惑。死亡迫近，势不可挡，却又无影无形。这种感受平抚了他那个种族与生俱来的骚动不安，也撩动了他灵魂深处的心弦。隐埋于内心的怀疑感，随时都让人备受折磨。这种怀疑感在他周围的沉寂中慢慢蔓延开来——那是一种深邃而又了无声息的寂静——顿然变得不可信赖，臭名昭著，就像是不正当暴力事件所做的伪装那样虽表面平静却令人难以揣测。他的内心掀起汹涌波涛，眼前沐浴在宁静的星光下的世界变成了一个虚幻的国度，那里是野蛮争斗的世界，是鬼魂厮杀的战场，惨不忍睹，却散发着魔力，威严而又可耻。他们为抢占我们无助的灵魂而殊死拼杀。这是一个动荡不安却神秘莫测的世界，充满了无法遏制的欲望和恐惧。

黑夜之中响起了一阵悲哀的呢喃声，那声音是那么哀伤，那么让人心惊肉跳，就好像周遭林中大片的荒山僻野在他的耳边低语，向他表白无边、庄严的冷漠与睿智。那些支支吾吾、隐隐约约的声音在他周围的空气中飘荡着，之后慢慢地化作词语，最后又轻轻地汇成一串轻柔而又单调的句子。他的身子动了一下，像要睡醒似的，然后又稍稍挪了挪位置。星空下，阿萨特纹丝不动地坐在那儿，耷拉着脑袋。他的身影朦朦胧胧，嘴里梦呓般地咕哝着——

"除了向朋友诉诉苦，还能如何呢？战争和爱情是男人必谈的话题。先生，战争对你来说并不陌生，你也目睹了我在危险面前是如何舍生取义的，不像其他人那样舍义求生！这种事书面写下来的话也许会丢失，也有可能被怀疑是瞎编乱造，但亲眼看到的事情可绝对错不了，那是刻骨铭心的！"

"我全都记得，"白人平静地说道。阿萨特继续以他那镇定而又哀伤的口吻说道——

"因此，我要跟你聊聊爱情，就在这深夜里向你倾诉，趁着黑夜和爱人还没有消逝之前，我得聊一聊它，让白昼去目睹我的痛苦，我的遗憾，我那饱经日晒的脸,还有我那颗破碎的心吧。"

他短叹了口气,声音很轻,几乎察觉不出来,随后又继续往下滔滔不绝地说了起来,连动也不动一下,也没什么手势。

"战乱结束后,为了梦想你离开了我的国家,这对我们这些在岛屿上生活的人来说是不可思议的。我和哥哥又像从前一样担任国王的护剑官。你知道我们是家族体系,受皇族统治,没人比我们更合适捍卫这权利的标志。太平盛世的时候,我们深得斯番鼎的宠爱,这要归功于在危难时期我们的表现让他信服了我们是多么的侠肝义胆。那是个和平年代。人们整天打打猎,斗斗鸡,相互扯扯淡,为鸡毛蒜皮的小事犯傻争吵;他们肚子吃得饱饱的,武器却锈迹斑斑;播种人可以安心地看着幼苗长大;商人们也来来往往地做生意。临走的时候他们几乎两手空空,回到这条和平之河的时候就会带着大包小裹。他们也会带来一些消息,但基本上真假参半,搞得谁也不知道啥时该高兴,啥时该难过。也能从他们那里听到你的消息,他们说在这儿见到你,又在那儿碰到你。我很高兴听到你的消息,因为我无法忘记那些动荡的年月,我一直都记得你,先生,直到有一天我发现我的眼睛看不到过去了,因为它们只停留在那个奄奄一息的人身上——那个还在屋里躺着的人。"

他停了下来,沉重地低喊道:"噢,玛拉,巴西亚!噢,灾难呀!"接着又继续他的讲述,声音抬高了些。

"先生,兄弟会成为你的最致命的敌人,也会是你最挚密的朋友,因为兄弟间彼此都很了解,如果你对对方百分百地了解,那么无论是行善还是施恶,你都拥有了制胜优势。我爱我哥。我去找他,告诉他我满眼只看得见一张脸,满耳只听得进一个声音。他就对我说:'敞开你的心扉,让她看到你的真心——然后等待。耐心等待是明智之举。印赤密塔总有一天会死去,或者等着我们的君主摆脱掉他对女人的恐惧。'……我就这样等着!……先生,还记不记得那个戴面纱的女人,她就是我们君主惧怕的女人,他惧怕她的智慧还有她的脾气。如果她想召唤她的仆人,我怎能拒绝得了?但我也只能快速地瞥她几眼,偷偷地说几句话来满足我内心的欲望。白天我在通往她浴室的路上徘徊;日落西山后,我蹑手蹑脚地沿着女人们庭院的茉莉花丛潜行。我们装作视而不见,透过花香交谈,透过遮蔽的树叶交谈,透过我们唇前静立的草叶交谈。我们特别谨言慎行,非常小声地互诉衷肠。时间飞逝……之后就听到女人们小声地闲言碎语——我们的敌人也警觉起来——我哥忧心忡忡,我想到了杀戮,想到了惨烈地死去……像你们白人一样,我们这个民族也会抢走自己想要的东西。人偶尔也会把忠诚和尊重抛到一边。强权和管辖权归统治者独有,而爱的感觉、力量和勇气是任何人都可以拥有的。我哥说:'你该把她从他们那里带走,我们兄弟俩一条心。'我回答道:

'我们尽快动手吧,因为我发现她的生活里没有阳光没有温暖。'当君主和所有大人物们都到河口夜钓的时候,我们的时机来了。河岸和森林之间的白沙滩上停放了上百只船,他们用树叶为拉扎霍王室一家搭建了临时憩所。炊烟缭绕,宛如弥散于夜间的蓝色迷雾,诸多的欢声笑语响彻其间。当他们备船打鱼的时候,我哥走过来对我说:'就今晚动手!'我留意了一下身上的武器,出发时我们的独木舟夹在火把船的中间行驶。河面上灯光闪耀,但船后却漆黑一片。趁着他们又呼又叫,兴奋得发狂的时候,我们偷偷撤了出来。我们把火把用水熄灭,又漂回岸边。岸上伸手不见五指,只有一些余烬散发出星星点点的光芒。我们听见女奴们在搭建的棚子间闲谈。随后我们找了个僻静之地停靠了下来,在那里等候。她来了,沿着河岸飞奔而来,没有留下一丝痕迹,就像一片树叶被风吹进了海里。我哥担忧地说:'快去迎一下,把她带到船上来。'我过去把她抱了起来,她气喘吁吁的,她的心紧贴着我的前胸,扑扑直跳。我对她说:'我要把你从那些人那儿带走,你应我心灵的呼唤而来,我要用船把你带离此地,违抗那些大人物们!''这就对了,'我哥说道,'我们就是这样的人,追求我们梦想的东西,为了守护它就是得罪再多的人也在所不惜。我们应该在光天化日下就把她带走。'我说:'我们赶紧离开此地吧,'因为自从她上船后,我的脑中就开始浮现君主手下的大批人马前来追杀的情景。'好吧,我们离开这儿,'我哥回应道:'我们已被驱逐出境了。现在这条船就是我们的王国,大海就是我们的避风之所。'他一只脚还在岸上磨蹭,想到胸前她那扑扑的心跳,我恳求哥哥动作快点儿,毕竟我们两个人不是上百个人的对手。我们出发了,沿着河堤顺流而下。当我们经过他们打鱼的河叉的时候,欢呼声已经停止了。但是他们嘈杂的说话声就像午间飞来飞去的虫子一样发出嗡嗡声。在火把的映照下,那些船聚成一团,漂浮在那里,上面浓烟缭绕。大家七嘴八舌地谈论着此次夜钓,相互炫耀着、吹捧着、嘲笑着。如果没有出逃,第二天早上他们还会是我们的朋友;然而在那天晚上,他们已经是我们的敌人了。我们快速地划了过去。从此我们出生的国度里已经不再有任何朋友了。她坐在独木舟的中间,脸上蒙着面纱,像现在一样默不作声,也像现在一样对什么都视而不见。虽然抛下了一切,但我并不后悔,因为我能听到她靠近我时的呼吸声,就像现在这样。"

他停了下来,耳朵朝门口的方向听了听,摇了摇头,又继续往下讲。

"我哥想大喊一声挑衅一下他们,他说喊一声就行,好让那些人知道我们是自由的强盗,靠的是我们手中的武器还有大海。我再次乞求他看在爱的份上不要出声。我还能不能听到她靠近我的呼吸声?我知道追击马上就会到来。我哥是爱我的。他小心地划动着船桨,不让它发出一丝的溅波声。他只说了句:'你现在也就算半个男人,另一半在那个女人那里。我可以等,等你完全变回男人,你会回到这儿跟我一起大喊,向他们挑战的。我们身上流的可是同一母亲的血!'我没作声,因为我全身的力气和精神全都集中在用来划桨的双手上了,一心想尽快找到一个安全之所与她安顿下来,从此远离男人们的愤怒和女人们的侮辱。当时的我爱得如痴如醉,坚信爱的力量能把我引向一个安全的国度,在那里不会遭到灭顶之灾,只要能让我逃过印赤密塔的愤怒和君主的利剑就好。我们咬紧牙关,快速向前划着,桨叶从平静的水面深深地浸入水中。我们划出了那条河,在浅滩清澈的水道中漂流。我们沿着黑暗的海岸前行,沿着沙滩前行。那里的海水向陆地倾诉着,白沙闪烁的光芒飞速地掠过我们的小船与海水交融。我们彼此都默不作声,我只说过一句话:'睡一觉吧,黛安米伦,很快你就会精疲力竭的。'我听到她应了一声,声音甜美而动听。但我从未回头看她一眼。太阳升起来了,我们丝毫没有停歇,汗水从我的脸上流淌下来,仿佛被云中倾盆而下的大雨淋浇了一般。我们头顶烈日,强忍着酷热向前行进。虽然我从未回头,但我感觉得到身后的哥哥沉稳地注视着前方,我们的船就像丛林人用毒矢吹管吹出的飞镖一样笔直地向前划动着。任何桨手或是舵手都不能与我哥媲美,我俩曾驾着这艘独木舟赢得过多次比赛的胜利。但我们从来没像那次逃跑那样拼尽全力——那次出逃是我们兄弟俩最后一次一起划船!我哥是我们国家最勇敢、最坚强的男子汉。我不能浪费任何体力回头看他,但我听得出他的呼吸越来越沉重。他却仍然一言不发。太阳高悬在天空上,我的后背仿佛着了火,肋骨也要累断了,我甚至连正常喘口气的力气也没有了。这时候我觉得必须用最后一口气喊一声'我们休息一下吧……''好吧。'我哥回答道,声音很坚定。他坚强而又勇敢,毫无畏惧也不知疲倦……我的哥哥呀!"

一阵低语声传来,强劲而又温和,向四处弥散开来,依稀可辨。那是震颤的树叶和晃动的树干发出的低鸣。那声音穿越幽深的密林,在星光闪耀、风平浪静的潟湖上回荡开来。木桩间的湖水轻拍了下细木,突然溅起一朵水花。一阵暖风拂面而来,发出一阵哀鸣——那声音洪亮而短促,宛如沉睡大地所发出的一声不安的叹息。

阿萨特继续讲述他的故事,嗓音压得低低的,显得很平和。

"我们把船停靠在一个小海湾的白色沙滩上。小海湾的旁边有一块狭长的陆地伸入海中,仿佛要挡住我们的去路。这是个很长的海角,丛林茂盛,向海里延伸了很远。我哥认识那个地方。在海角的那一边有一条河与大海交汇。海角的密林中有一条狭窄的小路贯穿其中。我们生起了一堆火,煮了些米饭。然后,在独木舟遮蔽的松软的沙滩上,我们俩躺下睡了。她负责给我们放哨。可还没等我合上眼,就听到了她的惊叫声。我们跳了起来。太阳已经西沉了一半,在海湾的入口处一艘大帆船映入眼帘,船上有许多桨手。我们马上认出那是拉扎霍王室的一艘船。他们向海滩上扫视着,之后便发现了我们。锣声四起,他们调转船头驶进海湾。我觉得胸口的心脏都要停止跳动了。黛安米伦坐在沙滩上,用手捂住了脸。从海上逃跑是徒劳的。我哥笑了,他手里有把枪,先生,那还是你临走时送给他的,但是只有少量的弹药。他赶紧对我说:'带她沿着小路快跑。我来拖住他们,他们手里没枪,敢在一个持枪人面前登陆对某些人来说那是必死无疑。赶紧带她跑吧。森林那边有一座渔夫的小屋,还有一艘独木舟,我把弹药打光后就会与你们汇合。我跑得很快,还没等他们追上我们就应该离开了。我尽量把他们拖得久点,因为她是个女人,既跑不快也打不了仗,但她那双脆弱的双手里却攥着你的心。'他跳到独木舟的后面。大帆船划进来了,我和她跑走了。当我们沿着林中小路奔跑的时候,我们听到了枪声。我哥开枪了,一枪——两枪——之后锣声停止了。我们身后寂静下来。那个海角很窄,还没等听到我哥放第三枪,我就看到了倾斜的海岸,接着又看到了水:那是一条大河的出口。我们穿过了一片草地,向水边跑去。我看见黑色的淤泥上立着一座低矮的小屋,还有一只独木舟泊在那里。身后又是一声枪响。我心想:'这是他最后的弹药了。'我们向独木舟飞奔过去。这时一个人从小屋那边冲了过来,我迅速扑向他,我们在烂泥里滚打起来。之后我站了起来,他倒在我的脚边不动了。我也不确定是否把他杀死了。我和黛安米伦把船推下了水。身后传来了尖叫声,我看见我哥正穿过那片草地。他的后面有很多人在穷追不舍。我把她抱上了船,随后也跳了上去。当我再回头看时,我哥已经倒在了地上。他摔倒了,之后又爬了起来,但那些人正把他团团围住。他大喊着:'我来了!'后面的人渐渐向他逼近,我在那儿看着,好多人啊!然后我又看了一眼她,先生,我竟然把船推走了!我把它推进了深水里,她跪在船头看着我。我边划桨边对她说:'把你的桨拿起来。'先生,我听到他在大喊,听到他大喊了两次我的名字。我也听到好多声音在喊'杀死他!揍他!'我不停地向前划着,丝毫没有回头。我听见他又一次尖声高叫了我的名字,那声音如同死前最后一声惨叫——我还是没有转身看上他一眼。我自己的名字!……我的哥哥呀!他喊了我三次——但我已经把一切都置之度外了。她不是还在船上吗?难道我不是要和她一起去追寻新的栖息之所,从而忘掉死亡的阴影、摆脱死亡的威胁吗?"

　　白人男子坐了起来。阿萨特起身站了起来,堆火的余烬映照出他那模糊、沉默的身影。潟湖之上,一团迷雾缓缓弥散开来,低低地,慢慢地把湖面上映射出的闪闪星光吞噬了。一大片白雾铺天盖地笼罩着陆地,黑暗之中感觉冷飕飕的,灰突突的。它绕着树干,围着屋前的平台悄然无声地打着转,就像在波涛汹涌、捉摸不定的大海上漂浮一样。只有远处的树冠在夜空的映衬下依稀可见,它们看上去如同阴森的海岸,令人望而生畏——那是一片布满欺骗、残酷无情、了无光明的海岸。

阿萨特的声音划破了沉寂,响亮地震颤着。

"我得到她了!我得到了!只要能得到她,就是与全人类为敌我也在所不惜。不管怎样我还是得到她了——还有——"

他的话在空旷的远方回荡着。他稍微顿了顿,似乎在倾听那些声音,直到它们逐渐消逝在很远的地方——从此它们变得孤立无援,无法回头。之后他平静地说——

"先生,我爱我哥。"

一阵风袭来,他打了个冷战。低垂的棕榈树叶高耸在他的头上,高耸在那片寂静无声的迷雾上空,震颤作响,听起来凄凄厉厉,奄奄一息。白人舒展了一下双腿。他的头低垂在胸前,忧伤地低语道——

"我们都爱自己的兄弟。"

阿萨特狂暴地咕哝着:

"谁死又如何?我自己心安就行。"

他好像听到屋里有什么响动,听了听,然后轻手轻脚地进屋去了。白人站了起来。阵阵微风吹过,星光暗淡了许多,仿佛星星们要隐匿到浩瀚无际的宇宙深处。一阵冷风吹过,万籁俱寂。数秒之后,原本黑漆漆、如波状起伏的树林后面射出一束金光,直冲云天,照亮了东方的半边天。太阳已经出来了。迷雾褪去了,先是散成片片碎块,飘在空中,之后化作薄薄的花环似的圆圈,无影无踪。卸去迷雾的泻湖在沿岸树丛浓荫的遮蔽下锃锃发亮,显得黝黑黝黑的。一只白头鹰在它的上空倾斜着缓缓翱翔,在明媚的阳光照耀下显得光辉灿烂。过了一会儿,它又展翅高飞,逐渐变成一个静止的黑点,最终消失在蓝天之中,仿佛永远离开了地球。白人站在门前凝望着天空,忽然听到小屋里传出一连串的胡言乱语,它们语无伦次、结结巴巴,最后是一声重重的呻吟。突然,阿萨特伸着双手跌跌撞撞地出来了。他浑身颤抖着,两眼发直,呆站在那里。过了一会儿,他说:"她不再烧了。"

太阳在树顶上微微探出点儿头来,平稳地向上攀升着。灿烂的阳光普照着泻湖,湖面上微波荡漾,熠熠生辉。林中树木卸去了清晨浓郁的阴影,变得清晰可见,仿佛猛然冲到你的面前又戛然而止,弄得树叶、弯曲的树干还有摇曳的树枝都骚动不已。在烈日骄阳下,昏迷者的低语声越来越大了。那声音含混难懂,在悲痛者孤寂的心灵深处萦绕着。阿萨特眼睛漫无目的地看着四周,之后便一动不动地盯着朝阳。

"我什么也看不见,"他低声自语。

"根本就没什么可看的,"白人说着走到平台边,向自己的船挥了挥手。泻湖那边隐隐传来一声喊,舢板向幽灵朋友这边划来。

"如果愿意跟我一起走的话,我会等你一上午。"白人说道,眼睛注视着湖水。

"不,先生,"阿萨特轻声说,"在这所房子里,我可以不吃、不睡,但我必须得先弄清路在何方。现在我什么也看不见——看不见任何东西!这个世界没有光明,也没有安宁可言;但却有死亡——这是许多人都必须面对的现实。我们可是同胞兄弟——而我却见死不救,我现在要回去了。"

他长吸了一口气,梦呓般地继续说道:"用不了多久我就能看清奋斗的方向——奋斗,而她却死了,现在……我眼前一片漆黑。"

他展开双臂,然后又放下,一动不动地站在那里,面无表情,两眼直勾勾地盯着太阳。白人上了船。撑船手们轻快地从船的两侧凑上前来,前呼后拥地看着他们疲惫之旅的起点。在高高的船尾,船老大头裹、白布闷闷不乐地坐着,船桨拖在水里。白人将双臂放在船舱的草顶上,回头望着船驶过的尾波泛起的一串串闪闪发亮的涟漪。直到舢板划出潟湖驶向河道的那一刻他才抬起头来。阿萨特仍旧一动不动地站在那里,形单影只地站在炎炎烈日下;他的视线跨越晴朗白昼的绚烂而投向虚幻世界的黑暗。

Il Conde: "Vedi Napoli e poi mori."

The following short story "Il Conde" written in the first person narration tells about an old Count who lives in Naples for his health and for the rest of his life, and who is then robbed by an Italian young man. Naples is the best place for people affected by rheumatic disease, and the old Count who also suffers from the disease comes here. The Count is convinced that if he leaves Naples he will die. Threatened by such an accident, the always kind-hearted Count could only choose to leave and walk into the shadow of death.

The first time we got into conversation was in the National Museum in Naples, in the rooms on the ground floor containing the famous collection of bronzes from Herculaneum and Pompeii: that marvelous legacy of antique art whose delicate perfection has been preserved for us by the catastrophic fury of a volcano.

He addressed me first, over the celebrated Resting Hermes which we had been looking at side by side. He said the right things about that wholly admirable piece. Nothing profound. His taste was natural rather than cultivated. He had obviously seen many fine things in his life and appreciated them; but he had no jargon of a dilettante or the connoisseur. A hateful tribe. He spoke like a fairly intelligent man of the world, a perfectly unaffected gentleman.

We had known each other by sight for some few days past. Staying in the same hotel—good, but not extravagantly up to date—I had noticed him in the vestibule going in and out. I judged he was an old and valued client. The bow of the hotelkeeper was cordial in its deference, and he acknowledged it with familiar courtesy. For the servants he was Il Conde. There was some squabble over a man's parasol—yellow silk with white lining sort of thing—the waiters had discovered abandoned outside the dining-room door. Our gold-laced doorkeeper recognized it and I heard him directing one of the lift boys to run after Il Conde with it. Perhaps he was the only Count staying in the hotel, or perhaps he had the distinction of being *the* Count *par excellence*, conferred upon him because of his tried fidelity to the house.

Having conversed at the Museo—(and by the by he had expressed his dislike of the busts and statues of Roman emperors in the gallery of marbles: their faces were too vigorous, too pronounced for him)—having conversed already in the morning I did not think I was intruding when in the evening, finding the dining room very full, I proposed to share his little table. Judging by the quiet urbanity of his consent he did not think so either. His smile was very attractive.

He dined in an evening waistcoat and a "smoking" (he called it so) with a black tie. All this of very good cut, not new—just as these things should be. He was, morning or evening, very correct in his dress. I have no doubt his whole existence had been correct, well ordered, and conventional, undisturbed by startling events. His white hair brushed upwards off a lofty forehead gave him the air of an idealist, of an imaginative man. His white moustache, heavy but carefully trimmed and arranged, was not unpleasantly tinted a golden yellow in the middle. The faint scent of some very good perfume, and of good cigars (that last an odor quite remarkable to come upon in Italy) reached me across the table. It was in his eyes that his age showed most. They were a little weary with creased eyelids. He must have been sixty or a couple of years more. And he was communicative. I would not go so far as to call it garrulous—but distinctly communicative.

He had tried various climates, of Abbazia, of the Riviera, of other places, too, he told me, but the only one which suited him was the climate of the Gulf of Naples. The ancient Romans, who, he pointed out to me, were men expert in the art of living, knew very well what they were doing when they built their villas on these shores, in Baiae, in Vico, in Capri. They came down to this seaside to get health, bringing with them their trains of mimes and flute-players to amuse their leisure. He thought it extremely probable that the Romans of the higher classes were specially predisposed to painful rheumatic affections.

This was the only personal opinion I heard him express. It was based on no special erudition. He knew no more of the Romans than an average informed man of the world is expected to know. He argued from personal experience. He had suffered himself from a painful and dangerous rheumatic affection till he found relief in this particular spot of Southern Europe.

This was three years ago, and ever since he had taken up his quarters on the shores of the gulf, either in one of the hotels in Sorrento or hiring a small villa in Capri. He had a piano, a few books; picked up transient acquaintances of a day, week, or month in the stream of travelers from all Europe. One can imagine him going out for his walks in the streets and lanes, becoming known to beggars, shopkeepers, children, country people; talking amiably over the walls to the *contadini*—and coming back to his rooms or his villa to sit before the piano, with his white hair brushed up and his thick orderly moustache, "to make a little music for myself." And, of course, for a change there was Naples near by—life, movement, animation, opera. A little amusement, as he said, is necessary for health. Mimes and flute-players, in fact. Only, unlike the magnates of ancient Rome, he had no affairs of the city to call him away from these moderate delights. He had no affairs at all. Probably he had never had any grave affairs to attend to in his life. It was a kindly existence, with its joys and sorrows regulated by the course of Nature—marriages, births, deaths—ruled by the prescribed usages of good society and protected by the State.

He was a widower; but in the months of July and August he ventured to cross the Alps for six weeks on a visit to his married daughter. He told me her name. It was that of a very aristocratic family. She had a castle—in Bohemia, I think. That is as near as I ever came to ascertaining his nationality. His own name, strangely enough, he never mentioned. Perhaps he thought I had seen it on the published list. Truth to say, I never looked. At any rate, he was a good European—he spoke four languages to my certain knowledge—and a man of fortune. Not of great fortune evidently and appropriately. I imagine that to be extremely rich would have appeared to him improper, outré—too blatant altogether. And obviously, too, the fortune was not of his making. The making of a fortune cannot be achieved without some roughness. It is a matter of temperament. His nature was too kindly for strife. In the course of conversation he mentioned his estate quite by the way, in reference to that painful and alarming rheumatic affection. One year, staying incautiously beyond the Alps as late as the middle of September, he had been laid up for three months in that lonely country house with no one but his valet and the caretaking couple to attend to him. Because, as he expressed it, he "kept no establishment there." He had only gone for a couple of days to confer with his land agent. He promised himself never to be so imprudent in the future. The first weeks of September would find him on the shores of his beloved gulf.

Sometimes in traveling one comes upon such lonely men, whose only business is to wait for the unavoidable. Deaths and marriages have made a solitude round them, and one really cannot blame their endeavors to make the waiting as easy as possible. As he remarked to me, "At my time of life freedom from physical pain is a very important matter."

It must not be imagined that he was a wearisome hypochondriac. He was really much too well bred to be a nuisance. He had an eye for the small weaknesses of humanity. But it was a good-natured eye. He made a restful, easy, pleasant companion for the hours between dinner and bedtime. We spent three evenings together, and then I had to leave Naples in a hurry to look after a friend who had fallen seriously ill in Taormina. Having nothing to do, *Il Conde* came to see me off at the station. I was somewhat upset, and his idleness was always ready to take a kindly form. He was by no means an indolent man.

He went along the train peering into the carriages for a good seat for me, and then remained talking from below. He declared he would miss me that evening very much and announced his intention of going after dinner to listen to the band in the public garden, the Villa Nazionale. He would amuse himself by hearing excellent music and looking at the best society. There would be a lot of people, as usual.

I seem to see him yet—his raised face with a friendly smile under the thick moustaches, and his kind fatigued eyes. As the train began to move, he addressed me in two languages: first in French saying, "*Bon voyage*"; then, in his very good, somewhat emphatic English, encouragingly, because he could see my concern: "All will—be—well—yet!"

My friend's illness having taken a decidedly favorable turn, I returned to Naples on the tenth day. I cannot say I had given much thought to *Il Conde* during my absence, but entering the dining-room I looked for him in his habitual place. I had an idea he might have gone back to Sorrento to his piano and his books and his fishing. He was great friends with all the boatmen, and fished a good deal with lines from a boat. But I made out his white head in the crowd of heads, and even from a distance noticed something unusual in his attitude. Instead of sitting erect, gazing all round with alert urbanity, he drooped over his plate. I stood opposite him for some time before he looked up, a little wildly, if such a strong word can be used in connection with his correct appearance.

"Ah, my dear sir! Is it you?" he greeted me. "I hope all is well."

He was very nice about my friend. Indeed he was always nice, with the niceness of people whose hearts are genuinely humane. But this time it cost him an effort. His attempts at general conversation broke down into dullness. It occurred to me he might have been indisposed. But before I could frame the inquiry he muttered:

"You find me here very sad."

"I am sorry for that," I said. "You haven't had bad news, I hope?"

It was very kind of me to take an interest. No. It was not that. No bad news, thank

God. And he became very still as if holding his breath. Then, leaning forward a little, and in an odd tone of awed embarrassment, he took me into his confidence.

"The truth is that I have had a very—a very—how shall I say?—abominable adventure happen to me."

The energy of the epithet was sufficiently startling in that man of moderate feelings and toned-down vocabulary. The word unpleasant I should have thought would have fitted amply the worst experience likely to befall a man of his stamp. And an adventure, too. Incredible! But it is in human nature to believe the worst; and I confess I eyed him stealthily, wondering what he had been up to. In a moment, however, my unworthy suspicions vanished. There was a fundamental refinement of nature about the man which made me dismiss all idea of some more or less disreputable scrape.

"It is very serious. Very serious." He went on nervously. "I will tell you after dinner, if you will allow me."

I expressed my perfect acquiescence by a little bow, nothing more. I wished him to understand that I was not likely to hold him to that offer, if he thought better of it. We talked of indifferent things, but with a sense of difficulty quite unlike our former easy, gossipy intercourse. The hand raising a piece of bread to his lips, I noticed, trembled slightly. This symptom, in regard to my reading of the man, was no less than startling.

In the smoking room he did not hang back at all. Directly we had taken our usual seats he leaned sideways over the arm of his chair and looked straight into my eyes earnestly.

"You remember," he began, "that day you went away? I told you then I would go to the Villa Nazionale to hear some music in the evening."

I remembered. His handsome old face, so fresh for his age, unmarked by any trying experience, appeared haggard for an instant. It was like the passing of a shadow. Returning his steadfast gaze, I took a sip of my black coffee. He was very systematically minute in his narrative, simply in order, I think, not to let his excitement get the better of him.

After leaving the railway station, he had an ice, and read the paper in a café. Then he went back to the hotel, dressed for dinner and dined with a good appetite. After dinner he lingered in the hall (there were chairs and tables there) smoking his cigar; talked to the little girl of the Primo Tenore of the San Carlo theatre, and exchanged a few words with that "amiable lady," the wife of the Primo Tenore. There was no performance that evening, and these people were going to the Villa also. They went out of the hotel. Very well.

At the moment of following their example—it was half-past nine already—he remembered he had a rather large sum of money in his pocket-book. He entered, therefore, the office and deposited the greater part of it with the book-keeper of the hotel. This done, he took a *carozella* and drove to the sea-shore. He got out of the cab and entered the Villa on foot from the Largo di Vittoria end.

He stared at me very hard. And I understood then how really impressionable he was. Every small fact and event of that evening stood out in his memory as if endowed with mystic significance. If he did not mention to me the color of the pony which drew the *carozella*, and the aspect of the man who drove, it was a mere oversight arising from his agitation, which he repressed manfully.

He had then entered the Villa Nazionale from the Largo di Vittoria end. The Villa Nazionale is a public pleasure-ground laid out in grass plots, bushes, and flower-beds between the houses of the Riviera di Chiaja and the waters of the bay. Alleys of trees, more or less parallel, stretch its whole length—which is considerable. On the Riviera di Chiaja side the electric tramcars run close to the railings. Between the garden and the sea is the fashionable drive, a broad road bordered by a low wall, beyond which the Mediterranean splashes with gentle murmurs when the weather is fine.

As life goes on late in the night at Naples, the broad drive was all astir with a brilliant swarm of carriage lamps moving in pairs, some creeping slowly, others running rapidly under the thin, motionless line of electric lamps defining the shore. And a brilliant swarm of stars hung above the land humming with voices, piled up with houses, glittering with lights—and over the silent flat shadows of the sea.

The gardens themselves are not very well lit. Our friend went forward in the warm gloom, with his eyes fixed upon a distant luminous region extending nearly across the whole width of the Villa, as if the air had glowed there with its own cold, bluish and dazzling light. This magic spot, behind the black trunks of trees and masses of inky foliage, breathed out sweet sounds mingled with bursts of brassy roar, sudden clashes of metal, and grave, vibrating thuds.

As he walked on, all these noises combined together into a piece of elaborate music whose harmonious phrases came persuasively through a great disorderly murmur of voices and shuffling of feet on the gravel of that open space. An enormous crowd immersed in the electric light, as if in a bath of some radiant and tenuous fluid shed upon their heads by luminous globes, drifted in hundreds round the band. Hundreds more sat on chairs in more or less concentric circles, receiving unflinchingly the great waves of sonority that ebbed out into the darkness. The Count penetrated the throng, drifted with it in tranquil enjoyment, listening and looking at the faces. All people of good society: mothers with their daughters, parents and children, young men and young women all talking, smiling, nodding to each other. Very many pretty faces, and very many pretty toilettes. There was, of course, a quantity of diverse types: showy old fellows with white mustaches, fat men, thin men, officers in uniform; but what predominated, he told me, was the South Italian type of young man, with a colorless, clear complexion, red lips, jet-black little mustache and liquid black eyes so wonderfully effective in leering or scowling.

Withdrawing from the throng, the Count shared a little table in front of the café with a young man of just such a type. Our friend had some lemonade. The young man was sitting moodily before an empty glass. He looked up once, and then looked down again. He also tilted his hat forward. Like this—

The Count made the gesture of a man pulling his hat down over his brow, and went on.

"I think to myself: He is sad, something is wrong with him, young men have their troubles. I take no notice of him, of course. I pay for my lemonade, and go away."

Strolling about in the neighborhood of the band, the Count thinks he saw twice that young man wandering alone in the crowd. Once their eyes met. It must have been the same young man, but there were so many there of that type that he could not be certain. Moreover, he was not very much concerned except in so far that he had been struck by the marked, peevish discontent of that face.

Presently, tired of the feeling of confinement one experiences in a crowd, the Count edged away from the band. An alley, very somber by contrast, presented itself invitingly with its promise of solitude and coolness. He entered it, walking slowly on till the sound of the orchestra became distinctly deadened. Then he walked back and turned about once more. He did this several times before he noticed that there was somebody occupying one of the benches.

The spot being midway between two lamp posts the light was faint.

The man lolled back in the corner of the seat, his legs stretched out, his arms folded and his head drooping on his breast. He never stirred, as though he had fallen asleep there, but when the Count passed by again he had changed his attitude. He sat leaning forward. His elbows were propped on his knees, and his hands were rolling a cigarette. He never looked up from that occupation.

The Count continued his stroll away from the band. He returned slowly, he said. I can imagine him enjoying to the full, but with his usual tranquility, the balminess of this southern night and the sounds of music softened delightfully by the distance.

Presently, he approached for the third time the man on the garden seat, still leaning forward with his elbows on his knees. It was a dejected pose. In the semi obscurity of the alley his high shirt collar and his cuffs made small patches of vivid whiteness. The Count said that he just noticed him getting up brusquely as if to walk away, but almost before he was aware of it the man stood before him asking in a low, gentle tone whether the signor would have the kindness to oblige him with a light.

The Count answered this request by a polite "Certainly," and dropped his hands with the intention of exploring both pockets of his trousers for the matches.

"I dropped my hands," he said, "but I never put them in my pockets. I felt a pressure there—"

He put the tip of his finger on a spot close under his breastbone, the very spot of the human body where a Japanese gentleman begins the operation of the hara-kiri, which is a form of suicide following upon dishonor, upon an intolerable outrage to the delicacy of one's feelings.

"I glance down," he continued in an awe-struck voice, "and what do I see? A knife! A long knife—"

"You don't mean to say," I exclaimed amazed, "that you were held up like this in the Villa at half-past ten o'clock, within a stone's throw of a thousand people!"

He nodded several times, staring at me with all his might.

"The clarinet," he declared solemnly, "was finishing its solo, and I assure you I could hear every note. Then the band crashed *fortissimo*, and that creature rolled its eyes and gnashed its teeth hissing at me with the greatest ferocity, 'Be silent! No noise or—'"

I could not get over my astonishment.

"What sort of knife was it?" I asked, stupidly.

"A long blade. A stiletto—perhaps a kitchen knife. A long narrow blade. It gleamed. And his eyes gleamed. His white teeth, too. I could see them. He was very ferocious. I thought to myself: 'If I hit him he will kill me.' How could I fight with him? He had the knife and I had nothing. I am nearly seventy, you know, and that was a young man. I seemed even to recognize him. The moody young man of the café. The young man I met in the crowd. But I could not tell. There are so many like him in this country."

The distress of that moment was reflected in his face. I should think that physically he must have been paralyzed by surprise. His thoughts, however, remained extremely active. They ranged over every alarming possibility. The idea of setting up a vigorous shouting occurred to him too. But he did nothing of the kind, and the reason why he refrained gave me a good opinion of his mental self-possession. He saw in a flash that nothing prevented the other from shouting, too.

"This young man might in an instant have thrown away his knife and pretended I was the aggressor. Why not? He might have said I attacked him. Why not? It was one incredible story against another! He might have said anything—bring some dishonoring charge against me—what do I know? By his dress he was no common robber. He seemed to belong to the better classes. What could I say? He was an Italian—I am a foreigner. Of course, I have a passport, and there is our consul—but to be arrested, dragged at night to the police office like a criminal!"

He shuddered. It was in his character to shrink from scandal, much more than from mere death. And certainly for many people this would have always remained—considering certain peculiarities of Neapolitan manners—a deucedly queer story. The Count was no fool. His belief in the respectable placidity of life having received this rude shock, he thought that now anything might happen. But also a notion came into his head that this young man was perhaps merely an infuriated lunatic.

This was for me the first hint of his attitude towards this adventure. In his exaggerated delicacy of sentiment he felt that nobody's self-esteem need be affected by what a madman may choose to do to one. It became apparent, however, that the Count was to be denied that consolation. He enlarged upon the abominably savage way in which that young man rolled his glistening eyes and gnashed his white teeth. The band was going now through a slow movement of solemn braying by all the trombones, with deliberately repeated bangs of the big drum.

"But what did you do?" I asked, greatly excited.

"Nothing," answered the Count. "I let my hands hang down very still. I told him quietly I did not intend making a noise. He snarled like a dog, then said in an ordinary voice:

'*Vostro portofolio.*'"

"So I naturally," continued the Count—and from this point acted the whole thing in pantomime. Holding me with his eyes, he went through all the motions of reaching into his inside breast pocket, taking out the pocket book and handing it over. But that young man, still bearing steadily on the knife, refused to touch it.

He directed the Count to take the money out himself, received it into his left hand, motioned the pocket-book to be returned to the pocket, all this being done to the thrilling of flutes and clarinets sustained by the emotional drone of the hautboys. And the "young man," as the Count called him, said: "This seems very little."

"It was, indeed, only 340 or 360 lire," the Count pursued. "I had left my money in the hotel, as you know. I told him this was all I had on me. He shook his head impatiently and said:

'*Vostro orologio.*'"

The Count gave me the dumb show of pulling out the watch, detaching it. But, as it happened, the valuable gold half-chronometer he possessed had been left at a watchmaker's for cleaning. He wore that evening (on a leather guard) the Waterbury fifty-franc thing he used to take with him on his fishing expeditions. Perceiving the nature of this booty, the well-dressed robber made a contemptuous clicking sound with his tongue like this, "Tse-Ah!" and waved it away hastily. Then, as the Count was returning the disdained object to his pocket, he demanded with a threateningly increased pressure of the knife on the epigastrium, by way of reminder:

"*Vostri anelli.*"

"One of the rings," went on the Count, "was given me many years ago by my wife; the other is the signet ring of my father. I said, 'No. That you shall not have!'"

Here the Count reproduced the gesture corresponding to that declaration by clapping one hand upon the other, and pressing both thus against his chest. It was touching in its resignation. "That you shall not have," he repeated, firmly, and closed his eyes, fully expecting—I don't know whether I am doing right by recording that such an unpleasant word had passed his lips—fully expecting to feel himself being—I really hesitate to say—being disemboweled by the push of the long, sharp blade resting murderously against the pit of his stomach—the very seat, in all human beings, of anguishing sensations.

Great waves of harmony went on flowing from the band.

Suddenly the Count felt the nightmarish pressure removed from the sensitive spot. He opened his eyes. He was alone. He had heard nothing. It is probable that "the young man" had departed, with light steps, some time before, but the sense of the horrid pressure had lingered even after the knife had gone. A feeling of weakness came over him. He had just time to stagger to the garden seat. He felt as though he had held his breath for a long time. He sat all in a heap panting with the shock of the reaction.

The band was executing, with immense bravura, the complicated finale. It ended with a tremendous crash. He heard it, unreal and remote, as if his ears had been stopped, and then the hard clapping of a thousand, more or less, pairs of hands, like a sudden hail shower passing away. The profound silence which succeeded recalled him to himself.

A tramcar resembling a long glass box wherein people sat with their faces strongly lighted, ran along swiftly within sixty yards of the spot where he had been robbed. Then another rustled by, and yet another going the other way. The audience about the band had broken up, and were entering the alley in small conversing groups. The Count sat up straight, and tried to think calmly of what had happened to him. The vileness of it took his breath away again. As far as I can make it out he was disgusted with himself. I do not mean to say with his behavior. Indeed, if his pantomimic rendering of it for my information was to be trusted, it was simply perfect. No, it was not that. He was not ashamed. He was shocked at being the selected victim, not of robbery so much as of contempt. His tranquility had been wantonly desecrated. His lifelong, kindly nicety of outlook had been defaced.

Nevertheless, at that stage, before the iron had time to sink deep, he was able to argue himself into comparative equanimity. As his agitation calmed down somewhat, he became aware that he was frightfully hungry. Yes, hungry. The sheer emotion had made him simply ravenous. He left the seat and, after walking for some time, found himself outside the gardens and before an arrested tramcar, without knowing very well how he came there. He got in as if in a dream, by a sort of instinct. Fortunately he found in his trouser pocket a copper to satisfy the conductor. Then the car stopped, and as everybody was getting out he got out, too. He recognized the Piazza San Ferdinando, but apparently it did not occur to him to take a cab and drive to the hotel. He remained in distress on the Piazza like a lost dog, thinking vaguely of the best way of getting something to eat at once.

Suddenly in a flash, he remembered his twenty-franc piece. He explained to me that he had that piece of French gold for something like three years. He used to carry it about with him as a sort of reserve in case of accident. Anybody is liable to have his pocket picked—a quite different thing from a brazen and insulting robbery.

The monumental arch of the Galleria Umberto faced him at the top of a vast flight of stairs. He climbed these without loss of time, and directed his steps towards the Café Umberto. All the tables outside were occupied by a lot of people who were drinking. But as he wanted something to eat, he went inside into the café, which is divided into aisles by square pillars set all round with long looking-glasses. The Count sat down on a red plush against one of these pillars, waiting for his *risotto*. And his mind reverted to his abominable adventure.

He thought of the moody, well-dressed young man, with whom he had exchanged glances in the crowd around the bandstand, and who, he felt confident, was the robber. Would he recognize him again? Doubtless. But he did not want ever to see him again. The best thing was to forget this humiliating episode.

The Count looked round anxiously for the coming of his *risotto*, and, behold! to the left against the wall—there was the young man! He sat alone at a table, with a bottle of some sort of wine or syrup and a carafe of iced water before him. The smooth olive cheeks, the red lips, the little jet-black mustache turned up gallantly, the fine black eyes a little heavy and shaded by long eyelashes, that peculiar expression of cruel discontent to be seen only in the busts of some Roman emperors—it was he, no doubt at all. But that was a type. The Count looked away hastily. The young officer over there reading a paper was like that, too. Same type. Two young men farther away playing checkers also resembled—

The Count lowered his head with the fear in his heart of being everlastingly haunted by the vision of that young man. He began to eat his *risotto*. Presently he heard the young man on his left call the waiter in a bad-tempered tone.

At the call, not only his own waiter, but two other idle waiters belonging to quite a different row of tables, rushed towards him with obsequious alacrity, which is not the general characteristic of the waiters in the Café Umberto. The young man muttered something and one of the waiters walking rapidly to the nearest door called out into the Galleria: "Pasquale! O! Pasquale!"

Everybody knows Pasquale, the shabby old fellow who, shuffling between the tables, offers for sale cigars, cigarettes, picture postcards, matches to the clients of the café. He is in many respects an engaging scoundrel. The Count saw the gray-haired, unshaven ruffian enter the café, the glass case hanging from his neck by a leather strap, and, at a word from the waiter, make his shuffling way with a sudden spurt to the young man's table. The young man was in need of a cigar with which Pasquale served him fawningly. The old peddler was going out, when the Count, on a sudden impulse, beckoned to him.

Pasquale approached, his smile of deferential recognition combining oddly with the ironic searching expression of the eyes. Leaning his case on the table, he lifted the glass lid without a word. The Count took a box of cigarettes and urged by a fearful curiosity, asked as casually as he could:

"Tell me, Pasquale, who is that young signor sitting over there?"

The other bent over his box at once.

"That, *Signor Conde*," he said, beginning to rearrange his wares busily and without looking up, "that is a young *Cavaliere* of a very good family from Bari. He studies in the university here, and is the chief, *capo*, of an association of young men— of very nice young men."

He paused, and then, with mingled discretion and pride of knowledge, murmured the explanatory word "*Camorra*" and shut down the lid. "A very powerful *Camorra*," he breathed out. "The professors themselves respect it greatly… *una lira e cinquante centesimi, Signor Conde*."

Our friend paid with the gold piece. While Pasquale was making up the change, he observed that the young man, of whom he had heard so much in so very few words, was watching the transaction covertly. After the old vagabond had withdrawn with a bow, the Count settled with the waiter and sat still. A numbness, he told me, had come over him.

The young man paid, too, got up and crossed over, apparently for the purpose of looking at himself in the mirror set in a pillar nearest to the Count's seat. He was dressed all in black with a dark green bow tie. The Count looked round, and was startled by meeting a vicious glance out of the corners of the other's eyes. The young *Cavaliere* from Bari, (according to Pasquale; but Pasquale is, of course, an accomplished liar) went on arranging his tie, settling his hat before the glass, and meantime he spoke just loud enough to be heard by the Count. He spoke through his teeth with the most insulting venom of contempt and gazing straight into the mirror.

"Ah! So you had some gold on you—you old liar—you *old birba*—you *furfante*! But you are not done with me yet."

The fiendishness of his expression vanished like lightning, and he lounged out of the café with a moody, impassive face.

The poor Count, when telling me this last episode, fell back trembling in his chair.

His forehead broke into perspiration. There was a wanton insolence in the spirit of this outrage which appalled even me. What it was to the Count's delicacy I won't attempt to guess. I am sure that if he had been not too refined, too correct to do such a blatantly vulgar thing as dying from apoplexy in a café, he would have had a fatal stroke there and then. All irony apart, my difficulty was to keep him from seeing the extent of my commiseration. He shrank from every excessive sentiment, and my commiseration was practically unbounded. It did not surprise me to hear that he had been in bed a week. Then he got up to make his arrangements for leaving Southern Italy at once and for ever.

And the man was convinced that he could not live through a whole year in any other climate!

No argument of mine had any effect. It was not timidity, though he did say to me once, "You do not know what a *Camorra* is, my dear sir. I am a marked man." He was not afraid of what could be done to him. His delicate conception of his dignity was defiled by a degrading experience. He couldn't stand that. No Japanese gentleman, outraged in his exaggerated sense of honor, could have gone about his preparations for hara-kiri with greater resolution. To go home really amounted to suicide for the poor Count.

There is a saying of Neapolitan patriotism, intended for the information of foreigners, I presume: "See Naples and then die." *Vedi Napoli e poi mori*. It is a saying of excessive vanity, and everything excessive was abhorrent to the nice moderation of the poor Count. Yet, as I was seeing him off at the railway station, I thought he was behaving with singular fidelity to its conceited spirit. *Vedi Napoli!*… He had seen it. He had seen it with a startling thoroughness—and now he was going to his grave. He was going to it by the *train de luxe* of the International Sleeping Car Company, via Trieste and Vienna. As the four long, somber coaches pulled out of the station I raised my hat with a solemn feeling of paying a last tribute of respect to a funeral cortège. *Il Conde's* profile, much aged already, glided away from me in stony immobility, behind the lighted pane of glass—*Vedi Napoli e poi mori*!

Questions

1. What impression does the Italian young man give to the old Count?
2. What does the Italian young man do to the old Count?
3. Why doesn't the old Count like the busts and statues of the Roman emperors?
4. What does the famous saying "*Vedi Napoli e poi mori*" imply in the short story?
5. What is the narrator's attitude toward the Count and what do we learn from the story?

艾尔伯爵："看到那不勒斯，死而无憾。"

下面的短篇小说"艾尔伯爵"采用第一人称的叙事手法，讲述了一个在那不勒斯休养、颐享天年的老伯爵如何被一个意大利的年轻男子打劫的故事。那不勒斯的海湾是治疗风湿病的最佳去处，身受风湿病折磨的老伯爵也来到这里。伯爵深信如果离开此地他将性命不保。一向心地善良的老伯爵面对这突如其来的变故，只能选择离开那不勒斯，走向死亡的阴影。

在那不勒斯的国家博物馆里我俩第一次见面并攀谈了起来。博物馆一楼的各个展厅里陈列着从赫库兰尼姆城和庞贝城出土的著名铜像收藏品，火山灾难性的爆发却为我们完好无损地保存了这些古代艺术遗产。

他主动上前跟我打招呼，谈论起我们正在一起欣赏着的著名的赫尔墨斯神休息的雕像。他对那件完美无瑕的艺术品的评价无可挑剔，但也无甚高见。他的审美情趣并非后天习得而是与生俱来的。显然他一生中曾欣赏过许多美好的艺术品，但从未说过业余艺术爱好者或专业鉴赏家们所说的那类行话。那些人真招人烦。听他说话就知道他是一位有识之士，一位不矫揉造作的绅士。

过去几天里我们彼此见过也算面熟，我们住同一家宾馆——虽说不错但奢华程度还算不上新潮——我见他在走廊里进进出出。据我判断他应该是此处一位年长、尊贵的客人。宾馆经理毕恭毕敬地向他鞠躬，他平易近人地予以回应。仆人们都尊称他为艾尔伯爵。服务生们在餐厅门外发现一把黄色丝绸做的有白色内衬的男士阳伞，还为这把伞的主人是谁争论了起来。身穿镶着金边外衣的看门人认出了那把伞，赶忙打发一个电梯员拿着那把伞去追赶艾尔伯爵。或许他是住在宾馆里的唯一一位伯爵，或许因为他是宾馆的常客，他获称此处最优秀的伯爵。

我们先前在博物馆打过交道——（当时过了一会儿，他告诉我说不喜欢那些摆放在画廊里的罗马皇帝的大理石半身像：他们的容貌显得过于精力充沛，太突出了）——早上我们还攀谈了一番，所以晚上餐厅客满的时候，我提议和他合用他那张小餐桌也不算唐突。他温文尔雅地表示同意，脸上露出迷人的微笑。

艾尔伯爵穿着西服马甲和一件"烟衣"（他就这么叫的），打一条黑领带。虽不是新衣服却穿着得体——正是这类衣服的本色。他早晚衣着得体。我毫不怀疑他的整个生活就是得体、整洁而传统，不受外界新鲜事物所动。他把白头发高高地梳在前额上，透出一种具有丰富想象力的理想主义者的气质。伯爵留着整齐浓密的白胡子，中间略带金黄色，看了令人赏心悦目。上好的香水和雪茄发出淡淡的香味（在意大利闻到这些香味实属罕见），从桌子另一边飘过来沁人心脾。他的眼睛最能表明他的年龄，在皱褶的眼帘下显得有些疲倦，想必已有六十出头。伯爵很健谈，但谈不上爱唠叨，只是喜欢和人聊天罢了。

伯爵见识过阿巴兹亚、里维埃拉和其他地方的种种气候，但唯一适合他的却是那不勒斯海湾气候。他告诉我说，古罗马人是生活艺术的专家，在巴耶、维柯和卡普里的海岸上建造别墅的时候，罗马人已对它们的功用胸有成竹。为获得健康他们来到这里，随行还带着哑剧演员和长笛吹奏手为他们的休闲时光平添乐趣。他认为那些罗马贵族很可能患有疼痛难忍的风湿病。

听他发表个人意见仅此一次，这并非来自于某种特有的博学，艾尔伯爵对罗马人的了解不比一个凡夫俗子多多少，他的观点源于个人经验。在找到这处南欧别致的度假地之前，他曾遭受痛苦不堪、危及生命的风湿病的折磨，可他的病情在这儿却有了好转。

那是三年前的事了，打那以后他就在沿着这个海湾边上的地方住了下来，要么在索伦托的宾馆里，要么在卡普里租一个小别墅。他有一架钢琴，几本书；每天、每周或每月伯爵都会在来自全欧洲的人流中结识几个转瞬即逝的朋友。可以想见，他走出去来到大街小巷，乞丐、店老板、小孩和乡下人都认识他；他隔着墙头和农夫唠嗑——回到宾馆房间或别墅里坐在钢琴前，花白的头发向上梳着，留着浓密整齐的胡子，"给自己弹首曲子。"当然，生活想要有所变化可以去附近的那不勒斯城——生活、运动、活力、歌剧。如他所说，小小的娱乐有益于身体健康，就像哑剧演员和长笛吹奏手们的演出一样。与古罗马巨头们唯一不同的是他不仅不会为城中事务所累还可以适度享乐。他根本没有操心事儿，或许这辈子都没遇到过劳神上火的大事。他惬意地生活着，生活的悲欢离合遵循着自然规律——婚姻、生育、死亡——有良好社会的规范和政府的佑护。

虽是个鳏夫可一到七八月份伯爵就会一连六个星期冒险穿越阿尔卑斯山区去看望自己已婚的女儿。他还把自己女儿的名字告诉了我。那是个贵族家庭，我记得她在波希米亚有个城堡，我对伯爵国籍的了解仅限于此。奇怪的是他从没提起过自己的名字，或许他以为我在公开的名单上已看见他的名字了。说实话，我没看过那个名单。不论如何，他是个体面的欧洲人——会说四种语言——是个有钱人，但并非大富大贵。我想大富大贵对他来说不合适，过犹不及——太显眼。毫无疑问，这些财富并非他发大财而得，这些财富的取得必是坎坷经历的结晶。这和个人气质有关，他性情温和，与世无争。谈话中他顺便提到自己的房产，还有那痛苦的风湿病。有一年他不经意间在阿尔卑斯山另一侧一直待到九月中旬，在那座孤零零的乡下房子里一连三个月卧床不起，身边只有一个贴身男仆和照顾他生活起居的一对夫妇。像他说的那样，他"在那儿没有房产"。其间他只离开了几天去和他的土地代理人见面。伯爵下定决心今后绝不能再这样鲁莽行事了。九月初的几个星期他已经回到自己最钟爱的海湾了。

旅行期间有时碰到这样一些孤独的人，他们唯一的营生就是坐等天命。死亡和婚嫁将他们包围在孤寂之中，他们尽量让这种等待变得容易，这无可挑剔。像伯爵对我说的那样："有生之年最重要的就是远离病痛的折磨。"

千万不要把伯爵想象成一个令人生厌的抑郁症患者。他受过良好的教养，从不惹人生厌。他敏锐、善良的目光能洞察人性中微小的软弱。在晚餐和睡觉之间的几个小时里，他是个安静、从容、悦人的伙伴。我们一起待了三个晚上，此后我不得不迅速离开那不勒斯去看望一位在陶尔米纳身患重病的朋友。艾尔伯爵无事可做便去车站为我送行，我有些感伤。虽说他悠然自得的样子总让人感到心情舒畅，可他绝不是个懒散的人。

伯爵沿着火车边走边从窗户向里张望要给我找个好座儿，我坐下后他便待在火车下面兴高采烈地和我聊天，郑重其事地说当晚他一定会想我的，还说打算晚餐后到国家别墅的公共花园里去听乐队演出。听着优美乐曲，看着最美好的社交聚会，其乐融融。像往常一样，届时那里将是高朋满座。

我仿佛又见他抬起头，看到他那慈祥、疲惫的双眼和浓密胡子下面露出的友好微笑。火车开动了，他用两种语言跟我道别：先用法语说"旅途顺利"；然后操着纯正略微强调的英语——他能看出我的心思——鼓励我说："一切会好起来的！"

我朋友的病有了明显好转，于是第十天我就返回了那不勒斯。虽说不在那不勒斯的这段日子里我未将艾尔伯爵记挂在心，可我一走进餐厅就径直走向他常坐的地方找他。我想他或许回索伦托弹钢琴、看书、钓鱼去了。伯爵已成了船夫们的好朋友，他从一条船借了鱼线经常钓鱼。可在人头攒动的人群里我还是看见了伯爵的满头白发，远远看去他的神情不同寻常。伯爵不是笔挺地坐在那里，温文尔雅、兴致勃勃地环顾四周，而是对着盘子沉思。我在他对面站了一会儿，他才抬起头来，表情古怪，或许只有这样一个强烈的词语才能恰如其分地描述他的神情。

"啊，我亲爱的先生！是你吗？"他跟我打招呼说。"我希望一切顺利。"

伯爵很关心我的朋友，实际上，他总是很热情，有一颗仁慈善良的心。此时他的一举一动都显得费力。他虽然也试图跟我谈些日常话题，但终究还是归于无聊的沉默。我突然想起他可能身体不适。可还没等我想好怎么问，伯爵已开始嘀咕了：

"你看，我在这儿很难过。"

"对此我很理解，"我说，"我想您总该不会有什么坏消息吧？"

伯爵非常感谢我的关心。不，不是那回事。没有坏消息，真是谢天谢地。他非常安静，仿佛屏住了呼吸。然后，向前倾了倾身体，话音古怪，神情凝重、尴尬地向我倾吐了心声。

"事实上我经历了一场非常——非常——该怎么说呢？——糟糕的冒险。"

这个向来性情温和、语调深沉的人用词如此有力，着实令人吃惊。我本以为不愉快这个词足以描述降临到像伯爵这种人身上最糟糕的事。况且还是次冒险，真是太不可思议了！但人的本性往往相信那些最糟糕的事。我承认曾怀着好奇心偷偷看了他两眼，想知道到底发生了什么。不一会儿，我那原本不值一提的疑问就烟消云散了。他与生俱来的优雅的言谈举止打消了我所有那些对或多或少不光彩事情的猜测。

"此事非常严重，非常严重。"他神情紧张，接着说，"如果你乐意的话，晚餐后我再告诉你。"

我微微点头表示赞许，除此之外没说别的。我希望伯爵能三思而后行，不一定非得履行这个提议。我们谈了些无关紧要的事，沟通起来比较费力，与我们先前轻松自如调侃的感觉全然不同。他抬起手拿片面包往嘴里送，手微微颤抖。根据我对伯爵的了解，此事并非只是令人吃惊那么简单。

在吸烟室里他毫不犹豫。我们直接走向他常坐的位子，他斜靠在自己座椅扶手上，凝视着我的眼睛。

"还记得，"他开始说，"你走的那天吗？我说晚上要去国家别墅听音乐。"

我还记得。他虽年事已高却仍显英俊，脸上丝毫没有饱经风霜的迹象，此时竟显得有些憔悴，那表情像影子一样转瞬即逝。我看着他坚定的目光，呷了口黑咖啡。伯爵按时间顺序讲述得有条不紊，我想，他之所以这么讲是担心自己感情不能自抑。

离开火车站，伯爵吃了个冰激凌，在咖啡馆读了会儿报纸。然后他回到宾馆，穿戴整齐去吃晚餐，那天晚上伯爵的食欲特别好。晚餐后他在大厅里边抽雪茄边闲逛（里面有桌椅），和圣卡洛剧院首席男高音的小女儿聊了几句，和首席男高音的妻子，"和蔼可亲的女士"攀谈了一会儿。因为晚上没有演出，所以这些人也要去别墅。他们离开了宾馆，感觉不错。

跟他们一起出去的时候——已是晚上九点半了——伯爵记得钱夹里有一大笔钱，于是走进办公室把大部分钱寄存在宾馆簿记员那里。此后，他乘一辆小马车来到海边，下了马车，从维多利亚广场步行走向别墅。

他紧紧地盯着我，当时我就发现他的确是个敏感的人。仿佛被某种神秘的力量控制着似的，那天晚上任何细小的事件都从他的记忆里浮现出来。如果说他没对我提及拉车的小马的毛色和驾车人相关情况的话，那仅是由于一时激动忽视罢了，他勇敢地控制着自己的情绪。

伯爵从维多利亚广场走进国家别墅。国家别墅是个公共娱乐场所，里面铺满草坪，海湾和里维埃拉·策佳房屋之间是灌木丛和花床。两边排列着树木的条条小巷，近乎平行，尽量向远处延伸——景色蔚为壮观。在里维埃拉·策佳一边，电车沿着栏杆运行。时尚的车道穿梭在花园和大海之间，靠地中海的一边是道小矮墙，风和日丽的日子里飞溅着的浪花轻轻地在那边吟唱。

那不勒斯的夜生活持续到很晚，马车在熙来攘往的宽阔大道上跑着，上面挂着的对对车灯给大道增色不少，有些车慢条斯理地跑着，有些则在岸边微暗静谧的灯光中奔跑。繁星满天，人声嘈杂，岸边盖满了房子，灯火辉煌——照耀在波澜不惊的大海上。

花园里光线幽暗而温暖，我们的朋友往前走着，眼睛注视着远处灯火通明的地方，灯光几乎覆盖了整个别墅。那里的空气仿佛在冰冷、蓝色耀眼的灯光照射下也发了光。这个神秘之所隐藏在漆黑的树木枝叶后面，悦耳的声音夹杂着粗声粗气的咆哮和金属突然碰撞的声音、低沉的打击声传了过来。

他向前走着，所有声音混合在一起组成精致的音乐，其间和谐的话语穿透响亮无序的低语和沙砾空地上杂乱的脚步声。灯下聚集了一大群人，他们仿佛沐浴在灿烂的光线中，照射在数百个人头顶上的发光球体在乐队上方摇曳着。另外几百人或多或少地围坐在一起形成几个同心圆，响亮的声音一阵阵传向在座的人，消散在漆黑的夜色中。伯爵走进人群，随人群而动，安静地享受着。听着音乐，看着人们的脸。人们都非常友好：母亲和女儿、父母和孩子、年轻男女有说有笑，彼此点头示意。漂亮的脸蛋和时尚的服饰。当然，人们的体态各有千秋：留着白胡子爱炫耀的老头、肥胖的男人、消瘦的男人、穿着制服的官员，但为数最多的还是来自意大利南方的年轻男人，淡淡的脸色，红红的嘴唇，浓黑的小胡子，清澈的黑眼睛最擅长目送秋波或是怒目相视。

从人群中走出来，伯爵在小咖啡馆前和这一类型的年轻男子坐在一张桌子边。我们的朋友要了些柠檬水。那个年轻小伙子气哼哼地坐在一个空玻璃杯前。他抬起头，又低下头，还把帽子向前斜了斜，就像这样——

伯爵做了个动作把帽子向额头拉了拉，接着说。

"我心想：他很悲伤，肯定出事了，年轻人有他们自己的麻烦事。当然我没注意他。我付了柠檬水的钱，就离开了。"

伯爵在乐队附近转悠着，记得曾两次看到那个年轻人独自在人群中徘徊。有一次他俩曾彼此对视。就是那个年轻人，可那里有许多同样类型的年轻人，他也不能肯定。另外，除了那张给他留下深刻印象的愤怒和不满的脸以外，他并没把他放在心上。

伯爵在人群里待了一会儿感到厌倦,慢慢离开了乐队。一条静谧、冷清的小巷子却引人入胜。伯爵走进巷子,缓缓前行直到演奏声听不见为止。然后他向回走,又转回去,一连走了几遍,才注意到其中一个长椅上坐着个人。

椅子位于两个街灯之间,光线昏暗。

坐在椅子上的男子懒洋洋地坐回椅子一角,向外伸着腿,胳膊叉在胸前,头低垂在胸前。他坐在那里纹丝不动,好像睡着了,可等伯爵再次路过的时候他的神态发生了变化。他朝前坐了起来,胳膊肘撑在膝盖上,手里卷着烟,头都没抬一下。

伯爵继续漫步离开乐队。他说自己又慢慢走回来。我可以想象伯爵是如何自得其乐、静静地享受这一切;这里南方夜间的芳香和音乐声被距离所冲淡,分外柔和。

不一会儿,伯爵第三次路过那条花园长椅。年轻人的胳膊肘仍撑在膝盖上,神情沮丧。在这条幽暗的小巷里他高高的白色领口、袖口露在外面分外显眼。伯爵说他看到那人突然起身仿佛要走,可还没来得及反应,那人已经站在了他面前,语调低沉缓和地问他是否能够好心地借火一用。

伯爵礼貌地答道"当然,可以",然后两手下垂要到口袋里找火柴。

"我垂下手,"他说,"可我的手还没来得及放进口袋里就感到有什么东西压迫在我身上——"

他用指尖指了指靠近胸骨下方的部位,也就是日本人开始剖腹自杀的地方。他们蒙耻之后,愤怒的感情无以言表,于是就剖腹自杀。

"我低头看了一眼,"伯爵接着说,让人听了不寒而栗,"我看见什么了?一把刀!一把长刀——"

"你不会是说,"我吃惊得大声喊道,"晚上十点半你在别墅区里被人打劫了,而不远处就有一千多人!"

他点了好几次头,努力看着我。

"单簧管,"他严肃地说,"正要结束独奏,我向你保证每个音符都听得清楚。随后乐队演奏到了高潮,那个畜生眼睛转来转去,咬牙切齿穷凶极恶地冲着我发出咝咝的声音。'安静!别出声,否则——'"

我惊恐万状。

"那是把什么样的刀?"我傻乎乎地问道。

"一把长刃刀。一把短剑——或许是把餐刀。有细长的刀刃,发着光。他的眼睛也发着光,还有他的白牙。我能看见他异常凶残的模样。我心想:'如果我跟他动手,他能把我给杀了。'我怎能和他拼呢?他手里有刀而我却赤手空拳。

我快70岁了，这你知道，而他是个年轻小伙子。我仿佛能认出他来，就是那个在咖啡馆里见过的神情忧郁的年轻人，我在人群里见过的那个年轻人，可我不能确定，因为在这里很多人和他长得相像。"

伯爵脸上浮现出紧张的神情。我以为他的身体定是由于惊吓动弹不得了，可他的思想仍旧异常活跃。他想到了所有可怕的可能后果，也曾想过大喊救命。可他没喊出来，他的自制力给我留下了一个好印象。他的脑海里闪过一个想法：对手也可能毫无顾忌地大喊救命。

"那个年轻人可以一瞬间扔掉手里的刀，假装说我是攻击者。怎么不可能呢？他可能说我袭击了他。怎么不可能呢？这只是相对于另一个的让人难以置信的故事！他什么都可能说——给我头上加上一些名誉扫地的罪名——我怎么知道？从穿着上看他不是个普通的抢匪，看上去出身较好。该怎么说呢？他是个意大利人——我是个外国人。当然，我有护照，这儿还有我们的领事馆——可就这么被捕，半夜三更像个罪犯一样被拖进警察局！"

说到这儿伯爵浑身发抖，他向来对流言蜚语退避三舍，对他来说流言蜚语比死亡更可怕。当然对很多人来说这种本性将永远——想想那不勒斯人某些独特的习俗——是个奇特的故事。伯爵不傻，他崇尚平静生活的思想受到了强烈刺激，他想现在凡事都有可能发生。可伯爵又有了另一个想法：这个年轻人或许只不过是个发了疯的精神病人。

他第一次暗示了对本次冒险经历的态度。对伯爵极为敏感的情绪来说，一个疯子的所作所为不会影响到任何人的名誉。显然，伯爵这种自我安慰并不奏效。他详细叙述了那个年轻人令人厌恶的野蛮行径：目露凶光，不停地转动，紧紧地咬着白牙。乐队正缓慢地演奏着肃穆的长号，其中夹杂着有意重复的敲鼓的声音。

"那你做什么了呢？"我非常激动地问道。

"什么都没做，"伯爵答道。"我的手静静地垂着，悄悄地告诉他说我没打算出声。他像条疯狗一样狂吼，接着平静地说：

'你的钱夹。'"

"所以我自然地，"伯爵接着说——从那一刻起他像演哑剧一样把事情的经过给我比画了一遍。他看着我的眼睛，手伸进胸前口袋里，拿出一个钱夹，把它递给对方。可那个年轻人手里仍握着刀子，拒绝碰钱夹。

他指挥伯爵把钱拿出来，左手接过钱，让伯爵把钱夹放回口袋，其间传来长笛和单簧管甜美的乐声及双簧管充满感情的低音。那个"年轻人"，伯爵是这么称呼他的，说："这些好像太少了。"

"确实不多，只有340或360里拉，"伯爵说，"我把钱放到宾馆里了，这你

知道。我说我身上就带了这么多,那个年轻人不耐烦地摇摇头说:

'你的手表。'"

伯爵哑口无言给我摘下他的手表来看。可碰巧原本戴在身上的价值不菲的纯金饰表留在表匠那儿清洗了。伯爵那天晚上戴着(皮表带)价值55法郎的防水表,去钓鱼的时候他总是戴着这块表。看了看这件战利品的成色,穿着体面的抢匪嘴里发出不屑一顾的声音,舌头像这样,"戚—啊!"对那块表挥挥手。伯爵把那块不起眼的手表放回口袋,年轻人更加用力地将刀子顶在伯爵腹部,提醒伯爵说:

"你的戒指。"

"其中一个戒指,"伯爵继续说,"是多年前我妻子给我的;另一个是我父亲留给我的。我说'不行,你不能拿走!'"

伯爵又给我演示了一下他当时的动作:双手合十放在胸前。他一副任人宰割的样子着实让人同情。"你不能拿走,"他闭上眼,坚定不移得重复说,完全准备着——我不确定是否听到他说出那个令人不愉快的词——完全准备好自己被——真是难以启齿——抵在胃部置人死命的锋利的长刀,捅进身体、开肠破肚的感觉——任何人都会感受到由那个位置剖腹而产生的极度疼痛。

乐队演奏的美妙和谐的乐曲不绝于耳。

伯爵突然间感到那个敏感部位上噩梦般的压迫消失了,睁眼一看发现只剩他独自一人,什么也没听见。或许那个"年轻人"早已悄悄溜走了,虽然顶着自己的刀已经不见了,可那种可怕的压迫感却挥之不去。伯爵顿时倍感虚弱,幸亏他及时蹒跚两步坐到了花园长椅上。他觉着自己仿佛很长一段时间里都在屏住呼吸。他一屁股坐下,惊恐于刚才那一反应,大声喘着粗气。

乐队正精彩地演奏着复杂的最后乐章。演奏在一阵巨大的打击乐声中结束。伯爵听着那虚无缥缈的音乐,仿佛自己的耳朵失去了听觉;接下来就听见从千人左右的人群里传出的雷鸣般的掌声,一双双鼓掌的手就像阵阵打过的冰雹。伯爵在此后的寂静中清醒过来。

一辆电车——像个长长的玻璃盒,乘客的脸被车里的灯光照得亮亮的——在离抢劫现场60码的地方飞快地开了过去。接着另一辆电车匆匆忙忙地向另一个方向开过去了。原本围坐在乐队旁边的观众已四散而去,三五成群地边说话边走进小巷。伯爵直直地坐在那里,想尽量镇定神情回想刚才那一幕。那令人厌恶的一幕压得他喘不上气来。在我看来他十分鄙视自己,我不是指他的举止。如果他对当时情景的哑剧模仿可信的话,那模仿也算惟妙惟肖了。不,不是那么回事。其实他并不感到耻辱,只是对自己被选为受害人感到震惊,不仅因为遭人抢劫,更因为由此而无故蒙羞。伯爵原本与世无争的温和本性给无情地玷污了,一生慈祥和蔼的面容已不再完美。

然而，当时一颗石头还没落地，他还能自己说服自己镇定下来。情绪缓和下来以后，伯爵感到饥饿难耐。没错，那是种饥肠辘辘的感觉，让他坐立不安。他起身离开椅子，走了一会儿，不知不觉发现自己已经出了花园，站在一辆停着的电车前。凭着某种知觉，仿佛在梦里一般上了电车。幸运的是他在裤兜里找到一枚铜币交给了售票员。车停了，他跟着人群一起下了车。伯爵认出了圣费尔南多广场，可他显然没想到乘出租马车或汽车返回宾馆。伯爵像条丧家犬一样，独自一人悲伤地在广场上待着，脑子里模模糊糊地合计着想找个最好的办法立刻弄点儿什么吃的东西。

伯爵突然想起了那块20法郎的金币。他给我解释说他已经把那块金币带在身上3年了，他常带在身上以防万一。任何人都有可能将他的钱包偷走——与厚颜无耻、威胁他人的抢劫不可同日而语。

安伯托风雨商业街上纪念碑式的拱形门坐落于几段楼梯上，迎面映入伯爵的眼帘。他毫不犹豫地上了楼，径直走进安伯托咖啡馆。外面的桌子周围满是喝咖啡的人。可他想吃东西，于是他进了咖啡馆，咖啡馆被正方形柱子和长玻璃镜分出几个走廊。伯爵靠着其中一个柱子坐在一个红色长毛绒的长椅上，等着他的意大利调味饭，那场令人憎恶的惊险经历在他的脑海里又浮现了出来。

他想到曾在乐队周围的人群里见过那个身着体面、表情阴郁的年轻人。伯爵确信，他就是那个劫匪。伯爵能再认出他来吗？毫无疑问。可伯爵甚至不想再见到他，最好是能忘掉这段令人羞耻的经历。

伯爵焦急地环顾四周看看自己点的意大利调味饭上来了没有，突然，一看！左边靠墙——坐着的就是那个青年人。他独自一人坐在一张桌子旁，面前放了一瓶酒或果汁之类的东西，还有一玻璃瓶冰水。细滑的橄榄色脸颊，红色的嘴唇，墨黑的胡子倔强得翘着，一双漂亮的黑眼睛在长长的眼睫毛映衬下阴沉沉的，这种特有的残酷不满的表情只有在罗马帝王的半身像上才能看得到——就是他，毋庸置疑。可那不过是个典型代表，伯爵于是匆忙转移视线。那边读报纸的年轻官员长得也一样，同样的类型。远处下棋的两个年轻人也像——

伯爵低下头，内心对那个年轻人形象的恐惧久久不能平息。伯爵开始吃意大利调味饭，此时伯爵听到左边那个年轻人没有好气地喊着服务员。

听到叫声，不光他自己的服务员，就连两个其他桌子的服务员都殷勤地急忙朝他那边奔了过去，这可不是安伯托咖啡店的一贯风格。那个年轻人嘀咕着说了些什么，于是其中一个服务员快步走到最近一扇门冲着街里喊："帕斯夸里！嘿！帕斯夸里！"

大家都认识帕斯夸里，他是个穿着破衣烂衫的老家伙，往来穿梭于桌子中间，向咖啡店的客人们兜售香烟、雪茄、明信片和火柴。从某些方面来看他是个相貌不错的无赖。伯爵看见一个灰白头发、胡子拉碴的无赖进了咖啡店，脖子上套根皮带，皮带上挂着一个玻璃盒子，听到服务员的喊声，他从桌子中间穿过，一下子飞奔到年轻人桌旁。那个年轻人要雪茄，帕斯夸里阿谀奉承地给他把雪茄点着。老无赖正要出门，伯爵一时冲动，招手示意让他过来。

帕斯夸里走过来，面带微笑毕恭毕敬，眼睛里却流露出愤世嫉俗、不断搜索的神情。他把箱子靠在桌子上，二话没说打开玻璃盖子。伯爵拿了一盒香烟，在恐惧的好奇心驱使下，尽量装作闲聊问道——

"告诉我，帕斯夸里，坐在那边的那个年轻先生是谁？"

帕斯夸里将身子俯在玻璃箱上面悄悄地说。

"那位，伯爵先生，"他低着头一边说一边忙活着重新收拾自己的东西，"他可是位家住巴里出身良好的绅士。他在这里一所大学里上学，还是个由年轻小伙子们组成的社团的领导，头目——他们是非常不错的年轻人。"

他顿了顿，然后一边低声说出这个解释性词语"克莫拉"，其间夹杂着炫耀判断力和学问的语气，一边盖上盖子。"一个非常强大的克莫拉组织，"他深吸一口气说，"就连教授们都十分尊重这个组织……1里拉50分，伯爵先生。"

我们的伯爵朋友用那块金币付了账。帕斯夸里在找钱的时候，伯爵注意到，那个年轻人正偷偷地看着他们之间的交易。简短的几句话让伯爵对他有了如此多的了解。那个老无赖鞠躬离开后，伯爵和服务员结了账，静静地坐在那里。他告诉我，一股浑身麻木的感觉突然袭来。

那个年轻人也付了账，起身朝这边走来，表面上看好像是想到离伯爵座位最近的柱子那里去照镜子。他身穿黑衣服，系着深绿色的蝴蝶结。伯爵环顾四周，被对方眼睛里流露出来的邪恶目光吓了一跳。那位来自巴里的绅士（帕斯夸里是这么说的，但帕斯夸里其实是个彻头彻尾的骗子）继续整理着自己的领结，对着镜子戴上帽子，与此同时，他说话的声音的大小正好能让伯爵听到。他的牙齿里挤出恶毒的话语，眼睛死死地盯着镜子。

"啊！你身上带着金子——你这个老骗子——老鬼——老滑头！可你和我的事还没完呢。"

那年轻人恶魔般的表情像闪电一样一闪即逝，他懒懒地走出咖啡馆，脸上一副忧郁冷漠的表情。

可怜的伯爵，将这最后一幕告诉我以后，一下子坐回椅子里浑身发抖，前额出汗。这次暴行给人带来的精神上的耻辱连我都感到惊恐万分。我不愿妄加猜测伯爵的情感细腻到何种程度，可我确信，即便当时他优雅的品质让他在咖啡馆里不会做出中风死去那样丢人现眼的低俗之事，但当时的那件事对他也是个致命的打击。讽刺的话暂且不论，问题是如何让伯爵明白我对他的同情是发自肺腑的。他不愿过度感伤，而我却给予他极大的同情。听到他一个星期卧床不起我并不感到吃惊。最后他还是起来了，为马上且永远离开南意大利做准备。

可伯爵已深信在其他任何一种气候中，自己都活不了一年！

我的劝说没有效果，伯爵那么做绝不是胆怯的表现，虽然他曾对我说："你不明白克莫拉到底是什么，我亲爱的先生。我已被他们盯上了。"至于会发生些什么他并不害怕，可他敏感的尊严却被这一令人羞耻的经历所玷污，这是他所无法容忍的。没有哪个日本绅士在自己强烈的荣誉感受损之际比伯爵能更加毅然决然地为自己剖腹自杀做准备。对可怜的伯爵来说回家实际上就等于自杀。

那不勒斯有句充满爱国激情的谚语，叫*Vedi Napoli e poi mori*，目的是为了能让外国人了解该地。我猜这句话的意思应该是："看到那不勒斯，死而无憾。"这句谚语显得过分虚荣，况且可怜的伯爵一向性情温和，他对任何过犹不及的东西都深恶痛绝。然而，我在车站为他送行的时候，我想他的举止异常真实地反映了那句谚语中自以为是的精神内核。*Vedi Napoli!*...看到那不勒斯！……伯爵见到那不勒斯了！他如此彻底地见识了那不勒斯着实让人吃惊——现在伯爵将走向自己的坟墓。他要乘坐国际卧铺公司的豪华列车完成自己的坟墓之旅，途经的里雅斯特和维也纳。随着四节长长的车厢缓缓开出车站，我怀着肃穆的心情举起手里的帽子向出葬的队列致以最后的敬意。车窗里亮着灯，艾尔伯爵像尊石像一样纹丝不动地坐在那里，他已显苍老的侧影慢慢地滑出了我的视线——*Vedi Napoli e poi mori*，看到那不勒斯，死而无憾！

Arthur Conan Doyle
(1859—1930)

Arthur Conan Doyle was most noted for his stories about the detective Sherlock Holmes, the best-known detective in literature. Doyle was born in Edinburgh, whose parents were Roman Catholics. From 1876 to 1881 he studied medicine at the University of Edinburgh Medical School. In 1882, he set up a medical practice in Southsea. The practice was initially not very successful; while waiting for patients, he wrote stories. He joined the Portsmouth Literary and Scientific Society in 1883 and seven years later he gave up his medical practice in favor of writing. He was knighted in 1902. From 1914, he turned to believe in Spiritualism, after his son's death in WWI. Arthur Conan Doyle married twice, and died in England after a heart attack.

His first significant work was *A Study in Scarlet*, which appeared in 1887 and featured the first appearance of Sherlock Holmes. Holmes is renowned for his skillful use of "deductive reasoning" to solve difficult cases. Conan Doyle wrote four novels and fifty-six short stories that featured Holmes. All but four stories are narrated by Holmes's friend and biographer, Dr. John H. Watson; two are narrated by Sherlock Holmes himself, and two others are written in the third person. Besides Sherlock Holmes, Conan Doyle also wrote a number of books on other subjects, including *The Great Boer War* (1900), *The Lost World* (1912), *The New Revelation* (1918), and *The History of Spiritualism* (1926).

The New Catacomb

The following from *Tales of Terror and Mystery* (1922) tells a story between Burger and Kennedy, both noted experts on Roman remains. Burger tells Kennedy of a new catacomb he has discovered, and offers to show it to him. Deep in the catacomb he leaves Kennedy to die in the dark. Compared with the complex plots that characterize the Holmes stories, the plot of this short story is quite simple. But with a vivid description, and an unexpected ending, the story becomes one of the most successful thrillers in the book.

"Look here, Burger," said Kennedy, "I do wish that you would confide in me."

The two famous students of Roman remains sat together in Kennedy's comfortable room overlooking the Corso. The night was cold, and they had both pulled up their chairs to the unsatisfactory Italian stove which threw out a zone of stuffiness rather than of warmth. Outside under the bright winter stars lay the modern Rome, the long, double chain of the electric lamps, the brilliantly lighted cafés, the rushing carriages, and the dense throng upon the footpaths. But inside, in the sumptuous chamber of the rich young English archaelogist, there was only old Rome to be seen. Cracked and timeworn friezes hung upon the walls, grey old busts of senators and soldiers with their fighting heads and their hard, cruel faces peered out from the corners. On the centre table, amidst a litter of inscriptions, fragments, and ornaments, there stood the famous reconstruction by Kennedy of the Baths of Caracalla, which excited such interest and admiration when it was exhibited in Berlin. Amphorae hung from the ceiling, and a litter of curiosities strewed the rich red Turkey carpet. And of them all there was not one which was not of the most unimpeachable authenticity, and of the utmost rarity and value; for Kennedy, though little more than thirty, had a European reputation in this particular branch of research, and was, moreover, provided with that long purse which either proves to be a fatal handicap to the student's energies, or, if his mind is still true to its purpose, gives him an enormous advantage in the race for fame. Kennedy had often been seduced by whim and pleasure from his studies, but his mind was an incisive one, capable of long and concentrated efforts which ended in sharp reactions of sensuous languor. His handsome face, with its high, white forehead, its aggressive nose, and its somewhat loose and sensual mouth, was a fair index of the compromise between strength and weakness in his nature.

Of a very different type was his companion, Julius Burger. He came of a curious blend, a German father and an Italian mother, with the robust qualities of the North mingling strangely with the softer graces of the South. Blue Teutonic eyes lightened his sun-browned face, and above them rose a square, massive forehead, with a fringe of close yellow curls lying round it. His strong, firm jaw was clean-shaven, and his companion had frequently remarked how much it suggested those old Roman busts which peered out from the shadows in the corners of his chamber. Under its bluff German strength there lay always a suggestion of Italian subtlety, but the smile was so honest, and the eyes so frank, that one understood that this was only an indication of his ancestry, with no actual bearing upon his character. In age and in reputation, he was on the same level as his English companion, but his life and his work had both been far more arduous. Twelve years before, he had come as a poor student to Rome, and had lived ever since upon some small endowment for research which had been awarded to him by the University of Bonn. Painfully, slowly, and doggedly, with extraordinary tenacity and single-mindedness, he had climbed from rung to rung of the ladder of fame, until now he was a member of the Berlin Academy, and there was every reason to believe that he would shortly be promoted to the Chair of the greatest of German Universities. But the singleness of purpose which had brought him to the same high level as the rich and brilliant Englishman, had caused him in everything outside their work to stand infinitely below him. He had never found a pause in his studies in which to cultivate the social graces. It was only when he spoke of his own subject that his face was filled with life and soul. At other times he was silent and embarrassed, too conscious of his own limitations in larger subjects, and impatient of that small talk which is the conventional refuge of those who have no thoughts to express.

And yet for some years there had been an acquaintanceship which appeared to be slowly ripening into a friendship between these two very different rivals. The base and origin of this lay in the fact that in their own studies each was the only one of the younger men who had knowledge and enthusiasm enough to properly appreciate the other. Their common interests and pursuits had brought them together, and each had been attracted by the other's knowledge. And then gradually something had been added to this. Kennedy had been amused by the frankness and simplicity of his rival, while Burger in turn had been fascinated by the brilliancy and vivacity which had made Kennedy such a favourite in Roman society. I say "had," because just at the moment the young Englishman was somewhat under a cloud. A love-affair, the details of which had never quite come out, had indicated a heartlessness and callousness upon his part which shocked many of his friends. But in the bachelor circles of students and artists in which he preferred to move there is no very rigid code of honour in such matters, and though a head might be shaken or a pair of shoulders shrugged over the flight of two and the return of one, the general sentiment was probably one of curiosity and perhaps of envy rather than of reprobation.

"Look here, Burger," said Kennedy, looking hard at the placid face of his companion, "I do wish that you would confide in me."

As he spoke he waved his hand in the direction of a rug which lay upon the floor. On the rug stood a long, shallow fruit-basket of the light wicker-work which is used in the Campagna, and this was heaped with a litter of objects, inscribed tiles, broken inscriptions, cracked mosaics, torn papyri, rusty metal ornaments, which to the uninitiated might have seemed to have come straight from a dustman's bin, but which a specialist would have speedily recognized as unique of their kind. The pile of odds and ends in the flat wicker-work basket supplied exactly one of those missing links of social development which are of such interest to the student. It was the German who had brought them in, and the Englishman's eyes were hungry as he looked at them.

"I won't interfere with your treasure-trove, but I should very much like to hear about it," he continued, while Burger very deliberately lit a cigar. "It is evidently a discovery of the first importance. These inscriptions will make a sensation throughout Europe."

"For every one here there are a million there!" said the German. "There are so many that a dozen savants might spend a lifetime over them, and build up a reputation as solid as the Castle of St. Angelo."

Kennedy sat thinking with his fine forehead wrinkled and his fingers playing with his long, fair moustache.

"You have given yourself away, Burger!" said he at last. "Your words can only apply to one thing. You have discovered a new catacomb."

"I had no doubt that you had already come to that conclusion from an examination of these objects."

"Well, they certainly appeared to indicate it, but your last remarks make it certain. There is no place except a catacomb which could contain so vast a store of relics as you describe."

"Quite so. There is no mystery about that. I HAVE discovered a new catacomb."

"Where?"

"Ah, that is my secret, my dear Kennedy. Suffice it that it is so situated that there is not one chance in a million of anyone else coming upon it. Its date is different from that of any known catacomb, and it has been reserved for the burial of the highest Christians, so that the remains and the relics are quite different from anything which has ever been seen before. If I was not aware of your knowledge and of your energy, my friend, I would not hesitate, under the pledge of secrecy, to tell you everything about it. But as it is I think that I must certainly prepare my own report of the matter before I expose myself to such formidable competition."

Kennedy loved his subject with a love which was almost a mania—a love which held him true to it, amidst all the distractions which come to a wealthy and dissipated young man. He had ambition, but his ambition was secondary to his mere abstract joy and interest in everything which concerned the old life and history of the city. He yearned to see this new underworld which his companion had discovered.

"Look here, Burger," said he, earnestly, "I assure you that you can trust me most implicitly in the matter. Nothing would induce me to put pen to paper about anything which I see until I have your express permission. I quite understand your feeling and I think it is most natural, but you have really nothing whatever to fear from me. On the other hand, if you don't tell me I shall make a systematic search, and I shall most certainly discover it. In that case, of course, I should make what use I liked of it, since I should be under no obligation to you."

Burger smiled thoughtfully over his cigar. "I have noticed, friend Kennedy, that when I want information over any point you are not always so ready to supply it."

"When did you ever ask me anything that I did not tell you? You remember, for example, my giving you the material for your paper about the temple of the Vestals."

"Ah, well, that was not a matter of much importance. If I were to question you upon some intimate thing would you give me an answer, I wonder! This new catacomb is a very intimate thing to me, and I should certainly expect some sign of confidence in return."

"What you are driving at I cannot imagine," said the Englishman, "but if you mean that you will answer my question about the catacomb if I answer any question which you may put to me I can assure you that I will certainly do so."

"Well, then," said Burger, leaning luxuriously back in his settee, and puffing a blue tree of cigar-smoke into the air, "tell me all about your relations with Miss Mary Saunderson."

Kennedy sprang up in his chair and glared angrily at his impassive companion. "What the devil do you mean?! What sort of a question is that? You may mean it as a joke, but you never made a worse one."

"No, I don't mean it as a joke," said Burger, simply. "I am really rather interested in the details of the matter. I don't know much about the world and women and social life and that sort of thing, and such an incident has the fascination of the unknown for me. I know you, and I knew her by sight—I had even spoken to her once or twice. I should very much like to hear from your own lips exactly what it was which occurred between you."

"I won't tell you a word."

"That's all right. It was only my whim to see if you would give up a secret as easily as you expected me to give up my secret of the new catacomb. You wouldn't, and I didn't expect you to. But why should you expect otherwise of me? There's Saint John's clock striking ten. It is quite time that I was going home."

"No; wait a bit, Burger," said Kennedy; "this is really a ridiculous caprice of yours to wish to know about an old love-affair which has burned out months ago. You know we look upon a man who kisses and tells as the greatest coward and villain possible."

"Certainly," said the German, gathering up his basket of curiosities, "when he tells anything about a girl which is previously unknown he must be so. But in this case, as you must be aware, it was a public matter that was the common talk of Rome, so that you are not really doing Miss Mary Saunderson any injury by discussing her case with me. But still, I respect your scruples; and so good night!"

"Wait a bit, Burger," said Kennedy, laying his hand upon the other's arm; "I am very keen upon this catacomb business, and I can't let it drop quite so easily. Would you mind asking me something else in return—something not quite so eccentric this time?"

"No, no; you have refused, and there is an end of it," said Burger, with his basket on his arm. "No doubt you are quite right not to answer, and no doubt I am quite right also—and so again, my dear Kennedy, good night!"

The Englishman watched Burger cross the room, and he had his hand on the handle of the door before his host sprang up with the air of a man who is making the best of that which cannot be helped.

"Hold on, old fellow," said he; "I think you are behaving in a most ridiculous fashion; but still; if this is your condition, I suppose that I must submit to it. I hate saying anything about a girl, but, as you say, it is all over Rome, and I don't suppose I can tell you anything which you do not know already. What was it you wanted to know?"

The German came back to the stove, and, laying down his basket, he sank into his chair once more.

"May I have another cigar?" said he. "Thank you very much! I never smoke when I work, but I enjoy a chat much more when I am under the influence of tobacco. Now, as regards this young lady, with whom you had this little adventure. What in the world has become of her?"

"She is at home with her own people."

"Oh, really—in England?"

"Yes."

"What part of England—London?"

"No, Twickenham."

"You must excuse my curiosity, my dear Kennedy, and you must put it down to my ignorance of the world. No doubt it is quite a simple thing to persuade a young lady to go off with you for three weeks or so, and then to hand her over to her own family at—what did you call the place?"

"Twickenham."

"Quite so—at Twickenham. But it is something so entirely outside my own experience that I cannot even imagine how you set about it. For example, if you had loved this girl your love could hardly disappear in three weeks, so I presume that you could not have loved her at all. But if you did not love her why should you make this great scandal which has damaged you and ruined her?"

"That's a logical way of looking at it, certainly." Kennedy looked moodily into the red eye of the stove. "Love is a big word, and it represents a good many different shades of feeling. I liked her, and—well, you say you've seen her—you know how charming she could look. But still I am willing to admit, looking back, that I could never have really loved her."

"Then, my dear Kennedy, why did you do it?"

"The adventure of the thing had a great deal to do with it."

"What! You are so fond of adventures!"

"Where would the variety of life be without them? It was for an adventure that I first began to pay my attentions to her. I've chased a good deal of game in my time, but there's no chase like that of a pretty woman. There was the piquant difficulty of it also, for, as she was the companion of Lady Emily Rood, it was almost impossible to see her alone. On the top of all the other obstacles which attracted me, I learned from her own lips very early in the proceedings that she was engaged."

"Mein Gott! To whom?"

"She mentioned no names."

"I do not think that anyone knows that. So that made the adventure more alluring, did it?"

"Well, it did certainly give a spice to it. Don't you think so?"

"I tell you that I am very ignorant about these things."

"My dear fellow, you can remember that the apple you stole from your neighbour's tree was always sweeter than that which fell from your own. And then I found that she cared for me."

"What—at once?"

"Oh, no, it took about three months of sapping and mining. But at last I won her over. She understood that my judicial separation from my wife made it impossible for me to do the right thing by her—but she came all the same, and we had a delightful time, as long as it lasted."

"But how about the other man?"

"I suppose it is the survival of the fittest." Kennedy shrugged his shoulders. "If he had been the better man she would not have deserted him. Let's drop the subject, for I have had enough of it!"

"Only one other thing. How did you get rid of her in three weeks?"

"Well, we had both cooled down a bit, you understand. She absolutely refused, under any circumstances, to come back to face the people she had known in Rome. Now, of course, Rome is necessary to me, and I was already pining to be back at my work—so there was one obvious cause of separation. Then, again, her old father turned up at the hotel in London, and there was a scene, and the whole thing became so unpleasant that really—though I missed her dreadfully at first—I was very glad to slip out of it. Now, I rely upon you not to repeat anything of what I have said."

"My dear Kennedy, I should not dream of repeating it. But all that you say interests me very much, for it gives me an insight into your way of looking at things, which is entirely different from mine, for I have seen so little of life. And now you want to know about my new catacomb. There's no use my trying to describe it, for you would never find it by that. There is only one thing, and that is for me to take you there."

"That would be splendid."

"When would you like to come?"

"The sooner the better. I am all impatience to see it."

"Well, it is a beautiful night—though a trifle cold. Suppose we start in an hour. We must be very careful to keep the matter to ourselves. If anyone saw us hunting in couples they would suspect that there was something going on."

"We can't be too cautious," said Kennedy. "Is it far?"

"Some miles."

"Not too far to walk?"

"Oh, no, we could walk there easily."

"We had better do so, then. A cabman's suspicions would be aroused if he dropped us both at some lonely spot in the dead of the night."

"Quite so. I think it would be best for us to meet at the Gate of the Appian Way at midnight. I must go back to my lodgings for the matches and candles and things."

"All right, Burger! I think it is very kind of you to let me into this secret, and I promise you that I will write nothing about it until you have published your report. Goodbye for the present! You will find me at the Gate at twelve."

The cold, clear air was filled with the musical chimes from that city of clocks as Burger, wrapped in an Italian overcoat, with a lantern hanging from his hand, walked up to the rendezvous. Kennedy stepped out of the shadow to meet him.

"You are ardent in work as well as in love!" said the German, laughing.

"Yes; I have been waiting here for nearly half an hour."

"I hope you left no clue as to where we were going."

"Not such a fool! By Jove, I am chilled to the bone! Come on, Burger, let us warm ourselves by a spurt of hard walking."

Their footsteps sounded loud and crisp upon the rough stone paving of the disappointing road which is all that is left of the most famous highway of the world. A peasant or two going home from the wine-shop, and a few carts of country produce coming up to Rome, were the only things which they met. They swung along, with the huge tombs looming up through the darkness upon each side of them, until they had come as far as the Catacombs of St. Calixtus, and saw against a rising moon the great circular bastion of Cecilia Metella in front of them. Then Burger stopped with his hand to his side.

"Your legs are longer than mine, and you are more accustomed to walking," said he, laughing. "I think that the place where we turn off is somewhere here. Yes, this is it, round the corner of the trattoria. Now, it is a very narrow path, so perhaps I had better go in front and you can follow."

He had lit his lantern, and by its light they were enabled to follow a narrow and devious track which wound across the marshes of the Campagna. The great Aqueduct of old Rome lay like a monstrous caterpillar across the moonlit landscape, and their road led them under one of its huge arches, and past the circle of crumbling bricks which marks the old arena. At last Burger stopped at a solitary wooden cow-house, and he drew a key from his pocket. "Surely your catacomb is not inside a house!" cried Kennedy.

"The entrance to it is. That is just the safeguard which we have against anyone else discovering it."

"Does the proprietor know of it?"

"Not he. He had found one or two objects that made me almost certain that his house was built on the entrance to such a place. So I rented it from him, and did my excavations for myself. Come in, and shut the door behind you."

It was a long, empty building, with the mangers of the cows along one wall. Burger put his lantern down on the ground, and shaded its light in all directions save one by draping his overcoat round it.

"It might excite remark if anyone saw a light in this lonely place," said he. "Just help me to move this boarding."

The flooring was loose in the corner, and plank by plank the two savants raised it and leaned it against the wall. Below there was a square aperture and a stair of old stone steps which led away down into the bowels of the earth.

"Be careful!" cried Burger, as Kennedy, in his impatience, hurried down them. "It is a perfect rabbits'-warren below, and if you were once to lose your way there the chances would be a hundred to one against your ever coming out again. Wait until I bring the light."

"How do you find your own way if it is so complicated?"

"I had some very narrow escapes at first, but I have gradually learned to go about. There is a certain system to it, but it is one which a lost man, if he were in the dark, could not possibly find out. Even now I always spin out a ball of string behind me when I am going far into the catacomb. You can see for yourself that it is difficult, but every one of these passages divides and subdivides a dozen times before you go a hundred yards."

They had descended some twenty feet from the level of the byre, and they were standing now in a square chamber cut out of the soft tufa. The lantern cast a flickering light, bright below and dim above, over the cracked brown walls. In every direction were the black openings of passages which radiated from this common centre.

"I want you to follow me closely, my friend," said Burger. "Do not loiter to look at anything upon the way, for the place to which I will take you contains all that you can see, and more. It will save time for us to go there direct."

He led the way down one of the corridors, and the Englishman followed closely at his heels. Every now and then the passage bifurcated, but Burger was evidently following some secret marks of his own, for he neither stopped nor hesitated. Everywhere along the walls, packed like the berths upon an emigrant ship, lay the Christians of old Rome. The yellow light flickered over the shrivelled features of the mummies, and gleamed upon rounded skulls and long, white armbones crossed over fleshless chests. And everywhere as he passed Kennedy looked with wistful eyes upon inscriptions, funeral vessels, pictures, vestments, utensils, all lying as pious hands had placed them so many centuries ago. It was apparent to him, even in those hurried, passing glances, that this was the earliest and finest of the catacombs, containing such a storehouse of Roman remains as had never before come at one time under the observation of the student.

"What would happen if the light went out?" he asked, as they hurried onwards.

"I have a spare candle and a box of matches in my pocket. By the way, Kennedy, have you any matches?"

"No; you had better give me some."

"Oh, that is all right. There is no chance of our separating."

"How far are we going? It seems to me that we have walked at least a quarter of a mile."

"More than that, I think. There is really no limit to the tombs—at least, I have never been able to find any. This is a very difficult place, so I think that I will use our ball of string."

He fastened one end of it to a projecting stone and he carried the coil in the breast of his coat, paying it out as he advanced. Kennedy saw that it was no unnecessary precaution, for the passages had become more complex and tortuous than ever, with a perfect network of intersecting corridors. But these all ended in one large circular hall with a square pedestal of tufa topped with a slab of marble at one end of it.

"By Jove!" cried Kennedy in an ecstasy, as Burger swung his lantern over the marble. "It is a Christian altar—probably the first one in existence. Here is the little consecration cross cut upon the corner of it. No doubt this circular space was used as a church."

"Precisely," said Burger. "If I had more time I should like to show you all the bodies which are buried in these upon the walls, for they are the early popes and bishops of the Church, with their mitres, their croziers, and full canonicals. Go over to that one and look at it!"

Kennedy went across, and stared at the ghastly head which lay loosely on the shredded and mouldering mitre.

"This is most interesting," said he, and his voice seemed to boom against the concave vault. "As far as my experience goes, it is unique. Bring the lantern over, Burger, for I want to see them all."

But the German had strolled away, and was standing in the middle of a yellow circle of light at the other side of the hall. "Do you know how many wrong turnings there are between this and the stairs? There are over two thousand. No doubt it was one of the means of protection which the Christians adopted. The odds are two thousand to one against a man getting out, even if he had a light; but if he were in the dark it would, of course, be far more difficult."

"So I should think."

"And the darkness is something dreadful. I tried it once for an experiment. Let us try it again!" He stooped to the lantern, and in an instant it was as if an invisible hand was squeezed tightly over each of Kennedy's eyes. Never had he known what such darkness was. It seemed to press upon him and to smother him. It was a solid obstacle against which the body shrank from advancing. He put his hands out to push it back from him. "That will do, Burger. Let's have the light again."

But his companion began to laugh, and in that circular room the sound seemed to come from every side at once. He said, "You seem uneasy, friend Kennedy."

"Go on, man, light the candle!" said Kennedy impatiently.

"It's very strange, Kennedy, but I could not in the least tell by the sound in which direction you stand. Could you tell where I am?"

"No; you seem to be on every side of me."

"If it were not for this string which I hold in my hand I should not have a notion which way to go."

"I dare say not. Strike a light, man, and have an end of this nonsense."

"Well, Kennedy, there are two things which I understand that you are very fond of. The one is an adventure, and the other is an obstacle to surmount. The adventure must be the finding of your way out of this catacomb. The obstacle will be the darkness and the two thousand wrong turns which make the way a little difficult to find. But you need not hurry, for you have plenty of time, and when you halt for a rest now and then,

I should like you just to think of Miss Mary Saunderson, and whether you treated her quite fairly."

"You devil, what do you mean?" roared Kennedy. He was running about in little circles and clasping at the solid blackness with both hands.

"Goodbye," said the mocking voice, and it was already at some distance. "I really do not think, Kennedy, even by your own showing that you did the right thing by that girl. There was only one little thing which you appeared not to know, and I can supply it. Miss Saunderson was engaged to a poor ungainly devil of a student, and his name was Julius Burger."

There was a rustle somewhere, the vague sound of a foot striking a stone, and then there fell silence upon that old Christian church—a stagnant, heavy silence which closed round Kennedy and shut him in like water round a drowning man.

Some two months afterwards the following paragraph made the round of the European Press:

"One of the most interesting discoveries of recent years is that of the new catacomb in Rome, which lies some distance to the east of the well-known vaults of St. Calixtus. The finding of this important burial-place, which is exceeding rich in most interesting early Christian remains, is due to the energy and sagacity of Dr. Julius Burger, the young German specialist, who is rapidly taking the first place as an authority upon ancient Rome. Although the first to publish his discovery, it appears that a less fortunate adventurer had anticipated Dr. Burger. Some months ago Mr. Kennedy, the well-known English student, disappeared suddenly from his rooms in the Corso, and it was conjectured that his association with a recent scandal had driven him to leave Rome. It appears now that he had in reality fallen a victim to that fervid love of archaeology which had raised him to a distinguished place among living scholars. His body was discovered in the heart of the new catacomb, and it was evident from the condition of his feet and boots that he had tramped for days through the tortuous corridors that make these subterranean tombs so dangerous to explorers. The deceased gentleman had, with inexplicable rashness, made his way into this labyrinth without, as far as can be discovered, taking with him either candles or matches, so that his sad fate was the natural result of his own temerity. What makes the matter more painful is that Dr. Julius Burger was an intimate friend of the deceased. His joy at the extraordinary find which he has been so fortunate as to make has been greatly marred by the terrible fate of his comrade and fellow-worker."

Questions

1. How do the descriptions of Burger and Kennedy establish the differences between them?
2. Why did Burger appear so unwilling to show the new catacomb to Kennedy?
3. What could be Kennedy's feeling after being informed that Burger was the fiance of Miss Saunderson? How does the description of Kennedy's reaction indicate his feeling inside?
4. What are the writing techniques used in the story to achieve the thrilling effect?
5. Explain the meaning of the story's title.

阿瑟·柯南·道尔
（1859—1930）

阿瑟·柯南·道尔爵士，因塑造了文学史上最著名的侦探人物夏洛克·福尔摩斯而闻名于世。柯南·道尔生于苏格兰的爱丁堡，其父母均为罗马天主教徒。1876年至1881年他在爱丁堡大学医学院学习医学。1882年柯南·道尔在南海城开始行医。其行医生涯最初并不顺利，在等候病人期间，他开始写作。1883年他加入朴次茅斯文学及科学协会，并于7年后放弃行医专心写作。1902年柯南·道尔被封为爵士。因为儿子在第一次世界大战中丧生，柯南·道尔从1914年开始相信唯灵论。他一生结婚两次，因心脏病在英格兰去世。

夏洛克·福尔摩斯在柯南·道尔的第一部重要作品《血字的研究》（1887）中首次亮相。福尔摩斯以其善于运用推理演绎法解决疑难案件而著称。柯南·道尔为福尔摩斯共写了4部小说、56个短篇小说；其中2篇以福尔摩斯的口吻写成，还有2篇以第三人称写成，其余都是以福尔摩斯的好友、传记作家华生医生的口吻写成。除了夏洛克·福尔摩斯，柯南·道尔还写过许多其他题材的作品，其中包括《伟大的布尔战争》（1900）、《失落的世界》（1912）、《新启示》（1918）以及《唯灵论史》（1926）。

新地下墓穴

下面的作品选自《恐怖疑案故事集》（1922），讲述了两个罗马遗迹研究专家伯格和肯尼迪之间的故事。伯格告诉肯尼迪自己发现了一个新的地下墓穴，并愿意带他同去。在墓穴深处，伯格将肯尼迪一人留在黑暗中死去。与情节复杂的福尔摩斯故事相比，本故事情节简单。但是凭借形象的描写和出人意料的结局，该故事成为这部作品集中最为成功的恐怖小说之一。

"你瞧，伯格，"肯尼迪说，"真希望你能信任我。"

两位罗马遗迹研究的著名学者一同坐在肯尼迪那舒适、可以鸟瞰整个卡尔索的房子里。夜很冷，俩人都把椅子拖近壁炉坐着。这个意大利式的壁炉并不让人觉得舒服，它散发出的热量让人觉得闷热而不是温暖。屋外，冬夜璀璨繁星下的现代罗马，流光溢彩，街道两旁的路灯犹如两条发光的流苏蜿蜒不绝，咖啡厅灯火通明。街上，马车疾驰；人行道上，人群熙攘。而屋内，在这个富有而年轻的英国考古学家那装饰奢华的房间里，满眼可见的却都是古罗马的遗物。墙上裂纹的带状装饰历经沧桑，角落里摆放着一些元老院议员和战士们的灰白而古老的半身像，他们昂着好战的头颅，表情冷酷而凶残，似乎正在窥视着什么。屋中央的桌子上，一堆诸如碑铭、碎片和饰品之中，立着肯尼迪复制的卡拉卡拉洗浴场微缩景观，这个复制品极具盛名，当年在柏林展出时，曾引发了人们极大的兴趣与赞叹。天棚上悬挂着几只双耳细颈椭圆土罐，华贵的红色土耳其地毯上散乱地放着各种古玩珍品，无一不是货真价实的稀世珍宝。虽然刚过30岁，肯尼迪在欧洲这一特殊研究领域却是很具威望，而且他具有相当的财力。雄厚的财力可能会严重分散他的研究精力，可如果他能够明确目标，坚定信念，这些就会为他在名誉角逐中提供巨大的有利条件。肯尼迪虽然经常会因奇思妙想和寻欢作乐而偏离研究工作，但他却拥有敏锐的头脑，能够长时间保持全神贯注的状态，直至对外界的反应都会变得极为迟缓。他英俊潇洒的脸庞，白皙高耸的额头，好勇斗胜的鼻子，松软性感的双唇，这一切都恰能体现出他性格中力量与软弱的妥协。

　　他的同伴，尤里乌斯·伯格却是完全另一种类型。他是个奇特的混血儿，爸爸是德国人，妈妈是意大利人，北方的强悍粗犷与南方的温柔优雅奇特地融合在一起。古铜色的面庞因那双蓝色日耳曼人的眼睛而神采奕奕，他前额宽阔方正，上面是一头浓密的黄色发卷。他的下巴强壮坚毅，刮得干干净净，他的同伴常说他的下巴总是让人想起房间角落里那些正在向外窥视的古老的罗马半身像。在刚毅的德国人的力量背后似乎又总隐藏着一丝意大利人的精明，可是他的笑容是那么的诚恳，目光又是那么的率真，所以人人都会认为那精明只是他血统上的一点印记，而同他的性格没有任何关系。两人年龄、声望相当，与他的同伴相比，只是他的生活与工作都曾更为艰辛。12年前，初到罗马之时，他还只是一个穷学生，一直靠着波恩大学给的那一小笔研究经费过活。历经艰辛，百折不挠，慢慢地，凭着超人的坚韧与专注，他沿着名誉之梯一层一层地向上攀登，直到现在成为柏林研究院的成员之一，而且极有可能在近期跻身于德国顶尖学府教授的行列。目标的单一性虽然使他能够与其富有且才华横溢的英国同伴享有同样的盛名，却使他在工作之外的任何方面都远不及后者。他从未片刻停下自己的研究，以便有时间培养一下社交举止与风度。只有当他谈论自己的专业时，脸上才会充满活力与热情。除此之外，由于自己对社会大事认识的局限性，他总是沉默寡言，局促不安，而对于掩饰空洞头脑的闲聊他又极为缺乏耐性。

　　然而几年之间，这两个截然不同的竞争对手却慢慢地从简单的相识变成了朋友。而这一转变的基础正在于他们彼此之间能够相互欣赏，因为他们都是各自领域里年轻一代的佼佼者，拥有可以相互匹敌的学识与激情。共同的兴趣与追求使他们走到了一起，又因彼此的学识而相互吸引。渐渐地，他们相互间又发现了更多的东西。肯尼迪觉得他对手身上的坦诚与率真甚为有趣，而伯格又被肯尼迪的才智与风趣所吸引，正是凭借这两点肯尼迪曾经成为罗马社交界的宠儿。用"曾经"是因为，现在这位年轻的英国人已经有点儿失宠了。一段细节从未被公开的桃色事件表明他是个无情无义的人，这令他的许多朋友感到震惊。但在他转而想要加入的单身学者与艺术家的圈子里，关于这类问题并没有十分严格的名誉准则。尽管人们对双飞单归或许也会摇摇头，耸耸肩，但更为普遍的态度是好奇，抑或是嫉妒，而绝不会是谴责。

"你瞧，伯格，"盯着同伴那张平静的脸，肯尼迪说，"真希望你能信任我。"

他一边说，一边挥手指向地板上的一块地毯，上面放着一个罗马周边平原地区常见的浅底柳条水果长篮。里面堆满了各种杂物，有刻了字的瓦片、破碎的碑文、裂纹的马赛克、撕碎的纸莎草纸、生锈的金属饰物。一般人会认为这些都是从垃圾箱里捡来的破烂，而专家会很快认出这些都是稀世珍宝。浅底柳编篮里的杂物正好可以延续上一段断代社会发展史，而这段历史刚好是这位学者的兴趣所在。正是这位德国人把它们带来的，英国人如饥似渴地看着这些宝物。

"我不会动你的这些珍宝，但我会很乐意听听它们的故事，"他继续说道，而此时，伯格不动声色地点燃了一根雪茄。"很明显，这是最重大的发现。这些碑铭将会在整个欧洲引起轰动。"

"那儿的东西是这些的百万倍！"德国人说道。"数量如此之大，就是派去十多个专家，恐怕也得研究上一辈子，而且个个都会享有像圣天使城堡一样牢不可摧的声望。"

肯尼迪坐在那里，紧蹙着俊美的额头，一边沉思，一边用手指捋弄着他那修长精致的胡须。

"你都说漏嘴了，伯格！"他终于说道，"你所说的只表明一件事，你发现了一座新的地下墓穴。"

"我肯定你在查看这些物件儿时就已经得出了这个结论。"

"是的，它们确实可以表明这一点，但是你最后的那句话证实了这一点。除了地下墓穴，不可能再在其他任何一个地方发现像你所说数量如此之多的古物。"

"确是如此。毫无秘密可言。我确实发现了一个新的地下墓穴。"

"在哪儿？"

"呵，这可是个秘密，我亲爱的肯尼迪。它所在的地方任何人都找不到，就连百万分之一的机会都没有。它的年代也不同于任何一个已知的地下墓穴。它是用来埋葬最高级别的基督徒的，所以那里的遗体和遗物同我们以前见过的任何一种都截然不同。如果我不了解你的水平和精力，我的朋友，你只要发誓保密，我会毫不犹豫地告诉你所有的事情。但是要知道，在向你这个强有力的竞争对手透露任何消息之前，我想我必须确保自己能就此完成一篇论文。"

肯尼迪对自己专业的热爱几近痴迷，尽管像他这样富有而浪荡的公子哥儿会遇到形形色色的诱惑和纷扰，可他对自己的专业仍是如痴如醉。他有雄心抱负，可同研究古罗马生活的方方面面所带来的不可言喻的快乐与兴趣相比，他的抱负也只能退而居其次。他渴望去他伙伴发现的这一新的地下世界一探究竟。

"你瞧，伯格，"他诚恳地说道，"我向你保证，这件事你可以百分之百地相信我。除非得到你的许可，否则无论受到何种诱惑，有关我所看到的一切，我是一个字也不会写的。我十分理解你的想法，而且我认为这种想法再自然不过了。但在我这方面你实在是没什么值得担忧的。再说，你要是不告诉我，我就会进行一番系统性的调查，而且很有可能会发现它。要是那样的话，我自然就会想怎么写就怎么写了，因为我根本就不欠你的。"

伯格吸着烟，若有所思地笑了笑，说道："我可早就注意到了，肯尼迪，我的朋友，当我需要一些信息时，你可没有总是那么痛快提供过。"

"你什么时候问我，我没告诉过你？你记不记得，你那次要写有关维斯塔圆庙的文章，我就给过你相关材料。"

"嗯，是的，但那东西并不怎么重要。要是我问你一些极为隐秘的问题你会告诉我答案吗？我怀疑！这个新地下墓穴对我来说就是个极为隐秘的东西，作为交换，我当然也希望得到同样的回报。"

"我不知道你到底想要什么，"英国人说，"但如果你是说，我要是回答你提出的任何问题，你就会告诉我有关地下墓穴的事，那我向你保证，我绝对会这么做的。"

"那么，好吧，"伯格一边说，一边懒洋洋地向后靠到长椅背上，又向空中吐出了一股蓝色的雪茄烟。"告诉我一切有关你和玛丽·桑德森小姐之间的事情。"

肯尼迪一下子从椅子上跳了起来，愤怒地瞪着他那表情冷漠的同伴。"你到底是什么意思？！这是个什么问题？你是在开玩笑吗？可没有比这更糟糕的玩笑了。"

"不，我不是在开玩笑，"伯格轻描淡写道，"我确实对这件事的细节极感兴趣。我对这个世界、女人、社交生活等等诸如此类的事情了解得并不多，而且这样的事情对我来说总是有种莫名其妙的魔力。我认识你，也见过她——我和她大概说过一两次话。我真的很想听你亲口说说你俩到底发生了些什么事。"

"我一个字也不会告诉你的。"

"那好吧。这只不过是我一时的怪念头。你希望我能一下子就说出有关地下墓穴的秘密,我只是想看看你是不是也能一下子就说出你的秘密。你不能,我也不指望你能。那你又凭什么认为我能?圣约翰大钟正敲响十点钟呢。我真的该回家了。"

"不,你等等,伯格,"肯尼迪说,"你可真够怪的,非要知道这几个月前就了结了的旧情事。你知道人们都认为一个人要是到处宣扬他吻过哪个女人,他就是最为无耻的懦夫、混蛋。"

"那是当然,"德国人说道,同时收拾起他那一篮古董,"如果他所谈论有关那女孩儿的事情还是别人一无所知的,那他的确是个混蛋。可就这件事来说,你也知道,已经是完全公开的了,整个罗马都在谈论这件事,所以同我谈论有关玛丽·桑德森小姐的事情,你压根儿就不会对她造成任何伤害。不过当然,我仍旧尊重你的顾忌,那么就晚安吧!"

"等等,伯格,"肯尼迪把手搭在对方的胳膊上,说道,"我对古墓这件事情确实很感兴趣,我是不会这么轻易放手的。作为回报,你能不能问我点儿其他事情——这次只要不是如此怪异的问题就行。"

"不行,不行,你都已经拒绝了,就这样吧,"伯格把篮子挎在胳膊上,说道,"毫无疑问,你不回答是正确的,同样我的猜测也是正确的——好了,我亲爱的肯尼迪,还是晚安吧!"

英国人看着伯格穿过房间,把手放在门把上。就在这时,房间的主人突然跳了起来,那架势就如同一个人在败局已定的情况下仍想要力挽狂澜。

"等一下,老伙计,"他说,"我觉得你现在的表现真的是再怪不过了,但如果这就是你的条件,我想我就只能告诉你了。我痛恨谈论有关一个女孩儿的任何事情,但是,就像你说的,现在全罗马都知道了,我想我也说不出什么你还不知道的东西了。你想知道什么?"

德国人走回到壁炉前,放下篮子,又陷到椅子里。

"我可以再来根雪茄吗?"他问道。"太谢谢你了!我工作的时候从不吸烟,不过聊天时抽点烟,会大大提高我的兴致。好了,说到这位年轻的女士,你同她共同经历了这段小小的冒险。她现在到底怎么样了?"

"她和她的家人住在一起。"

"噢,是吗——在英格兰?"

"是的。"

"英格兰的什么地方——伦敦?"

"不,是特威肯汉。"

"千万别介意我的好奇心,我亲爱的肯尼迪,要知道这完全是因为我对这个世界的无知。毫无疑问这件事做起来相当简单，去说服一个年轻的女士跟你一起远走高飞三个星期左右的时间，然后再把她交回给她的家人——你刚才说那地方叫什么来着？"

"特威肯汉。"

"啊，对——在特威肯汉。但我对这种事情实在是太没经验，所以根本无法想象你是怎么搞的。比如说，你要是爱过这个女孩儿，你的爱很难在三个星期后就消失得无影无踪，所以我估计你压根儿就不曾爱过她。但你要是不爱她，为何又要搞出如此丑闻伤了自己又毁了她？"

"你这样看是合乎情理的，当然。"肯尼迪忧郁地望着壁炉里的那团红火。"爱是个很大的字眼儿，它涵盖了多种不同的情感。我喜欢过她，而且——哎，你说你曾见过她的——你知道她看起来是多么的迷人。但回头想想，我还是得承认，我可能真的就没爱过她。"

"那么，我亲爱的肯尼迪，你为什么还要这么做？"

"主要是因为这件事很具冒险性。"

"什么？你可真是太爱冒险了！"

"生活要是没了冒险还有什么意思？正是因为这种冒险性，我才会第一次去关注她。我曾追逐过很多猎物，但没有比追逐一个漂亮女人更刺激的了。这事并不那么好做，这也正是令人兴奋的地方。她是艾米莉·路德夫人的侍伴，所以几乎就找不到她独处的机会。而在所有这些令人兴奋的障碍中，最吸引我的一点是，她当时已经订婚了。这是我们交往之初她亲口告诉我的。"

"我的天哪！和谁？"

"她没说过名字。"

"我想没人知道这一点。这让整个冒险更有吸引力了，是不是？"

"嗯，确实更有味道了。你不这么认为吗？"

"跟你说，我对这类事确实很无知。"

"我亲爱的朋友，你一定知道从邻居树上偷来的苹果总是比自己树上掉下来的甜。后来我就发现她喜欢上我了。"

"什么——马上？"

"哦，不，费了大概三个月的工夫。不过最后还是把她搞定了。她也知道我当时和妻子是法定分居，所以不可能和她结婚，可她还是义无反顾地来了，我们过得还是很快乐的，至少在那段时间里。"

"可那个男人怎么办？"

"我认为这就是适者生存。"肯尼迪耸了耸肩。"如果他更为优秀，她也不会抛弃他。不谈这事了，我已经说够了！"

"再说一件事。你是怎么在三个星期后就甩掉她的?"

"唉,你知道,我们后来都恢复了点理智。不论怎样,她断然拒绝来罗马见她曾经认识的人。可是,罗马对我来说当然是必去之地,而且当时我也开始极其渴望回去工作——这就是个再明显不过的分手理由。而且接着她的老爹突然出现在伦敦的旅馆里面,大吵了一架,整个事情变得如此令人不悦,我真觉得——虽然一开始,我还想她想得要命——从这件事里脱身还真是件快事。好了,我相信你是不会把我的话讲出去的。"

"我亲爱的肯尼迪,我就是做梦也不会讲出去的。但你所说的真的让我很感兴趣,我还了解了你看问题的方式,和我的完全不同,因为我对生活了解得实在太少了。好了,你不是想知道我新发现的地下墓穴吗?描述是没有用的,这样做你什么也得不到。只有一种办法,那就是我把你带去。"

"那可太棒了。"

"你想什么时候去?"

"越早越好。我都等不及要去瞧瞧它了。"

"好吧,这是一个美妙的夜晚——虽说有点冷。那就一个小时以后出发吧。我们必须小心,不能让别人知道。要是有人看见咱俩一起出巡,肯定会起疑心。"

"再怎么小心也不为过,"肯尼迪说。"远吗?"

"几英里吧。"

"走起来也不算太远?"

"哦,是的,很轻松就能走到。"

"那最好还是走着去。咱俩一起在一个僻静的地方下车,又是大半夜的,很容易引起马车夫的怀疑。"

"的确如此。那咱俩最好在午夜时分在亚壁古道的大门口会面。我得回去取些火柴、蜡烛之类的东西。"

"那行,伯格!你真是太好了,让我知道这个秘密。我向你保证,在你发表论文之前,我是一个字也不会写的。那先就此道别!12点的时候我肯定会在大门那儿等你的。"

罗马城里的大钟悠扬奏响,钟声在寒冷而清爽的空气里飘荡着。伯格裹着一件意大利大衣,一手提着灯,向约定地点走去。肯尼迪从黑影里走出来见他。

"你对工作和爱情拥有同样的激情!"德国人笑着说道。

"是的,我在这儿都等了快半个小时了。"

"希望你没被人看见。"

"没那么傻!哎呀,我都冻透了!来吧,伯格,让我们疾步向前,把自己暖起来吧。"

这段由粗石铺就的马路是仅存于世并正在消失的曾经最为著名的公路,他们踏于其上的脚步声响亮而清脆。俩人在路上只是碰见了一两个从酒馆回家的农夫,以及一些往罗马城运送农产品的大车。他们大步前行,路两边许多巨大的坟墓,在黑暗中若隐若现。俩人一直走到了圣卡利斯托斯的地下墓穴。衬着月光,西西莉亚·梅泰拉陵墓那宏伟的圆形堡垒耸立在他们的面前。伯格停下了脚步,一只手叉着腰。

"你的腿比我的长,而且你更习惯于走路,"他笑着说,"我想我们要拐弯的地方就在这附近。是的,就是这儿,就在那家饮食店的拐角处。那条路很窄,最好我在前面走,你在后面跟着。"

他点亮了提灯,那点儿光亮足以让他们沿着这条狭窄曲折的小径,在罗马城郊平原地带的沼泽地里迂回前行。月光下,古罗马时期的导水沟渠就像是一条巨大而可怖的毛毛虫匍匐在地里。他们从这毛毛虫的一处拱起下穿过,又经过了曾是古代竞技场的一圈儿破碎的砖堆。终于,伯格在一处孤零零的木头牛舍前停了下来,并从口袋里掏出了一把钥匙。"你的地下墓穴肯定不是在一所房子里吧!"肯尼迪大叫道。

"这是它的入口。这牛棚正可以保证除了我们谁也别想发现它。"

"牛棚的主人知道吗?"

"他不知道。他曾发现过一两件东西,所以我几乎可以肯定,他的房子就建在一处陵寝的入口处。我就从他那儿把房子租了过来,自己开始挖掘。进来吧,把门关上。"

这房子进深很长,空荡荡的,只是沿着一面墙放着些牛槽。伯格把提灯放到地上,用外套把灯的三面罩住,只留一面取光。

"在这偏僻的地方,一点光亮都会引人注意的,"他说道,"帮我把这些地板挪开。"

地板的边缘已经松动了。两位专家将板子一块块地揭开,靠在墙边。底下露出一个方形洞口,一段古老的石阶从洞口一直延伸到洞内。

肯尼迪耐不住性子,冲下了石阶。"要小心!"伯格叫道,"这底下可绝对是个兔子洞,只要一迷路,就只有百分之一的机会再走出来。等我拿了灯再走。"

"要是这么复杂,你是怎么找到路的?"

"一开始也险得很,不过逐渐就摸出门道儿了。还是有规律的。可一个人要是在这里迷了路,而且还是在黑暗之中,恐怕就很难出去了。就是现在我要是在这墓穴里走得远了,也总要在身后拖个线球。你也知道,这样做很麻烦,可再往里走不到一百码,这里的每条通道都能一分再分地分出十多条岔道来。"

他们已从牛棚处往下走了大约20英尺,进入了一间在软石灰岩中凿出的正方形的房间。提灯的光线摇曳不定,下明上昏,映着那裂了纹的褐色墙面。房间的四面八方都是黑洞洞的路口,从这个中心延伸出去。

"你要紧紧地跟着我,我的朋友,"伯格说道。"路上看见什么都不许停,我领你去的地方什么都有,更好更全。我们抓紧时间,直奔重点。"

他带路走进其中一条通道,英国人紧随其后。这条路时不时地就会分叉,伯格明显是沿着他自己的秘密标记前行,因为他既不曾停下脚步也不曾犹豫不决。沿着墙壁,到处都塞满了古罗马时期基督教徒的遗骸,就像是移民船上的卧铺,密密麻麻的。昏黄的灯光闪烁不定,映照着木乃伊那干枯褶皱的面皮,闪烁着那一个个圆圆的头颅,那细长、惨白的臂骨,交叉在干瘪无肉的胸前。每路过一处,肯尼迪都要用渴求的眼神扫视着那些碑铭、殡葬器皿、画卷、法衣、各种用具,所有的东西都一如几百年前经由那一双双虔诚的双手放置的那样摆在那里。即便只是匆忙地瞄上几眼,肯尼迪也能一眼看出这是所有地下墓穴中年代最久,最为精美的一个,里面塞满了各种罗马古物,数量如此之多是他以前从未见过的。

"灯要是灭了怎么办?"他问道,他们疾行的脚步并未停止。

"我口袋里还有一根备用蜡烛和一盒火柴。对了,肯尼迪,你带火柴了吗?"

"没有,你最好给我几根。"

"呵,没事儿。反正咱俩也不会分开。"

"还有多远?感觉咱们至少都走了四分之一英里了。"

"比那多,我想。这墓穴就没个尽头——至少,我是没发现过。这地方可真是不好走,我看还是用线球吧。"

他把线球的一端系在一块凸起的石头上,把线球揣在大衣的胸兜里,边走边往外拖线。肯尼迪也瞧出来这种谨慎并非多余,通道已变得极为复杂曲折,交错纵横的岔道形成完美的网络。而这所有的通道均在一处宽敞的圆形大厅交汇。大厅一端有个四方形的台子,石灰岩底座,大理石台面。

伯格拎着提灯晃了晃这块儿大理石。"天啊!"肯尼迪跟着狂喜道,"这是基督徒的祭坛,很可能是现存最早的。这个角上还刻着一个小小的祭祀十字。这个圆形大厅以前肯定是用来作教堂的。"

"完全正确,"伯格说,"就是时间太少了,要不我就领你看看墙上壁龛里所有的遗体,全都是早期的教皇和主教,还有他们的法冠、牧杖、全套的法衣。快去看看那边那个!"

肯尼迪走了过去，瞪大了眼睛瞅着那可怖的头颅，头颅底下散布着腐朽破碎的法冠。

"这真是太有趣了，"他说道。他的声音似乎与拱顶相撞而隆隆作响。"依我的经验，这很独特。把提灯拿过来，伯格，我想把他们都看看。"

可那德国人早已悠悠地走开，正站在大厅的另一头，罩在那黄色光圈的中央。"你知道从这到入口的那段楼梯之间有多少假岔道吗？超过两千个。毫无疑问这是基督徒采取的保护措施之一。即使有灯，一个人能活着走出去的概率也就是两千分之一；可要是没灯，当然，就要更困难一些了。"

"我也是这么想的。"

"而且黑暗是个很可怕的东西。我曾经试过一次。咱们再试一次吧！"他俯身吹灭了提灯，瞬时间，就好像有一只看不见的手紧紧地捂住了肯尼迪的眼睛。他从未经历过如此的黑暗。这黑暗像是在向他挤压过来，让他窒息。这黑暗就像是有形的障碍挡在身前，让他无法前行。他伸出手想将这黑暗推开。"行了，伯格，把灯点上吧。"

可他的同伴却笑了起来。在圆形的大厅里，这笑声似乎来自四面八方。他说："你有些不安呀，我的朋友肯尼迪。"

"快点，伙计，把蜡烛点上！"肯尼迪有些不耐烦了。

"真是太怪了，肯尼迪，听你的声音我根本说不出你在哪儿。你知道我在哪儿吗？"

"不知道，好像我的周围全是你。"

"要不是我手里有这根线，我根本不可能知道走哪条路。"

"确是如此。划个火吧，伙计，别无聊了。"

"你瞧，肯尼迪，有两件事我知道你特别喜欢。一个是冒险，再一个就是逾越障碍。冒险，就是摸索着走出这地下墓穴。障碍，就是黑暗和两千个假岔道，这会让寻路变得有些费劲。不过你也不用着急，反正有的是时间。当你停下来休息的时候，我希望你倒是想想玛丽·桑德森小姐，想想你是不是对得起她。"

"你个混蛋，你是什么意思？"肯尼迪怒吼道。他绕着圈子，没头脑地乱跑乱撞，在凝固了的黑暗中挥着双手，乱抓乱扯。

"再见啦，"一个嘲弄的声音从远处说道。"肯尼迪，即便是根据你自己的说法，我也不认为你对那女孩儿做的是对的。还有一件小事看来你并不知道，我倒是可以告诉你。和桑德森小姐订婚的是一个其貌不扬的穷鬼学者，而他的名字是尤利乌斯·伯格。"

某处隐约传来脚踩在石头上的窸窣声，接着这古老的基督教堂就陷入一片死寂——那么的凝滞、沉重。肯尼迪被这沉寂包裹着，就像溺水之人，瞬间被这死寂吞没。

大约两个月以后，下面这段文字被欧洲的各大报刊转载：

"罗马最新发现一座地下墓穴，这是近几年来最令人兴奋的发现之一。该墓穴位于著名的圣卡利斯托斯墓穴以东，里面拥有大量极具研究价值的早期基督徒遗骸。这一重要埋葬地点的发现要归功于尤利乌斯·伯格博士，一位精力充沛、聪慧睿智、年轻有为的德国专家，他已迅速成为古罗马研究的学术泰斗。尽管他是公开发布这一发现的第一人，但在伯格博士之前还有一个不太幸运的冒险家先期到达过古墓。数月前，肯尼迪先生，著名的英国学者，在他位于卡尔索的房子里突然失踪。据当时推测，可能因为一桩丑闻，他不得不离开罗马。现在看来，他实际已在古墓中遇难。他对考古学的热衷使他成为该领域中的佼佼者，亦使他付出了生命的代价。他的尸体是在新地下墓穴的中心地带发现的。从他双脚及靴子的磨损情况可以明显看出他在那些迂回曲折的通道里曾连续行走多日。对于探险者来说，正是这些通道让地下坟墓变得极为危险。据目前调查表明，这位先生既没拿蜡烛也没带火柴，单凭令人费解的冲动，就走进了地下迷宫。他的悲惨命运自然是这一冲动的必然后果。尤为痛心的是，尤利乌斯·伯格博士还是这位已故先生的亲密朋友。他万分幸运取得这一卓越发现的喜悦也因其伙伴兼同事的可怕命运而大减。"

H. G. Wells
(1866—1946)

H. G. Wells (Herbert George Wells) is an English novelist, journalist, sociologist, and historian, but he is best known for his science fiction novels. Wells was born in Bromley, Kent. His father was a shopkeeper and a professional cricketer, and his mother served from time to time as a housekeeper. In his early childhood, Wells developed love for literature. Later he obtained a scholarship to the Normal School of Science in London and studied biology there under T. H. Huxley. However, his interest faltered and in 1887 he left without a degree. He taught in private schools for four years, not taking his B. S. degree until 1890. Wells lived through World War II in his house on Regent's Park and he died in London.

Wells's best-known works are *The Time Machine* (1895), one of the first modern science fiction stories, *The Invisible Man* (1897), and *The War of the Worlds* (1898). His novels are among the classics of science fiction. Later in his life Wells's romantic and enthusiastic conception of technology turned more doubtful. Wells also published critical pamphlets attacking the Victorian social order, including *Anticipations* (1901), *Mankind in the Making* (1903), and *A Modern Utopia* (1905). His last book, *Mind at the End of Its Tether* (1945), is about mankind's future prospects, which he always viewed with pessimism.

The Stolen Bacillus

In the following story, a man forges the letter of introduction, meets the bacteriologist, steals the bacillus and runs away with it. Then follows a dramatic cab chase between the visitor, the bacteriologist and his wife. The visitor turns out to be an anarchist and he drinks the drops of the bacillus in order to spread it widely when the tube breaks by accident although ironically it is not the deadly bacillus of cholera in the end. Besides the dramatic tension and comical effect, the story implies certain dark conflicts between science, politics and the well-being of society.

"This again," said the bacteriologist, slipping a glass slide under the microscope, "is a preparation of the celebrated bacillus of cholera—the cholera germ."

The pale-faced man peered down the microscope. He was evidently not accustomed to that kind of thing, and held a limp white hand over his disengaged eye. "I see very little," he said.

"Touch this screw," said the bacteriologist; "perhaps the microscope is out of focus for you. Eyes vary so much. Just the fraction of a turn this way or that."

"Ah! now I see," said the visitor. "Not so very much to see after all. Little streaks and shreds of pink. And yet those little particles, those mere atomies, might multiply and devastate a city! Wonderful!"

He stood up, and releasing the glass slip from the microscope, held it in his hand towards the window. "Scarcely visible," he said, scrutinizing the preparation. He hesitated, "Are these—alive? Are they dangerous now?"

"Those have been stained and killed," said the bacteriologist. "I wish, for my own part, we could kill and stain every one of them in the universe."

"I suppose," the pale man said with a slight smile, "that you scarcely care to have such things about you in the living—in the active state?"

"On the contrary, we are obliged to," said the bacteriologist. "Here, for instance—" He walked across the room and took up one of several sealed tubes. "Here is the living thing. This is a cultivation of the actual living disease bacteria." He hesitated. "Bottled cholera, so to speak."

A slight gleam of satisfaction appeared momentarily in the face of the pale man. "It's a deadly thing to have in your possession," he said, devouring the little tube with his eyes. The bacteriologist watched the morbid pleasure in his visitor's expression. This man, who had visited him that afternoon with a note of introduction from an old friend, interested him from the very contrast of their dispositions. The lank black hair and deep grey eyes, the haggard expression and nervous manner, the fitful yet keen interest in his visitor, were a novel change from the phlegmatic deliberations of the ordinary scientific worker with whom the bacteriologist chiefly associated. It was perhaps natural, with a hearer evidently so impressionable to the lethal nature of his topic, to take the most effective aspect of the matter.

He held the tube in his hand thoughtfully. "Yes, here is the pestilence imprisoned. Only break such a little tube as this into a supply of drinking-water, say to these minute particles of life that one must needs stain and examine with the highest powers of the microscope even to see, and that one can neither smell nor taste—say to them, 'Go forth, increase and multiply, and replenish the cisterns, 'and death—mysterious, untraceable death, death swift and terrible, death full of pain and indignity—would be released upon this city, and go hither and thither seeking his victims. Here he would take the husband from the wife, here the child from its mother, here the statesman from his duty, and here the toiler from his trouble. He would follow the water-mains, creeping along streets, picking out and punishing a house here and a house there where they did not boil their drinking-water, creeping into the wells of the mineral-water makers, getting washed into salad and lying dormant in ices. He would wait ready to be drunk in the horse-troughs and by unwary children in the public fountains. He would soak into the soil, to reappear in springs and wells at a thousand unexpected places. Once start him at the water supply, and before we could ring him in, and catch him again, he would have decimated the metropolis." He stopped abruptly. He had been told rhetoric was his weakness. "But he is quite safe here, you know—quite safe."

The pale-faced man nodded. His eyes shone. He cleared his throat. "These anarchist—rascals," said he, "are fools, blind fools—to use bombs when this kind of thing is attainable. I think—"

A gentle rap, a mere light touch of the fingernails was heard at the door. The bacteriologist opened it.

"Just a minute, dear," whispered his wife.

When he re-entered the laboratory his visitor was looking at his watch. "I had no idea I had wasted an hour of your time," he said. "Twelve minutes to four. I ought to have left here by half-past three. But your things were really too interesting. No, positively I cannot stop a moment longer. I have an engagement at four."

He passed out of the room, reiterating his thanks, and the bacteriologist accompanied him to the door, and then returned thoughtfully along the passage to his laboratory. He was musing on the ethnology of his visitor. Certainly the man was not a Teutonic type nor a common Latin one. "A morbid product, anyhow, I am afraid," said the bacteriologist to himself. "How he gloated on those cultivations of disease-germs!" A disturbing thought struck him. He turned to the bench by the vapour-bath, and then very quickly to his writing-table. Then he felt hastily in his pockets, and then rushed to the door. "I may have put it down on the hall table," he said.

"Minnie!" he shouted hoarsely in the hall.

"Yes, dear," came a remote voice.

"Had I anything in my hand when I spoke to you, dear, just now?"

Pause.

"Nothing, dear, because I remember—"

"Blue ruin!" cried the bacteriologist, and incontinently ran to the front door and down the steps of his house to the street.

Minnie, hearing the door slam violently, ran in alarm to the window. Down the street a slender man was getting into a cab. The bacteriologist, hatless, and in his carpet slippers, was running and gesticulating wildly towards this group. One slipper came off, but he did not wait for it. "He has gone *mad*!" said Minnie, "it's that horrid science of his;" and, opening the window, would have called after him. The slender man, suddenly glancing round, seemed struck with the same idea of mental disorder. He pointed hastily to the bacteriologist, said something to the cabman, the apron of the cab slammed, the whip swished, the horse's feet clattered, and in a moment the cab, bacteriologist hotly in pursuit, had receded up the vista of the roadway and disappeared round the corner.

Minnie remained straining out of the window for a minute. Then she drew her head back into the room again. She was dumbfounded. "Of course he is eccentric," she meditated. "But running about London—in the height of the season, too—in his socks!" A happy thought struck her. She hastily put her bonnet on, seized his shoes, went into the hall, took down his hat and light overcoat from the pegs, emerged upon the doorstep, and hailed a cab that opportunely crawled by. "Drive me up the road and round Havelock Crescent, and see if we can find a gentleman running about in a velveteen coat and no hat."

"Velveteen coat, ma'am and no' at. Very good, ma'am." And the cabman whipped up at once in the most matter-of-fact way, as if he drove to this address every day in his life.

Some few minutes later the little group of cabmen and loafers that collects round the cabmen's shelter at Haverstock Hill were startled by the passing of a cab with a ginger-coloured screw of a horse, driven furiously.

They were silent as it went by, and then as it receded—"That's 'Arry' Icks. Wot's *he* got?" said the stout gentleman known as Old Tootles.

"He's a-using his whip, he is, *to* rights," said the ostler boy.

"Hallo!" said poor old Tommy Byles, "here's another bloomin' loonatic. Blowed if there ain't."

"It's Old George," said Old Tootles, "and he's drivin' a loonatic, as you say. Ain't he a-clawin' out of the keb? Wonder if he's after 'Arry 'Icks?"

The group round the cabmen's shelter became animated. Chorus: "Go it, George!" "It's a race!" "You'll ketch 'em!" "Whip up!"

"She's a goer, she is!" said the ostler boy.

"Strike me giddy!" cried Old Tootles. "Here! *I'm* a-goin' to begin in a minute. Here's another comin'. If all the kebs in Hampstead ain't gone mad this morning!"

"It's a female this time," said the ostler boy.

"She's a-following *him*," said Old Tootles. "Usually the other way about."

"What's she got in her 'and?"

"Looks like a 'igh 'at."

"What a bloomin' lark it is! Three to one on old George," said the ostler boy. "Next!"

Minnie went by in a perfect roar of applause. She did not like it but she felt that she was doing her duty, and whirled on down Haverstock Hill and Camden Town High Street with her eyes ever intent on the animated back of Old George, who was driving her vagrant husband so incomprehensively away from her.

The man in the foremost cab sat crouched in the corner, his arms tightly folded, and the little tube that contained such vast possibilities of destruction gripped in his hand. His mood was a singular mixture of fear and exultation. Chiefly he was afraid of being caught before he could accomplish his purpose, but behind this was a vaguer but larger fear of the awfulness of his crime. But his exultation far exceeded his fear. No anarchist before him had ever approached this conception of his. Ravachol, Vaillant, all those distinguished persons whose fame he had envied, dwindled into insignificance beside him. He had only to make sure of the water-supply, and break the little tube into a reservoir. How brilliantly he had planned it, forged the letter of introduction, and got into the laboratory, and how brilliantly he had seized his opportunity! The world should hear of him at last. All those people who had sneered at him, neglected him, preferred other people to him, found his company undesirable, should consider him at last. Death, death, death! They had always treated him as a man of no importance. All the world had been in a conspiracy to keep him under. He would teach them yet what it is to isolate a man. What was this familiar street? Great St Andrew's Street, of course! How fared the chase? He craned out of the cab. The bacteriologist was scarcely fifty yards behind. That was bad. He would be caught and stopped yet. He felt in his pocket for money, and found half a sovereign. This he thrust up through the trap in the top of the cab into the man's face. "More," he shouted, "if only we get away."

The money was snatched out of his hand. "Right you are," said the cabman, and the trap slammed, and the lash lay along the glistening side of the horse. The cab swayed, and the anarchist, half-standing under the trap, put the hand containing the little glass tube upon the apron to preserve his balance. He felt the brittle thing crack, and the broken half of it rang upon the floor of the cab. He fell back into the seat with a curse, and stared dismally at the two or three drops of moisture on the apron.

He shuddered.

"Well! I suppose I shall be the first. *Phew*! Anyhow, I shall be a martyr. That's something. But it is a filthy death, nevertheless. I wonder if it hurts as much as they say."

Presently a thought occurred to him—he groped between his feet. A little drop was still in the broken end of the tube, and he drank that to make sure. It was better to make sure. At any rate, he would not fail.

Then it dawned upon him that there was no further need to escape the bacteriologist. In Wellington Street he told the cabman to stop and got out. He slipped on the step, his head felt queer. It was rapid stuff this cholera poison. He waved his cabman out of existence, so to speak, and stood on the pavement with his arms folded upon his breast, awaiting the arrival of the bacteriologist. There was something tragic in his pose. The sense of imminent death gave him a certain dignity. He greeted his pursuer with a defiant laugh.

"*Vive l'anarchie*! You are too late, my friend. I have drunk it. The cholera is abroad!"

The bacteriologist from his cab beamed curiously at him through his spectacles. "You have drunk it! An anarchist! I see now." He was about to say something more, and then checked himself. A smile hung in the corner of his mouth. He opened the apron of his cab as if to descend, at which the anarchist waved him a dramatic farewell and strode off towards Waterloo Bridge, carefully jostling his infected body against as many people as possible.

The bacteriologist was so preoccupied with the vision of him that he scarcely manifested the slightest surprise at the appearance of Minnie upon the pavement with his hat and shoes and overcoat. "Very good of you to bring my things," he said, and remained lost in contemplation of the receding figure of the anarchist. "You had better get in," he said, still staring. Minnie felt absolutely convinced now that he was mad, and directed the cabman home on her own responsibility.

"Put on my shoes? Certainly, dear," said he, as the cab began to turn and hid the strutting black figure, now small in the distance, from his eyes. Then suddenly something grotesque struck him, and he laughed. Then he remarked, "It is really very serious, though. You see, that man came to my house to see me, and he is an anarchist. No—don't faint, or I cannot possibly tell you the rest. And I wanted to astonish him, not knowing he was an anarchist, and took up a cultivation of that new species of bacterium I was telling you of, that infests, and I think causes the blue patches upon, various monkeys; and, like a fool, I said it was Asiatic cholera. And he ran away with it to poison the water of London, and he certainly might have made things look blue for this civilised city. But instead he has swallowed it. Of course, I cannot say what will happen, but you know it turned that kitten blue, and the three puppies—in patches, and the sparrow—bright blue. But the bother is, I shall have all the trouble and expense of preparing some more."

"Put on my coat on this hot day! Why? Because we might meet Mrs Jabber? My dear, Mrs Jabber is not a draught. But why should I wear a coat on a hot day because of Mrs—? Oh! *very well*."

Questions

1. Who stole the bacillus?
2. Compared with the scientist, what do you think of the man who stole the bacillus?
3. What would be the harm of the bacillus if it was broken?
4. What actually happened at the end of this story?
5. What do you learn from this story?

赫·乔·威尔斯
（1866—1946）

　　赫·乔·威尔斯（赫伯特·乔治·威尔斯）是英国小说家、记者、社会学家和历史学家，但他最著名的头衔是科幻小说家。威尔斯出生在肯特郡勃朗里城。他父亲既是一家商店店主又是一位专业板球手，母亲时常给人做管家。威尔斯早在童年时期就开始热爱文学。后来他获得伦敦师范学院奖学金，在著名的赫胥黎教授指导下学习生物学。可在学校他的兴趣发生了变化，于1887年他没拿到学位就离开了学校，直到在私立学校教了四年书后的1890年才获得理学士学位。第二次世界大战期间他一直住在伦敦摄政公园附近的家里，并在那里去世。

　　威尔斯的最著名作品有：最早的现代科幻小说之一《时间机器》（1895）、《隐形人》（1897）和《世界之战》（1898）。他的小说是科幻经典。晚年他对于技术的浪漫情结与热情的态度更多地变成了怀疑。威尔斯还发表了一些评论作品，抨击维多利亚社会现状，其中有《期待》（1901）、《创造中的人类》（1903），以及《现代乌托邦》（1905）。他的最后一部作品是《无计可施的大脑》（1945），其中展望了人类的将来，充满了他惯有的悲观论调。

被盗的细菌

　　下面的故事讲述了一个人拿着伪造的介绍信，会见了一位细菌学家，偷了他的细菌，然后逃之夭夭这么一件怪事。然后是细菌学家乘马车追来访者、妻子追丈夫，一连串戏剧性的追逐。原来，来访者是个无政府主义者。半路上细菌试管突然破裂，这个无政府主义极端分子就喝了剩下的几滴，为的是要将细菌传播得更广，而颇具讽刺意味的是，他最终所偷走的并不是致命的霍乱病菌。故事除了戏剧性的紧张情节和某种滑稽效果之外，同时还暗示出科学、政治与社会福祉间的某种隐秘的矛盾。

　　"这又是一次著名的霍乱细菌——霍乱病菌胚芽的试验。"细菌学家把一个载玻片放在显微镜下说道。

　　一个面色苍白的来访者透过显微镜仔细观察。很显然，他对这类东西并不熟悉，他用苍白无力的手遮住另外一只眼睛说："我几乎什么都看不见。"

细菌学家说:"转动一下这个螺丝,或许你看的时候显微镜的焦距没有调好。不同的眼睛的差距是很大的。往这边或者那边稍稍调一下。"

"啊,我看见了!"这个来访者说,"但是并不太清晰。一条条粉色的。还有那些微粒,那些原子,可能会不断增多直至摧毁这座城市,真是太棒了!"

他站起来,把载玻片从显微镜下拿开,放在手里并朝窗户走去,"几乎看不见,"他仔细检查着制剂说。他犹豫了:"这些细菌是活的吗?现在有危险吗?"

"那些都是被染了色并且杀死了的,"细菌学家说,"对于我来说,我希望能杀死宇宙中的每一个这样的微粒并给它们染色。"

"我想你总不愿意有这些活的——处于激活状态的细菌在你周围吧?"那个面色苍白的人带着一丝微笑说。

"恰恰相反,我们必须面对,"细菌学家说,"比如说,"他穿过房间,从几个密封的试管中拿起一个,"这就是活的,这是病菌的活体繁殖的,"他犹豫了一下,"可以说是瓶装霍乱病菌。"

那个苍白的人脸上瞬间流露出一丝满意。"对你来说这是致命的东西,"他眼睛注视着小试管说。细菌学家观察着这位来访者脸上病态的喜悦。这个下午来拜访他的人是个老朋友介绍来的,由于他们完全不同的性格使得他对这个拜访者很感兴趣。来访者头发柔软乌黑,双眼深陷,表情憔悴,举止紧张,这些与同细菌学家经常打交道的普通科学工作者的冷静思考截然不同,很是新奇,因而激起细菌学家阵阵强烈的好奇。面对这样一位对他实验的破坏性的本质如此敏感的听众,大肆渲染一番这桩事或许是很自然的。

他手拿着试管陷入沉思。"是啊,这是被囚禁的病菌,只要打破这个小试管并将它投入饮用水中,对这些微小的生命粒子说,人只能用高倍显微镜才能看得见、给它们染色并检验,这些东西既无色也无味——对它们说,'继续增长、繁殖,填满整个蓄水池',这样,神秘的死亡,不可追踪的死亡,迅速可怕的死亡,充满痛苦与屈辱的死亡——将会在这座城市中爆发,到处蔓延,去寻找它的受害者。它会使妻子失去丈夫,使母亲失去孩子,使政客离职,使劳作者摆脱苦役。它会顺着水管,潜伏在街道上,选择并惩罚那些没有把饮用水烧开的家庭,潜入矿泉水工厂的井里,随水进入沙拉里,蛰伏于冰冻食品中。它会在马槽中等待着被马饮用,或者在喷泉中等待着被毫无警惕的孩子喝到。它会渗透到土壤中,并重现于千万处意想不到的泉水或是水井中。一旦它进入供水系统,在我们遏制住并抓住它之前,它早就摧毁了整座城市。"他突然停下来,意识到虚夸的言辞是他的弱点。"不过,它现在是非常安全的,放心吧,非常安全。"

那个面色苍白的人点点头。他眼睛发亮，清了清嗓子说："这些无政府主义者——无赖和流氓，真愚蠢，太愚蠢了，有这种病菌可以使用还用炸弹！我觉得……"

门被轻轻敲响，只听得见手指甲轻轻的触碰声，细菌学家打开门。

"打扰一下，亲爱的，"他的妻子低声说。

他再次回到实验室时，拜访者正在看手表。"我没有注意到我已经浪费您一小时的时间了，"他说，"差十二分钟四点，我本应三点半走。但是你的东西真是太有趣了。啊，不，我绝不能再待在这儿了，我四点还有预约。"

他走出房间，再次表示感谢，细菌学家送他到门口，若有所思地回到他的实验室。他在思考来访者的人种，他肯定既不是德意志人种也不是拉丁人种。"不管怎样，这个人恐怕都是个怪物，"他自言自语，"他怎么能对病毒的繁殖如此幸灾乐祸！"他突然有个不安的想法。他转向蒸汽浴室旁边的长凳，很快又回到他的书桌。他突然快速摸了下口袋，随即冲向房门。"我可能把它放在大厅的桌子上了，"他说。

"米妮！"他在大厅里嘶哑地喊道。

"什么事？亲爱的！"一个声音在远处应答着。

"刚刚我和你说话的时候手里拿着什么东西吗？"

妻子停顿了一下。

"什么也没有啊，亲爱的，因为我记得……"

"糟了！"细菌学家大叫，完全失控地向前门跑去，下了台阶，冲向街道。

米妮听到门砰的一声重重地关上，她惊恐地冲到窗旁。街上，一个瘦弱的男人上了一辆马车，细菌学家未戴帽子，穿着拖鞋，一边跑一边向马车招手叫停。一只鞋跑掉了，但是他并没有停下来。"他一定是疯了！"米妮说，"准是他那可怕的科学实验。"她打开窗户想大声喊他。那个瘦弱的男人突然回过头看，似乎也被同样的神经错乱所震惊。他匆匆指向那个细菌学家，对马夫说了些什么，马车的帘子突然放了下来，鞭子开始嗖嗖作响，马蹄也嗒嗒地响起来。瞬间，细菌学家苦苦追赶的马车便渐渐远去，最后消失在街角。

米妮继续向窗外看了一会儿，然后转向房间。她直发愣。"他的确另类，"她这么想着。"但在这样的季节，穿着袜子在伦敦城里跑来跑去……"这时她又忽然有个快活的想法。她迅速戴上帽子，抓起他的鞋子，走进大厅，从衣帽架上拿下他的帽子和外衣，走向门阶，叫住了一辆碰巧缓缓而来的马车。"走这条路去哈夫洛克·克雷森特街，看看能否找到一个穿着平绒上衣没戴帽子的男人。"

"平绒上衣,没戴帽子,好的,夫人。"车夫立刻像往常一样挥起鞭子,好像他每天都去这个地方似的。

几分钟后,在哈佛斯托克山庄的车夫休息处,聚集在那里的一小撮车夫和游手好闲之徒,被一辆疾驶而来的马车惊呆了。辕马呈姜黄色,疲倦不堪,暴躁如雷。

马车过来时他们都安静下来,当车跑远时,一个绰号叫老唠叨的壮汉说:"那是艾瑞·伊克斯,他怎么了?"

"他正挥舞着马鞭,向右转呢。"一个小马夫说。

"哎!"穷汉老汤米·拜尔斯说,"这儿又来了匹胡蹦乱跳的疯马。看那马喘的。"

"是老乔治,"老唠叨说,"你说得对,他驾了匹疯马。他在用马车追人吧?我怀疑他是不是在追艾瑞·伊克斯。"

在车夫休息处的一群人开始活跃起来,一起喊着:"快跑啊,乔治!""追啊!""你要追上他们了!""快啊!"

"那马真快,真快!"那个小马夫说。

"看得我直晕,"老唠叨说,"来吧!我也马上就出发了,又来一个,今早是不是汉普斯特德所有马车都疯了!"

"这次是个娘们儿!"那个小马夫说。

"她在追那个男的,"老唠叨说,"可一般是男追女啊。"

"她手里拿着什么?"

"看起来是顶高帽。"

"真像个云雀!老乔治是三比一啊!"小马夫说,"下一个!"

米妮经过时,响起一片震耳欲聋的掌声。她不喜欢这样,但是她觉得这是她的职责,并继续在哈佛斯托克山庄和卡姆登城高街上疾行,眼睛注视着老乔治上下颠簸的背,就是他驾车带着她狠狠的丈夫离她不知有多远。

最前面马车里的人蜷缩在一角,手臂紧紧地交叉着,那充满毁灭性的试管死死地被他握在手里。他现在的心情是既恐惧又兴奋。他主要是害怕在实现目标之前被抓住,但隐藏在背后的还有更模糊但也更大的恐惧,即对自己罪行严重性的恐惧。但此时,他的兴奋远远大于恐惧。在他之前,没有哪个无政府主义者的想法曾接近他的想法。拉瓦肖尔、瓦扬,这些人的名声他都曾嫉妒过,但现在都无法与他相比。他只需要找到供应水源,把小试管打破,投入水源地。他计划得多么聪明,伪造介绍信,进入实验室,他是多么完美地抓住了机会!全世界的人都会对他有所耳闻。所有那些嘲笑过他、忽视过他、喜欢别人胜过他、认为他的陪伴不称心如意的人，到最后都会对他刮目相看。去死，去死，去死吧！人们总是把他看得无足轻重。全世界的人都在共谋把他压在底下。他要好好教训教训他们，让他们知道孤立一个人将会怎样。这条熟悉的街道叫什么来着？当然是大圣安德鲁街！追得怎么样啦？他把头伸出马车观望。那个细菌学家也就在50码以外。糟糕，他会被赶上、抓住。他在口袋里找到了半英镑的金币，把钱从马车上方的活板门塞出去，直对着车夫的脸，喊道："只要甩掉他们，给你更多钱！"

钱从他的手里被抢走了，"放心吧，您！"马车夫说，活板门砰地关上了，鞭子抽打着油亮的马背。马车摇晃着，那个盗走细菌的人半蹲在车内，拿试管的手扶着马车围栏以保持平衡。他感觉到易碎的试管开始断裂，断了的一半掉到马车板上。他趔趄着坐回到位子上，嘴里诅咒着，盯着马车围栏上的两三滴水滴。

他战栗起来。

"我想我可能是第一个，咻！不管怎么样，我也算是个烈士。算是件了不起的事。可这么死也太肮脏了。不知是否像他们所说的那么痛苦。"

很快一个想法涌入他的脑中——他在两脚之间摸索着。在试管底部的裂痕处还有一滴，他喝下那一滴以确保万无一失。最好要万无一失。无论如何，他都不要失败。

这时他逐渐意识到已经没有必要再躲避那个细菌学家了。在威灵顿大街，他叫停车夫，下了马车。他在台阶上滑了一下，头有点儿眩晕。霍乱病菌发作得真快。可以说是他挥手叫车夫走了，叫他彻底消失了，随后他站在人行道上，双手交叉在胸前，等待着细菌学家的到来。他的姿势有一点儿悲剧的味道。死亡逼近的意识给了他些许尊严。他轻蔑地大笑着向追逐者打招呼。

"无政府主义万岁！你太迟了，我的朋友。我已经把它喝了！霍乱已经开始扩散了！"

透过眼镜，细菌学家从他的马车里好奇地看着他。"你把它喝了！真是个无政府主义之徒，我现在知道了。"他正想再说些什么，但又戛然而止，嘴角露出一丝微笑。他打开马车的帘子仿佛要下车，正在这时，那个人剧烈地向他挥手告别并朝着滑铁卢大桥大步走去，将他已感染的身体竭力挤入尽可能多的人群中。

细菌学家全神贯注于那人的身影，他对米妮拿着他的衣帽和鞋子出现在街道上并没有表现出多大的惊讶。"太好了，你把我的东西都拿来了，"他说着，还深陷于对那个无政府主义者消失的身影的沉思中。"你最好上车，"他的眼睛仍盯着。米妮现在绝对相信他已经疯了，于是她自作主张告诉车夫驾车回家。

"穿上鞋？当然，亲爱的，"他说，此时车夫调转车头，那个趾高气扬的背影在他眼中渐渐变小直至消失。突然，他想起一件稀奇古怪的事，于是大笑起来。然后他说:"这可的确很严重,你知道,那个人来我家看我,他是个无政府主义者。别——先别晕倒,否则我就不能告诉你其他的了。我想让他震惊,但我并不知道他是个无政府主义者,于是我拿了一个曾跟你说过的新品种的细菌,我想那些细菌能大批滋生在猴子身上并且在它们身上长蓝色块斑。我像个傻子一样说它是亚细亚霍乱菌。他拿着跑了,要污染伦敦的水,他当然也可能让这座文明城市里的东西变成蓝色。可是,他自己却把它喝了。当然,我说不准会发生什么事,但你知道它让那只小猫变成了蓝色,三只小狗长了块斑,让麻雀变成了明蓝色。可问题是,我还得费事、费钱再重新培养细菌。"

"这么热的天还穿外套!为什么?因为我们可能会碰见喳喳太太?亲爱的,喳喳太太又不是寒流。可为什么我得因为喳喳太太在这么大热天穿上外套呢?啊!那好吧。"

James Joyce
(1882—1941)

James Joyce, Irish novelist, was noted for his experimental use of language in such works as *Ulysses* (1922) and *Finnegans Wake* (1939). During his literary career Joyce suffered rejections from publishers, suppression by censors, attacks by critics, and misunderstanding by readers. He was born in Dublin and from 1902 Joyce led a nomadic life. Although he spent long times in Paris, Trieste, Rome, and Zürich, with only occasional brief visits to Ireland, his native country remained basic to all his writings.

His first important novel is *A Portrait of the Artist as a Young Man* (1914—1915). The book follows the life of the protagonist, Stephen Dedalus, from childhood towards maturity, his education at University College, Dublin, and his rebellion to free himself from the claims of his family and Irish nationalism. His most influential book, *Ulysses*, centers around Leopold Bloom, a Jewish advertising canvasser, his wife Molly, and Stephen Dedalus. The story, using stream-of-consciousness technique, parallels the major events in Odysseus' journey home. *Finnegans Wake* presents the dreams and nightmares of H. C. Earwicker and his family, and remains one of the most baffling works of the 20th century. His short story collection is *Dubliners*.

Araby

James Joyce is best-known for his modernistic narrative style of stream-of-consciousness. However, in the following story, we witness his early lucid and impressionist descriptions of a youth's desire and emotions. The youth in the story has "confused adoration" for his friend Mangan's sister. He strives to do everything to get close to her and to cater for her liking. Knowing that she loves to go to Araby but she can't actually go, the youth volunteers to go for her and promises to bring her something. Despite some difficulties, he eventually reaches the bazaar. However, in the hall of the bazaar, the youth feels total contempt from the adult world as well as his own disappointment and vanity. Thus, his heart is filled with anguish and anger.

North Richmond Street, being blind, was a quiet street except at the hour when the Christian Brothers' School set the boys free. An uninhabited house of two storeys stood at the blind end, detached from its neighbours in a square ground. The other houses of the street, conscious of decent lives within them, gazed at one another with brown imperturbable faces.

The former tenant of our house, a priest, had died in the back drawing-room. Air, musty from having been long enclosed, hung in all the rooms, and the waste room behind the kitchen was littered with old useless papers. Among these I found a few paper-covered books, the pages of which were curled and damp: *The Abbot*, by Walter Scott, *The Devout Communicant*, and *The Memoirs of Vidocq*. I liked the last best because its leaves were yellow. The wild garden behind the house contained a central apple-tree and a few straggling bushes, under one of which I found the late tenant's rusty bicycle-pump. He had been a very charitable priest; in his will he had left all his money to institutions and the furniture of his house to his sister.

When the short days of winter came, dusk fell before we had well eaten our dinners. When we met in the street the houses had grown sombre. The space of sky above us was the colour of ever-changing violet and towards it the lamps of the street lifted their feeble lanterns. The cold air stung us and we played till our bodies glowed. Our shouts echoed in the silent street. The career of our play brought us through the dark muddy lanes behind the houses, where we ran the gauntlet of the rough tribes from the cottages, to the back doors of the dark dripping gardens where odours arose from the ashpits, to the dark odorous stables where a coachman smoothed and combed the horse or shook music from the buckled harness. When we returned to the street, light from the kitchen windows had filled the areas. If my uncle was seen turning the corner, we hid in the shadow until we had seen him safely housed. Or if Mangan's sister came out on the doorstep to call her brother in to his tea, we watched her from our shadow peer up and down the street. We waited to see whether she would remain or go in and, if she remained, we left our shadow and walked up to Mangan's steps resignedly. She was waiting for us, her figure defined by the light from the half-opened door. Her brother always teased her before he obeyed, and I stood by the railings looking at her. Her dress swung as she moved her body, and the soft rope of her hair tossed from side to side.

Every morning I lay on the floor in the front parlour watching her door. The blind was pulled down to within an inch of the sash so that I could not be seen. When she came out on the doorstep my heart leaped. I ran to the hall, seized my books and followed her. I kept her brown figure always in my eye and, when we came near the point at which our ways diverged, I quickened my pace and passed her. This happened morning after morning. I had never spoken to her, except for a few casual words, and yet her name was like a summons to all my foolish blood.

Her image accompanied me even in places the most hostile to romance. On Saturday evenings when my aunt went marketing I had to go to carry some of the parcels. We walked through the flaring streets, jostled by drunken men and bargaining women, amid the curses of labourers, the shrill litanies of shop-boys who stood on guard by the barrels of pigs' cheeks, the nasal chanting of street-singers, who sang a *come-all-you* about O'Donovan Rossa, or a ballad about the troubles in our native land. These noises converged in a single sensation of life for me: I imagined that I bore my chalice safely through a throng of foes. Her name sprang to my lips at moments in strange prayers and praises which I myself did not understand. My eyes were often full of tears (I could not tell why) and at times a flood from my heart seemed to pour itself out into my bosom. I thought little of the future. I did not know whether I would ever speak to her or not or, if I spoke to her, how I could tell her of my confused adoration. But my body was like a harp and her words and gestures were like fingers running upon the wires.

One evening I went into the back drawing-room in which the priest had died. It was a dark rainy evening and there was no sound in the house. Through one of the broken panes I heard the rain impinge upon the earth, the fine incessant needles of water playing in the sodden beds. Some distant lamp or lighted window gleamed below me. I was thankful that I could see so little. All my senses seemed to desire to veil themselves and, feeling that I was about to slip from them, I pressed the palms of my hands together until they trembled, murmuring: "*O love! O love!*" many times.

At last she spoke to me. When she addressed the first words to me I was so confused that I did not know what to answer. She asked me was I going to *Araby*. I forgot whether I answered yes or no. It would be a splendid bazaar, she said she would love to go.

"And why can't you?" I asked.

While she spoke she turned a silver bracelet round and round her wrist. She could not go, she said, because there would be a retreat that week in her convent. Her brother and two other boys were fighting for their caps, and I was alone at the railings. She held one of the spikes, bowing her head towards me. The light from the lamp opposite our door caught the white curve of her neck, lit up her hair that rested there and, falling, lit up the hand upon the railing. It fell over one side of her dress and caught the white border of a petticoat, just visible as she stood at ease.

"It's well for you," she said.

"If I go," I said, "I will bring you something."

What innumerable follies laid waste my waking and sleeping thoughts after that evening! I wished to annihilate the tedious intervening days. I chafed against the work of school. At night in my bedroom and by day in the classroom her image came between me and the page I strove to read. The syllables of the word *Araby* were called to me through the silence in which my soul luxuriated and cast an Eastern enchantment over me. I asked for leave to go to the bazaar on Saturday night. My aunt was surprised, and hoped it was not some Freemason affair. I answered few questions in class. I watched my master's face pass from amiability to sternness; he hoped I was not beginning to idle. I could not call my wandering thoughts together. I had hardly any patience with the serious work of life which, now that it stood between me and my desire, seemed to me child's play, ugly monotonous child's play.

On Saturday morning I reminded my uncle that I wished to go to the bazaar in the evening. He was fussing at the hallstand, looking for the hat-brush, and answered me curtly:

"Yes, boy, I know."

As he was in the hall I could not go into the front parlour and lie at the window. I left the house in bad humour and walked slowly towards the school. The air was pitilessly raw and already my heart misgave me.

When I came home to dinner my uncle had not yet been home. Still it was early. I sat staring at the clock for some time and, when its ticking began to irritate me, I left the room. I mounted the staircase and gained the upper part of the house. The high, cold, empty, gloomy rooms liberated me and I went from room to room singing. From the front window I saw my companions playing below in the street. Their cries reached me weakened and indistinct and, leaning my forehead against the cool glass, I looked over at the dark house where she lived. I may have stood there for an hour, seeing nothing but the brown-clad figure cast by my imagination, touched discreetly by the lamplight at the curved neck, at the hand upon the railings and at the border below the dress.

When I came downstairs again I found Mrs Mercer sitting at the fire. She was an old, garrulous woman, a pawnbroker's widow, who collected used stamps for some pious purpose. I had to endure the gossip of the tea-table. The meal was prolonged beyond an hour and still my uncle did not come. Mrs Mercer stood up to go: she was sorry she couldn't wait any longer, but it was after eight o'clock and she did not like to be out late, as the night air was bad for her. When she had gone I began to walk up and down the room, clenching my fists. My aunt said:

"I'm afraid you may put off your bazaar for this night of Our Lord."

At nine o'clock I heard my uncle's latchkey in the hall door. I heard him talking to himself and heard the hallstand rocking when it had received the weight of his overcoat. I could interpret these signs. When he was midway through his dinner I asked him to give me the money to go to the bazaar. He had forgotten.

"The people are in bed and after their first sleep now," he said.

I did not smile. My aunt said to him energetically:

"Can't you give him the money and let him go? You've kept him late enough as it is."

My uncle said he was very sorry he had forgotten. He said he believed in the old saying: "All work and no play makes Jack a dull boy." He asked me where I was going and, when I told him a second time, he asked me did I know *The Arab's Farewell to His Steed*. When I left the kitchen he was about to recite the opening lines of the piece to my aunt.

I held a florin tightly in my hand as I strode down Buckingham Street towards the station. The sight of the streets thronged with buyers and glaring with gas recalled to me the purpose of my journey. I took my seat in a third-class carriage of a deserted train. After an intolerable delay the train moved out of the station slowly. It crept onward among ruinous houses and over the twinkling river. At Westland Row Station a crowd of people pressed to the carriage doors; but the porters moved them back, saying that it was a special train for the bazaar. I remained alone in the bare carriage. In a few minutes the train drew up beside an improvised wooden platform. I passed out on to the road and saw by the lighted dial of a clock that it was ten minutes to ten. In front of me was a large building which displayed the magical name.

I could not find any sixpenny entrance and, fearing that the bazaar would be closed, I passed in quickly through a turnstile, handing a shilling to a weary-looking man. I found myself in a big hall girded at half its height by a gallery. Nearly all the stalls were closed and the greater part of the hall was in darkness. I recognized a silence like that which pervades a church after a service. I walked into the centre of the bazaar timidly. A few people were gathered about the stalls which were still open. Before a curtain, over which the words *Café Chantant* were written in coloured lamps, two men were counting money on a salver. I listened to the fall of the coins.

Remembering with difficulty why I had come, I went over to one of the stalls and examined porcelain vases and flowered tea-sets. At the door of the stall a young lady was talking and laughing with two young gentlemen. I remarked their English accents and listened vaguely to their conversation.

"O, I never said such a thing!"

"O, but you did!"

"O, but I didn't!"

"Didn't she say that?"

"Yes. I heard her."

"O, there's a... fib!"

Observing me, the young lady came over and asked me did I wish to buy anything. The tone of her voice was not encouraging; she seemed to have spoken to me out of a sense of duty. I looked humbly at the great jars that stood like eastern guards at either side of the dark entrance to the stall and murmured:

"No, thank you."

The young lady changed the position of one of the vases and went back to the two young men. They began to talk of the same subject. Once or twice the young lady glanced at me over her shoulder.

I lingered before her stall, though I knew my stay was useless, to make my interest in her wares seem the more real. Then I turned away slowly and walked down the middle of the bazaar. I allowed the two pennies to fall against the sixpence in my pocket. I heard a voice call from one end of the gallery that the light was out. The upper part of the hall was now completely dark.

Gazing up into the darkness I saw myself as a creature driven and derided by vanity; and my eyes burned with anguish and anger.

Questions

1. What was the narrator's living environment like? And how did it help to depict the boy's mood and emotions?

2. How did the boy feel about Mangan's sister?
3. How did the boy get the idea of going to Araby and what did he promise Mangan's sister if he did go there?
4. Why was the boy late for Araby? And what was the market like?
5. How did the adults behave towards him at the market and how did he feel intensely?

詹姆斯·乔伊斯
（1882—1941）

爱尔兰小说家詹姆斯·乔伊斯以在小说《尤利西斯》（1922）和《芬尼根守夜人》（1939）中运用实验性语言而闻名于世。在其文学生涯中，乔伊斯不断遭到出版商的退稿、审查部门的压制、批评家的攻击以及读者的误解。他生于都柏林，从1902年开始过着四处漂泊的生活。尽管他在巴黎、的里雅斯特、罗马和苏黎世长期生活，只是偶尔回到爱尔兰，但是他的作品全部以他的祖国为题材。

他的第一部重要的小说是《青年艺术家的画像》（1914—1915）。作品描述了主人公斯蒂芬·迪达勒斯的童年和青年时期、在都柏林的大学学院所接受的教育，以及他如何反抗、摆脱家庭的束缚和狭隘的民族主义情绪。他最有影响的作品《尤利西斯》以一名犹太广告经纪人利奥波德·布卢姆、他的妻子莫莉及斯蒂芬·迪达勒斯为中心。故事采用了意识流手段，主要事件与奥德修斯的返乡之旅类似。《芬尼根守夜人》展现了H.C.伊尔维克和家人的梦境与噩梦，是20世纪最为难懂的作品之一。他的短篇小说集是《都柏林人》。

阿拉比

詹姆斯·乔伊斯以其现代主义意识流叙述风格闻名于世。然而在他的这篇早期作品中，我们所领略的是他对少年欲望与情感明晰而又颇具印象派色彩的描绘。故事里的少年对他同学曼根的姐姐有一种"懵懂的爱慕"。他竭力靠近、讨好她。得知她特别想去阿拉比集市但又没去成，这位少年自告奋勇前去，并许诺为她带东西回来。经过一番周折，少年终于到了阿拉比集市。然而，在集市大厅里，少年深感成人世界对他的蔑视，同时也感到无尽的失望和空虚。此时，只有痛苦与愤怒充满他的胸膛。

北里奇蒙德街是条死胡同，很安静，只有在基督兄弟学校放学的时刻除外。矗立在死胡同的堵头有一幢无人居住的两层楼房，楼房与邻里被一个正方形广场隔开。街上其他房子里的人家彼此感觉生活得都不错，而这些呈棕褐色的房子，在冷峻的外表下面面相对。

我们家从前的房客，一位牧师，就死在后面起居室里。由于房子长期门窗紧闭，空气中发霉的气息弥漫所有房间，厨房后的废置房间里丢弃着废旧报纸和书籍。在其中我发现几本包了纸皮的书，书页卷曲、潮湿：有瓦尔特·司各特的《修道院》，《虔诚的教友》，还有《维多克回忆录》。我最喜欢最后一本，因为那本书页发黄。房屋后荒芜的园子中央有一棵苹果树和几簇稀稀落落的灌木丛，在灌木丛中我发现了已故房客生锈的自行车打气筒。牧师为人非常慷慨，他在遗嘱中将自己的全部积蓄都留给了教会，只将屋里的家具留给了自己的妹妹。

　　冬天来临，白昼变短，还没等我们完全吃完晚饭，黄昏就降临了。当我们在街上碰面，四周的房子已经变得昏暗下来。我们头顶上那片天空呈现出不断变换的紫色，街灯朝向天空微微发光。寒风袭人，我们玩耍着，直到浑身发热。我们的叫喊声在寂静的街道上回荡。我们玩耍的路径穿过房后黑暗、泥泞的小巷通到一座座小屋，在那儿我们扮演野蛮部落交叉射击；我们还经过黑暗、湿漉漉的园子后门，那里传出一股股炉灰味，又到黑暗、泛味的马厩，那儿有车夫伺候、梳理马匹，有时他们晃动扣好的马具，发出悦耳的声响。待我们回到街上，厨房窗户里的灯光已经照遍四处。如果这时看见我大伯正拐弯过来，我们就藏在黑影里，直到他完全进屋。如果这时曼根的姐姐出来站在台阶上，叫她弟弟回家吃茶点，我们就从黑影里看她朝街上四处张望。我们等着看她是要再多待一会儿，还是进去，如果她待在那里，我们就离开黑影，老老实实地走向曼根家的台阶。她在那儿等我们，她的腰身由半开的门里射出来的灯光显露出来。她弟弟在服从之前总要逗弄她一把，我就站在栏杆边看她。她身子一动，裙子就摆动起来，还有她那条柔软的发辫也随之左右摇摆起来。

　　我每天早上都趴在前厅的地板上观察她家的门。窗帘拉下来离窗框保持在一英寸之内，这样我就不会被看见。当她从台阶上一出来，我的心跳就加速。我急忙跑到门厅，抓起书，赶紧跟着她。我总是使她棕褐色的身形保持在我的视线之内，当我们接近岔路口时，我就快步超过她。这样的事每天早晨都同样发生。我从未同她说过话，只是不经意地冒出过几个词儿，但她的名字对于我整个鲁莽、冲动的身体就像是号令。

　　她的形象甚至在最有悖于浪漫的地方都会伴随着我。星期六晚上我伯母去市场，我得去帮着拿东西。我们走过光彩照人的街道，街道上挤满了醉汉和讨价还价的女人，四处是苦力的咒骂声，还有男店员尖声尖气、乏味的重复声，他们站在那里看守着几桶猪头肉，街头歌手哼唱着，他们唱着一首有关奥多诺万·罗莎的民歌，或者有关本国的一些艰难困苦的歌谣。这些嘈杂声汇合在一起构成了我对生活单一的感知：我想象着自己高举圣杯安全地从一群魔鬼身边穿过。在连我自己都不明白的奇怪祷告和赞美声中，她的名字会突然间蹦到我嘴边。我的双眼常常会热泪盈眶（我也不知是为什么），有时候一股热流似乎会从心房涌出来流进胸膛。我很少想到未来。我不知自己究竟会不会和她说话，假如对她说话，我又如何告诉她我对她充满困惑的爱慕之情。可是我的身体就像一张竖琴，而她的话和手势就像弹拨其弦上的手指。

一天夜里，我进入牧师去世的那间起居室。那是一个漆黑、阴雨的夜晚，屋里无任何声音。透过一片打碎的窗格玻璃，我听见雨水撞击地面的声响，细针状的雨水不断地淋在已经浸透了的床上。一些远处的街灯或是窗户里的灯光在我下面闪烁着微光。我看不见什么，对此我心存感激。我的一切感官似乎都渴望掩藏起自己，正当我感觉自己即将摆脱这一切之时，我双掌合一，直到手掌颤动，喃喃自语："啊，爱情！啊，爱情！"就这样重复了许多次。

最终她对我说话了。当她对我说第一句话时，我头脑发懵，不知回答什么。她问我去不去"阿拉比"。我忘了回答是去还是不去。那会是一个特棒的集市，她说她很想去。

"那你为什么不能去？"我问。

她说话间将自己手腕上的银镯子转啊转。她不能去，她说，因为那个星期她所在的修道院里有静修。她的弟弟和其他两个男孩在抢帽子玩，我独自站在栏杆旁。她翘起一只高跟鞋，头弓向我。我家门对面的灯光照在她脖颈白白的曲线上，照亮了落在那儿垂下来的头发，照亮了她扶在栏杆上的手。她悠闲地站在那儿，灯光洒在她裙子的一边，照在她隐约可见的衬裙白边上。

"你可以去啊，"她说。

"我要是去的话，"我说，"我给你带点儿东西回来。"

自从那夜之后，我日日夜夜冥思苦想，不知有多少傻念头浪费掉我的大好时光！我真想去除这期间讨厌的天数。我对上学也感到烦躁。晚上在卧室，白天在教室，她的形象总是横在我和我竭力要读的书页之间。"阿拉比"这个词的每一个音节都透过寂静向我呼唤，我的灵魂沉溺其中，使我笼罩在东方魔法之中。我请求星期六晚上去阿拉比集市。我伯母感到惊讶，她希望那不是什么共济会之类的事。我在课上很少回答问题。我注视着教书先生的面部表情从和蔼可亲变成严厉苛刻；他希望我不会从此游手好闲。我总是走神，招不回来。我对生活中的正经事少有耐心，这些事横在我和欲望之间，因而显得像孩子的把戏，可恶、乏味的孩子把戏。

星期六早上我提醒大伯我晚上要去集市。他对着衣帽架吹毛求疵，边找帽刷边简短地回了我一句：

"好，孩子，我知道。"

由于他在走廊里，我无法进入前厅趴在窗户旁。于是我心情沮丧地离开家，慢腾腾地向学校走去。空气阴冷无情，我早已心事重重。

当我回家吃晚饭时，大伯还没回家。时间还早，我坐着盯了一会儿钟表，它的滴答声很快使我急躁起来，于是我离开了房间。我爬上楼梯，来到楼上。那儿顶棚高高，冷飕飕、空荡荡、阴森森的房间使我自由自在，我从一间屋窜到另一间，唱着歌。从前窗我看见同伴们在下面的街上玩耍。他们的叫喊声传到我耳朵里，变得微弱不清；我额头顶着清凉的玻璃，朝她所住的昏暗不清的房子张望。我在那儿站了有一个钟头，什么也没有看见，只是在想象中憧憬着那棕褐色的身影、被灯光微微照亮的曲线优美的脖颈、扶在栏杆上的手，还有裙子的裙沿。

当我再下楼的时候，发现默瑟夫人坐在火炉边。她是个年老、多嘴的女人，一个典当商的寡妇，为某种善事收集旧邮票。我还得忍受她在茶几旁的闲聊。晚饭拖了一个钟头，我大伯还没回来。默瑟夫人起身要走：她说对不起不能再等了，但已经过了八点钟，她不愿意晚出门，夜晚的空气不利于她的身体。当她走后，我开始在屋里来回走动，紧紧攥着拳头。我伯母说：

"天哪，恐怕你得推迟今晚去集市的时间了。"

到了九点钟我听见大伯在门厅开锁的声音。我听见他自言自语，听见衣帽架承受他的大衣重量时一直晃动。我太熟悉这些动静了。晚饭吃到一半，我管他要去集市的钱。他早忘了。

"人家都上床了，现在都睡过一觉了，"他说。

我没笑。伯母热心地对他说：

"你能不能给他钱让他去？你现在已经耽搁他够晚的了。"

我大伯说对不起，他忘了。他说他信老话儿："整天学习不玩耍，杰克变成笨小孩。"他问我去哪儿，当我第二次回答他后，他问我知不知道《阿拉伯人向坐骑告别》。当我离开厨房，他正准备向伯母背诵那作品的开头几行。

我手里紧攥着一弗罗林银币，沿着白金汉街大步走向车站。街道挤满了顾客，汽灯照得一片通明，这景象叫我想起自己行程的目的。我上了一辆破旧的火车，在一节三等车厢的座位上坐下。在一阵难耐的拖延之后，火车慢慢地驶离了车站。火车向前爬行着，两旁是破损废弃的房屋，然后通过一条亮闪闪的河流。在西部道车站，一群人挤向车厢的门，但乘务员将他们拦了回去，说这是去集市的专用车。我一直独自一人坐在空荡荡的车厢里。几分钟后火车在一个临时搭建的木站台旁停下来。我穿过站台来到路上，借着发亮的钟表盘看见时间是差十分钟十点钟。在我前面是一幢大楼，上面显示着那魔法般的名字。

我找不到只花六便士就可以进去的入口，怕集市关门，就快速通过一个十字转门进去了，向一个面容疲惫的人交了一先令。我不知不觉进入一个大厅里，四周围绕着长廊，向上伸到大厅的一半。几乎所有货摊都关了，厅里的大部分地方一片黑暗。我感觉到一片寂静，就像做礼拜之后笼罩在教堂里的静谧气氛。我胆怯地走到集市当中。有几个人聚在还开着的货摊旁。有一个门帘上方用彩灯写着

"歌咏咖啡厅",门帘前两个人在托盘上数钱。我听着硬币落下的声响。

好不容易记起我为何来这儿,于是我走到一家货摊前,细看了看瓷花瓶和花茶具。在一家货摊门旁,一位年轻女士在和两位年轻男士说话、逗笑。我注意到他们的英国口音,含含糊糊地听见他们的交谈。

"哦,我从没说过那事儿!"

"哦,可你说过!"

"哦,可我没说过!"

"她没说过那事儿吗?"

"说过。我听见过。"

"哦,那是……撒谎!"

看见我,那位年轻女士过来问我要买什么。她的腔调表明她并不指望我买什么;她只是例行公事地对我说话。我老实巴交地看了看货摊入口处两侧的大坛子,坛子矗立在那儿就像东方的卫兵,然后咕哝道:

"不了,谢谢。"

那年轻的女士换了一个花瓶的位置,走回到那两位男子身旁。他们又开始谈同一个话题。有一两次,那年轻的女士回过头来瞥我一眼。

我徘徊在她的货摊前,虽然自己知道逗留也是徒劳,可让自己对她的陶器感兴趣似乎才是更真格的事儿。之后我慢慢走开,走到集市的中央。我任凭兜里的两便士碰击着一个六便士的银币。我听见长廊一头传来灭灯的喊叫声。大厅的上半部现在完全黑下来了。

向上凝视着黑暗的深处,我看见自己就像一个被虚荣驱使和嘲弄的家伙;我的双眼里燃烧着愤恨与痛苦的火焰。

The Boarding House

In the following story from *Dubliners*, we meet Mrs. Mooney, a working-class woman who rents rooms in her house to young male lodgers. Her daughter, Polly, becomes involved with one of the boarders, a clerk in his mid-thirties named Mr. Doran. Mrs. Mooney allows the affair to continue until other lodgers at the house have observed it. Then she insists that Doran marry her daughter. Despite the fact that he does not love her, and that his family will look down on the marriage, Doran agrees to wed Polly. Paralysis, death, and corruption, which pervade all the fifteen tales in *Dubliners*—and symbolism and storytelling craftsmanship—are evident in "The Boarding House".

Mrs. Mooney was a butcher's daughter. She was a woman who was quite able to keep things to herself: a determined woman. She had married her father's foreman and opened a butcher's shop near Spring Gardens. But as soon as his father-in-law was dead Mr. Mooney began to go to the devil. He drank, plundered the till, ran headlong into debt. It was no use making him take the pledge: he was sure to break out again a few days after. By fighting his wife in the presence of customers and by buying bad meat he ruined his business. One night he went for his wife with the cleaver and she had to sleep in a neighbour's house.

After that they lived apart. She went to the priest and got a separation from him with care of the children. She would give him neither money nor food nor house-room; and so he was obliged to enlist himself as a sheriff's man. He was a shabby stooped little drunkard with a white face and a white moustache and white eyebrows, pencilled above his little eyes, which were pink-veined and raw; and all day long he sat in the bailiff's room, waiting to be put on a job. Mrs. Mooney, who had taken what remained of her money out of the butcher business and set up a boarding house in Hardwicke Street, was a big imposing woman. Her house had a floating population made up of tourists from Liverpool and the Isle of Man and, occasionally, *artistes* from the music halls. Its resident population was made up of clerks from the city. She governed the house cunningly and firmly, knew when to give credit, when to be stern and when to let things pass. All the resident young men spoke of her as *The Madam*.

Mrs. Mooney's young men paid fifteen shillings a week for board and lodgings (beer or stout at dinner excluded). They shared in common tastes and occupations and for this reason they were very chummy with one another. They discussed with one another the chances of favourites and outsiders. Jack Mooney, the Madam's son, who was clerk to a commission agent in Fleet Street, had the reputation of being a hard case. He was fond of using soldiers' obscenities; usually he came home in the small hours. When he met his friends he had always a good one to tell them and he was always sure to be on to a good thing—that is to say, a likely horse or a likely *artiste*. He was also handy with the mits and sang comic songs. On Sunday nights there would often be a reunion in Mrs. Mooney's front drawing-room. The music-hall *artistes* would oblige; and Sheridan played waltzes and polkas and vamped accompaniments. Polly Mooney, the Madam's daughter, would also sing. She sang:

>"*I'm a... naughty girl.*
>
>*You needn't sham*:
>
>*You know I am.*"

Polly was a slim girl of nineteen; she had light soft hair and a small full mouth. Her eyes, which were grey with a shade of green through them, had a habit of glancing upwards when she spoke with anyone, which made her look like a little perverse madonna. Mrs. Mooney had first sent her daughter to be a typist in a corn-factor's office, but as a disreputable sheriff's man used to come every other day to the office, asking to be allowed to say a word to his daughter, she had taken her daughter home again and set her to do housework. As Polly was very lively the intention was to give her the run of the young men. Besides, young men like to feel that there is a young woman not very far away. Polly, of course, flirted with the young men, but Mrs. Mooney, who was a shrewd judge, knew that the young men were only passing the time away: none of them meant business. Things went on so for a long time, and Mrs. Mooney began to think of sending Polly back to typewriting when she noticed that something was going on between Polly and one of the young men. She watched the pair and kept her own counsel.

Polly knew that she was being watched, but still her mother's persistent silence could not be misunderstood. There had been no open complicity between mother and daughter, no open understanding, but though people in the house began to talk of the affair, still Mrs. Mooney did not intervene. Polly began to grow a little strange in her manner, and the young man was evidently perturbed. At last, when she judged it to be the right moment, Mrs. Mooney intervened. She dealt with moral problems as a cleaver deals with meat: and in this case she had made up her mind.

It was a bright Sunday morning of early summer, promising heat, but with a fresh breeze blowing. All the windows of the boarding house were open and the lace curtains ballooned gently towards the street beneath the raised sashes. The belfry of George's Church sent out constant peals, and worshippers, singly or in groups, traversed the little circus before the church, revealing their purpose by their self-contained demeanour no less than by the little volumes in their gloved hands. Breakfast was over in the boarding house, and the table of the breakfast-room was covered with plates on which lay yellow streaks of eggs with morsels of bacon-fat and bacon-rind. Mrs. Mooney sat in the straw arm-chair and watched the servant Mary remove the breakfast things. She made Mary collect the crusts and pieces of broken bread to help to make Tuesday's bread-pudding. When the table was cleared, the broken bread collected, the sugar and butter safe under lock and key, she began to reconstruct the interview which she had had the night before with Polly. Things were as she had suspected: she had been frank in her questions and Polly had been frank in her answers. Both had been somewhat awkward, of course. She had been made awkward by her not wishing to receive the news in too cavalier a fashion or to seem to have connived, and Polly had been made awkward not merely because allusions of that kind always made her awkward, but also because she did not wish it to be thought that in her wise innocence she had divined the intention behind her mother's tolerance.

Mrs. Mooney glanced instinctively at the little gilt clock on the mantelpiece as soon as she had become aware through her revery that the bells of George's Church had stopped ringing. It was seventeen minutes past eleven: she would have lots of time to have the matter out with Mr. Doran and then catch short twelve at Marlborough Street. She was sure she would win. To begin with, she had all the weight of social opinion on her side: she was an outraged mother. She had allowed him to live beneath her roof, assuming that he was a man of honour, and he had simply abused her hospitality. He was thirty-four or thirty-five years of age, so that youth could not be pleaded as his excuse; nor could ignorance be his excuse, since he was a man who had seen something of the world. He had simply taken advantage of Polly's youth and inexperience: that was evident. The question was: What reparation would he make?

There must be reparation made in such a case. It is all very well for the man: he can go his ways as if nothing had happened, having had his moment of pleasure, but the girl has to bear the brunt. Some mothers would be content to patch up such an affair for a sum of money: she had known cases of it. But she would not do so. For her only one reparation could make up for the loss of her daughter's honour: marriage.

She counted all her cards again before sending Mary up to Mr. Doran's room to say that she wished to speak with him. She felt sure she would win. He was a serious young man, not rakish or loud-voiced like the others. If it had been Mr. Sheridan or Mr. Meade or Bantam Lyons her task would have been much harder. She did not think he would face publicity. All the lodgers in the house knew something of the affair; details had been invented by some. Besides, he had been employed for thirteen years in a great Catholic wine-merchant's office, and publicity would mean for him, perhaps, the loss of his job. Whereas if he agreed all might be well. She knew he had a good screw for one thing, and she suspected he had a bit of stuff put by.

Nearly the half-hour! She stood up and surveyed herself in the pier-glass. The decisive expression of her great florid face satisfied her, and she thought of some mothers she knew who could not get their daughters off their hands.

Mr. Doran was very anxious indeed this Sunday morning. He had made two attempts to shave, but his hand had been so unsteady that he had been obliged to desist. Three days' reddish beard fringed his jaws, and every two or three minutes a mist gathered on his glasses so that he had to take them off and polish them with his pocket-handkerchief. The recollection of his confession of the night before was a cause of acute pain to him; the priest had drawn out every ridiculous detail of the affair, and in the end had so magnified his sin that he was almost thankful at being afforded a loophole of reparation. The harm was done. What could he do now but marry her or run away? He could not brazen it out. The affair would be sure to be talked of, and his employer would be certain to hear of it. Dublin is such a small city: everyone knows everyone else's business. He felt his heart leap warmly in his throat as he heard in his excited imagination old Mr. Leonard calling out in his rasping voice: "Send Mr. Doran here, please."

All his long years of service gone for nothing! All his industry and diligence thrown away! As a young man he had sown his wild oats, of course; he had boasted of his free-thinking and denied the existence of God to his companions in public-houses. But that was all passed and done with... nearly. He still bought a copy of *Reynolds's Newspaper* every week, but he attended to his religious duties, and for nine-tenths of the year lived a regular life. He had money enough to settle down on; it was not that.

But the family would look down on her. First of all there was her disreputable father, and then her mother's boarding house was beginning to get a certain fame. He had a notion that he was being had. He could imagine his friends talking of the affair and laughing. She was a little vulgar; sometimes she said "I seen" and "If I had've known." But what would grammar matter if he really loved her? He could not make up his mind whether to like her or despise her for what she had done. Of course he had done it too. His instinct urged him to remain free, not to marry. Once you are married you are done for, it said.

While he was sitting helplessly on the side of the bed in shirt and trousers, she tapped lightly at his door and entered. She told him all, that she had made a clean breast of it to her mother and that her mother would speak with him that morning. She cried and threw her arms round his neck, saying:

"O Bob! Bob! What am I to do? What am I to do at all?"

She would put an end to herself, she said.

He comforted her feebly, telling her not to cry, that it would be all right, never fear. He felt against his shirt the agitation of her bosom.

It was not altogether his fault that it had happened. He remembered well, with the curious patient memory of the celibate, the first casual caresses her dress, her breath, her fingers had given him. Then late one night as he was undressing for bed she had tapped at his door, timidly. She wanted to relight her candle at his for hers had been blown out by a gust. It was her bath night. She wore a loose open combing jacket of printed flannel. Her white instep shone in the opening of her furry slippers and the blood glowed warmly behind her perfumed skin. From her hands and wrists too as she lit and steadied her candle a faint perfume arose.

On nights when he came in very late it was she who warmed up his dinner. He scarcely knew what he was eating feeling her beside him alone, at night, in the sleeping house. And her thoughtfulness! If the night was anyway cold or wet or windy there was sure to be a little tumbler of punch ready for him. Perhaps they could be happy together....

They used to go upstairs together on tiptoe, each with a candle, and on the third landing exchange reluctant good nights. They used to kiss. He remembered well her eyes, the touch of her hand and his delirium....

But delirium passes. He echoed her phrase, applying it to himself: "*What am I to do?*" The instinct of the celibate warned him to hold back. But the sin was there; even his sense of honour told him that reparation must be made for such a sin.

While he was sitting with her on the side of the bed Mary came to the door and said that the missus wanted to see him in the parlour. He stood up to put on his coat and waistcoat, more helpless than ever. When he was dressed he went over to her to comfort her. It would be all right, never fear. He left her crying on the bed and moaning softly: "*O my God!*"

Going down the stairs his glasses became so dimmed with moisture that he had to take them off and polish them. He longed to ascend through the roof and fly away to another country where he would never hear again of his trouble, and yet a force pushed him downstairs step by step. The implacable faces of his employer and of the Madam stared upon his discomfiture. On the last flight of stairs he passed Jack Mooney, who was coming up from the pantry nursing two bottles of *Bass*. They saluted coldly; and the lover's eyes rested for a second or two on a thick bulldog face and a pair of thick short arms. When he reached the foot of the staircase he glanced up and saw Jack regarding him from the door of the return-room.

Suddenly he remembered the night when one of the music-hall *artistes*, a little blond Londoner, had made a rather free allusion to Polly. The reunion had been almost broken up on account of Jack's violence. Everyone tried to quiet him. The music-hall *artiste*, a little paler than usual, kept smiling and saying that there was no harm meant; but Jack kept shouting at him that if any fellow tried that sort of a game on with his sister he'd bloody well put his teeth down his throat, so he would.

Polly sat for a little time on the side of the bed, crying. Then she dried her eyes and went over to the looking-glass. She dipped the end of the towel in the water-jug and refreshed her eyes with the cool water. She looked at herself in profile and readjusted a hairpin above her ear. Then she went back to the bed again and sat at the foot. She regarded the pillows for a long time, and the sight of them awakened in her mind secret, amiable memories. She rested the nape of her neck against the cool iron bed-rail and fell into a revery. There was no longer any perturbation visible on her face.

She waited on patiently, almost cheerfully, without alarm, her memories gradually giving place to hopes and visions of the future. Her hopes and visions were so intricate that she no longer saw the white pillows on which her gaze was fixed or remembered that she was waiting for anything.

At last she heard her mother calling. She started to her feet and ran to the banisters.

"Polly! Polly!"

"Yes, mamma?"

"Come down, dear. Mr. Doran wants to speak to you."

Then she remembered what she had been waiting for.

Questions

1. The author was educated in a traditional Catholic way, which, however, fostered his strong distaste for religion. How does he reveal his attitude towards Catholicism in the story?
2. Paralysis is a recurrent theme in the stories in *Dubliners*. "The Boarding House" is no exception. How is the theme of paralysis reflected in the three major characters, Mrs. Mooney, Polly, and Mr. Doran?
3. How many different points of view are adopted? Why do you think the writer organizes the story this way?
4. How is flashback employed? How does it help in the development of the story?
5. Comment on the society of Dublin described in the story.

寄宿旅馆

下面这个故事选自《都柏林人》。穆尼太太是位工人阶级的妇女。她将家里的房间租给年轻的男性房客。她的女儿波莉与其中一位房客,一个三十多岁的叫杜兰先生的职员发生了关系。穆尼太太任凭事情发展下去,直到其他的房客都注意到了这件事。然后她要求杜兰与自己的女儿结婚。尽管杜兰不爱她,他的家人也会瞧不起这门婚姻,他还是同意和她结婚。《都柏林人》中的全部十五个故事都充斥着瘫痪、死亡、腐败的主题;除此之外,象征主义和叙事技巧在《寄宿旅馆》中也体现得很明显。

穆尼太太是屠夫的女儿,她是个很能藏得住心事的女人,十分决绝。她嫁给了父亲的工头,在斯普林花园附近开了间肉铺。但是岳父一死,穆尼先生就开始堕落了。他喝酒,洗劫自家的钱箱,欠了一屁股债。让他起誓根本没什么用,几天后他一定会再犯。他在顾客面前与妻子打架,购入坏肉,生意一落千丈。一天夜里他用切肉刀追打妻子,逼得她只能在邻居家过夜。

从那以后他们分居了。她找到牧师,得到和他分居的许可,独自抚养子女。她不给他钱,也不提供食物或住处,所以他不得不应征为郡治安官做事。他是个衣衫褴褛、佝偻着腰的小个子酒鬼,长着白脸、白胡子,眉毛也是白的,就像描上去似的,一双小眼睛里突起粉红色的血管,显得阴冷、粗野。他整天坐在法警办公室里等差事。穆尼太太是个引人注目的大个子女人。她把肉铺剩下的钱取出来在哈德维克街开了间寄宿旅馆。旅馆里流动的客人包括从利物浦和曼岛来的游客,偶尔也有音乐厅的演员。常住的客人是城里的职员。她治理旅馆的风格既狡诈又坚决,清楚什么时候允许赊账,什么时候寸步不让,什么时候大事化小,小事化了。所有常住的年轻人都叫她"夫人"。

穆尼太太的年轻客人一周为住宿和膳食付15先令(不包括晚餐的啤酒或烈性黑啤酒)。他们的品位与职业都相似,因此关系十分密切。他们讨论谁最受宠,谁和大家格格不入。夫人的儿子,杰克·穆尼是弗利特街一家代理事务所的职员。他是个难对付的家伙,喜欢像士兵那样骂脏话,通常三更半夜回家。遇到朋友时,他总有故事讲,而且一定有好事——比如说,一匹胜算很大的马,或是一个不错的歌舞演员。他还很擅长拳击,唱逗乐的歌。周日晚上穆尼太太的前客厅常会有联欢活动。音乐厅的演员会来助阵,谢里丹演奏华尔兹、波尔卡舞曲或是即席伴奏。夫人的女儿波莉·穆尼也会唱歌。她唱道:

"我是个……顽皮的姑娘,

你不用装：
你知道我就这样。"

波莉19岁，是个苗条的姑娘。她长着浅色柔软的头发，小巧丰满的嘴。她的眼睛灰中带着一抹绿，说话的时候习惯向上望，这使她看起来像个任性的小夫人。穆尼太太一开始送女儿去一个谷物商那里做打字员，可是郡治安官那里有个臭当差的每隔一天就去求见她的女儿。于是她又把女儿领回了家做家务。因为波莉很活泼，夫人的本意是能让她随意与小伙子们接触。而且，他们喜欢身边有个年轻女子。当然波莉常和小伙子们打情骂俏，但是穆尼太太有精明的判断力，她知道年轻人只是在打发时间，没有一个是真心的。就这样过了很长时间，后来穆尼太太注意到波莉和其中一个年轻人的关系有点特别，于是她又开始考虑让波莉重操打字的行当。她监视着这一对年轻人，并没有给予任何忠告。

波莉知道自己被监视，但是母亲持续的缄默，其意图不言而喻。母女间互不沟通，也没有共识。尽管旅馆的住客开始谈论此事，穆尼太太还是没有干预。波莉的举止变得有些奇怪，年轻人也很明显地变得心绪不宁。最后，穆尼太太觉得时机成熟，可以干预了。她处理道德问题就如用切肉刀切肉一样。在这件事上，她已经下定决心了。

那是初夏一个明媚的周日上午，看起来会很热，但却吹着清爽的微风。旅馆的所有窗户都开着，窗扇被抬起，蕾丝窗帘被风吹得向街上轻轻地展开。乔治教堂的钟楼发出持续的钟鸣，做礼拜的人独自或成群穿过教堂前面的环形小广场，戴着手套的手中握着的小册子和他们持重的举止都表明了他们的目的。旅馆中的早餐已经结束，早餐室的桌子上满是盘子。盘中有一道道黄色的蛋液，一块块熏肉的脂肪和肉皮。穆尼太太坐在草编的扶手椅中，看着仆人玛丽收东西。她让玛丽把面包皮和一块块的碎面包收起来，留着周二做面包布丁。当桌子清干净了，碎面包收好了，白糖黄油安全地锁起来后，她开始回想起前晚和波莉的谈话。事情正如她所怀疑的那样：她问得很直接，波莉答得很坦白。当然，双方都有些尴尬。她尴尬是因为她不希望得知这事时显得很漫不经心，或者似乎是纵容这事发生。波莉尴尬不仅是因为提到那种事总会让她尴尬，还因为她不希望别人觉得她精明的单纯已使她猜到母亲宽容背后的本意。

穆尼太太在沉思中意识到乔治教堂的钟声已经停了，她出于本能急忙向壁炉上小小的镀金钟看去。11点过17分了：她有足够的时间和杜兰先生开诚布公，赶得及12点前到达玛尔波罗街。她确信会赢。首先她这方有社会舆论的支持：她是被侮辱的母亲。她觉得杜兰先生是个体面人才让他住在家里，可他却辜负了她的热情好客。他有三十四五岁了，所以也不能推说自己年轻不懂事，无知也不好用，因为他见过些世面了。他就是利用了波莉的年轻单纯：这很明显。问题在于：他会怎么补救呢？

这种事情一定要有所补救。男方完全没问题：他可以占了便宜，却当什么都没发生过，但女孩会成为众矢之的。有些母亲对这种事用笔钱来补救就满足了，她就知道几桩。但是她不会这么做。对她来说，只有一种措施能弥补女儿名誉的损失：结婚。

她把胜算又估量了一遍，才让玛丽到楼上杜兰先生的房间说要和他谈谈。她确信会赢。他是个严肃的年轻人，不像其他人那样，或放荡随便或高声大气。如果是谢里丹先生、米德先生或是本特·莱恩斯，她的任务会艰巨得多。她觉得他不会愿意张扬出去。所有的房客都对此略有所知，一些人还添油加醋。而且，他13年来都为一家很大的天主教酒商工作，事情张扬出去也许他会被解雇。相反，如果他同意了，一切都好说。一方面她知道他工资不菲，她还怀疑他有些积蓄。

快11点半了！她站起身，在大穿衣镜前审视着自己。她红润的大脸盘儿上决绝的表情让她很满意，她想起自己认识的一些母亲连女儿都嫁不出去。

这个周日上午杜兰先生十分焦虑。他两次打算刮胡子，但手抖得太厉害，不得不放弃。他下巴周围长着三天没刮的发红的胡子，每两三分钟他眼镜上就起了一层雾，他不得不摘下眼镜用手绢擦干净。回想起前一晚的忏悔，他就感到一阵剧痛。牧师刨根问底，挖出了每一个可笑的细节，最后说他实在是罪孽深重，他几乎是心怀感激地接受了补救的建议。错已铸成。他现在除了娶她或是逃走之外还能干什么呢？他不可能厚着脸皮不承认。人们一定会议论纷纷，他的老板一定会有所耳闻。都柏林太小了：大家彼此都一清二楚。他想象自己听到老莱昂纳多先生厉声喊道："请把杜兰先生叫过来。"他感觉到自己的心在喉咙里激烈地跳动着。

他多年的工作将一无所获！他的辛苦勤奋全白费了！当然年轻时他也放荡过；他在酒馆里向伙伴吹嘘自己的自由思想，否认上帝的存在，但那些全都过去了，结束了……几乎是这样。他每周还是会买一份《雷诺德报》，但他履行自己的宗教职责，一年里十分之九的时间都规规矩矩。他的钱足够安定下来的，这个倒不是问题。但是他家人会瞧不起她。首先，她父亲声名狼藉，其次她母亲的旅馆也开始有点不好的名声。他觉得自己上当受骗了。他能想象朋友们如何谈起这事，如何嘲笑他。她有点儿土气：有时她会说："我那啥瞅见了""我要是那个知道了的话"但是他要是真爱她，语法又算得了什么？他没法决定依照她的所为应该喜欢她还是瞧不起她。当然他也有份。他的本能敦促他保持自由身，不要结婚。本能警告他：一旦结婚，你就完了。

就在他穿着衬衫长裤无助地坐在床边时,她轻轻地敲门进来了。她告诉了他一切,她已经向母亲和盘托出,她母亲那天上午就要和他谈。她哭着搂住他的脖子:

"哦,鲍勃,鲍勃!我该怎么做?我究竟该怎么做?"

她说要自我了断。

他无力地安慰她,告诉她不要哭,会好起来的,别害怕。隔着衬衫他感觉到她胸部的起伏。

这件事不全是他的错。以独身男子那种奇特而持久的记忆力,他清楚地记得她的衣裙、她的呼吸、她的指尖所给予他的第一次漫不经心的爱抚。然后一天深夜在他脱衣准备睡觉时,她羞怯地敲了敲他的房门。因为她的蜡烛被风吹熄了,她想要在他的蜡烛上借个火。那晚是她惯例洗澡的日子。她穿了一件松垮的印花法兰绒外衣。她白色的脚背从毛皮拖鞋的开口处闪露出来,芳香的肌肤下面透出温暖的血色。在她点燃蜡烛后拿手稳住时,从她的手和手腕也透出一阵清香。

他晚归时,她为他热饭。夜里在沉寂的房子里,感觉到她在身边,他食不知味。她还很体贴!如果夜里稍有些寒冷潮湿或是刮风,她一定会为他准备一小杯潘趣酒。也许他们在一起会幸福……

他们常常一人拿一支蜡烛,踮着脚尖一起上楼,在第三个楼梯平台处不情愿地互道晚安。他们常会接吻。他清楚地记得她的眼睛,她手的抚摸和他的狂喜。

但是狂喜的心情已经消失。他重复着她的话,但说的是自己:"我该怎么办?"独身男子的本能警告他后撤。但是罪过已经犯下了;甚至出于荣誉感,他也一定要对这种罪过做出补救。

就在他和她坐在床边时,玛丽来到门前说太太在起居室要见他。他站起身穿上外套、马甲,从没这样无助过。穿好后他走过去安慰她。会没事的,别害怕。他离开时,她在床上哭泣,轻声地呜咽着:"哦,上帝!"

下楼时,他的眼镜起雾变得模糊不清,他不得不摘下眼镜擦拭。他渴望腾空穿越屋顶,飞到另一个国家,在那里他再也不用面对这个难题。然而一股力量把他一步步推下楼。他的老板和夫人的脸无情地看着他的窘状。在最后一段楼梯上他与杰克·穆尼擦身而过。杰克抱着两瓶巴斯酒从食品储藏室走上来。他们冷淡地打了招呼;有一两秒,这位情人的眼睛打量着一张粗壮的斗牛犬似的脸和短粗的手臂。走到楼梯底部时他向上望,看到杰克正从整理室的门边注视着他。

突然他记起有一晚,一个音乐厅的演员,个子小小的金发伦敦人很随便地开波莉的玩笑。杰克暴跳如雷,几乎破坏了联欢。大家都试图安抚他。音乐厅的演员脸色比平常苍白,不断地笑着说他没有恶意。但是杰克不断地咆哮着,要是任何家伙想玩弄他妹妹,他会咬断他的喉咙,他会的。

波莉在床边坐着哭了一会儿。然后她擦干眼睛走到镜子前。她把毛巾的一端浸在水罐里用凉水抹了抹眼睛。她照了照自己的侧面，调了调耳朵上方的发夹。然后她又走回去坐在床脚。她盯着枕头看了好长时间。枕头勾起了她隐秘而亲切的回忆，她把颈背靠在冰凉的床侧铁栏杆上陷入沉思。她脸上再看不出一些的烦恼。

她耐心地，甚至是兴高采烈地等待着，不知不觉地她不再回忆，而开始憧憬与展望未来。她的憧憬和展望细致入微、复杂异常，她已经看不见自己盯着的枕头，也不记得在等待什么了。

最后她听到母亲在叫她。她蓦地站起身跑到楼梯栏杆旁。

"波莉！波莉！"

"什么事，妈妈？"

"下来，亲爱的。杜兰先生要跟你谈谈。"

这时她才记起来自己一直在等待的是什么。

Ivy Day in the Committee Room

This story is set in the Committee Room on Wicklow Street where several men are taking a break from canvassing for the politician Richard J. Tierney. Their discussions mainly revolve about politics. "Ivy Day in the Committee Room" serves primarily to commemorate Charles Stewart Parnell, a much loved Irish politician who fought for Ireland. The story also conveys the corrupt nature of the politics at the time, which in turn contributes to Joyce's overall theme of paralysis in *Dubliners*—in this case being political paralysis.

Old Jack raked the cinders together with a piece of cardboard and spread them judiciously over the whitening dome of coals. When the dome was thinly covered his face lapsed into darkness but, as he set himself to fan the fire again, his crouching shadow ascended the opposite wall and his face slowly re-emerged into light. It was an old man's face, very bony and hairy. The moist blue eyes blinked at the fire and the moist mouth fell open at times, munching once or twice mechanically when it closed. When the cinders had caught he laid the piece of cardboard against the wall, sighed and said:

"That's better now, Mr. O'Connor."

Mr. O'Connor, a grey-haired young man, whose face was disfigured by many blotches and pimples, had just brought the tobacco for a cigarette into a shapely cylinder, but when spoken to he undid his handiwork meditatively. Then he began to roll the tobacco again meditatively and after a moment's thought decided to lick the paper.

"Did Mr. Tierney say when he'd be back?" he asked in a husky falsetto.

"He didn't say."

Mr. O'Connor put his cigarette into his mouth and began to search his pockets. He took out a pack of thin pasteboard cards.

"I'll get you a match," said the old man.

"Never mind, this'll do," said Mr. O'Connor.

He selected one of the cards and read what was printed on it:

MUNICIPAL ELECTIONS

ROYAL EXCHANGE WARD

Mr. Richard J. Tierney, P.L.G., respectfully solicits the favour of your vote and influence at the coming election in the Royal Exchange Ward.

Mr. O'Connor had been engaged by Tierney's agent to canvass one part of the ward but, as the weather was inclement and his boots let in the wet, he spent a great part of the day sitting by the fire in the Committee Room in Wicklow Street with Jack, the old caretaker. They had been sitting thus since the short day had grown dark. It was the sixth of October, dismal and cold out of doors.

Mr. O'Connor tore a strip off the card and, lighting it, lit his cigarette. As he did so the flame lit up a leaf of dark glossy ivy in the lapel of his coat. The old man watched him attentively and then, taking up the piece of cardboard again, began to fan the fire slowly while his companion smoked.

"Ah, yes," he said, continuing, "it's hard to know what way to bring up children. Now who'd think he'd turn out like that! I sent him to the Christian Brothers and I done what I could for him, and there he goes boozing about. I tried to make him somewhat decent."

He replaced the cardboard wearily.

"Only I'm an old man now I'd change his tune for him. I'd take the stick to his back and beat him while I could stand over him—as I done many a time before. The mother, you know, she cocks him up with this and that..."

"That's what ruins children," said Mr. O'Connor.

"To be sure it is," said the old man. "And little thanks you get for it, only impudence. He takes th'upper hand of me whenever he sees I've a sup taken. What's the world coming to when sons speak that way to their fathers?"

"What age is he?" said Mr. O'Connor.

"Nineteen," said the old man.

"Why don't you put him to something?"

"Sure, amn't I never done at the drunken bowsy ever since he left school? 'I won't keep you,' I says. 'You must get a job for yourself.' But, sure, it's worse whenever he gets a job; he drinks it all."

Mr. O'Connor shook his head in sympathy, and the old man fell silent, gazing into the fire. Someone opened the door of the room and called out:

"Hello! Is this a Freemason's meeting?"

"Who's that?" said the old man.

"What are you doing in the dark?" asked a voice.

"Is that you, Hynes?" asked Mr. O'Connor.

"Yes. What are you doing in the dark?" said Mr. Hynes, advancing into the light of the fire.

He was a tall, slender young man with a light brown moustache. Imminent little drops of rain hung at the brim of his hat and the collar of his jacket-coat was turned up.

"Well, Mat," he said to Mr. O'Connor, "how goes it?"

Mr. O'Connor shook his head. The old man left the hearth, and after stumbling about the room returned with two candlesticks which he thrust one after the other into the fire and carried to the table. A denuded room came into view and the fire lost all its cheerful colour. The walls of the room were bare except for a copy of an election address. In the middle of the room was a small table on which papers were heaped.

Mr. Hynes leaned against the mantelpiece and asked:

"Has he paid you yet?"

"Not yet," said Mr. O'Connor. "I hope to God he'll not leave us in the lurch tonight."

Mr. Hynes laughed.

"O, he'll pay you. Never fear," he said.

"I hope he'll look smart about it if he means business," said Mr. O'Connor.

"What do you think, Jack?" said Mr. Hynes satirically to the old man.

The old man returned to his seat by the fire, saying:

"It isn't but he has it, anyway. Not like the other tinker."

"What other tinker?" said Mr. Hynes.

"Colgan," said the old man scornfully.

"It is because Colgan's a working-man you say that? What's the difference between a good honest bricklayer and a publican — eh? Hasn't the working-man as good a right to be in the Corporation as anyone else — ay, and a better right than those shoneens that are always hat in hand before any fellow with a handle to his name? Isn't that so, Mat?" said Mr. Hynes, addressing Mr. O'Connor.

"I think you're right," said Mr. O'Connor.

"One man is a plain honest man with no hunker-sliding about him. He goes in to represent the labour classes. This fellow you're working for only wants to get some job or other."

"Of course, the working-classes should be represented," said the old man.

"The working-man," said Mr. Hynes, "gets all kicks and no halfpence. But it's labour produces everything. The working-man is not looking for fat jobs for his sons and nephews and cousins. The working-man is not going to drag the honour of Dublin in the mud to please a German monarch."

"How's that?" said the old man.

"Don't you know they want to present an address of welcome to Edward Rex if he comes here next year? What do we want kowtowing to a foreign king?"

"Our man won't vote for the address," said Mr. O'Connor. "He goes in on the Nationalist ticket."

"Won't he?" said Mr. Hynes. "Wait till you see whether he will or not. I know him. Is it Tricky Dicky Tierney?"

"By God! perhaps you're right, Joe," said Mr. O'Connor. "Anyway, I wish he'd turn up with the spondulics."

The three men fell silent. The old man began to rake more cinders together. Mr. Hynes took off his hat, shook it and then turned down the collar of his coat, displaying, as he did so, an ivy leaf in the lapel.

"If this man was alive," he said, pointing to the leaf, "we'd have no talk of an address of welcome."

"That's true," said Mr. O'Connor.

"Musha, God be with them times!" said the old man. "There was some life in it then."

The room was silent again. Then a bustling little man with a snuffling nose and very cold ears pushed in the door. He walked over quickly to the fire, rubbing his hands as if he intended to produce a spark from them.

"No money, boys," he said.

"Sit down here, Mr. Henchy," said the old man, offering him his chair.

"O, don't stir, Jack, don't stir," said Mr. Henchy.

He nodded curtly to Mr. Hynes and sat down on the chair which the old man vacated.

"Did you serve Aungier Street?" he asked Mr. O'Connor.

"Yes," said Mr. O'Connor, beginning to search his pockets for memoranda.

"Did you call on Grimes?"

"I did."

"Well? How does he stand?"

"He wouldn't promise. He said: 'I won't tell anyone what way I'm going to vote.' But I think he'll be all right."

"Why so?"

"He asked me who the nominators were; and I told him, I mentioned Father Burke's name. I think it'll be all right."

Mr. Henchy began to snuffle and to rub his hands over the fire at a terrific speed. Then he said:

"For the love of God, Jack, bring us a bit of coal. There must be some left."

The old man went out of the room.

"It's no go," said Mr. Henchy, shaking his head. "I asked the little shoeboy, but he said: 'O, now, Mr. Henchy, when I see the work going on properly I won't forget you, you may be sure.' Mean little tinker! 'Usha, how could he be anything else?"

"What did I tell you, Mat?" said Mr. Hynes. "Tricky Dicky Tierney."

"O, he's as tricky as they make 'em," said Mr. Henchy. "He hasn't got those little pigs' eyes for nothing. Blast his soul! Couldn't he pay up like a man instead of: 'O, now Mr. Henchy, I must speak to Mr. Fanning... I've spent a lot of money'? Mean little schoolboy of hell! I suppose he forgets the time his little old father kept the hand-me-down shop in Mary's Lane."

"But is that a fact?" asked Mr. O'Connor.

"God, yes," said Mr. Henchy. "Did you never hear that? And the men used to go in on Sunday morning before the houses were open to buy a waistcoat or a trousers — moya! But Tricky Dicky's little old father always had a tricky little black bottle up in a corner. Do you mind now? That's that. That's where he first saw the light."

The old man returned with a few lumps of coal which he placed here and there on the fire.

"That's a nice how-do-you-do," said Mr. O'Connor. "How does he expect us to work for him if he won't stump up?"

"I can't help it," said Mr. Henchy. "I expect to find the bailiffs in the hall when I go home."

Mr. Hynes laughed and, shoving himself away from the mantelpiece with the aid of his shoulders, made ready to leave.

"It'll be all right when King Eddie comes," he said. "Well, boys, I'm off for the present. See you later. 'Bye, 'bye."

He went out of the room slowly. Neither Mr. Henchy nor the old man said anything, but, just as the door was closing, Mr. O'Connor, who had been staring moodily into the fire, called out suddenly:

"'Bye, Joe."

Mr. Henchy waited a few moments and then nodded in the direction of the door.

"Tell me," he said across the fire, "what brings our friend in here? What does he want?"

"'Usha, poor Joe!" said Mr. O'Connor, throwing the end of his cigarette into the fire, "he's hard up, like the rest of us."

Mr. Henchy snuffled vigorously and spat so copiously that he nearly put out the fire, which uttered a hissing protest.

"To tell you my private and candid opinion," he said. "I think he's a man from the other camp. He's a spy of Colgan's, if you ask me. Just go round and try and find out how they're getting on. They won't suspect you. Do you twig?"

"Ah, poor Joe is a decent skin," said Mr. O'Connor.

"His father was a decent, respectable man," Mr. Henchy admitted. "Poor old Larry Hynes! Many a good turn he did in his day! But I'm greatly afraid our friend is not nineteen carat. Damn it, I can understand a fellow being hard up, but what I can't understand is a fellow sponging. Couldn't he have some spark of manhood about him?"

"He doesn't get a warm welcome from me when he comes," said the old man. "Let him work for his own side and not come spying around here."

"I don't know," said Mr. O'Connor dubiously, as he took out cigarette-papers and tobacco. "I think Joe Hynes is a straight man. He's a clever chap, too, with the pen. Do you remember that thing he wrote... ?"

"Some of these hillsiders and fenians are a bit too clever if you ask me," said Mr. Henchy. "Do you know what my private and candid opinion is about some of those little jokers? I believe half of them are in the pay of the Castle."

"There's no knowing," said the old man.

"O, but I know it for a fact," said Mr. Henchy. "They're Castle hacks... I don't say Hynes... No, damn it, I think he's a stroke above that... But there's a certain little nobleman with a cock-eye — you know the patriot I'm alluding to?"

Mr. O'Connor nodded.

"There's a lineal descendant of Major Sirr for you if you like! O, the heart's blood of a patriot! That's a fellow now that'd sell his country for fourpence — ay — and go down on his bended knees and thank the Almighty Christ he had a country to sell."

There was a knock at the door.

"Come in!" said Mr. Henchy.

A person resembling a poor clergyman or a poor actor appeared in the doorway. His black clothes were tightly buttoned on his short body and it was impossible to say whether he wore a clergyman's collar or a layman's, because the collar of his shabby frock-coat, the uncovered buttons of which reflected the candle-light, was turned up about his neck. He wore a round hat of hard black felt. His face, shining with raindrops, had the appearance of damp yellow cheese save where two rosy spots indicated the cheek-bones. He opened his very long mouth suddenly to express disappointment and at the same time opened wide his very bright blue eyes to express pleasure and surprise.

"O Father Keon!" said Mr. Henchy, jumping up from his chair. "Is that you? Come in!"

"O, no, no, no!" said Father Keon quickly, pursing his lips as if he were addressing a child.

"Won't you come in and sit down?"

"No, no, no!" said Father Keon, speaking in a discreet, indulgent, velvety voice. "Don't let me disturb you now! I'm just looking for Mr. Fanning..."

"He's round at the *Black Eagle*," said Mr. Henchy. "But won't you come in and sit down a minute?"

"No, no, thank you. It was just a little business matter," said Father Keon. "Thank you, indeed."

He retreated from the doorway and Mr. Henchy, seizing one of the candlesticks, went to the door to light him downstairs.

"O, don't trouble, I beg!"

"No, but the stairs is so dark."

"No, no, I can see... Thank you, indeed."

"Are you right now?"

"All right, thanks... Thanks."

Mr. Henchy returned with the candlestick and put it on the table. He sat down again at the fire. There was silence for a few moments.

"Tell me, John," said Mr. O'Connor, lighting his cigarette with another pasteboard card.

"Hm?"

"What is he exactly?"

"Ask me an easier one," said Mr. Henchy.

"Fanning and himself seem to me very thick. They're often in Kavanagh's together. Is he a priest at all?"

"'Mmmyes, I believe so... I think he's what you call a black sheep. We haven't many of them, thank God! but we have a few... He's an unfortunate man of some kind..."

"And how does he knock it out?" asked Mr. O'Connor.

"That's another mystery."

"Is he attached to any chapel or church or institution or —"

"No," said Mr. Henchy, "I think he's travelling on his own account... God forgive me," he added, "I thought he was the dozen of stout."

"Is there any chance of a drink itself?" asked Mr. O'Connor.

"I'm dry too," said the old man.

"I asked that little shoeboy three times," said Mr. Henchy, "would he send up a dozen of stout. I asked him again now, but he was leaning on the counter in his shirt-sleeves having a deep goster with Alderman Cowley."

"Why didn't you remind him?" said Mr. O'Connor.

"Well, I wouldn't go over while he was talking to Alderman Cowley. I just waited till I caught his eye, and said: 'About that little matter I was speaking to you about...' 'That'll be all right, Mr. H.,' he said. Yerra, sure the little hop-o'-my-thumb has forgotten all about it."

"There's some deal on in that quarter," said Mr. O'Connor thoughtfully. "I saw the three of them hard at it yesterday at Suffolk Street corner."

"I think I know the little game they're at," said Mr. Henchy. "You must owe the City Fathers money nowadays if you want to be made Lord Mayor. Then they'll make you Lord Mayor. By God! I'm thinking seriously of becoming a City Father myself. What do you think? Would I do for the job?"

Mr. O'Connor laughed.

"So far as owing money goes..."

"Driving out of the Mansion House," said Mr. Henchy, "in all my vermin, with Jack here standing up behind me in a powdered wig—eh?"

"And make me your private secretary, John."

"Yes. And I'll make Father Keon my private chaplain. We'll have a family party."

"Faith, Mr. Henchy," said the old man, "you'd keep up better style than some of them. I was talking one day to old Keegan, the porter. 'And how do you like your new master, Pat?' says I to him. 'You haven't much entertaining now,' says I. 'Entertaining!' says he. 'He'd live on the smell of an oil-rag.' And do you know what he told me? Now, I declare to God, I didn't believe him."

"What?" said Mr. Henchy and Mr. O'Connor.

"He told me: 'What do you think of a Lord Mayor of Dublin sending out for a pound of chops for his dinner? How's that for high living?' says he. 'Wisha! wisha,' says I. 'A pound of chops,' says he, 'coming into the Mansion House.' 'Wisha!' says I, 'What kind of people is going at all now?'"

At this point there was a knock at the door, and a boy put in his head.

"What is it?" said the old man.

"From the *Black Eagle*," said the boy, walking in sideways and depositing a basket on the floor with a noise of shaken bottles.

The old man helped the boy to transfer the bottles from the basket to the table and counted the full tally. After the transfer the boy put his basket on his arm and asked:

"Any bottles?"

"What bottles?" said the old man.

"Won't you let us drink them first?" said Mr. Henchy.

"I was told to ask for the bottles."

"Come back tomorrow," said the old man.

"Here, boy!" said Mr. Henchy, "will you run over to O'Farrell's and ask him to lend us a corkscrew—for Mr. Henchy, say. Tell him we won't keep it a minute. Leave the basket there."

The boy went out and Mr. Henchy began to rub his hands cheerfully, saying:

"Ah, well, he's not so bad after all. He's as good as his word, anyhow."

"There's no tumblers," said the old man.

"O, don't let that trouble you, Jack," said Mr. Henchy. "Many's the good man before now drank out of the bottle."

"Anyway, it's better than nothing," said Mr. O'Connor.

"He's not a bad sort," said Mr. Henchy, "only Fanning has such a loan of him. He means well, you know, in his own tinpot way."

The boy came back with the corkscrew. The old man opened three bottles and was handing back the corkscrew when Mr. Henchy said to the boy:

"Would you like a drink, boy?"

"If you please, sir," said the boy.

The old man opened another bottle grudgingly, and handed it to the boy.

"What age are you?" he asked.

"Seventeen," said the boy.

As the old man said nothing further, the boy took the bottle, said: "Here's my best respects, sir, to Mr. Henchy," drank the contents, put the bottle back on the table and wiped his mouth with his sleeve. Then he took up the corkscrew and went out of the door sideways, muttering some form of salutation.

"That's the way it begins," said the old man.

"The thin edge of the wedge," said Mr. Henchy.

The old man distributed the three bottles which he had opened and the men drank from them simultaneously. After having drunk each placed his bottle on the mantelpiece within hand's reach and drew in a long breath of satisfaction.

"Well, I did a good day's work to-day," said Mr. Henchy, after a pause.

"That so, John?"

"Yes. I got him one or two sure things in Dawson Street, Crofton and myself. Between ourselves, you know, Crofton (he's a decent chap, of course), but he's not worth a damn as a canvasser. He hasn't a word to throw to a dog. He stands and looks at the people while I do the talking."

Here two men entered the room. One of them was a very fat man, whose blue serge clothes seemed to be in danger of falling from his sloping figure. He had a big face which resembled a young ox's face in expression, staring blue eyes and a grizzled moustache. The other man, who was much younger and frailer, had a thin, clean-shaven face. He wore a very high double collar and a wide-brimmed bowler hat.

"Hello, Crofton!" said Mr. Henchy to the fat man. "Talk of the devil..."

"Where did the booze come from?" asked the young man. "Did the cow calve?"

"O, of course, Lyons spots the drink first thing!" said Mr. O'Connor, laughing.

"Is that the way you chaps canvass," said Mr. Lyons, "and Crofton and I out in the cold and rain looking for votes?"

"Why, blast your soul," said Mr. Henchy, "I'd get more votes in five minutes than you two'd get in a week."

"Open two bottles of stout, Jack," said Mr. O'Connor.

"How can I?" said the old man, "when there's no corkscrew?"

"Wait now, wait now!" said Mr. Henchy, getting up quickly. "Did you ever see this little trick?"

He took two bottles from the table and, carrying them to the fire, put them on the hob. Then he sat down again by the fire and took another drink from his bottle. Mr. Lyons sat on the edge of the table, pushed his hat towards the nape of his neck and began to swing his legs.

"Which is my bottle?" he asked.

"This, lad," said Mr. Henchy.

Mr. Crofton sat down on a box and looked fixedly at the other bottle on the hob. He was silent for two reasons. The first reason, sufficient in itself, was that he had nothing to say; the second reason was that he considered his companions beneath him. He had been a canvasser for Wilkins, the Conservative, but when the Conservatives had withdrawn their man and, choosing the lesser of two evils, given their support to the Nationalist candidate, he had been engaged to work for Mr. Tierney.

In a few minutes an apologetic "Pok!" was heard as the cork flew out of Mr. Lyons' bottle. Mr. Lyons jumped off the table, went to the fire, took his bottle and carried it back to the table.

"I was just telling them, Crofton," said Mr. Henchy, "that we got a good few votes to-day."

"Who did you get?" asked Mr. Lyons.

"Well, I got Parkes for one, and I got Atkinson for two, and I got Ward of Dawson Street. Fine old chap he is, too—regular old toff, old Conservative! 'But isn't your candidate a Nationalist?' said he. 'He's a respectable man,' said I. 'He's in favour of whatever will benefit this country. He's a big ratepayer,' I said. 'He has extensive house property in the city and three places of business, and isn't it to his own advantage to keep down the rates? He's a prominent and respected citizen,' said I , 'and a Poor Law Guardian, and he doesn't belong to any party, good, bad, or indifferent.' That's the way to talk to 'em."

"And what about the address to the King?" said Mr. Lyons after drinking and smacking his lips.

"Listen to me," said Mr. Henchy. "What we want in this country, as I said to old Ward, is capital. The King's coming here will mean an influx of money into this country. The citizens of Dublin will benefit by it. Look at all the factories down by the quays there, idle! Look at all the money there is in the country if we only worked the old industries, the mills, the ship-building yards and factories. It's capital we want."

"But look here, John," said Mr. O'Connor. "Why should we welcome the King of England? Didn't Parnell himself..."

"Parnell," said Mr. Henchy, "is dead. Now, here's the way I look at it. Here's this chap come to the throne after his old mother keeping him out of it till the man was grey. He's a man of the world, and he means well by us. He's a jolly fine, decent fellow, if you ask me, and no damn nonsense about him. He just says to himself: 'The old one never went to see these wild Irish. By Christ, I'll go myself and see what they're like.' And are we going to insult the man when he comes over here on a friendly visit? Eh? Isn't that right, Crofton?"

Mr. Crofton nodded his head.

"But after all now," said Mr. Lyons argumentatively, "King Edward's life, you know, is not the very..."

"Let bygones be bygones," said Mr. Henchy. "I admire the man personally. He's just an ordinary knockabout like you and me. He's fond of his glass of grog and he's a bit of a rake, perhaps, and he's a good sportsman. Damn it, can't we Irish play fair?"

"That's all very fine," said Mr. Lyons. "But look at the case of Parnell now."

"In the name of God," said Mr. Henchy, "where's the analogy between the two cases?"

"What I mean," said Mr. Lyons, "is we have our ideals. Why, now, would we welcome a man like that? Do you think now after what he did Parnell was a fit man to lead us? And why, then, would we do it for Edward the Seventh?"

"This is Parnell's anniversary," said Mr. O'Connor, "and don't let us stir up any bad blood. We all respect him now that he's dead and gone — even the Conservatives," he added, turning to Mr. Crofton.

Pok! The tardy cork flew out of Mr. Crofton's bottle. Mr. Crofton got up from his box and went to the fire. As he returned with his capture he said in a deep voice:

"Our side of the house respects him, because he was a gentleman."

"Right you are, Crofton!" said Mr. Henchy fiercely. "He was the only man that could keep that bag of cats in order. 'Down, ye dogs! Lie down, ye curs!' That's the way he treated them. Come in, Joe! Come in!" he called out, catching sight of Mr. Hynes in the doorway.

Mr. Hynes came in slowly.

"Open another bottle of stout, Jack," said Mr. Henchy. "O, I forgot there's no corkscrew! Here, show me one here and I'll put it at the fire."

The old man handed him another bottle and he placed it on the hob.

"Sit down, Joe," said Mr. O'Connor, "we're just talking about the Chief."

"Ay, ay!" said Mr. Henchy.

Mr. Hynes sat on the side of the table near Mr. Lyons but said nothing.

"There's one of them, anyhow," said Mr. Henchy, "that didn't renege him. By God, I'll say for you, Joe! No, by God, you stuck to him like a man!"

"O, Joe," said Mr. O'Connor suddenly. "Give us that thing you wrote — do you remember? Have you got it on you?"

"O, ay!" said Mr. Henchy. "Give us that. Did you ever hear that, Crofton? Listen to this now: splendid thing."

"Go on," said Mr. O'Connor. "Fire away, Joe."

Mr. Hynes did not seem to remember at once the piece to which they were alluding, but, after reflecting a while, he said:

"O, that thing is it... Sure, that's old now."

"Out with it, man!" said Mr. O'Connor.

"'Sh, 'sh," said Mr. Henchy. "Now, Joe!"

Mr. Hynes hesitated a little longer. Then amid the silence he took off his hat, laid it on the table and stood up. He seemed to be rehearsing the piece in his mind. After a rather long pause he announced:

THE DEATH OF PARNELL
6th October, 1891

He cleared his throat once or twice and then began to recite:

He is dead. Our Uncrowned King is dead.
O, Erin, mourn with grief and woe
For he lies dead whom the fell gang
Of modern hypocrites laid low.

He lies slain by the coward hounds
He raised to glory from the mire;

And Erin's hopes and Erin's dreams
Perish upon her monarch's pyre.

In palace, cabin or in cot
The Irish heart where'er it be
Is bowed with woe—for he is gone
Who would have wrought her destiny.

He would have had his Erin famed,
The green flag gloriously unfurled,
Her statesmen, bards, and warriors raised
Before the nations of the World.

He dreamed (alas, 'twas but a dream!)
Of Liberty: but as he strove
To clutch that idol, treachery
Sundered him from the thing he loved.

Shame on the coward, caitiff hands
That smote their Lord or with a kiss
Betrayed him to the rabble-rout
Of fawning priests—no friends of his.

May everlasting shame consume
The memory of those who tried
To befoul and smear the exalted name
Of one who spurned them in his pride.

He fell as fall the mighty ones,
Nobly undaunted to the last,
And death has now united him
With Erin's heroes of the past.

No sound of strife disturb his sleep!

Calmly he rests: no human pain
Or high ambition spurs him now
The peaks of glory to attain.

They had their way: they laid him low.
But Erin, list, his spirit may
Rise, like the Phoenix from the flames,
When breaks the dawning of the day,

The day that brings us Freedom's reign.
And on that day may Erin well
Pledge in the cup she lifts to Joy
One grief—the memory of Parnell.

Mr. Hynes sat down again on the table. When he had finished his recitation there was a silence and then a burst of clapping: even Mr. Lyons clapped. The applause continued for a little time. When it had ceased all the auditors drank from their bottles in silence.

Pok! The cork flew out of Mr. Hynes' bottle, but Mr. Hynes remained sitting flushed and bare-headed on the table. He did not seem to have heard the invitation.

"Good man, Joe!" said Mr. O'Connor, taking out his cigarette papers and pouch the better to hide his emotion.

"What do you think of that, Crofton?" cried Mr. Henchy. "Isn't that fine? What?"

Mr. Crofton said that it was a very fine piece of writing.

Questions

1. How does Joyce suggest the political decay of "modern" Ireland in this short story? What does the title suggest about the political situation in Ireland?
2. How do Henchy, O'Connor, Lyons, and Crofton differ from Joe Hynes in their political views?
3. How is Mr. Hynes's poem related to the story?
4. What are the main recurring images described in the story? How do they highlight the major themes of the story?
5. Why do you think the author develops the story mostly by means of dialogue instead of narrative?

委员会办公室里的常春藤日

本故事发生在威克罗街的委员会办公室。几个为政客理查德·J. 提尔尼游说的人在那里休息。他们的谈话主要是围绕政治问题。《委员会办公室里的常春藤日》主要是为了纪念一位广受爱戴、为爱尔兰而战的政治家查尔斯·帕耐尔。故事还展现出当时腐败的政治局势,从而反映出乔伊斯在《都柏林人》一书中总的主题——瘫痪,这里是指政治上的瘫痪。

老杰克用一块纸板把煤渣拢到一起,然后把它们仔细地铺在烧得发白的煤堆上。当煤堆被薄薄地覆盖了一层之后,他的脸陷入了黑暗之中,但是随即他又开始起劲地扇火,他蹲着的身影爬上了对面的墙,他的脸又慢慢在火光中出现。这是一张老人的脸,颧骨突出,胡子拉碴。潮湿的蓝眼睛迎着火光眨动,湿润的嘴巴不时地张开,闭上时会机械地咀嚼一两次。煤渣着起来后,他把纸板靠在墙上,叹了口气说:

"现在好多了,奥康纳先生。"

奥康纳先生是个灰头发的年轻人,他的脸上长了许多红斑和粉刺,相貌难看。他刚把烟叶用烟纸卷成一个匀称的圆筒,听到这话,又沉思着把圆筒打开。然后他又开始沉思着把烟叶卷起来,想了一会儿,才舔了舔纸。

"提尔尼先生说他什么时候回来了吗?"他用沙哑的假声问。

"他没说。"

奥康纳先生把烟放到嘴里,开始翻自己的口袋。他拿出一包薄卡片。

"我给你拿根火柴,"老头儿说。

"不用了,这就行,"奥康纳先生说。

他选了一张卡读上面印的字:

市长选举

皇家交易所选区

在皇家交易所选区即将举行的选举中,济贫会委员理查德·J. 提尔尼先生恭请您投票并鼎力相助。

提尔尼先生的竞选经理人雇用了奥康纳先生在选区的一部分地方游说,但是因为天气太糟,他的靴子又透水,他一天的大部分时间都和老门房杰克坐在威克罗街委员会办公室的火炉旁。自从短暂的白天黑下来,他们就一直这么坐着。这是10月6日,户外十分阴冷。

奥康纳先生从一张卡片上撕下一个纸条,引着火,用它点烟。他点烟时,火苗照亮了外套翻领上一枚光洁的深色常春藤叶。老头儿注意地盯着他,然后又拿起那块纸板,在他的伙伴抽烟时开始慢慢地扇火。

"啊,是的,"他接着说,"真不知道该怎么抚养孩子。现在谁会想到他会变成那样。我送他去天主教平信徒社团。我能为他做的都做了。他却到处喝酒。我尽力想让他成器。"

他疲惫地把纸板放回去。

"只是我现在老了,不然我能让他改过来。我会像以前好多次做过的那样,拿着棍子到他背后,趁我还能管得住他,打他一顿。他妈,你知道,这样那样地把他惯坏了……"

"就是这样才把孩子宠坏了,"奥康纳先生说。

"就是,"老头儿说,"你得到的只有无礼放肆,没什么感激。不管什么时候他看见我喝上一杯就会教训我。儿子那样跟老子讲话,这都成了什么世道?"

"他多大了?"奥康纳先生说。

"19,"老头儿说。

"你怎么不让他干点什么?"

"当然了,自从那个醉鬼离开学校我就跟他说过,'我不会养着你',我说,'你得自己找个工作'。但是,当然了,他找到工作就更糟;他把钱都喝掉了。"

奥康纳先生同情地摇了摇头,老头儿盯着炉火沉默下来。有人打开房门喊道:

"喂,是共济会在开会吗?"

"谁呀?"老头儿说。

"你们摸黑干嘛呢?"一个声音问道。

"是你吗,海因斯?"奥康纳先生问。

"是。你们摸黑干嘛呢?"海因斯先生说着,走到炉火的亮处。

他是个高挑苗条的年轻人,长着浅棕色的胡须。他的帽檐上垂着小雨滴,外套的领子也竖了起来。

"那么,麦特,"他对奥康纳先生说,"进行得怎么样?"

奥康纳先生摇了摇头。老头儿离开火炉,蹒跚着在屋里找了两个插在烛台上的蜡烛又走回来。他把蜡烛先后伸进炉火里点着,然后端到桌上。一个光秃秃的房间出现了，炉火不再显得生气勃勃。房间的墙上只有一份竞选讲稿。屋子的中间是张小桌子，上面堆着文件。

海因斯先生靠着壁炉台问道：

"他付钱了吗？"

"还没，"奥康纳先生说，"我真希望今晚他不会让我们白等。"

海因斯先生笑起来。

"哦，他会付你钱的，别担心，"他说。

"我希望如果他是认真的，他就会精明点，"奥康纳先生说。

"你觉得呢，杰克？"海因斯先生语含讥讽地问老头儿。

老头儿坐回到炉火边说：

"倒不是，但是，不管怎样，他有实力。不像那个生手。"

"哪个生手？"海因斯先生说。

"科尔根，"老头儿轻蔑地说。

"因为科尔根是个工人你才那么说吗？一个优秀诚实的砌砖工人和酒馆老板之间有什么不同——哼？工人不是和别人一样有权利进入市政府吗——是的，工人比那些一见到大人物就脱帽的势利小人更有权利。不对吗，麦特？"海因斯先生对奥康纳先生说。

"我想你是对的，"奥康纳先生说。

"那个人是个从不趋炎附势、朴素又诚实的人。他代表劳动阶级参选。你的老板只想得到份工作。"

"当然，应该有人代表劳动阶级，"老头儿说。

"工人，"海因斯先生说，"得到的只有苛待，没有优遇。但是劳动创造了一切。工人不是为儿子、侄子、表亲找肥差的。工人不会玷污都柏林的荣誉去取悦德国来的国王。"

"那是怎么回事？"老头儿说。

"你不知道，如果爱德华国王明年来这儿的话，他们想上呈一份欢迎辞吗？我们向一个外国国王卑躬屈膝是为了什么？"

"我们的候选人不会投赞成票的，"奥康纳先生说，"他是以民族党的候选人身份参选的。"

"他不会吗？"海因斯先生说，"等着看他会不会吧。我了解他。不就是滑头鬼提尔尼吗？"

"老天作证！也许你是对的，乔，"奥康纳先生说，"不管怎样，我希望他会带着钱出现。"

三个人沉默下来。老头儿开始把更多的炉渣拢到一起。海因斯先生脱掉帽子晃了晃，然后折下外套的领子，露出翻领上的常春藤叶。

"要是这个人还活着，"他指着叶子说，"我们根本不会谈到欢迎辞的事。"

"的确。"奥康纳先生说。

"天哪，上帝与他们同在。"老头儿说。"那时多有起色呀。"

房间又一次沉默下来。然后一个匆忙的小个子推门进来。他抽着鼻子，耳朵也冻红了。他很快走到火边，摩擦着手，好像要擦出火花来。

"没钱，孩子们，"他说。

"坐这儿，亨奇先生，"老头儿说着把自己的椅子让给他。

"哦，别忙了，杰克，别忙了，"亨奇先生说。

他简单地对海因斯先生点了个头，坐在老头儿空出来的椅子上。

"你去过安吉尔街了吗？"他问奥康纳先生。

"是的，"奥康纳先生边说边开始在口袋里找备忘录。

"你拜访格莱姆斯了吗？"

"是的。"

"哦？他什么立场？"

"他不愿承诺什么。他说：'我不会告诉任何人我会怎么投票。'但我想他没什么问题。"

"为什么？"

"他问我提名的都是谁，我告诉他了。我提到伯克神甫的名字。我想没什么问题。"

亨奇先生开始抽鼻子，以惊人的速度在火上搓着手。然后他说：

"看在上帝的份上，杰克，给我们拿点煤来。一定还有剩的。"

老人走出房间。

"不成呀，"亨奇先生摇着头说。"我问了那小子，但是他说：'哦，亨奇先生，我要是看到一切都做得好好的我是不会忘记你的。你尽管放心。'抠门的小子！也是，他也不可能是别的样子！"

"我怎么跟你说的，麦特？"海因斯先生说，"滑头鬼提尔尼。"

"哦，他是滑头到一定程度了，"亨奇先生说，"他那双小猪眼不是白长的。去他的！他就不能像个男人那样把钱付了，而不是说些'哦，亨奇先生，我得跟法宁先生谈谈……我已经花了很多了'？抠门的小王八蛋！我想他忘了他老爸在玛丽巷开旧衣店的时候了。"

"那是真的吗？"奥康纳先生问。

"上帝，是真的，"亨奇先生说，"你没听说过吗？人们过去都在周日早上其他商店没开门时进去买马甲或长裤——还真像那么回事!但是滑头鬼的小老爸总在角落里放个小黑瓶子。你记得吗?就那样。他就在那里出生的。"

老头儿拿着几块煤回来了,他把煤块铺在炉火上。

"那可真够意思,"奥康纳先生说,"他不肯出钱,我们怎么给他干活?"

"我可帮不了,"亨奇先生说,"我回家后就会发现司法官在厅里等着我呢。"

海因斯先生笑了,肩膀一挺,从壁炉旁直起身来,准备离开。

"艾迪国王来了就会好起来,"他说,"好吧,孩子们,我先走一步。回见,回见。"

他慢慢走出房间。亨奇先生和老头儿什么也没说,但就在门快关上时,本来一直阴郁地盯着炉火的奥康纳先生突然喊道,

"回见,乔。"

亨奇先生等了一会儿,然后向门的方向点点头。

"告诉我,"他隔着炉火说,"什么风把我们的朋友吹来的?他想要什么?"

"唉,可怜的乔!"奥康纳先生说着把烟头扔进火里,"他和我们一样缺钱。"

亨奇先生大声地抽了抽鼻子,向炉火吐了一大口痰,几乎把火浇灭,炉火发出"嗞"的一声抗议。

"实话只说给你听,"他说,"我想他是从那边阵营来的。要是你问我,我认为他是科尔根的间谍。到处走走,看看他们进展如何。他们不会怀疑你的。你明白吗?"

"啊,可怜的乔是个体面人,"奥康纳先生说。

"他父亲是个体面可敬的人,"亨奇先生承认。"可怜的老拉里·海因斯!他活着时做了多少好事!但是恐怕我们的朋友就不是什么好料了。去他的,一个人穷我能理解,但当寄生虫我就不懂了。他就不能有点尊严吗?"

"他来的时候我不欢迎他,"老头儿说,"让他给他自己那边工作吧,别在这里打探消息。"

"我不清楚,"奥康纳先生疑惑地说着,拿出烟纸和烟叶。"我觉得乔·海因斯是个正直的人。他笔头也很灵光。你记得他写的那个……?"

"要是你问我的话,我认为有些山里人和芬尼亚会会员聪明得过了头,"亨奇先生说。"实话告诉你,我相信这些讨厌鬼有一半都是给总督府工作的。"

"这可无法知道。"老头儿说。

"哦,但我可知道这是真的,"亨奇先生说。"他们是总督府的雇佣文

人……我不是说海因斯……不，妈的，我觉得他还不至于……但有个斗鸡眼的小贵族——你知道我说的那个爱国者吧？"

奥康纳先生点点头。

"换句话说，这就是瑟尔上校的直系子孙！哦，一个爱国者的骨血！那就是个为四便士就能卖国的家伙——唉——还会跪下感谢上天他还有国可卖。"

门口有人敲门。

"进来！"亨奇先生说。

一个像个穷牧师或是穷演员的人出现在门口。他的黑衣服紧紧扣在矮小的身体上，没法判断他穿的衣服是牧师的衣领还是平信徒的，因为他破旧的大衣领子竖了起来，上面没有被包裹的纽扣反射着烛光。他戴了顶硬黑毡做的圆帽。脸上有雨滴在闪光，除了颧骨的两块玫瑰红，他的脸就像块潮湿的黄奶酪。他突然张开大嘴表示失望，同时睁大明亮的蓝眼睛表示惊喜。

"哦！纪昂神甫！"亨奇先生说着从椅子上跳起来。"是你吗？进来！"

"哦！不！不！"纪昂神甫快速地说，好像同孩子讲话那样噘着嘴。

"你不进来坐吗？"

"不，不，不！"纪昂神甫以一种谨慎、纵容又软绵绵的嗓音说。"别让我打扰了你们！我只是在找法宁先生……"

"他在黑鹰酒馆那里，"亨奇先生说，"但是你不进来坐会儿吗？"

"不，不，谢谢你。只是点公事，"纪昂神甫说。"非常感谢。"

他从门口退去，亨奇先生抓起一根蜡烛，走到门边照着他下楼。

"哦，请别麻烦了！"

"不麻烦，楼梯太黑了。"

"别，别，我能看见……太谢谢你了。"

"现在行了吗？"

"好了，谢谢……谢谢。"

亨奇先生拿着蜡烛回来，把它放在桌子上。他又在火边坐下。大家沉默了一会儿。

"告诉我，约翰，"奥康纳先生说着又用一张卡片点燃了烟。

"什么？"

"他到底是干什么的？"

"你还是问我一个简单点的吧，"亨奇先生说。

"在我看来法宁和他非常亲密。他们常常一起在卡瓦纳出现。他真是个牧师吗？"

"嗯，是的，我觉得……我想他是你们叫败家子的那种人。这种人不太多，感谢上帝！但还是有几个……他是个有点不幸的人……"

"他是怎么潦倒的？"奥康纳先生问。

"那是另一个谜了。"

"他属于某个教堂、教会、机构或——"

"不，"亨奇先生说，"我想他是为自己的事儿在奔波……上帝饶恕我，"他又说，"我刚才还以为他是送黑啤酒的呢。"

"真有酒喝吗？"奥康纳先生问。

"我也渴了，"老头儿说。

"我问了那小子三次了，"亨奇先生说，"他能不能给我们送一打黑啤酒来。我刚才又问了他，但是他穿着衬衫靠在柜台上和艾尔德曼·考利在深谈着什么。"

"为什么你不提醒他？"奥康纳先生说。

"哦，他和艾尔德曼·考利谈话时我不能过去。我就等着直到他看到我，然后说，'我刚才跟你说的那件小事……''没问题，H先生，'他说。嗯，那个小矮子肯定已经忘得一干二净了。"

"那一区有点什么猫腻，"奥康纳先生若有所思地说。"昨天我在萨福克街角处看见他们三个在起劲地商量。"

"我想我知道他们在玩什么把戏，"亨奇先生说。"现在你想当市长大人就得欠市议员钱。然后他们就让你当市长。上帝作证！我自己也正在考虑当个市议员。你觉得呢？我能胜任吗？"

奥康纳先生笑起来。

"就欠钱这一点来说……"

"开车出市长官邸，"亨奇先生说，"穿着气派，杰克戴着搽了粉的假发站在我身后——嗯？"

"让我做你的私人秘书，约翰。"

"是的，我也会让纪昂神甫做我的私人牧师。我们会来个家庭聚会。"

"千真万确，亨奇先生，"老头儿说，"你会比他们有些人还有气派。有天我和门房老纪根聊天。'你觉得你的新主人怎么样，派特？'我跟他说。'你现在没什么油水了。'我说。'油水，'他说，'他靠油布的味儿就能过活。'你们知道他告诉我什么了吗？我跟上帝说，我真不信他的话。"

"什么？"亨奇先生和奥康纳先生说。

"他告诉我：'都柏林的市长大人订购了一磅排骨的晚餐，你怎么看？那就是上等生活？'他说。'哎呀！哎呀！'我说。'一磅排骨，'他说。'送进市长官邸。''哎呀！'我说，'到底现在是什么样的人当政呀？'"

这时有人敲门，一个男孩子伸进头。

"什么事？"老头儿说。

"从黑鹰酒馆来的，"男孩说着侧身走进来，把一个篮子放在地板上，里面传出瓶子晃动的声音。

老头儿帮男孩把瓶子从篮子里移到桌上，点了总数。

搬完以后男孩把篮子挎到胳膊上问：

"有瓶子吗？"

"什么瓶子？"老头说。

"你不让我们先喝吗？"亨奇先生说。

"人家告诉我要瓶子。"

"明天来拿吧，"老头儿说。

"哎，孩子！"亨奇先生说，"你能跑到奥法罗家让他借我们一个螺丝起子吗？你就说亨奇先生借的。告诉他我们一会儿就还。把篮子留那儿。"

男孩出去了，亨奇先生开始高兴地搓手，说：

"呵，毕竟他没那么糟。不管怎么说，他言出必行。"

"没有杯子，"老头儿说。

"哦，不用为这个心烦，杰克，"亨奇先生说。"许多英雄都是用瓶喝的。"

"不管怎样，也比没有强，"奥康纳先生说。

"他不是个坏人，"亨奇先生说，"只是法宁向他借了一大笔钱。你知道，他的行事方式虽上不得台面，但本意不坏。"

男孩拿着螺丝起子回来了。老头儿开了三瓶，正要递回起子时，亨奇先生对男孩说，

"你想喝点吗，孩子？"

"那敢情好，先生，"男孩说。

老头儿不情愿地又开了一瓶，递给男孩。

"你多大了？"他问。

"17，"孩子说。

因为老头儿没再说什么，男孩拿起酒瓶，说："致亨奇先生，我最大的敬意。"喝了酒，把瓶子放回到桌上，用袖子擦了擦嘴，然后他拿起起子，侧身走出门去，咕哝着告别的话。

"人就这么学坏的，"老头儿说。

"小恶慢慢会铸大错，"亨奇先生说。

老头儿把开的三瓶酒分了，大家同时喝了一口。喝完后，每个人都把瓶子放

在壁炉台上够得着的地方，满意地吸了口气。

"嗯，我今天没白忙，"亨奇先生顿了顿说道。

"是吗，约翰？"

"是的，我在道森街给他争取了一两票，科罗夫顿和我。也就我们说说，你知道，科罗夫顿（当然是个体面人），但是他当个游说者一文不值。他绷着脸不说话。我讲话时他就站着看着人群。"

这时两个人走进房间。一个非常胖，他的蓝哔叽衣服似乎快要从倾斜的身体上滑下来。他长着张大脸，表情像头小牛，蓝色的眼睛瞪着，长着花白的胡子。另一个年轻得多，也瘦得多，一张瘦脸，刮得干干净净。他穿着非常高的双领，戴着宽檐圆顶硬礼帽。

"嗨，科罗夫顿？"亨奇先生对胖男人说，"说谁谁就到……"

"酒从哪儿来的？"年轻人问。"母牛产崽了吗？"

"哦，当然，莱恩斯一眼就会看到酒！"奥康纳先生笑着说。

"你们这些家伙就这么游说吗，"莱恩斯先生说，"而我和科罗夫顿就得站在冷风冷雨里拉选票？"

"嘿，去你的，"亨奇先生说，"我五分钟内获得的选票比你们俩一星期得的还多。"

"开两瓶黑啤酒，杰克，"奥康纳先生说。

"怎么开？"老头儿说，"没起子了。"

"等等，等等，"亨奇先生说着很快起身，"你们看过这个小把戏吗？"

他从桌上拿了两瓶到炉火边，把它们放在壁炉搁架上。然后他又坐在火边，从他的瓶子里喝了一口。莱恩斯先生坐在桌边，把帽子朝颈背推去，开始晃荡腿。

"哪个是我那瓶？"他问。

"这个，小伙子，"亨奇先生说。

科罗夫顿坐在一个箱子上，目不转睛地盯着搁架上的另一瓶。他沉默是出于两个原因。第一个相当充分，就是他没什么可说的；第二个就是他瞧不起这些伙伴。他本是保守党人威尔金斯的游说人，但是保守党退出选举后，选择了没那么讨厌的一方，转而支持民族党候选人，他就受雇于提尔尼先生。

几分钟后，大家听到充满歉意的"噗"的一声，塞子飞出了莱恩斯先生的瓶子。莱恩斯先生从桌子上跳下来，走到火边，拿起酒瓶又走回桌边。

"我刚才正说着，科罗夫顿，"亨奇先生说，"我们今天拉到了不少票。"

"你们争取到谁了？"莱恩斯先生问。

"嗯，先是帕克斯，然后是阿特金森，还有道森街的监管人。他也是个不错的老家伙——普通的老花花公子，老保守党！'你们的候选人不是民族党的吗？'他说。'他是个可敬的人，'我说。'他赞成一切对国家有利的事。他是个纳税大户，'我说，'他在市里有很多房产以及三处生意。税率下降不是也对他有好处吗？他是个地位显赫，广受尊敬的市民，'我说，'还是济贫会委员，他不属于任何党派，好的，坏的，或是中间派的。'跟他们就得这么说。"

"给国王的欢迎辞呢？"莱恩斯先生喝了一口，咂了咂嘴说道。

"听我说，"亨奇先生说。"就像我跟老监管说的那样，我们国家需要的是资金。国王来这里意味着现金的流入。都柏林的市民会因此受益。看看码头那边的所有工厂，都没活儿干！看看，我们只要让老工业，面粉厂、造船厂、工厂运转起来我们就能赚到钱。我们需要的是资金。"

"但是这么想想，约翰，"奥康纳先生说。"我们为什么要欢迎英格兰国王？帕耐尔自己难道不是……"

"帕耐尔，"亨奇先生说，"已经死了。听听我的看法。这个家伙的老妈一直占着王位，直到头发白了他才登了基。他见过世面，对我们没有恶意。要是你问我的话，他就是个快活体面的家伙，没其他废话。他就是这么想的：'老妈从没去看看这些不服管的爱尔兰人。基督作证，我自己要去看看他们什么样子。'这样一个来友好访问的人，我们难道要侮辱他吗？嗯？不对吗，科罗夫顿？"

科罗夫顿先生点点头。

"但是，毕竟，"莱恩斯先生反驳道，"爱德华国王的生活，你知道，不是非常……"

"过去的就让它过去吧，"亨奇先生说。"我个人很崇拜这个人。他和你我一样只是个普通的家伙。他爱喝点酒，也许有点像花花公子，他还是个不错的运动员。妈的，我们爱尔兰人就不能公平些吗？"

"那都没问题，"莱恩斯先生说，"但是看看帕耐尔的情况。"

"看在上帝的份上，"亨奇先生说，"这两件事有什么相似之处？"

"我的意思是，"莱恩斯先生说，"我们都有理想。为什么我们现在要欢迎那样的一个人？你觉得做了那样的事之后，帕耐尔还是领导我们的合适人选吗？那为什么我们要迁就爱德华七世呢？"

"今天是帕耐尔的周年，"奥康纳先生说，"我们不要搞僵气氛。他已去世，我们都很尊敬他——甚至保守党人，"他转向科罗夫顿先生，补充道。

噗！慢一些的那个塞子飞出了科罗夫顿先生的瓶子。科罗夫顿先生从箱子上站起来走向炉火。他拿着瓶子走回来时以低沉的声音说道：

"我们这边尊敬他，因为他是个绅士。"

"正是如此，科罗夫顿！"亨奇先生激动地说。"他是唯一一个能让混乱局势稳定下来的人。'趴下,你们这些狗!下来,你们这些混蛋!'他就是这么对待他们的。进来!乔!进来!"他看到海因斯先生站在门口就喊了出来。

海因斯先生慢慢走进来。

"再开瓶黑啤酒,杰克,"亨奇先生说。"哦,我忘了没起子了。嗯,递给我一瓶,我把它放在火上。"

老头儿又递给他一瓶,他把它放在炉架上。

"坐下,乔,"奥康纳先生说,"我们正在谈领袖。"

"是的,是的!"亨奇先生说。

海因斯先生靠着莱恩斯先生坐在桌边,但一言未发。

"毕竟还有一个人,"亨奇先生说,"没有背弃他。上帝作证,我是在说你,乔!不,上帝作证!你像个男子汉那样忠于他!"

"哦,乔,"奥康纳先生突然说。"给我们朗诵一下你写的那个——记得吗?你带着吗?"

"哦,是的!"亨奇先生说。"给我们念那个。你听过吗?科罗夫顿,现在听听:非常棒的作品。"

"来吧,"奥康纳先生说。"开火吧,乔。"

海因斯先生似乎没有立刻记起他们在指哪篇,但是,想了一会儿后,他说:

"哦,那个……当然了,现在已经过时了。"

"念吧,伙计!"奥康纳先生说。

"嘘,嘘,"亨奇先生说。"念吧,乔!"

海因斯先生又犹豫了一会儿。然后在沉寂中,他摘下帽子,放在桌上,之后站起来。他似乎在脑海中排练这首诗。过了很长时间,他朗诵道:

帕耐尔之死

1891年10月6日

他清了清嗓子,然后开始背诵:

他死了,我们的无冕之王死了。
哦,爱尔兰,以悲愁哀悼。
他已逝,残暴之徒,
现代的伪君子们将他击倒。

他被懦夫们所杀害。

而他曾将他们从泥沼带向荣光。
爱尔兰的希望与梦想
在国王的坟墓上消亡。

宫廷、木房、村舍,
哪里有爱尔兰的心脏,
哪里就因他的逝去而忧伤。
因为他本可操纵爱尔兰的方向。

他本会使爱尔兰天下知名,
绿旗光荣地迎风飘展,
政治家、诗人、勇士
骄傲地立于世界面前。

他梦想着自由,
可惜那只是个梦。
他为了理想奋斗,
背叛却使他远离爱着的所有。

那些不知羞耻的懦夫
击倒了他们的主人。
或以一个吻将他出卖给牧师,
那些谄媚的、煽动民众的敌人。

愿永久的羞愧磨损那些人的记忆,
他们试图将他的英名玷污,
因他如此骄傲,
不屑与他们为伍。

他像所有的勇士一样倒下,
直至最后仍英勇高贵。
死亡将他带走,
与爱尔兰昔日的英雄相会。

不会有冲突之声惊扰他的沉睡,
他平静地歇息。
不再有雄心壮志或人间的苦痛
推动他到达光荣的顶峰。

他们得偿所愿:他们将他击倒。
但是爱尔兰会铭记,
当破晓之时,
他的灵魂会像凤凰从火焰中飞起。

那是会带给我们自由的一天。
那一天,爱尔兰人欢庆的酒杯上,
仍会留有一丝悲伤,
那是对帕耐尔的怀念。

海因斯先生又坐在桌边。他背诵完的时候,房间里先是一片沉默,然后爆发出一阵掌声;甚至莱恩斯先生也鼓掌了。掌声持续了一会儿。掌声停止之后,所有的听众都沉默地喝了一口。

噗!塞子飞出了海因斯先生的瓶子,但是海因斯先生仍坐在桌边,满脸通红,光着头。他似乎没听到瓶子发出的这声邀请。

"好样的,乔!"奥康纳先生说着拿出烟纸和荷包来掩饰自己的情感。

"你觉得怎么样呢,科罗夫顿?"亨奇先生喊道。"难道不好吗?怎么样?"

科罗夫顿先生说写得真好。

Virginia Woolf
(1882—1941)

Virginia Woolf, British novelist, literary critic, feminist and a central figure of Bloomsbury group, was the daughter of the well-known English essayist, critic and biographer, Sir Leslie Stephen. She was born in London and was educated at home by private teachers. In 1912 she married the political theorist Leonard Woolf. Virginia Woolf had recurring bouts of depression. The outbreak of the World War II increased her mental turmoil, and she committed suicide by drowning herself in the Ouse, Sussex.

Woolf published her first book *The Voyage Out* in 1915. In 1919 appeared a realistic novel, *Night and Day*. *Jacob's Room* (1922) was based upon the life and death of her brother Toby. In *Mrs. Dalloway* (1925), she experimented with her new style of writing, "stream of consciousness." She explored this technique in: *To the Lighthouse* (1927), *Orlando* (1928), *The Waves* (1931), *The Years* (1938) and *Between the Acts* (1941). These novels, aside from their great psychological depths, contain much poetic and lyrical factors in them. With *To the Lighthouse* and *The Waves* Woolf established herself as one of the leading writers of modernism. She was also a literary critic whose reviews and other essays were collected and published in *The Common Reader* (1925) and *The Second Common Reader* (1932). As a feminist, Virginia Woolf's concern with feminist thematics are dominant in *A Room of One's Own* (1929). Her feministic essays were also collected and published in *Three Guineas* (1938). Virginia Woolf published only one book of short stories *Monday or Tuesday* (1921) early in her career. After her death, her husband published another collection *A Haunted House and Other Stories* (1953).

The Mark on the Wall

The following story, a masterpiece of "stream of consciousness", concludes with the dramatic identification of that mark as a snail after several pages of digressive thinking in terms of history, reality, society, art, writing, and life itself, and fully shows her affluent imagination and incredible creativity.

Perhaps it was the middle of January in the present year that I first looked up and saw the mark on the wall. In order to fix a date it is necessary to remember what one saw. So now I think of the fire; the steady film of yellow light upon the page of my book; the three chrysanthemums in the round glass bowl on the mantelpiece. Yes, it must have been the winter time, and we had just finished our tea, for I remember that I was smoking a cigarette when I looked up and saw the mark on the wall for the first time. I looked up through the smoke of my cigarette and my eye lodged for a moment upon the burning coals, and that old fancy of the crimson flag flapping from the castle tower came into my mind, and I thought of the cavalcade of red knights riding up the side of the black rock. Rather to my relief the sight of the mark interrupted the fancy, for it is an old fancy, an automatic fancy, made as a child perhaps. The mark was a small round mark, black upon the white wall, about six or seven inches above the mantelpiece.

How readily our thoughts swarm upon a new object, lifting it a little way, as ants carry a blade of straw so feverishly, and then leave it.... If that mark was made by a nail, it can't have been for a picture, it must have been for a miniature—the miniature of a lady with white powdered curls, powder-dusted cheeks, and lips like red carnations. A fraud of course, for the people who had this house before us would have chosen pictures in that way—an old picture for an old room. That is the sort of people they were—very interesting people, and I think of them so often, in such queer places, because one will never see them again, never know what happened next. They wanted to leave this house because they wanted to change their style of furniture, so he said, and he was in process of saying that in his opinion art should have ideas behind it when we were torn asunder, as one is torn from the old lady about to pour out tea and the young man about to hit the tennis ball in the back garden of the suburban villa as one rushes past in the train.

But as for that mark, I'm not sure about it; I don't believe it was made by a nail after all; it's too big, too round, for that. I might get up, but if I got up and looked at it, ten to one I shouldn't be able to say for certain; because once a thing's done, no one ever knows how it happened. Oh! dear me, the mystery of life; The inaccuracy of thought! The ignorance of humanity! To show how very little control of our possessions we have—what an accidental affair this living is after all our civilization—let me just count over a few of the things lost in one lifetime, beginning, for that seems always the most mysterious of losses—what cat would gnaw, what rat would nibble—three pale blue canisters of book-binding tools? Then there were the bird cages, the iron hoops, the steel skates, the Queen Anne coal-scuttle, the bagatelle board, the hand organ—all gone, and jewels, too. Opals and emeralds, they lie about the roots of turnips. What a scraping paring affair it is to be sure! The wonder is that I've any clothes on my back, that I sit surrounded by solid furniture at this moment. Why, if one wants to compare life to anything, one must liken it to being blown through the Tube at fifty miles an hour—landing at the other end without a single hairpin in one's hair! Shot out at the feet of God entirely naked! Tumbling head over heels in the asphodel meadows like brown paper parcels pitched down a shoot in the post office! With one's hair flying back like the tail of a race-horse. Yes, that seems to express the rapidity of life, the perpetual waste and repair; all so casual, all so haphazard....

But after life. The slow pulling down of thick green stalks so that the cup of the flower, as it turns over, deluges one with purple and red light. Why, after all, should one not be born there as one is born here, helpless, speechless, unable to focus one's eyesight, groping at the roots of the grass, at the toes of the Giants? As for saying which are trees, and which are men and women, or whether there are such things, that one won't be in a condition to do for fifty years or so. There will be nothing but spaces of light and dark, intersected by thick stalks, and rather higher up perhaps, rose-shaped blots of an indistinct colour—dim pinks and blues which will, as time goes on, become more definite, become—I don't know what....

And yet that mark on the wall is not a hole at all. It may even be caused by some round black substance, such as a small rose leaf, left over from the summer, and I, not being a very vigilant housekeeper—look at the dust on the mantelpiece, for example, the dust which, so they say, buried Troy three times over, only fragments of pots utterly refusing annihilation, as one can believe.

The tree outside the window taps very gently on the pane... I want to think quietly, calmly, spaciously, never to be interrupted, never to have to rise from my chair, to slip easily from one thing to another, without any sense of hostility, or obstacle. I want to sink deeper and deeper, away from the surface, with its hard separate facts. To steady myself, let me catch hold of the first idea that passes... Shakespeare... Well, he will do as well as another. A man who sat himself solidly in an arm-chair, and looked into the fire, so—A shower of ideas fell perpetually from some very high Heaven down through his mind. He leant his forehead on his hand, and people, looking in through the open door—for this scene is supposed to take place on a summer's evening—But how dull this is, this historical fiction! It doesn't interest me at all. I wish I could hit upon a pleasant track of thought, a track indirectly reflecting credit upon myself, for those are the pleasantest thoughts, and very frequent even in the minds of modest mouse-coloured people, who believe genuinely that they dislike to hear their own praises. They are not thoughts directly praising oneself; that is the beauty of them; they are thoughts like this:

"And then I came into the room. They were discussing botany. I said how I'd seen a flower growing on a dust heap on the site of an old house in Kingsway. The seed, I said, must have been sown in the reign of Charles the First. What flowers grew in the reign of Charles the First?" I asked— (but I don't remember the answer). Tall flowers with purple tassels to them perhaps. And so it goes on. All the time I'm dressing up the figure of myself in my own mind, lovingly, stealthily, not openly adoring it, for if I did that, I should catch myself out, and stretch my hand at once for a book in self-protection. Indeed, it is curious how instinctively one protects the image of oneself from idolatry or any other handling that could make it ridiculous, or too unlike the original to be believed in any longer. Or is it not so very curious after all? It is a matter of great importance. Suppose the looking glass smashes, the image disappears, and the romantic figure with the green of forest depths all about it is there no longer, but only that shell of a person which is seen by other people—what an airless, shallow, bald, prominent world it becomes! A world not to be lived in. As we face each other in omnibuses and underground railways we are looking into the mirror; that accounts for the vagueness, the gleam of glassiness, in our eyes. And the novelists in future will realize more and more the importance of these reflections, for of course there is not one reflection but an almost infinite number; those are the depths they will explore, those the phantoms they will pursue, leaving the description of reality more and more out of their stories, taking a knowledge of it for granted, as the Greeks did and Shakespeare perhaps—but these generalizations are very worthless. The military sound of the word is enough. It recalls leading articles, cabinet ministers—a whole class of things indeed which as a child one thought the thing itself, the standard thing, the real thing, from which one could not depart save at the risk of nameless damnation. Generalizations bring back somehow Sunday in London, Sunday afternoon walks, Sunday luncheons, and also ways of speaking of the dead, clothes, and habits—like the habit of sitting all together in one room until a certain hour, although nobody liked it. There was a rule for everything. The rule for tablecloths at that particular period was that they should be made of tapestry with little yellow compartments marked upon them, such as you may see in photographs of the carpets in the corridors of the royal palaces. Tablecloths of a different kind were not real tablecloths. How shocking, and yet how wonderful it was to discover that these real things, Sunday luncheons, Sunday walks, country houses, and tablecloths were not entirely real, were indeed half phantoms, and the damnation which visited the disbeliever in them was only a sense of illegitimate freedom. What now takes the place of those things I wonder, those real standard things? Men perhaps, should you be a woman; the masculine point of view which governs our lives, which sets the standard, which establishes Whitaker's Table of Precedency, which has become, I suppose, since the war half a phantom to many men and women, which soon, one may hope, will be laughed into the dustbin where the phantoms go, the mahogany sideboards and the Landseer prints, Gods and Devils, Hell and so forth, leaving us all with an intoxicating sense of illegitimate freedom—if freedom exists....

In certain lights that mark on the wall seems actually to project from the wall. Nor is it entirely circular. I cannot be sure, but it seems to cast a perceptible shadow, suggesting that if I ran my finger down that strip of the wall it would, at a certain point, mount and descend a small tumulus, a smooth tumulus like those barrows on the South Downs which are, they say, either tombs or camps. Of the two I should prefer them to be tombs, desiring melancholy like most English people, and finding it natural at the end of a walk to think of the bones stretched beneath the turf... There must be some book about it. Some antiquary must have dug up those bones and given them a name... What sort of a man is an antiquary, I wonder? Retired Colonels for the most part, I daresay, leading parties of aged labourers to the top here, examining clods of earth and stone, and getting into correspondence with the neighbouring clergy, which, being opened at breakfast time, gives them a feeling of importance, and the comparison of arrow-heads necessitates cross-country journeys to the county towns, an agreeable necessity both to them and to their elderly wives, who wish to make plum jam or to clean out the study, and have every reason for keeping that great question of the camp or the tomb in perpetual suspension, while the Colonel himself feels agreeably philosophic in accumulating evidence on both sides of the question. It is true that he does finally incline to believe in the camp; and, being opposed, indites a pamphlet which he is about to read at the quarterly meeting of the local society when a stroke lays him low, and his last conscious thoughts are not of wife or child, but of the camp and that arrowhead there, which is now in the case at the local museum, together with the foot of a Chinese murderess, a handful of Elizabethan nails, a great many Tudor clay pipes, a piece of Roman pottery, and the wine-glass that Nelson drank out of — proving I really don't know what.

No, no, nothing is proved, nothing is known. And if I were to get up at this very moment and ascertain that the mark on the wall is really—what shall we say?—the head of a gigantic old nail, driven in two hundred years ago, which has now, owing to the patient attrition of many generations of housemaids, revealed its head above the coat of paint, and is taking its first view of modern life in the sight of a white-walled fire-lit room, what should I gain?—Knowledge? Matter for further speculation? I can think sitting still as well as standing up. And what is knowledge? What are our learned men save the descendants of witches and hermits who crouched in caves and in woods brewing herbs, interrogating shrew-mice and writing down the language of the stars? And the less we honour them as our superstitions dwindle and our respect for beauty and health of mind increases.... Yes, one could imagine a very pleasant world. A quiet, spacious world, with the flowers so red and blue in the open fields. A world without professors or specialists or house-keepers with the profiles of policemen, a world which one could slice with one's thought as a fish slices the water with his fin, grazing the stems of the water-lilies, hanging suspended over nests of white sea eggs.... How peaceful it is down here, rooted in the centre of the world and gazing up through the grey waters, with their sudden gleams of light, and their reflections—if it were not for Whitaker's Almanack—if it were not for the Table of Precedency!

I must jump up and see for myself what that mark on the wall really is—a nail, a rose-leaf, a crack in the wood?

Here is nature once more at her old game of self-preservation. This train of thought, she perceives, is threatening mere waste of energy, even some collision with reality, for who will ever be able to lift a finger against Whitaker's Table of Precedency? The Archbishop of Canterbury is followed by the Lord High Chancellor; the Lord High Chancellor is followed by the Archbishop of York. Everybody follows somebody, such is the philosophy of Whitaker; and the great thing is to know who follows whom. Whitaker knows, and let that, so Nature counsels, comfort you, instead of enraging you; and if you can't be comforted, if you must shatter this hour of peace, think of the mark on the wall.

I understand Nature's game—her prompting to take action as a way of ending any thought that threatens to excite or to pain. Hence, I suppose, comes our slight contempt for men of action—men, we assume, who don't think. Still, there's no harm in putting a full stop to one's disagreeable thoughts by looking at a mark on the wall.

Indeed, now that I have fixed my eyes upon it, I feel that I have grasped a plank in the sea; I feel a satisfying sense of reality which at once turns the two Archbishops and the Lord High Chancellor to the shadows of shades. Here is something definite, something real. Thus, waking from a midnight dream of horror, one hastily turns on the light and lies quiescent, worshipping the chest of drawers, worshipping solidity, worshipping reality, worshipping the impersonal world which is a proof of some existence other than ours. That is what one wants to be sure of... Wood is a pleasant thing to think about. It comes from a tree; and trees grow, and we don't know how they grow. For years and years they grow, without paying any attention to us, in meadows, in forests, and by the side of rivers—all things one likes to think about. The cows swish their tails beneath them on hot afternoons; they paint rivers so green that when a moorhen dives one expects to see its feathers all green when it comes up again. I like to think of the fish balanced against the stream like flags blown out; and of water-beetles slowly raising domes of mud upon the bed of the river. I like to think of the tree itself—first the close dry sensation of being wood; then the grinding of the storm; then the slow, delicious ooze of sap. I like to think of it, too, on winter's nights standing in the empty field with all leaves close-furled, nothing tender exposed to the iron bullets of the moon, a naked mast upon an earth that goes tumbling, tumbling, all night long. The song of birds must sound very loud and strange in June; and how cold the feet of insects must feel upon it, as they make laborious progresses up the creases of the bark, or sun themselves upon the thin green awning of the leaves, and look straight in front of them with diamond-cut red eyes... One by one the fibres snap beneath the immense cold pressure of the earth, then the last storm comes and, falling, the highest branches drive deep into the ground again. Even so, life isn't done with; there are a million patient, watchful lives still for a tree, all over the world, in bedrooms, in ships, on the pavement, lining rooms, where men and women sit after tea, smoking cigarettes. It is full of peaceful thoughts, happy thoughts, this tree. I should like to take each one separately—but something is getting in the way... Where was I? What has it all been about? A tree? A river? The Downs? Whitaker's Almanack? The fields of asphodel? I can't remember a thing. Everything's moving, falling, slipping, vanishing... There is a vast upheaval of matter. Someone is standing over me and saying—

"I'm going out to buy a newspaper."

"Yes?"

"Though it's no good buying newspapers.... Nothing ever happens. Curse this war; God damn this war!... All the same, I don't see why we should have a snail on our wall."

Ah, the mark on the wall! It was a snail.

Questions

1. What viewpoints did Virginia Woolf hold concerning life? What analogue did she employ in the illustration of her thoughts?
2. Virginia Woolf is renowned as a feminist. Point to sentences that show her feministic attitude toward the society of her age.
3. How did Virginia Woolf judge antiquaries's work? Do they make contribution to the progress of society? Why or why not?
4. This story concludes with a surprising ending. What effect does it achieve?
5. Illustrate the characteristics of "stream of consciousness" and how the author used it tactfully in this work.

弗吉尼亚·伍尔夫
(1882—1941)

弗吉尼亚·伍尔夫是英国小说家、文学评论家、女权主义者、布卢姆斯伯里集团的核心成员。她的父亲莱斯利·斯蒂芬爵士是著名的传记作家和文学批评家。伍尔夫出生于伦敦,在家中接受了私塾教育。1912年她嫁给了政治理论家伦纳德·伍尔夫。弗吉尼亚·伍尔夫患有间歇性抑郁症。第二次世界大战的爆发加重了她的精神错乱,以至于她最终在苏塞克斯郡家附近的欧塞河投河自尽。

1915年,弗吉尼亚·伍尔夫出版了她的第一本书《出航》。1919年她出版了现实主义小说《夜与日》。1922年弗吉尼亚·伍尔夫以她弟弟托比的生死为原型创作了《雅各的房间》。1925年她尝试用"意识流"的手法创作了《达洛维夫人》。在下面的小说中,她开始了"意识流"手法的运用与创新:《到灯塔去》(1927),《奥兰多》(1928),《海浪》(1931),《岁月》(1938)和《幕间》(1941)。作者在小说中除了进行深度的心灵探索外,还将一些抒情和诗歌的因素融入其中。《到灯塔去》和《海浪》的出版使弗吉尼亚·伍尔夫成为现代主义代表性作家之一。弗吉尼亚·伍尔夫还是一名文学评论家,她的评论和随笔收集在《普通读者Ⅰ》(1925)和《普通读者Ⅱ》(1932)中。她也是一名女权主义者,她的女权主义观点突出地反映在《自己的一间屋》(1929)一书中,同时在其随笔集《三个畿尼》(1938)中也有所反映。伍尔夫生前只出版了一部短篇小说集《星期一或星期二》(1921),死后由其丈夫整理出版了另一部集子《闹鬼的房子与其他故事》。

墙上的斑点

在下面这篇"意识流"经典短篇小说中,作者从墙上的斑点出发,展开联想,表达了她对历史、现实、社会、艺术、创作以及生活的思考,文章最后极具戏剧性地揭示了墙上的斑点实际上只不过是一只蜗牛而已。这篇作品堪称意识流手法的佳作,充分展现了作者丰富的想象力和惊人的创作才华。

也许是在今年的一月中旬,我抬起头来,第一次看到了墙上的斑点。为了确定是哪一天,很有必要回想一下当时我看到了什么。于是我想到了炉火,想到了一缕黄色的光稳稳地落在我的书页上;还有壁炉台上的圆玻璃碗里的三朵菊花。

是啊，那时准是冬天，我们刚刚喝完了茶，因为我记得当时我正在抽烟，抬起头，第一次看到了墙上的那个斑点。透过香烟的雾气望去，我的目光在燃烧的煤块上停留了片刻，旧时的那个在城堡塔楼飘拂的深紫色的旗帜的幻影又涌入了我的脑海。我想起了一队红衣骑士正骑马登上了满是黑色岩石的山坡。斑点的那个样子打断了我的幻想，使我松了口气，因为那是一个旧日的幻觉，一个无意识的幻觉，大约起始于我的孩提时代。那个斑点是白色墙壁上的一个黑色小圆点，在壁炉上方大约六到七英寸处。

　　我们的思绪是多么容易聚集到一个新的事物上啊，像一群蚂蚁兴奋地搬运一根稻草，搬了一会儿，就丢弃了……如果那个斑点是一个钉子的印迹，那它不可能是用来挂景物画的，而是用来挂微型人物画像的——一位卷发上沾了粉，面颊上涂了粉，嘴唇像红色康乃馨的贵妇人的微型画像。当然这是一幅赝品，这所房子以前的主人总选择这样的画——一间老式的屋里挂一幅旧式的画像。他们就是这种人——很有趣的人，在这样奇怪的地方，我经常想起他们，因为没有人能再见到他们，也永远不知道后来发生了什么事情。他是这么说的，他们从这座房子里搬走，是因为他们想要改变一下他们的家具风格。他正说着，以他之见，艺术的形式背后应该富含思想，正在此时我们就突然分开了，就像一个人在火车上看到郊区别墅的后花园里，一个老太太正要去倒茶，一个年轻人正要打网球，这一切一闪而过。

　　但是对于那个斑点，我也不敢肯定它是什么；我觉得它不是钉子的印迹，它太大，太圆了。我可以站起来，但是如果我站起来看，十之八九我也不敢肯定它是什么；因为一旦一件事发生，没有人会知道它是怎样发生的。噢，天啊，生命的神秘，思想的误区！人类的无知！为了证明我们对自己所拥有的控制力是多么的微弱——文明背后，我们的生存是多么偶然的事情——让我先列举一下我们一生中丢失的几件东西吧。它们似乎总是最神秘的失踪物——三个装着订书工具的浅蓝色的罐子，那只猫会去咬、耗子会去啃的罐子？然后有几个鸟笼、铁环、钢制的溜冰鞋、安妮女王时期的煤斗、弹子球台、手摇风琴——全都丢失了，还有珠宝。猫眼石和翡翠在萝卜根的四周散失了。毫无疑问那些是节衣缩食才积蓄下来的啊！神奇的是，我坐在那里，身上披了几件衣服，四周是殷实的家具。哎呀，如果一个人想要把生活比作什么，可以把它比作以一小时50英里的速度穿越地铁的人——在地铁的另一端着陆的时候，头发上没有剩下一支发夹！完全裸露地飞射到上帝的脚下！大头朝下地跌落在开满水仙花的草地上，就像一捆捆褐色的纸包裹被扔进邮局的输物管道一样！头发像赛马的尾巴一样在脑后飞扬。是啊，那似乎表达了生活的快节奏，永不停止的损耗和修复；所有的一切是如此的随意，如此的偶然……

可是，在来生。粗大的绿色的茎秆被拖得慢慢垂了下来，杯形的花朵翻转过来，溢满了紫红色的光。噢，当一个人在这里出生，无依无靠又不能说话，目光游移，无法集中，在草根的四周摸索，在巨人的脚趾上摸索，他为什么不可以在别处投生呢？至于说哪些是树，哪些是男人和女人，或者是否存在这样的事物，人们再过50年左右也还是无法说清楚的。什么都没有，只有光和黑暗的空间，粗大的茎秆交错在其中，也许更高处有一些玫瑰花形的色彩模糊的点——淡粉色的和淡蓝色的——一切都随着时间的流逝，变得更加清晰，变得——我也不知道是什么……

然而那墙上的斑点根本不是一个小洞。它也许是由某个黑色的圆形物体导致的，比如是一片经历了一个夏天而存留下来的玫瑰花的叶子，我可不是一个警惕性很高的管家——看看壁炉台上的灰尘就知道了，正如他们所说的那样，这样的尘土三次埋葬了特洛伊，只有那些瓶瓶罐罐的碎片完全无法湮灭，这一点人们是相信的。

窗外的树轻柔地敲打着玻璃……我希望能够静静地思考，心情平静，思绪驰骋，永远没有人来打扰，永远不需要从座椅里站起，让思绪从一件事滑入另一件事，没有感觉到一丝的敌意或阻隔。我希望自己沉下去，越沉越深，离开表面那些严酷的、孤立的事实。为了稳定我的思绪，抓住闪过脑际的第一个念头……莎士比亚……嗯，他和别人都行。这个人稳稳地坐在扶手椅里，凝望着炉火，于是——思绪如阵雨般永不停歇地从某个高高的天堂落下，进入他的大脑。他用手撑着额头，人们正透过开着的门向屋里望去——这一场景应该发生在某个夏日的傍晚——可是，这样的历史故事多么的枯燥无味啊！我对它一点儿兴趣也没有。我希望能偶然踏上一条令人愉悦的思想轨迹，这一思想轨迹能间接地为我增添光彩，因为那是些最令人愉悦的思想，甚至在谦逊的、鼠色的人们的脑海里也经常出现。他们真挚地认为，他们是不愿意听到别人的赞扬的。那些思想不是直接赞美自己的，这才是它们的美丽之处；那些思想是这样的：

"然后，我走进一个房间。他们正在谈论植物学。我给他们描述了一只花是怎样在金斯威的一处老房子的土堆上长出的。我说花的种子准是在查理一世统治时期种下的。在查理一世统治时期有什么样的花呢？"我问道——（但是我记不住答案了）。也许是那种高大的有着紫色花穗的花吧。于是我的思绪继续前进。我总是在脑海里钟爱地、偷偷地装扮着我的形象，却从来没有公开地崇拜自己的形象。因为，如果我那样做了，我自己就会意识到，立即伸出手来拿本书掩饰我自己。神奇的是，一个人能够本能地保护自己的形象，避免它被过度地崇拜或因为其他的操作而显得滑稽可笑，或者使它太不像原来的自己以至于不被别人所接受。或者说这并不十分神奇？这个问题非常重要。假设穿衣镜破碎了，形象消失了，那个浪漫的形象和四周浓密的绿色的森林也不复存在了，只有那个人的外壳可以被别人看到——这个世界将会变得多么的沉闷，多么的浅薄，多么的光秃，多么的突出啊！一个将不能居住的世界。当我们在公共汽车和地铁里面对彼此的时候，我们其实就是在照镜子；那就是为什么我们的眼里会有迷茫、呆滞的目光。未来的小说家们将会越来越意识到这些想法的重要性，因为肯定不会只有一个想法，而是会有无数个想法；那些就是他们要挖掘的深度，那些就是他们要捕捉的幻影，而他们的故事却越来越远离现实，他们把对这一切的认知当成想当然，希腊人是这样的，也许还有莎士比亚——但是这些结论是多么的没有价值。这个词的军事味道已经足够了。它让人想起社论，想起内阁大臣们——想起一系列事物，就像孩提时代，人们认为这些事物是标准的，是真实的，他们不能够违背，否则就要冒不得好死的诅咒的危险。总结不知怎么地让人回忆起伦敦的周日，周日午后的散步，周日的午餐，还让人想起逝去的人的说话方式、衣着和习惯——就像尽管没有一个人喜欢，但是大家却会在同一个房间里坐上一个小时这样的习惯。一切事物都有一个规则。在那个特定的时期，桌布的规则是它们应该是由花毯做的，上面装饰着黄色的小格子，就像你在照片里看到的皇宫走廊里的地毯那样。换一种不同的桌布就不算是真桌布了。当人们发现这些真实的事物、周日的午餐、周日的散步、乡村的房舍，还有桌布都完全不是真实的，实际上只是半个幻影，而对怀疑这些的人的惩罚其实也只不过是一种非法的自由感的时候，他们感到这一切是多么的令人惊讶而又绝妙啊！我想知道，现在是什么取代了那些事物，取代了那些真正标准的事物？也许是男人，如果你是个女人的话；男性的观点统治着我们的生活，制定着标准，建立着惠特克的尊卑序列表；我猜测，自战争之后它对许多男人、女人来说多少是幻影，而且人们希望它将会像幻影、红木碗橱、兰西尔版画、上帝、魔鬼和地狱之类东西一样被嘲笑着扔进垃圾箱，给我们所有的人留下一个令人陶醉的非法的自由感——如果自由存在的话……

在某种光线下，墙上的斑点似乎从墙上凸起。它不完全是圆形的。我不敢肯定，但是它好像投下了一个可见的影子，那暗示着如果我用手指沿着那面墙摸下去，在某一时刻，手指会在一个小小的古冢上上下移动，一个光滑的古冢，就像南部丘陵的那些古冢一样。据说，它们或者是坟墓，或者是露营地。在这两个当中，我宁愿它们是坟墓，我像大多数英国人一样渴望忧伤，于是在一次散步就要结束的时候自然而然地就想起了草地下面埋着尸骨……肯定有一本书写过这件事。肯定有那么一位古文物研究者把这些尸骨挖掘出来，并给它们起了名字……我想知道，古文物研究者是什么样的人呢？我猜，他们大都是些退了役的上校，领着一群上了年纪的工人到这上面来，检查土块和石头，和附近的牧师相互通了信。牧师在早餐的时候拆开了信，感觉到自己很受重视。为了将箭头进行比较，他们需要作多次越野旅行，到乡下的小镇去，这种必要的旅行对于牧师和他们的老伴来说都是很惬意的，老伴们正想要做梅子酱，或者想要打扫书房。他们有充足的理由使得那个露营地或者古冢的重大问题成为永远的悬疑。而上校本人在收集这个问题的两方面的证据上表现出愉悦和达观。事实上，他最终倾向于认为它们是露营地；遭到反对后，他写了一本小册子，打算在当地协会的一个季度会议上宣读，正好这时他中风病倒了，他的最后一个有意识的念头不是想起了妻子和孩子，而是想起了露营地和那里的箭头，那个箭头现在被放在当地博物馆的箱子里，放在一起的还有一只中国女杀人犯的脚、一把伊丽莎白时期的钉子、许多都铎王朝的土制烟斗、一块罗马时期的陶片，以及纳尔逊喝酒用过的酒杯——我不知道这些到底证明了什么。

不，不，什么也不证明，什么也不知道。如果我在这一时刻站起来，确定墙上的斑点真的是——我们说是什么呢？——那个巨大的破旧的钉子头，在二百年前被钉到墙上，现在由于几代家庭主妇的耐心擦拭，这个钉子头已经露在油漆的外面了，正在一间有着雪白的墙壁，燃烧着炉火的房间里第一次目睹了现代生活，我将会得到什么？——知识？还是进行深入的思考的材料？无论是静静地坐着还是站起来，我都能思考。知识是什么？我们的学者除了是蹲在山洞里和在森林里制作草药、审问地鼠、记载星宿的语言的那些巫婆和隐士的后代，还能是什么呢？当我们的迷信逐渐减少，我们对他们的信奉越来越少，我们对美和思想的尊重就增加了……是的，人们能想象出一个十分令人愉悦的世界。一个宁静、广袤的世界，旷野里开满了红色和蓝色的花朵。一个没有教授、专家或长着警察面孔的管家的世界，在那里人们可以像鱼儿用鳍划过水面那样，用他们的思想划过世界，掠过荷花的茎梗，在满是白色海鸟蛋的鸟巢上方停泊……这下面是多么的平静啊，它深深扎根于世界的中心，透过灰色的，突然光影重重的海水向上望去——如果没有惠特克年鉴——如果没有尊卑序列表！

我必须跳起来，亲自看看墙上的斑点到底是什么——一枚钉子？一片玫瑰花瓣？还是木头的裂纹？

这是大自然又一次玩了一把自我保护的游戏。她察觉到这一连串的思想可能是纯粹地在损耗精力，甚至与现实发生点儿冲突，因为谁会去冒犯惠特克的尊卑序列表呢？继大法官位列坎特伯雷大主教之后，约克大主教又位列大法官之后。每个人都位列某人之后，这是惠特克的哲学。最重要的是要知道谁位列谁的后面。惠特克知道，正如大自然忠告的，让那个来安慰你而不是让你愤怒；如果你不能得到安慰，如果你一定要破坏这宁静的一小时，那么就想想墙上的斑点吧。

我明白大自然的把戏——她催促人们采取行动，结束那些易于让人兴奋或痛苦的思想。因此，我以为，我们对于行动中的男人都带有些许的轻蔑——我们认为他们是不思考的人。不过，通过看一下墙上的斑点，来结束人们的不悦思想，这样做毫无害处。

其实，即使我专心致志地看着它，我也感觉我好像在大海里抓住了一块木板。我对能立刻使两位大主教和那位大法官变成了虚无的现实充满了满足感。这是肯定而真实的事物。因而，人们从午夜可怕的梦魇中醒来，匆忙打开灯，静静地躺着，赞美衣柜，赞美实在的物体，赞美现实，赞美客观世界，它证明了除了我们自身之外还有其他物质存在。那就是我们想确认的事情——木头是一个让人想起来很愉悦的事物。它来自于树；树木生长，而我们不知道它们是怎么生长的。它们在草地，在森林，在河边一年一年地生长，并没有注意我们——这些全是我们喜欢去思考的事物。在炎热的午后，牛儿在树下摇着尾巴；树儿把河水都染绿了，以至于当一只雌红松鸡一头扎进水里的时候，我们希望它出来的时候羽毛会变绿。我喜欢想起像随风飘扬的旗帜般逆流而上的鱼儿；我喜欢想起那些在河床上慢慢堆起土丘的水甲虫。我喜欢想起那棵树：——首先是它的紧致，干燥的木质感，然后想起暴风雨对它的折磨，再想起它缓慢流出的树汁。我也喜欢想起，在冬日的夜晚它矗立在空旷的田野里，树上所有的叶子都卷了起来，没有一个柔弱的部分暴露在如铁弹般射出的月光中，像一根光秃的旗杆矗立在整夜滚动的大地上。六月里，鸟儿的歌声听起来是那么的高亢而陌生；当那些昆虫沿着树皮的褶皱费力地向上爬，或者当他们在绿色的薄薄的叶片上晒太阳，用红宝石般的眼睛径直地看着前方的时候，它们放在树上的脚会感觉到多么的寒冷啊……在大地严寒的巨大压力下，树的纤维一根接一根地断裂。最后一场暴风雨来临了，树倒下去了，最高处的树枝再一次深深地插入泥土里。即使这样，生命也并没有完结。这棵树的成千上万条坚韧而警醒的生命分散在世界各地。它们分散在卧室里、轮船上、人行道上，有的还落在了房间的分割板上，男男女女在喝了茶之后坐在这间屋子里抽烟。这棵树让人们充满了平和而幸福的联想。我想把握住每一个想法，单独思考一番——可是有东西阻碍了我的思路……我想到哪里了？都想了什么啊？一棵树？一条河？丘陵地带？惠特克年鉴？开满水仙花的田野？我什么也想不起来了。一切都在移动，下沉，滑动，消失……一切都陷入了广泛的剧变中。有人正在俯身对我说：

"我要出去买份报纸。"

"啊？"

"不过买份报纸也没有什么用……一切照常。这场该死的战争；让这场战争见鬼去吧！……不论怎么样，我认为我们不应该让一只蜗牛在我们的墙上爬。"

哦，墙上的斑点！那是一只蜗牛。

The Duchess and the Jeweller

The main character in the story is a jeweller who pursues wealth and social status. Though rich, the jeweller cannot get away from the memory of his poor childhood. To become a member of the aristocracy, the jeweller buys fake pearls from the duchess again and again. The story critically depicts earned wealth, inherited aristocracy, and a desire of an aristocratic marriage.

Oliver Bacon lived at the top of a house overlooking the Green Park. He had a flat; chairs jutted out at the right angles—chairs covered in hide. Sofas filled the bays of the windows—sofas covered in tapestry. The windows, the three long windows, had the proper allowance of discreet net and figured satin. The mahogany sideboard bulged discreetly with the right brandies, whiskeys and liqueurs. And from the middle window he looked down upon the glossy roofs of fashionable cars packed in the narrow straits of Piccadilly. A more central position could not be imagined. And at eight in the morning he would have his breakfast brought in on a tray by a man-servant: the man-servant would unfold his crimson dressing-gown; he would rip his letters open with his long pointed nails and would extract thick white cards of invitation upon which the engraving stood up roughly from duchesses, countesses, viscountesses and Honourable Ladies. Then he would wash; then he would eat his toast; then he would read his paper by the bright burning fire of electric coals.

"Behold Oliver," he would say, addressing himself. "You who began life in a filthy little alley, you who…" and he would look down at his legs, so shapely in their perfect trousers; at his boots; at his spats. They were all shapely, shining; cut from the best cloth by the best scissors in Savile Row. But he dismantled himself often and became again a little boy in a dark alley. He had once thought that the height of his ambition—selling stolen dogs to fashionable women in Whitechapel. And once he had been done. "Oh, Oliver," his mother had wailed. "Oh, Oliver! When will you have sense, my son?" Then he had gone behind a counter; had sold cheap watches; then he had taken a wallet to Amsterdam… At that memory he would chuckle—the old Oliver remembering the young. Yes, he had done well with the three diamonds; also there was the commission on the emerald. After that he went into the private room behind the shop in Hatton Garden; the room with the scales, the safe, the thick magnifying glasses. And then… and then…He chuckled. When he passed through the knots of jewellers in the hot evening who were discussing prices, gold mines, diamonds, reports from South Africa, one of them would lay a finger to the side of his nose and murmur, "Hum-m-m," as he passed. It was no more than a murmur; no more than a nudge on the shoulder, a finger on the nose, a buzz that rant through the cluster of jewellers in Hatton Garden on a hot afternoon—oh, many years ago now! But still Oliver felt it purring down his spine, the nudge, the murmur that meant, "Look at him—young Oliver, the young jeweller—there he goes." Young he was then. And he dressed better and better; and had, first a hansom cab; then a car; and first he went up to the dress circle, then down into the stalls. And he had a villa at Richmond, overlooking the river, with trellises of red roses; and Mademoiselle used to pick one every morning and stick it in his buttonhole.

"So," said Oliver Bacon, rising and stretching his legs. "So…"

And he stood beneath the picture of an old lady on the mantelpiece and raised his hands. "I have kept my word," he said, laying his hands together, palm to palm, as if he were doing homage to her. "I have won my bet." That was so; he was the richest jeweller in England; but his nose, which was long and flexible, like an elephant's trunk, seemed to say by its curious quiver at the nostrils (but it seemed as if the whole nose quivered, not only the nostrils) that he was not satisfied yet; still smelt something under the ground a little further off. Imagine a giant hog in a pasture rich with truffles; after unearthing this truffle and that, still it smells a bigger, a blacker truffle under the ground further off. So Oliver snuffed always in the rich earth of Mayfair another truffle, a blacker, a bigger further off.

Now then he straightened the pearl in his tie, cased himself in his smart blue overcoat; took his yellow gloves and his cane; and swayed as he descended the stairs and half snuffed, half sighed through his long sharp nose as he passed out into Piccadilly. For was he not still a sad man, a dissatisfied man, a man who seeks something that is hidden, though he had won his bet?

He swayed slightly as he walked, as the camel at the zoo sways from side to side when it walks along the asphalt paths laden with grocers and their wives eating from paper bags and throwing little bits of silver paper crumpled up on to the path. The camel despises the grocers; the camel is dissatisfied with its lot; the camel sees the blue lake and the fringe of palm trees in front of it. So the great jeweller, the greatest jeweller in the whole world, swung down Piccadilly, perfectly dressed, with his gloves, with his cane; but dissatisfied still, till he reached the dark little shop, that was famous in France, in Germany, in Austria, in Italy, and all over America—the dark little shop in the street off Bond Street.

As usual, he strode through the shop without speaking, though the four men, the two old men, Marshall and Spencer, and the two young men, Hammond and Wicks, stood straight and looked at him, envying him. It was only with one finger of the amber-coloured glove, waggling, that he acknowledged their presence. And he went in and shut the door of his private room behind him.

Then he unlocked the grating that barred the window. The cries of Bond Street came in; the purr of the distant traffic. The light from reflectors at the back of the shop struck upwards. One tree waved six green leaves, for it was June. But Mademoiselle had married Mr. Pedder of the local brewery—no one stuck roses in his buttonhole now.

"So," he half sighed, half snorted, "so—"

Then he touched a spring in the wall and slowly the panelling slid open, and behind it were the steel safes, five, no, six of them, all of burnished steel. He twisted a key; unlocked one; then another. Each was lined with a pad of deep crimson velvet; in each lay jewels—bracelets, necklaces, rings, tiaras, ducal coronets; loose stones in glass shells; rubies, emeralds, pearls, diamonds. All safe, shining, cool, yet burning, eternally, with their own compressed light.

"Tears!" said Oliver, looking at the pearls.

"Heart's blood!" he said, looking at the rubies.

"Gunpowder!" he continued, rattling the diamonds so that they flashed and blazed.

"Gunpowder enough to blow Mayfair—sky high, high, high!" He threw his head back and made a sound like a horse neighing as he said it.

The telephone buzzed obsequiously in a low muted voice on his table. He shut the safe.

"In ten minutes," he said. "Not before." And he sat down at his desk and looked at the heads of the Roman emperors that were graved on his sleeve links. And again he dismantled himself and became once more the little boy playing marbles in the alley where they sell stolen dogs on Sunday. He became that wily astute little boy, with lips like wet cherries. He dabbled his fingers in ropes of tripe; he dipped them in pans of frying fish; he dodged in and out among the crowds. He was slim, lissome, with eyes like licked stones. And now—now—the hands of the clock ticked on, one two, three, four…The Duchess of Lambourne waited his pleasure; the Duchess of Lambourne, daughter of a hundred Earls. She would wait for ten minutes on a chair at the counter. She would wait his pleasure. She would wait till he was ready to see her. He watched the clock in its shagreen case. The hand moved on. With each tick the clock handed him—so it seemed—pate de foie gras, a glass of champagne, another of fine brandy, a cigar costing one guinea. The clock laid them on the table beside him as the ten minutes passed. Then he heard soft slow footsteps approaching; a rustle in the corridor. The door opened. Mr. Hammond flattened himself against the wall.

"Her Grace!" he announced.

And he waited there, flattened against the wall.

And Oliver, rising, could hear the rustle of the dress of the Duchess as she came down the passage. Then she loomed up, filling the door, filling the room with the aroma, the prestige, the arrogance, the pomp, the pride of all the Dukes and Duchesses swollen in one wave. And as a wave breaks, she broke, as she sat down, spreading and splashing and falling over Oliver Bacon, the great jeweller, covering him with sparkling bright colours, green, rose, violet; and odours; and iridescences; and rays shooting from fingers, nodding from plumes, flashing from silk, for she was very large, very fat, tightly girt in pink taffeta, and past her prime. As a parasol with many flounces, as a peacock with many feathers, shuts its flounces, folds its feathers, so she subsided and shut herself as she sank down in the leather armchair.

"Good morning, Mr. Bacon," said the Duchess. And she held out her hand which came through the slit of her white glove. And Oliver bent low as he shook it. And as their hands touched the link was forged between them once more. They were friends, yet enemies, he was master, she was mistress; each cheated the other, each needed the other, each feared the other; each felt this and knew this every time they touched hands thus in the little back room with the white light outside, and the tree with its six leaves, and the sound of the street in the distance and behind them the safes.

"And to-day, Duchess—what can I do for you to-day?" said Oliver, very softly.

The Duchess opened her heart, her private heart, gaped wide. And with a sign but no words she took from her bag a long washleather pouch—it looked like a lean yellow ferret. And from a slit in the ferret's belly she dropped pearls—ten pearls. They rolled from the slit in the ferret's belly—one, two, three, four—like the eggs of some heavenly bird.

"All's that's left me, dear Mr. Bacon," she moaned. Five, six, seven—down they rolled, down the slopes of the vast mountain sides that fell between her knees into one narrow valley—the eighth, the ninth, and the tenth. There they lay in the glow of the peach-blossom taffeta. Ten pearls.

"From the Appleby cincture," she mourned. "The last…the last of them all."

Oliver stretched out and took one of the peals between finger and thumb. It was round, it was lustrous. But real was it, or false? Was she lying again? Did she dare?

She laid her plump padded finger across her lips. "If the Duke knew…" she whispered. "Dear Mr. Bacon, a bit of bad luck…"

Been gambling again, had she?

"That villain! That sharper!" she hissed.

The man with the chipped cheek bone? A bad'un. And the Duke was straight as a poker; with side whiskers; would cut her off, shut her up down there if he knew—what I know, thought Oliver, and glanced at the safe.

"Araminta, Daphne, Diana," she moaned. "It's for *them*."

The ladies Araminta, Daphne, Dianna—her daughters. He knew them; adored them. But it was Diana he loved.

"You have all my secrets," she leered. Tears slid; tears fell; tears, like diamonds, collecting powder in the ruts of her cherry blossom cheeks.

"Old friend," she murmured, "old friend."

"Old friend," he repeated, "old friend," as if he licked the words.

"How much?" he queried.

She covered the pearls with her hand.

"Twenty thousand," she whispered.

But was it real or false, the one he held in his hand? The Appleby cincture—hadn't she sold it already? He would ring for Spencer or Hammond. "Take it and test it," he would say. He stretched to the bell.

"You will come down to-morrow?" she urged, she interrupted. "The Prime Minister—His Royal Highness…" She stopped. "And Diana…" she added.

Oliver took his hand off the bell.

He looked past her, at the backs of the houses in Bond Street. But he saw, not the houses in Bond Street, but a dimpling river; and trout rising and salmon; and the Prime Minister; and himself too, in white waistcoat; and then, Diana. He looked down at the pearl in his hand. But how could he test it, in the light of the river, in the light of the eyes of Diana? But the eyes of the Duchess were on him.

"Twenty thousand," she moaned. "My honour!"

The honour of the mother of Diana! He drew his cheque book towards him; he took out his pen.

"Twenty——" he wrote. Then he stopped writing. The eyes of the old woman in the picture were on him—of the old woman his mother.

"Oliver!" she warned him. "Have sense! Don't be a fool!"

"Oliver!" the Duchess entreated—it was "Oliver" now, not "Mr. Bacon." "You'll come for a long weekend?"

Alone in the woods with Diana! Riding alone in the woods with Diana!

"Thousand," he wrote, and signed it.

"Here you are," he said.

And there opened all the flounces of the parasol, all the plumes of the peacock, the radiance of the wave, the swords and spears of Agincourt, as she rose from her chair. And the two old men and the two young men, Spencer and Marshall, Wicks and Hammond, flattened themselves behind the counter envying him as he led her through the shop to the door. And he waggled his yellow glove in their faces, and she held her honour—a cheque for twenty thousand pounds with his signature—quite firmly in her hands.

"Are they false or are they real?" asked Oliver, shutting his private door. There they were, ten pearls on the blotting-paper on the table. He took them on the window. He held them under his lens to the light….This, then, was the truffle he had routed out of the earth! Rotten at the centre—rotten at the core!

"Forgive me, oh, my mother!" he sighed, raising his hand as if he asked pardon of the old woman in the picture. And again he was a little boy in the alley where they sold dogs on Sunday.

"For," he murmured, laying the palms of his hands together, "it is to be a long week-end."

Questions

1. Why does Oliver Bacon accept the pearls even though he suspects they might be fake?
2. How are the animal metaphors used in this story to portray Oliver Bacon as highly arrogant and ambitious?
3. How are the details of sight, hearing and smell used in this story? And how do these senses contribute to the character portrayal?
4. How is the indirect stream-of-consciousness technique used in this story?
5. Woolf depicts Oliver Bacon as a many-sided man: He is both ambitious and sympathetic. Do you agree or disagree?

公爵夫人与珠宝商

　　这篇小说中的主人公是一位追求财富和地位的珠宝商。他虽然富有,但总是无法摆脱对童年贫穷生活的回忆。为了成为贵族,珠宝商一次又一次地收购公爵夫人的假珍珠。故事批判性地描述了积累的财富、世袭的贵族和对贵族婚姻的渴望。

　　奥利弗·培根住在一所房子的顶楼,在那里可以俯瞰格林公园。他拥有一套公寓;椅子靠前摆放着,角度得当——上面铺着皮革。沙发靠凸窗摆放着,上面铺着花毯。三面长窗上垂着精致的网状花缎窗帘,颇为适宜。桃花心木的餐具柜上陈列考究:上等的白兰地、威士忌和利口酒。他从中间的窗户看下去,皮卡迪利大街的狭窄街道上停满了时尚轿车,车顶闪闪发光。这里是顶级黄金地段。早上8点,男仆会用托盘把早餐端进来,为他展开深红色的晨衣。他会用长而尖的指甲挑开来信,抽出厚厚的白色请柬,请柬上印着公爵夫人、伯爵夫人、子爵夫人以及众多名媛淑女的名字。然后他去沐浴,享用吐司,在明亮的灯光下看报。

　　"看呀,奥利弗,"他会对自己说,"你出身肮脏的小巷,你……"他会低头看看双腿,衬着合体、考究的裤子,这双腿那么匀称、好看;然后再看看靴子,还有鞋罩。它们全都有型有款、闪闪发亮,用了上好的料子,由萨维尔街的名师剪裁。但是,他常常卸下行头,把自己还原成黑暗巷子里的小男孩。曾几何时,他最高的志向就是把偷来的狗卖给白教堂区的时尚女郎们。有一次他被抓了,母亲号啕大哭:"哎,奥利弗!你什么时候才能懂事呀,儿子?"从那以后,他站过柜台,卖过廉价手表,偷过钱包,带着钱去了阿姆斯特丹……每每想到这儿,他就会暗自笑起来——老奥利弗在回想小奥利弗呢。是啊,那三颗钻石让他狠赚了一笔;卖那块祖母绿得到的佣金也不少。之后,他便来到了哈顿花园店铺后面的密室,房间里摆着天平、保险箱、厚厚的放大镜。然后……然后……他又窃笑。炎热的晚上,珠宝商们成群结伙聚在一起讨论价格、金矿、钻石以及来自南非的消息。他从他们身边走过,其中必定有人用手指按住鼻翼,悄悄地"嗯"一声。那不过是轻声低语,不过是碰一下肩膀,用手指按一下鼻子,不过是炎热的下午聚集在哈顿花园的珠宝商们互相叽叽喳喳——啊,那是多年以前的事了!可是奥利弗仍然感觉心头一震,那触碰、那低语是在说:"瞧他——年轻的奥利弗,那个年轻的珠宝商,他来啦。"那时他真的很年轻。他的衣着越来越讲究;先是有了双轮双座小马车,接着有了轿车;最初去戏院时坐楼厅前座,后来坐到了正厅前座。他在里士满有座别墅,可以俯瞰河景,院中搭着玫瑰花架;

那时，法国小姐每天早上都会摘一朵玫瑰花，别在他胸前的纽扣孔里。

"就这样……"奥利弗·培根站起来，伸了伸腿。"就这样……"

壁炉上方有一位老妇人的画像。他站在画像前，举起双手。"我实现了诺言，"他双手合十，仿佛在向她顶礼膜拜，"我赌赢了。"事实的确如此；他是英格兰最富有的珠宝商；然而，他那如同大象鼻子一样柔韧的长鼻子鼻孔（可看上去似乎不仅是鼻孔，而是整个鼻子）奇怪地颤抖了一下，好像是在说他仍不满足；他仍嗅到前面不远处的地下有些什么。想象一头硕大的公猪，在一块富产松露的草地上拱出了无数块松露，但它仍然嗅到前方地下还藏着更大、更黑的松露。同样，奥利弗总能在梅菲尔区肥沃的土地上嗅到另一块松露，前方更黑、更大的松露。

他扶正领带上的珍珠，套上时髦的蓝色大衣，拿过黄色手套和手杖，摇摇摆摆地下了楼，一路上用他又长又尖的鼻子嗅着、叹着，来到了皮卡迪利大街。他虽然赌赢了，可仍然不快活、不满足，仍然寻求尚未挖掘的东西。

他一摇一摆地走着，像动物园里的骆驼一摇一摆地走在沥青路上。沥青路上挤满了杂货商和他们的老婆，他们从纸袋里掏出东西吃，把锡箔纸片揉成团扔到路上。骆驼瞧不起杂货商，也不满意自己的命运，它憧憬着前方湛蓝的湖水和棕榈树林。于是，这位大珠宝商，全世界最大的珠宝商，一摇一摆地走在皮卡迪利大街上，衣着考究，戴着手套，拄着手杖，却仍不满足。他就这样来到了距离邦德大街不远的一条街上的一家又暗又小的店铺。虽然又暗又小，这家店铺却闻名于法国、德国、奥地利、意大利和整个美洲。

他像往常一样，大步穿过店堂，一言不发。四个店员：两老——马歇尔和斯潘塞，两小——哈蒙德和威克斯都站得笔直，注视着他，羡慕着他。他只晃了晃琥珀色手套里的一根手指，表示知道他们在那里，然后就走进他的密室，关上门。

他打开窗栅栏，外面立刻传来了邦德大街的喧闹和远处车辆的轰鸣。光从店铺后面反射上来。树上长满了绿色的叶子，已经是六月了。然而法国小姐已经嫁给了当地酒厂的佩德先生，再没人往他的胸前别玫瑰花了。

"就这样，"他似在低声叹息，又似在嗤之以鼻，"就这样……"

他触摸了一下墙上的发条，镶板徐徐打开，里面是钢制的保险箱，有五个，不，是六个，都是锃亮的钢制保险箱。他转动钥匙；打开了一个；又一个。每个箱子里面都垫衬着深红色的天鹅绒，每个都装有珠宝——手镯、项链、戒指、冠状头饰、公爵冠冕；宝石放在玻璃罩下；红宝石、绿宝石、珍珠、钻石。件件都保管得安全妥当，件件都熠熠发光，摸起来凉丝丝的，却积聚着内在的火焰，永不熄灭地燃烧着。

"泪水啊!"奥利弗看着珍珠说。

"心血啊!"他看着红宝石说。

"火药!"他接着说,边说边拨弄着钻石,它们光芒四射、熠熠生辉。

"这些火药能把梅菲尔区——炸上天!上天!上天!"他仰起头,边说边发出马一样的嘶鸣。

桌上的电话似乎也在讨好,低声下气地嗡嗡响着。他关上保险箱。

"十分钟之后,"他说,"之前不行。"他在写字台前坐下,双眼注视着袖扣上刻着的罗马皇帝头像。他又一次卸下行头,把自己还原成了巷子里弹球的小男孩。星期天人们在那条巷子里出售偷来的狗。他又变成了那个狡猾的机灵鬼了,嘴唇如湿漉漉的樱桃般红润。他把手伸进羊下水里,或伸手去捞锅里的炸鱼。他在人群中窜来窜去。他瘦小机敏,眼睛好像光滑的宝石。而如今——如今——时钟的指针"嘀嗒"地走着,一、二、三、四……兰伯恩公爵夫人正在等待他的召见。兰伯恩公爵夫人,她的父亲比一百个伯爵还要尊贵,她会在柜台边的椅子上等上10分钟,等待他的召见。她要等到他愿意见她的时候。他看了看绿皮罩里的时钟,指针还在不停地走着。指针边走,他边拿出各样东西:肥鹅肝酱、一杯香槟、一杯上好的白兰地、一支价值一基尼(注:英国的旧金币,值一镑一先令)的雪茄。这些东西随着时钟的嘀嗒声一一出现在桌上,十分钟之内全摆在了他的身边。这时他听到轻缓的脚步声由远及近,过道里一阵窸窸窣窣。门开了,哈蒙德贴着墙站着。

"公爵夫人驾到!"他通告道。

他贴着墙,等候着。

奥利弗站起身。公爵夫人从过道那头走来,他能听见裙子的沙沙声。她越走越近,显现在门口,带来了一阵香气,带来了她的显赫、傲慢、浮华,以及所有公爵和公爵夫人加在一起的高傲,所有这些汇成一股巨浪,冲进了房间。她坐下了,就像波浪退却一样,她也松弛下来。她刚坐下,巨浪随即扩展开来,溅起层层浪花,淹没了奥利弗·培根这位大珠宝商。各种光闪闪的明亮颜色:绿色、玫瑰红、紫罗兰,各种袭人的芬芳,各种令人眼花缭乱的斑斓,手上的戒指光芒四射,头上的羽毛微微颤动,身上的绸缎闪闪发光,大珠宝商被笼罩其中。她是个庞然大物,紧紧地裹在塔夫绸里,青春已逝。她陷在皮椅里坐下,也收敛了自己的锋芒,就像一把阳伞收起了荷叶边,又像一只孔雀敛起了羽毛。

"早上好,培根先生。"公爵夫人说着,从白手套里抽出手来,奥利弗俯身握住这只手。两只手相握,他们之间的关系又建立起来了。他们是朋友,也是敌人;他是男主人,她是女主人;他们相互欺骗,相互需要,相互惧怕,这一点两人都感觉得到,清楚得很:在这间小小的里屋,外面阳光灿烂、绿树成荫,远处车水马龙，身后则是保险箱。每到这个时候，两人都能意识到这一点。

"今天，公爵夫人——今天有何为您效劳？"奥利弗轻声问。

公爵夫人打开了她的心扉，敞开了她很少向人透露的心声。她叹了口气，默默地从包里掏出一只狭长的软皮口袋，它看上去像一只瘦长的黄色雪貂。顺着袋口，她从雪貂的肚皮里倒出了珍珠——十颗珍珠，它们从雪貂肚皮里顺着袋口滚出来——一颗、两颗、三颗、四颗——像某种仙鸟的卵。

"我只有这些了，亲爱的培根先生，"她哀怨道。五颗、六颗、七颗——珍珠一颗颗顺着她的双膝间滚落下来，像是从巨大的两座山坡上滚进峡谷里——八颗、九颗、十颗，它们躺在耀眼的桃红色塔夫绸里，共十颗。

"这是阿普尔比束带上的，"她咕哝着，"就这几颗了。"

奥利弗伸出手，用食指和拇指拈起其中一颗珠子，的确是珠圆玉润。可它是真的，还是假的？她又在撒谎吗？她敢吗？

她把肉鼓鼓的手指按在嘴唇上，"如果公爵知道了……"她轻声说，"亲爱的培根先生，我有点儿不走运……"

她又去赌钱了？

"是那个恶棍！那个老千！"她恨恨地说。

那个颧骨尖如刀片的家伙？一个十足的坏蛋。奥利弗想着，要是腰板挺直、留着络腮胡子的公爵知道了，一定会剥夺她的继承权，再关她禁闭，他边想边用眼睛瞟了瞟保险箱。

"阿拉明塔、达夫妮、黛安娜，"她哀叹道，"是为了她们。"

阿拉明塔小姐、达夫妮小姐、黛安娜小姐——她的女儿们。他认识她们，喜欢她们。他爱的人正是黛安娜！

"我的秘密您全都知道了，"她用挑逗的眼光看着他说。泪珠滑落；泪珠滚落；泪珠，像一颗颗钻石黏下了脂粉，在红如樱桃的双颊上冲出了一道道泪沟。

"老朋友，"她喃喃地说，"老朋友！"

"老朋友，"他重复着，"老朋友，"似乎在玩味这个词。

"多少钱？"他问。

她用手盖住珍珠。

"两万。"她悄声说。

然而，他手里拿的是真的，还是假的？阿普尔比束带上的珠子——她不是已经卖过了吗？他想按铃叫斯潘塞和哈蒙德来，然后对他们说："拿去验验。"他的手伸向了电铃。

"明天你来吧？"她急切地打断了他。"首相阁下要来……"她顿了顿，接着说，"还有黛安娜……"

奥利弗把手从电铃上移开。

他的目光越过她,停在了邦德大街的房子背面。但他看到的不是邦德大街的房子,而是一条泛着涟漪的小溪,溪中鳟鱼腾跃,还有鲑鱼;他看到了首相,还有自己,穿着白色背心;之后,看到了黛安娜。他低头看着手中的珠子。在小溪的熠熠波光中,在黛安娜的盈盈顾盼下,他如何能检验这颗珍珠是真是假?此时,公爵夫人的眼睛正盯着他。

"两万,"她哀求道,"以我的名誉担保。"

以黛安娜母亲的名誉担保!他拿过支票簿,取出钢笔。

"贰——"他写着,却又停下来,画像中的老妇人正盯着他——那是母亲的眼睛。

"奥利弗!"她发出警告,"清醒点!别做傻瓜!"

"奥利弗!"公爵夫人恳求道——现在是"奥利弗"了,不再是"培根先生"。"来我家度一个长长的周末吧?"

单独和黛安娜待在林子里!单独和黛安娜在林中骑马!

"——万,"他写完,签上名。

"给您。"他说。

她从椅子上站了起来,霎时太阳伞所有的荷叶边都打开了,孔雀所有的羽毛也都展开了,巨浪的光辉,阿金库尔战役上的利剑和长矛——她又恢复了雍容华贵、锋芒毕露。他引夫人穿过店堂来到门口,斯潘塞和马歇尔这两位老伙计,威克斯和哈蒙德这两位小伙计都在柜台后站得笔直,羡慕着他。他在他们面前晃了晃黄色手套,而她则紧紧攥着她的名誉——他签了名的20000英镑的支票。

"它们是假的,还是真的呢?"奥利弗关上自己的房门,暗自问道。那十颗珍珠正躺在桌上的吸墨纸上。他拿起珠子走到窗口,对着阳光用透镜照着……那么,这就是他从泥中掘出的松露了!烂了心的松露——烂了根的松露!

"哦,原谅我,母亲!"他叹道,举起一只手,好像在乞求画中老妇人的原谅。他又变成了巷子里的小男孩,星期天人们就在那巷子里出售偷来的狗。

"因为,"他双手合十喃喃地说,"那将是一个长长的周末啊!"

Virginia Woolf

Kew Gardens

The following story ingeniously combines the descriptions of human beings and nature together. The omniscient narrator follows four different groups of visitors, depicting a set of related and also independent pictures with Kew Gardens as the setting, a snail as the clue and the stories of four groups of people as the plot. Through the interlaced descriptions of nature and the dialogues of people, Woolf penetrates into the philosophical question of human alienation and loneliness.

From the oval-shaped flower-bed there rose perhaps a hundred stalks spreading into heart-shaped or tongue-shaped leaves half way up and unfurling at the tip red or blue or yellow petals marked with spots of colour raised upon the surface; and from the red, blue or yellow gloom of the throat emerged a straight bar, rough with gold dust and slightly clubbed at the end. The petals were voluminous enough to be stirred by the summer breeze, and when they moved, the red, blue and yellow lights passed one over the other, staining an inch of the brown earth beneath with a spot of the most intricate colour. The light fell either upon the smooth, grey back of a pebble, or the shell of a snail with its brown, circular veins, or, falling into a raindrop, it expanded with such intensity of red, blue and yellow the thin walls of water that one expected them to burst and disappear. Instead, the drop was left in a second silver grey once more, and the light now settled upon the flesh of a leaf, revealing the branching thread of fibre beneath the surface, and again it moved on and spread its illumination in the vast green spaces beneath the dome of the heart-shaped and tongue-shaped leaves. Then the breeze stirred rather more briskly overhead and the colour was flashed into the air above, into the eyes of the men and women who walk in Kew Gardens in July.

The figures of these men and women straggled past the flower-bed with a curiously irregular movement not unlike that of the white and blue butterflies who crossed the turf in zig-zag flights from bed to bed. The man was about six inches in front of the woman, strolling carelessly, while she bore on with greater purpose, only turning her head now and then to see that the children were not too far behind. The man kept this distance in front of the woman purposely, though perhaps unconsciously, for he wished to go on with his thoughts.

"Fifteen years ago I came here with Lily," he thought. "We sat somewhere over there by a lake and I begged her to marry me all through the hot afternoon. How the dragon-fly kept circling round us: how clearly I see the dragon-fly and her shoe with the square silver buckle at the toe. All the time I spoke I saw her shoe and when it moved impatiently I knew without looking up what she was going to say: the whole of her seemed to be in her shoe. And my love, my desire, were in the dragon-fly; for some reason I thought that if it settled there, on that leaf, the broad one with the red flower in the middle of it, if the dragonfly settled on the leaf she would say 'Yes' at once. But the dragon-fly went round and round: it never settled anywhere—of course not, happily not, or I shouldn't be walking here with Eleanor and the children—Tell me, Eleanor, d'you ever think of the past?"

"Why do you ask, Simon?"

"Because I've been thinking of the past. I've been thinking of Lily, the woman I might have married... Well, why are you silent? Do you mind my thinking of the past?"

"Why should I mind, Simon? Doesn't one always think of the past, in a garden with men and women lying under the trees? Aren't they one's past, all that remains of it, those men and women, those ghosts lying under the trees... one's happiness, one's reality?"

"For me, a square silver shoe-buckle and a dragon-fly—"

"For me, a kiss. Imagine six little girls sitting before their easels twenty years ago, down by the side of a lake, painting the water-lilies, the first red water-lilies I'd ever seen. And suddenly a kiss, there on the back of my neck. And my hand shook all the afternoon so that I couldn't paint. I took out my watch and marked the hour when I would allow myself to think of the kiss for five minutes only—it was so precious—the kiss of an old grey-haired woman with a wart on her nose, the mother of all my kisses all my life. Come Caroline, come Hubert."

They walked on past the flower-bed, now walking four abreast, and soon diminished in size among the trees and looked half transparent as the sunlight and shade swam over their backs in large trembling irregular patches.

In the oval flower-bed the snail, whose shell had been stained red, blue, and yellow for the space of two minutes or so, now appeared to be moving very slightly in its shell, and next began to labour over the crumbs of loose earth which broke away and rolled down as it passed over them. It appeared to have a definite goal in front of it, differing in this respect from the singular high stepping angular green insect who attempted to cross in front of it, and waited for a second with its antenna trembling as if in deliberation, and then stepped off as rapidly and strangely in the opposite direction. Brown cliffs with deep green lakes in the hollows, flat, blade-like trees that waved from root to tip, round boulders of grey stone, vast crumpled surfaces of a thin crackling texture—all these objects lay across the snail's progress between one stalk and another to his goal. Before he had decided whether to circumvent the arched tent of a dead leaf or to breast it there came past the bed the feet of other human beings.

This time they were both men. The younger of the two wore an expression of perhaps unnatural calm; he raised his eyes and fixed them very steadily in front of him while his companion spoke, and directly his companion had done speaking he looked on the ground again and sometimes opened his lips only after a long pause and sometimes did not open them at all. The elder man had a curiously uneven and shaky method of walking, jerking his hand forward and throwing up his head abruptly, rather in the manner of an impatient carriage horse tired of waiting outside a house; but in the man these gestures were irresolute and pointless. He talked almost incessantly; he smiled to himself and again began to talk, as if the smile had been an answer. He was talking about spirits—the spirits of the dead, who, according to him, were even now telling him all sorts of odd things about their experiences in Heaven.

"Heaven was known to the ancients as Thessaly, William, and now, with this war, the spirit matter is rolling between the hills like thunder." He paused, seemed to listen, smiled, jerked his head and continued: —

"You have a small electric battery and a piece of rubber to insulate the wire—isolate?—insulate?—well, we'll skip the details, no good going into details that wouldn't be understood—and in short the little machine stands in any convenient position by the head of the bed, we will say, on a neat mahogany stand. All arrangements being properly fixed by workmen under my direction, the widow applies her ear and summons the spirit by sign as agreed. Women! Widows! Women in black—"

Here he seemed to have caught sight of a woman's dress in the distance, which in the shade looked a purple black. He took off his hat, placed his hand upon his heart, and hurried towards her muttering and gesticulating feverishly. But William caught him by the sleeve and touched a flower with the tip of his walking-stick in order to divert the old man's attention. After looking at it for a moment in some confusion the old man bent his ear to it and seemed to answer a voice speaking from it, for he began talking about the forests of Uruguay which he had visited hundreds of years ago in company with the most beautiful young woman in Europe. He could be heard murmuring about forests of Uruguay blanketed with the wax petals of tropical roses, nightingales, sea beaches, mermaids, and women drowned at sea, as he suffered himself to be moved on by William, upon whose face the look of stoical patience grew slowly deeper and deeper.

Following his steps so closely as to be slightly puzzled by his gestures came two elderly women of the lower middle class, one stout and ponderous, the other rosy cheeked and nimble. Like most people of their station they were frankly fascinated by any signs of eccentricity betokening a disordered brain, especially in the well-to-do; but they were too far off to be certain whether the gestures were merely eccentric or genuinely mad. After they had scrutinised the old man's back in silence for a moment and given each other a queer, sly look, they went on energetically piecing together their very complicated dialogue:

"Nell, Bert, Lot, Cess, Phil, Pa, he says, I says, she says, I says, I says, I says—"
"My Bert, Sis, Bill, Grandad, the old man, sugar,

Sugar, flour, kippers, greens
Sugar, sugar, sugar."

The ponderous woman looked through the pattern of falling words at the flowers standing cool, firm, and upright in the earth, with a curious expression. She saw them as a sleeper waking from a heavy sleep sees a brass candlestick reflecting the light in an unfamiliar way, and closes his eyes and opens them, and seeing the brass candlestick again, finally starts broad awake and stares at the candlestick with all his powers. So the heavy woman came to a standstill opposite the oval-shaped flower-bed, and ceased even to pretend to listen to what the other woman was saying. She stood there letting the words fall over her, swaying the top part of her body slowly backwards and forwards, looking at the flowers. Then she suggested that they should find a seat and have their tea.

The snail had now considered every possible method of reaching his goal without going round the dead leaf or climbing over it. Let alone the effort needed for climbing a leaf, he was doubtful whether the thin texture which vibrated with such an alarming crackle when touched even by the tip of his horns would bear his weight; and this determined him finally to creep beneath it, for there was a point where the leaf curved high enough from the ground to admit him. He had just inserted his head in the opening and was taking stock of the high brown roof and was getting used to the cool brown light when two other people came past outside on the turf. This time they were both young, a young man and a young woman. They were both in the prime of youth, or even in that season which precedes the prime of youth, the season before the smooth pink folds of the flower have burst their gummy case, when the wings of the butterfly, though fully grown, are motionless in the sun.

"Lucky it isn't Friday," he observed.

"Why? D'you believe in luck?"

"They make you pay sixpence on Friday."

"What's sixpence anyway? Isn't it worth sixpence?"

"What's 'it'—what do you mean by 'it'?"

"O, anything—I mean—you know what I mean."

Long pauses came between each of these remarks: they were uttered in toneless and monotonous voices. The couple stood still on the edge of the flower-bed, and together pressed the end of her parasol deep down into the soft earth. The action and the fact that his hand rested on the top of hers expressed their feelings in a strange way, as these short insignificant words also expressed something, words with short wings for their heavy body of meaning, inadequate to carry them far and thus alighting awkwardly upon the very common objects that surrounded them, and were to their inexperienced touch so massive: but who knows (so they thought as they pressed the parasol into the earth) what precipices aren't concealed in them, or what slopes of ice don't shine in the sun on the other side? Who knows? Who has ever seen this before? Even when she wondered what sort of tea they gave you at Kew, he felt that something loomed up behind her words, and stood vast and solid behind them; and the mist very slowly rose and uncovered—O Heavens,—what were those shapes?—little white tables, and waitresses who looked first at her and then at him; and there was a bill that he would pay with a real two shilling piece, and it was real, all real, he assured himself, fingering the coin in his pocket, real to everyone except to him and to her; even to him it began to seem real; and then—but it was too exciting to stand and think any longer, and he pulled the parasol out of the earth with a jerk and was impatient to find the place where one had tea with other people, like other people.

"Come along Trissie; it's time we had our tea."

"Wherever does one have one's tea?" she asked with the oddest thrill of excitement in her voice, looking vaguely round and letting herself be drawn on down the grass path, trailing her parasol, turning her head this way and that way, forgetting her tea, wishing to go down there and then down there, remembering orchids and cranes among wild flowers, a Chinese pagoda and a crimson-crested bird; but he bore her on.

Thus one couple after another with much the same irregular and aimless movement passed the flower-bed and were enveloped in layer after layer of green-blue vapour, in which at first their bodies had substance and a dash of colour, but later both substance and colour dissolved in the green-blue atmosphere. How hot it was! So hot that even the thrush chose to hop, like a mechanical bird, in the shadow of the flowers, with long pauses between one movement and the next; instead of rambling vaguely the white butterflies danced one above another, making with their white shifting flakes the outline of a shattered marble column above the tallest flowers; the glass roofs of the palm house shone as if a whole market full of shiny green umbrellas had opened in the sun; and in the drone of the aeroplane the voice of the summer sky murmured its fierce soul. Yellow and black, pink and snow white, shapes of all these colours, men, women, and children were spotted for a second upon the horizon, and then, seeing the breadth of yellow that lay upon the grass, they wavered and sought shade beneath the trees, dissolving like drops of water in the yellow and green atmosphere, staining it faintly with red and blue. It seemed as if all gross and heavy bodies had sunk down in the heat motionless and lay huddled upon the ground, but their voices went wavering from them as if they were flames lolling from the thick waxen bodies of candles. Voices, yes, voices, wordless voices, breaking the silence suddenly with such depth of contentment, such passion of desire, or, in the voices of children, such freshness of surprise; breaking the silence? But there was no silence; all the time the motor omnibuses were turning their wheels and changing their gear; like a vast nest of Chinese boxes all of wrought steel turning ceaselessly one within another the city murmured; on the top of which the voices cried aloud and the petals of myriads of flowers flashed their colours into the air.

Questions

1. Compare the four different groups of people who stroll through Kew Gardens. Do

you see any similarities among them?
2. Why is so much attention paid to a snail walking across the garden?
3. Analyze in detail the scene of Trissie and the young man standing by the flower-bed. What does the umbrella symbolize? What does the two-shilling piece in the young man's pocket symbolize?
4. What is unique about this story? Can you formulate a plot? What is the story trying to do by skipping around from group to group and why doesn't the story tell the reader more about what happens to each of its characters?
5. How would you characterize the descriptive language Woolf uses here and the way in which she presents the thoughts and speech of her characters?

邱　园

下面的故事巧妙地把对人与自然的描写联系在一起。全知的叙述者伴随着四组不同人物的步伐，以邱园为舞台背景、一只蜗牛为线索、人物对话为主要情节，向读者展示了一幅幅相关又独立的画面。通过对自然和人物的交叉描写，伍尔夫探索了人的孤独与异化问题。

椭圆形的花坛里长有上百株花儿，花梗中上段冒出片片绿叶，有心形的也有舌状的；梢头冒出一簇簇花瓣，有红的、蓝的、还有黄的，花瓣上还有一颗颗斑点，十分显眼。不管是红的、蓝的、还是黄的，那影影绰绰的底盘儿里总是伸起一根直直的花柱，粗头细身，上面沾着一层金粉。花瓣开得很丰满，在夏日微风的吹拂下微微摆动；花瓣一动，红的、蓝的、黄的光亮交相辉映，使底下褐色的寸寸泥土沾上杂色的斑点。光亮或是落在光滑灰白色的鹅卵石背上，或是落在蜗牛壳棕色的螺旋纹上，要不就落在一滴雨点上，画出一道道薄薄的水墙，红的、蓝的、黄的，雨点胀得很大，真叫人担心它会迸裂，转瞬即逝。然而雨点并没有胀裂，转眼光亮一过，雨点便又恢复了银灰色的原样。光亮落到了一张叶片上，照出叶子表皮底下枝枝杈杈的叶脉。光亮又继续前移，照射到心形叶和舌状叶子构成的穹顶下，在那一大片绿影里放出光明。这时高处的风吹得略微强了些，于是光亮便转而反射到顶上广阔的天空，映入了七月来游邱园的男男女女的眼帘。

花坛旁三三两两地走过男男女女的身影，他们闲逛着，脚步不定，跟草坪上那些迂回穿飞、逐坛周游的蓝白蝴蝶倒不无相似之处。其中一位男士走在一位女士的前面，相隔大约六英尺；男的是随意漫步，女的比较专心，只是常常回过头去，留心别让孩子们落下太远。那男士是故意要这样走在女的前面，也有可能他是无意识的，因为他想一路走一边想想自己的心事。

"15年前我跟莉莉一块儿来过这里，"他心想。"我们坐在那边的湖畔，那天天气很热，我向她求婚，求了整整一下午。记得当时有只蜻蜓老是绕着我们飞个没完。那蜻蜓的模样我至今还记得清清楚楚，我还记得她的鞋头上有个方方的银扣。我在说话的时候，眼睛看得见她的鞋子，只要看见她的鞋子不耐烦地一动，我连头也不用抬，就知道她要说什么：她的全部心思似乎都集中在那双鞋里。我呢，却把我的爱情、我的心愿，都寄托在那只蜻蜓身上。不知怎么我忽然心血来潮，认定那只蜻蜓要是停下来，停在那边的叶子上，停在那中间有一朵红花的阔叶上，那她马上就会答应我的婚事。可是蜻蜓却转了一圈又一圈，哪儿也不肯停下——当然没停下，幸好没停下，要不今天我也不会同埃莉诺带着孩子在这儿散步了。告诉我,埃莉诺,你想不想过去的事?"

"你问这个干什么,西蒙?"

"因为我正在想过去的事。我在想莉莉,当初我也许会娶的那个女孩。……咦,你怎么不说话了?我想起过去的事,你不高兴了?"

"我干嘛要不高兴呢,西蒙?到了这儿能不想起过去吗?有多少男男女女躺在这园子的大树底下,他们不就是人们的过去吗?人们的过去不就只留下了这么一点点陈迹?那些男男女女,大树下的那些魂灵……人们的幸福?人们的现实?"

"对我,是鞋头上一颗方方的银扣和一只蜻蜓——"

"对我,是亲吻。回想20年前,6个小姑娘在那边的一个小湖畔,坐在画架前画睡莲,那是我生平第一次看到开红花的睡莲。突然,有人在我脖颈儿上轻轻地吻了一下。我的手因此抖了一个下午,连画都不能画了。我取出表来,看着时间,限定自己只能对这个吻回味五分钟——这个吻太宝贵了——吻我的是一位鼻子上长着个瘊子的鬓发半白的老太太,这个吻可以说是我生命中所有亲吻的始祖。快来呀,卡洛琳,快来呀,休伯特。"

于是他们四个人并排走过了花坛,不一会儿在大树间就只留下了四个大小不一的身影,阳光和树荫在他们背上拂动,投下了摇曳不定的大块斑驳的碎影。

椭圆形的花坛里,那红的、蓝的、黄的光彩刚才在蜗牛壳上停留了有两三分钟光景,这会儿蜗牛似乎在壳里微微地动了起来,然后就费力地在松软的泥土上爬了起来,一路走过去,松土翻起又倒下。这蜗牛心中似乎有个明确的去处,在这一点上可就跟前面一只怪模怪样的青虫不一样了,那青虫高高地抬起了腿,起初打算从蜗牛面前穿过去,但是转而又抖动着触须等了一会儿,像是故意考虑了一下,最后还是迈着快速而古怪的步子,回头向相反的方向而去。褐色的峭壁下临沟壑,沟内有一池池深绿的湖水,宛如利剑似的树木,从根到梢一起摆动,灰白色的浑圆大石立在路上,还有那薄薄脆脆的、又大又皱的表面——所有这些障碍横在一株株花梗之间,阻碍了蜗牛到达它的目的地。蜗牛来到了一张圆顶帐篷般的枯叶前,还没有来得及决定是绕道而过还是往前直闯,花坛跟前又有人来了。

这一次来的两个都是男的。年轻的那位表情平静得似乎有点不大自然。同行的另一个说话时,他就抬起眼来,直直地一个劲儿地盯着前方,同行的那位话一说完,他就又看着地下,有时过了大半晌才开口,有时则干脆不说话。另一位年纪大些,走起路来高一脚低一脚,摇晃得厉害,他朝前一甩手、猛地一抬头的样子,很像一匹性子急躁的拉车大马,在房子外面等得不耐烦了,不过对他来说,他这些动作却是犹犹豫豫的,也没有什么含义。他不停地说着话,自得其乐地笑笑，又接着说了起来，仿佛这一笑回答了他自己的问题。他在谈论灵魂——死者的灵魂。据他说，那些死者的灵魂一直在向他诉说他们在天国千奇百怪的事儿。

"天国，古人认为就是塞萨利，威廉。如今战争一起，灵物就常在那里的山间徘徊出没，所过之处声震如雷。"他说到这里停了一下，像在听着什么，然后微微一笑，猛然把头一仰，又接着说：

"只要一个小电池，另外还要一段胶布包扎电线，以免走电——叫漏电？还是走电？——不管它，这些细节就不用说了，说了也没用，反正人家也听不懂——总之，把这个小机关装在床头方便的位置，比方说，可以搁在一只干净的红木小几上。让工匠把这一切都按照我的指示装配齐全，寡妇虔心静听，约好的信号一发出，她们丈夫的亡灵就会被召来。只有女人才行！死了丈夫的女人！还没有脱下孝服的女人！"

刚说到这儿，他似乎在远处看到了一个女人的衣服，在阴影里看来像是紫黑色的。他摘下帽子，一手按在心口，嘴里咕哝着什么，做出兴冲冲的手势，匆忙向她走去。可是威廉一把抓住了他的袖子，为了把老头儿的注意力吸引过来，又举起手杖在一朵花上点了点。老头儿一时似乎有些困惑，他对着那朵花瞅了一阵，凑过耳朵去听，好像听到花儿里有个声音在说话。于是他就大谈起乌拉圭的森林，说是在几百年前他曾经同欧洲最美丽的一位小姐一起去过那里。只听他嘟嘟囔囔，说起乌拉圭的森林里满地都是热带玫瑰如蜡一般的花瓣，还说起夜莺、海滩、美人鱼和海里淹死的女人。他一边说着，一边很不情愿地被威廉推着往前走，威廉脸上那种冷漠自若的表情也慢慢地变得愈来愈深沉了。

接踵而来的是两个上了年纪的妇女，因为跟老头儿离得很近，所以看见老头儿的举动，有点摸不着头脑。这两个女人都属于下层中产阶级，一个体形发胖，十分笨重，另一个两颊红润，手脚麻利。她们这种身份的人往往有这么个特点，就是看见有人——特别是有钱人——举止古怪，可能脑子不大正常，就立刻有了兴致。可是这一回离老头儿终究还不够近，没法肯定这人到底只是行为怪僻，还是当真发了疯。她们对着老头儿的背影默默端详了好一会儿，彼此交换了一个古怪的眼色，然后又兴致勃勃地继续她们那复杂的对话：

"内尔，伯特，罗特，萨斯，菲尔，爸爸，他说，我说，她说，我说，我说，我说——"

"我的伯特，妹妹，比尔，爷爷，那老头子，糖，

糖，面粉，鲱鱼，蔬菜，
糖，糖，糖。"

就在这一大串话落下时,那个胖女人看见这些花朵冷淡、坚定而笔直地挺立在泥土里,便带着好奇的神情盯着看了起来。那模样儿就像一个人从沉睡中醒来,看到黄铜烛台的反光有些异样,便把眼睛闭了闭再睁开,看到的还是黄铜烛台,这才完全醒了过来,于是就全神贯注地盯着烛台看。所以那个大块头女人干脆就对着椭圆形花坛站住不动了,她本来还装作像在听对方说话,现在索性连点儿样子都不装了。她由着对方的话雨点般地向她打来,她只管站在那里,晃动着上半身,时而前俯,时而后仰,一心赏她的花。赏够了,这才提出,还是去找个座位喝点茶吧。

蜗牛这时已经考虑过了所有的可行办法:既不绕道而行,也不爬上枯叶。且不说爬上枯叶得费那么大的劲儿,就看这薄薄的叶子吧,才拿触角的尖头轻轻一碰,就摇摆了半天,稀里哗啦好不吓人,是不是能担得起自己的那点分量,实在是个疑问;所以蜗牛终于还是决定往叶子底下爬,因为那枯叶有个翘起的地方,离地够高,蜗牛完全钻得进去。蜗牛刚刚把头伸进缺口,正在打量那高高的褐色的顶棚,对那里冷森森的褐赤赤的光线还没有怎么适应,外边草坪上又有两个人过来了。这一回两个都是年轻人,一男一女。两人都正当青春妙龄,甚至可能还要年轻些,正如粉红鲜润的蓓蕾含苞待放,长成了翅膀的彩蝶尚未在艳阳下展翅飞舞。

"走运,今天不是星期五,"那男的说。

"怎么?你也相信运气?"

"星期五来就得破费六个便士。"

"六个便士算得了什么?那还不值六个便士吗?"

"什么叫'那'呀——你这'那'字,指啥意思呀?"

"啊,说说罢了——我的意思——你应该明白我的意思。"

这几句对话,每一句说完之后总要歇上好大一会儿,口气也都很平淡、单调。这一对儿静静地站在花坛边上,一起按着她那把阳伞,把伞尖都深深地按进了松软的泥土里。他把手搁在她的手上,两人一起把伞尖按进了泥土里,这不寻常地表明了他们的感情。其实他们这短短几句无关紧要的话也一样大有深意,只是意重情厚,话的翅膀太短,承载不起这么大的分量,勉强起飞也飞不远,只能就近找个普通话题尴尬地落下脚来,可他们那稚嫩的心灵却已经感受到这话的分量了。他们一边把阳伞尖往泥土里按,一边暗暗琢磨:谁说得准这些话里不是藏着万丈深崖呢?谁说得准这丽日之下,背面坡上不是一片冰天雪地呢?谁说得准?这种事儿谁经历过?甚至就当她不过随便说了一句,不知邱园的茶怎么样,他一听立刻觉得这话的背后像是朦胧浮现起一个幽影,似乎有个庞大而结实的东西矗立在那儿。好不容易薄雾慢慢地散去,天哪,那是些什么玩意儿?——是雪白的小桌子，还有女服务员，先瞅瞅她，又瞅瞅他。一会儿付账的话，得两个先令，可不是假的。他摸了摸口袋里那个两先令的硬币，暗暗安慰自己：不是做梦，绝对不是做梦。这种事本来谁都觉得不足为怪，唯有他和她是例外，如今可连他也感到这似乎不是非分之想了，后来——想到这里他兴奋得站也站不住、想也没心想了，于是他猛地拔出阳伞尖，急不可耐地要去找喝茶的地方，如别人一样，和大家在一起喝茶。

"来吧，特丽西，咱们该喝茶去了。"

"这喝茶的地方在哪儿？"她口气激动得甚至有些古怪，两眼迷惘四顾，任凭他牵着走，把阳伞拖在背后，顺着草坪上的小径而去。她把头这边转转那边转转，这里也想去那里也想去，喝茶也不在心上了，只记得那儿野花丛中有兰花和仙鹤，有一座中国式的宝塔，还有一头红冠鸟。他还是领着她继续走。

就这样，一双双，一对对，从花坛旁不断过去，走路的样子差不多都是这样不拘一格，漫无目的。一层又一层青绿色的雾霭，渐渐把他们裹了起来，起初还看得见他们的形体，色彩分明，可是随后形体和色彩就全都消融在青绿色的大气里了。天气实在太热了！热得连画眉鸟都宁可躲在花荫里，要隔上大半天才蹦跶一下，跳起来像个自动玩具一样。白蝴蝶也不再随处飞舞，而是上下盘旋，宛如撒下了白花花的一片片，飘荡在最高一层鲜花的顶上，勾勒出一副轮廓，活像半截颓败的大理石圆柱。栽培棕榈的温室玻璃顶，光芒四射，仿佛阳光下开辟了好大一个露天市场，摆满了闪闪发亮的绿伞。在飞机的嗡嗡声中，夏日的天空在喃喃地诉说自己炽热的情怀。远远的天边，一时间出现了五光十色的许多人影，有黄的也有黑的，有粉红的也有雪白的，看得出有男，有女，还有孩子，他们一看见草地上金灿灿的一片，马上就动摇了，都纷纷躲进树荫里，像水滴一样融入了这金灿灿、绿茸茸的世界，只留下了淡淡的红的、蓝的痕迹。看来一切庞然大物似乎都已被热气熏倒，一动不动，蜷缩成一团，可是他们的嘴里仍然吐出颤颤悠悠的声音，好似粗大的蜡烛吐着火苗儿一样。声音，对，是声音，是无言的声音，含着那样酣畅的快意，也含着那样炽烈的欲望，孩子的声音里则含着那样稚气的惊奇，这样的声音一下子把沉寂都打破了。打破了沉寂？但是这里没有沉寂。公共汽车的轮子一直在飞转，排档一直在变换。城市发出嗡嗡声，就像一大套中国套盒玩具，全是铸钢锻造的，一盒套一盒，每盒都在那里转个不停。可是那无言的声音却响亮得压过了城市的声音，万紫千红的花瓣也把自己的光彩射入了辽阔的空中。

D. H. Lawrence
(1885—1930)

D. H. Lawrence (David Herbert Lawrence), English novelist, poet, playwright, essayist, literary critic and painter was from a coal miner's family in Eastwood, Nottinghamshire, England. His mother was from a middle class family and supported her son's education. After completing high school and receiving a teaching certificate from college, Lawrence began teaching in South London but soon devoted himself to writing. *Sons and Lovers* (1913) made him first established as a major literary figure. His other major novels include *The Rainbow* (1915), *Women in Love* (1920) and *Lady Chatterley's Lover* (1928). Much of his fiction is about characters caught between their unsatisfactory relationships with others and their struggle to break free. Lawrence sought an ideal balance in which two beings are attracted to each other but never lose their individuality. A virulent social critic, he was frequently harassed by censorship because his short stories, novels, and poetry were often explicitly sexual and he always challenged conventional moral attitudes. His collected works represent an extended reflection upon the dehumanising effects of modernity and industrialisation. Lawrence suffered from both tuberculosis and harassment from the British authorities, and spent years wandering in Italy, Australia, Mexico, New Mexico, seeking a warm, sunny climate and free land. He died in Vence, France.

Lawrence wrote short stories all his life, publishing the first collection, *The Prussian Officer and Other Stories* (1914), and then, *England, My England and Other Stories* (1922), *The Woman Who Rode Away* (1928), *Love among the Haystacks and Other Stories* (1930). The style of his early stories was harshly realistic, but Lawrence's depiction of his characters' emotional situations changed in his later works, where he created fantasies like his famous and chilling story "The Rocking-Horse Winner".

Rawdon's Roof

The central character Rawdon repeats his vow that "No woman shall sleep again under my roof!" This repetition irritates his friend Joe, the narrator of the story, because Rawdon in fact has an attractive woman named Janet Drummond whose husband is away on business constantly. Rawdon loves Janet's children and her husband has a bad reputation, so even if they have an affair, nobody would mind. However, Rawdon insists on his vow. Then one day Janet shows up very late at Rawdon's house because she gets in a fight with her husband, and then Rawdon and Hawken the butler escort her home because of the vow. While Rawdon and the butler are away, and Joe is preparing to spend the night, Joe accidentally bumps into Hawken's girlfriend, who has, unknown to Rawdon, spent many a night under the roof. The story strongly satirizes the human vices of hypocrisy, pretentiousness and infidelity.

Rawdon was the sort of man who said, privately, to his men friends, over a glass of wine after dinner: "No woman shall sleep again under my roof!"

He said it with pride, rather vaunting, pursing his lips. "Even my housekeeper goes home to sleep."

But the housekeeper was a gentle old thing of about sixty, so it seemed a little fantastic. Moreover, the man had a wife, of whom he was secretly rather proud, as a piece of fine property, and with whom he kept up a very witty correspondence, epistolary, and whom he treated with humorous gallantry when they occasionally met for half an hour. Also he had a love affair going on. At least, if it wasn't a love affair, what was it? However!

"No, I've come to the determination that no woman shall ever sleep under my roof again—not even a female cat!"

One looked at the roof, and wondered what it had done amiss. Besides, it wasn't his roof. He only rented the house. What does a man mean, anyhow, when he says "my roof"? *My* roof! The only roof I am conscious of having, myself, is the top of my head. However, he hardly can have meant that no woman should sleep under the elegant dome of his skull. Though there's no telling. You see the top of a sleek head through a window, and you say: "By Jove, what a pretty girl's head!" And after all, when the individual comes out, it's in trousers.

The point, however, is that Rawdon said so emphatically—no, not emphatically, succinctly: "No woman shall ever again sleep under my roof." It was a case of futurity. No doubt he had had his ceilings whitewashed, and their memories put out. Or rather, repainted, for it was a handsome wooden ceiling. Anyhow, if ceilings have eyes, as walls have ears, then Rawdon had given his ceilings a new outlook, with a new coat of paint, and all memory of any woman's having slept under them—for after all, in decent circumstances we sleep under ceilings, not under roofs—was wiped out for ever.

"And will you neither sleep under any woman's roof?"

That pulled him up rather short. He was not prepared to sauce his gander as he had sauced his goose. Even I could see the thought flitting through his mind, that some of his pleasantest holidays depended on the charm of his hostess. Even some of the nicest hotels were run by women.

"Ah! Well! That's not quite the same thing, you know. When one leaves one's own house one gives up the keys of circumstance, so to speak. But, as far as possible, I make it a rule not to sleep under a roof that is openly, and obviously, and obtrusively a woman's roof!"

"Quite!" said I with a shudder. "So do I!"

Now I understood his mysterious love affair less than ever. He was never known to speak of this love affair: he did not even write about it to his wife. The lady—for she was a lady—lived only five minutes' walk from Rawdon. She had a husband, but he was in diplomatic service or something like that, which kept him occupied in the sufficiently-far distance. Yes, far enough. And, as a husband, he was a complete diplomat. A balance of power. If he was entitled to occupy the wide field of the world, she, the other and contrasting power, might concentrate and consolidate her position at home.

She was a charming woman, too, and even a beautiful woman. She had two charming children, long-legged, stalky, clove-pink-half-opened sort of children. But really charming. And she was a woman with a certain mystery. She never talked. She never said anything about herself. Perhaps she suffered; perhaps she was frightfully happy, and made *that* her cause for silence. Perhaps she was wise enough even to be beautifully silent about her happiness. Certainly she never mentioned her sufferings, or even her trials: and certainly she must have a fair handful of the latter, for Alec Drummond sometimes fled home in the teeth of a gale of debts. He simply got through his own money and through hers, and, third and fatal stride, through other people's as well. Then something had to be done about it. And Janet, dear soul, had to put her hat on and take journeys. But she never said anything of it. At least, she did just hint that Alec didn't *quite* make enough money to meet expenses. But after all, we don't go about with our eyes shut, and Alec Drummond, whatever else he did, didn't hide his prowess under a bushel.

Rawdon and he were quite friendly, but really! None of them ever talked. Drummond didn't talk, he just went off and behaved in his own way. And though Rawdon would chat away till the small hours, *he* never "talked". Not to his nearest male friend did he ever mention Janet save as a very pleasant woman and his neighbour: he admitted he adored her children. They often came to see him.

And one felt about Rawdon, he was making a mystery of something. And that was rather irritating. He went every day to see Janet, and of course we saw him going: going or coming. How can one help but see? But he always went in the morning, at about eleven, and did not stay for lunch: or he went in the afternoon, and came home to dinner. Apparently he was never there in the evening. Poor Janet, she lived like a widow.

Very well, if Rawdon wanted to make it so blatantly obvious that it was only platonic, purely platonic, why wasn't he natural? Why didn't he say simply: "I'm very fond of Janet Drummond, she is my very dear friend"? Why did he sort of curl up at the very mention of her name, and curdle into silence: or else say rather forcedly: "Yes, she is a charming woman. I see a good deal of her, but chiefly for the children's sake. I'm devoted to the children!" Then he would look at one in such a curious way, as if he were hiding something. And after all, what was there to hide? If he was the woman's friend, why not? It could be a charming friendship. And if he were her lover, why, heaven bless me, he ought to have been proud of it, and showed just a glint, just an honest man's glint.

But no, never a glint of pride or pleasure in the relation either way. Instead of that, this rather theatrical reserve. Janet, it is true, was just as reserved. If she could, she avoided mentioning his name. Yet one knew, sure as houses, she felt something. One suspected her of being more in love with Rawdon than ever she had been with Alec. And one felt that there was a hush put upon it all. She had had a hush put upon her. By whom? By both the men? Or by Rawdon only? Or by Drummond? Was it for her husband's sake? Impossible! For her children's? But why! Her children were devoted to Rawdon.

It had now become the custom for them to go to him three times a week, for music. I don't mean he taught them the piano. Rawdon was a very refined musical amateur. He had them sing, in their delicate girlish voices, delicate little songs, and really he succeeded wonderfully with them; he made them so true, which children rarely are, musically, and so pure and effortless, like little flamelets of sound. It really was rather beautiful, and sweet of him. And he taught them *music*, the delicacy of the feel of it. They had a regular teacher for the practice.

Even the little girls, in their young little ways, were in love with Rawdon! So if their mother were in love too, in her ripened womanhood, why not?

Poor Janet! She was so still, and so elusive: the hush upon her! She was rather like a half-opened rose that somebody had tied a string round, so that it couldn't open any more. But why? Why? In her there was a real touch of mystery. One could never ask her, because one knew her heart was too keenly involved: or her pride.

Whereas there was, really, no mystery about Rawdon, refined and handsome and subtle as he was. He had no mystery: at least, to a man. What *he* wrapped himself up in was a certain amount of mystification.

Who wouldn't be irritated to hear a fellow saying, when for months and months he has been paying a daily visit to a lonely and very attractive woman—nay, lately even a twice-daily visit, even if always before sundown—to hear him say, pursing his lips after a sip of his own very moderate port: "I've taken a vow that no woman shall sleep under my roof again!"

I almost snapped out: "Oh, what the hell! And what about your Janet?" But I remembered in time, it was not *my* affair, and if he wanted to have his mystifications, let him have them.

If he meant he wouldn't have his wife sleep under his roof again, that one could understand. They were really very witty with one another, he and she, but fatally and damnably married.

Yet neither wanted a divorce. And neither put the slightest claim to any control over the other's behaviour. He said: "Women live on the moon, men on the earth." And she said: "I don't mind in the least if he loves Janet Drummond, poor thing. It would be a change for him, from loving himself. And a change for her, if somebody loved her—"

Poor Janet! But he wouldn't have her sleep under his roof, no, not for any money. And apparently he never slept under hers—if she could be said to have one. So what the deuce?

Of course, if they were friends, just friends, all right! But then in that case, why start talking about not having a woman sleep under your roof? Pure mystification!

The cat never came out of the bag. But one evening I distinctly heard it mewing inside its sack, and I even believe I saw a claw through the canvas.

It was in November—everything much as usual—myself pricking my ears to hear if the rain had stopped, and I could go home, because I was just a little bored about "cornemuse" music. I had been having dinner with Rawdon, and listening to him ever since on his favourite topic: not, of course, women, and why they shouldn't sleep under his roof, but fourteenth-century melody and windbag accompaniment.

It was not late—not yet ten o'clock—but I was restless, and wanted to go home. There was no longer any sound of rain. And Rawdon was perhaps going to make a pause in his monologue.

Suddenly there was a tap at the door, and Rawdon's man, Hawken, edged in. Rawdon, who had been a major in some fantastic capacity during the war, had brought Hawken back with him. This fresh-faced man of about thirty-five appeared in the doorway with an intensely blank and bewildered look on his face. He was really an extraordinarily good actor.

"A lady, sir!" he said, with a look of utter blankness.

"A what?" snapped Rawdon.

"A lady!"—then with a most discreet drop in his voice: "Mrs. Drummond, sir!" He looked modestly down at his feet.

Rawdon went deathly white, and his lips quivered.

"Mrs. Drummond! Where?"

Hawken lifted his eyes to his master in a fleeting glance.

"I showed her into the dining-room, there being no fire in the drawing-room."

Rawdon got to his feet and took two or three agitated strides. He could not make up his mind. At last he said, his lips working with agitation:

"Bring her in here."

Then he turned with a theatrical gesture to me.

"What this is all about, I *don't* know," he said.

"Let me clear out," said I, making for the door.

He caught me by the arm.

"No, for God's sake! For God's sake, stop and see me through!"

He gripped my arm till it really hurt, and his eyes were quite wild. I did not know my Olympic Rawdon.

Hastily I backed away to the side of the fire—we were in Rawdon's room, where the books and piano were—and Mrs. Drummond appeared in the doorway. She was much paler than usual, being a rather warm-coloured woman, and she glanced at me with big reproachful eyes, as much as to say: You intruder! You interloper! For my part, I could do nothing but stare. She wore a black wrap, which I knew quite well, over her black dinner-dress.

"Rawdon!" she said, turning to him and blotting out my existence from her consciousness. Hawken softly closed the door, and I could feel him standing on the threshold outside, listening keen as a hawk.

"Sit down, Janet," said Rawdon, with a grimace of a sour smile, which he could not get rid of once he had started it, so that his face looked very odd indeed, like a mask which he was unable either to fit on or take off. He had several conflicting expressions all at once, and they had all stuck.

She let her wrap slip back on her shoulders, and knitted her white fingers against her skirt, pressing down her arms, and gazing at him with a terrible gaze. I began to creep to the door.

Rawdon started after me.

"No, don't go! Don't go! I specially want you not to go," he said in extreme agitation.

I looked at her. She was looking at him with a heavy, sombre kind of stare. Me she absolutely ignored. Not for a second could she forgive me for existing on the earth. I slunk back to my post behind the leather armchair, as if hiding.

"Do sit down, Janet," he said to her again. "And have a smoke. What will you drink?"

"No, thanks!" she said, as if it were one word slurred out. "No, thanks."

And she proceeded again to fix him with that heavy, portentous stare.

He offered her a cigarette, his hand trembling as he held out the silver box.

"No, thanks!" she slurred out again, not even looking at the box, but keeping him fixed with that dark and heavy stare.

He turned away, making a great delay lighting a cigarette, with his back to her, to get out of the stream of that stare. He carefully went for an ash-tray, and put it carefully within reach—all the time trying not to be swept away on that stare. And she stood with her fingers locked, her straight, plump, handsome arms pressed downwards against her skirt, and she gazed at him.

He leaned his elbow on the mantelpiece abstractedly for a moment—then he started suddenly, and rang the bell. She turned her eyes from him for a moment, to watch his middle finger pressing the bell-button. Then there was a tension of waiting, an interruption in the previous tension. We waited. Nobody came. Rawdon rang again.

"That's very curious!" he murmured to himself. Hawken was usually so prompt. Hawken, not being a woman, slept under the roof, so there was no excuse for his not answering the bell. The tension in the room had now changed quality, owing to this new suspense. Poor Janet's sombre stare became gradually loosened, so to speak. Attention was divided. Where was Hawken? Rawdon rang the bell a third time, a long peal. And now Janet was no longer the centre of suspense. Where was Hawken? The question loomed large over every other.

"I'll just look in the kitchen," said I, making for the door.

"No, no. I'll go," said Rawdon.

But I was in the passage—and Rawdon was on my heels. The kitchen was very tidy and cheerful, but empty; only a bottle of beer and two glasses stood on the table. To Rawdon the kitchen was as strange a world as to me—he never entered the servants' quarters. But to me it was curious that the bottle of beer was empty, and both the glasses had been used. I knew Rawdon wouldn't notice.

"That's very curious!" said Rawdon: meaning the absence of his man.

At that moment we heard a step on the servants' stairs, and Rawdon opened the door to reveal Hawken descending with an armful of sheets and things.

"What are you doing?"

"Why!—" and a pause. "I was airing the clean laundry, like not to waste the fire last thing."

Hawken descended into the kitchen with a very flushed face and very bright eyes and rather ruffled hair, and proceeded to spread the linen on chairs before the fire.

"I hope I've not done wrong, sir," he said in his most winning manner. "Was you ringing?"

"Three times! Leave that linen and bring a bottle of the fizz."

"I'm sorry, sir. You can't hear the bell from the front, sir."

It was perfectly true. The house was small, but it had been built for a very nervous author, and the servants' quarters were shut off, padded from the rest of the house.

Rawdon said no more about the sheets and things, but he looked more peaked than ever.

We went back to the music-room. Janet had gone to the hearth, and stood with her hand on the mantel. She looked round at us, baffled.

"We're having a bottle of fizz," said Rawdon. "Do let me take your wrap."

"And where was Hawken?" she asked satirically.

"Oh, busy somewhere upstairs."

"He's a busy young man, that!" she said sardonically. And she sat uncomfortably on the edge of the chair where I had been sitting.

When Hawken came with the tray, she said:

"I'm not going to drink."

Rawdon appealed to me, so I took a glass. She looked inquiringly at the flushed and bright-eyed Hawken, as if she understood something.

The manservant left the room. We drank our wine, and the awkwardness returned.

"Rawdon!" she said suddenly, as if she were firing a revolver at him. "Alec came home tonight in a bigger mess than ever, and wanted to make love to me to get it off his mind. I can't stand it any more. I'm in love with you, and I simply can't stand Alec getting too near to me. He's dangerous when he's crossed-and when he's worked up. So I just came here. I didn't see what else I could do."

She left off as suddenly as a machine-gun leaves off firing. We were just dazed.

"You are quite right," Rawdon began, in a vague and neutral tone...

"I am, am I not?" she said eagerly.

"I'll tell you what I'll do," he said. "I'll go round to the hotel tonight, and you can stay here."

"Under the kindly protection of Hawken, you mean!" she said, with quiet sarcasm.

"Why!—I could send Mrs. Betts, I suppose," he said.

Mrs. Betts was his housekeeper.

"You couldn't stay and protect me yourself?" she said quietly.

"I! I! Why, I've made a vow—haven't I, Joe?"—he turned to me—"not to have any woman sleep under my roof again."—He got the mixed sour smile on his face.

She looked up at the ceiling for a moment, then lapsed into silence. Then she said:

"Sort of monastery, so to speak!"

And she rose and reached for her wrap, adding:

"I'd better go, then."

"Joe will see you home," he said.

She faced round on me.

"Do you mind *not* seeing me home, Mr. Bradley?" she said, gazing at me.

"Not if you don't want me," said I.

"Hawken will drive you," said Rawdon.

"Oh, no, he won't!" she said. "I'll walk. Goodnight."

"I'll get my hat," stammered Rawdon, in an agony. "Wait! Wait! The gate will be locked."

"It was open when I came," she said.

He rang for Hawken to unlock the iron doors at the end of the short drive, whilst he himself huddled into a greatcoat and scarf, fumbling for a flashlight.

"You won't go till I come back, will you?" he pleaded to me. "I'd be awfully glad if you'd stay the night. The sheets *will* be aired."

I had to promise—and he set off with an umbrella, in the rain, at the same time asking Hawken to take a flashlight and go in front. So that was how they went, in single file along the path over the fields to Mrs. Drummond's house, Hawken in front, with flashlight and umbrella, curving round to light up in front of Mrs. Drummond, who, with umbrella only, walked isolated between two lights, Rawdon shining his flashlight on her from the rear from under his umbrella. I turned indoors.

So that was over! At least, for the moment!

I thought I would go upstairs and see how damp the bed in the guest-chamber was before I actually stayed the night with Rawdon. He never had guests—preferred to go away himself.

The guest-chamber was a good room across a passage and round a corner from Rawdon's room—its door just opposite the padded service-door. This latter service-door stood open, and a light shone through. I went into the spare bedroom, switching on the light.

To my surprise, the bed looked as if it had just been left—the sheets tumbled, the pillows pressed. I put in my hands under the bedclothes, and it was warm. Very curious!

As I stood looking round in mild wonder, I heard a voice call softly: "Joe!"

"Yes!" said I instinctively, and, though startled, strode at once out of the room and through the servants' door, towards the voice. Light shone from the open doorway of one of the servants' rooms.

There was a muffled little shriek, and I was standing looking into what was probably Hawken's bedroom, and seeing a soft and pretty white leg and a pretty feminine posterior very thinly dimmed in a rather short night-dress, just in the act of climbing into a narrow little bed, and, then arrested, the owner of the pretty posterior burying her face in the bed-clothes, to be invisible, like the ostrich in the sand.

I discreetly withdrew, went downstairs and poured myself a glass of wine. And very shortly Rawdon returned looking like Hamlet in the last act.

He said nothing, neither did I. We sat and merely smoked. Only as he was seeing me upstairs to bed, in the now immaculate bedroom, he said pathetically:

"Why aren't women content to be what a man wants them to be?"

"Why aren't they!" said I wearily.

"I thought I had made everything clear," he said.

"You start at the wrong end," said I.

And as I said it, the picture came into my mind of the pretty feminine butt-end in Hawken's bedroom. Yes, Hawken made better starts, wherever he ended.

When he brought me my cup of tea in the morning, he was very soft and cat-like. I asked him what sort of day it was, and he asked me if I'd had a good night, and was I comfortable?

"Very comfortable!" said I. "But I turned you out, I'm afraid."

"Me, sir?" He turned on me a face of utter bewilderment.

But I looked him in the eye.

"Is your name Joe?" I asked him.

"You're right, sir."

"So is mine," said I. "However, I didn't see her face, so it's all right. I suppose you *were* a bit tight, in that little bed!"

"Well, sir!" and he flashed me a smile of amazing impudence, and lowered his tone to utter confidence. "This is the best bed in the house, this is." And he touched it softly.

"You've not tried them all, surely?"

A look of indignant horror on his face!

"No, sir, indeed I haven't."

That day, Rawdon left for London, on his way to Tunis, and Hawken was to follow him. The roof of his house looked just the same.

The Drummonds moved too—went away somewhere, and left a lot of unsatisfied tradespeople behind.

Questions

1. What sort of motto did Rawdon keep before his men friends? And what marital status did he have?
2. With what kind of woman did Rawdon have a love affair? Or is it a love affair at all?
3. The story was told in the first person point of view. What tone or style did the narrator use in telling the story?
4. What kind of relationship did Rawdon keep with his wife?
5. Then what happened to Rawdon and Janet one November evening? And what did the narrator discover about Hawken?

戴·赫·劳伦斯
(1885—1930)

戴·赫·劳伦斯（戴维·赫伯特·劳伦斯）是英国小说家、诗人、剧作家、散文家、文学评论家及画家。他出生于英格兰诺丁汉郡伊斯特伍德镇的一个矿工家庭。他的母亲来自中产阶级家庭，非常重视儿子的教育。劳伦斯中学毕业后又在大学获得教师资格证，之后他开始在南伦敦教学，但很快便专注于写作。《儿子与情人》（1913）的出版使他一举成名。他的主要小说还包括《虹》（1915）、《恋爱中的女人》（1920）、《查泰莱夫人的情人》（1928）等。劳伦斯的大部分作品描述了饱受人际关系困扰而试图解脱的人物。他在人际关系中寻求理想化的平衡，即两个人彼此吸引但却不丧失自我。劳伦斯是无情的社会批评家，由于他在小说、诗歌中经常直接描写性，总是挑战传统道德观，因而常常受到书籍审查的侵扰。他的作品体现了现代性与工业化对人的异化。劳伦斯患有肺结核，同时还受到英国当局的侵扰，他常年游历于意大利、澳大利亚、墨西哥、美国的新墨西哥等地，寻求温暖、阳光充足的气候与自由的土地。他最终死于法国旺斯。

劳伦斯一生都在写短篇小说，出版的第一部集子是《普鲁士军官与其他故事》（1914），之后还有《英格兰，我的英格兰与其他故事》（1922）、《骑马出走的女人》（1928）、《干草堆中的爱情与其他故事》（1930）等。他早期的短篇小说风格严峻、写实，而后期作品对于人物情感的描写则转变为奇思妙想，其著名的惊悚故事《木马赢家》即是如此。

罗登的屋顶

　　该故事主角罗登反复发誓"绝对不再允许女人睡在我的屋顶下！"罗登的反复发誓使其朋友乔，即讲本故事的人，大为恼火，因为罗登事实上有一位很漂亮的女人叫珍妮特·德拉蒙德，该女人的丈夫经常出差。罗登很喜欢珍妮特的孩子，珍妮特的丈夫又名声很臭，因此即使他们俩有什么关系，别人也不会怎样。然而，罗登却刻意坚持他的誓约。直到有一天，珍妮特很晚来到罗登家，因为她同丈夫打了起来。于是为了不破誓约，罗登和其男仆霍肯只得护送珍妮特回家。当罗登和男仆离开之际，乔准备就寝，无意中却撞见霍肯的女友。这位女友在罗登不知情的情况下，在他的屋顶下度过了无数个夜晚。故事辛辣地讽刺了人与人之间的虚伪、做作与不忠。

　　罗登是这么一种人，晚餐后他会借着一杯葡萄酒私下里对其男性朋友说："绝对不再允许女人睡在我的屋顶下！"

　　他说这话时很自豪，撅起嘴唇，自吹自擂。"连我的女管家都得回家睡觉。"

　　不过那位管家是个六十多岁温和的老妇人，因而这话也就似乎有点儿离谱。此外，罗登这个人有妻子，对此他背地里感到很得意，他妻子就是一份可观的资产，他以书信形式同妻子保持着很巧妙的往来，偶尔他们也会见上半个钟头，这时他会以幽默殷勤相待。同时他还有风流韵事进行着。至少，假如那不叫风流韵事，又叫什么呐？真是的！

　　"不，我下定了决心，绝对不允许女人再睡在我的屋顶下——连母猫都不行！"

　　我看了看屋顶，想知道那儿出了什么毛病。再说，那也不是他的屋顶。他只是租了那房子。可是当一个人说"我的屋顶"，他到底是什么意思呢？我的屋顶！我自己明明白白所拥有的顶只是我的头顶。不过他的意思大概不会是说，绝不允许女人睡在他优雅的天灵盖下吧。可那也说不定。你透过窗户看见一个圆溜溜的头顶，你会说："天哪，瞧那女孩的头多漂亮啊！" 不管怎么说吧，谁出门都得穿裤子。

　　但问题是罗登说这话时强调得很——不，不是强调，是简洁："绝不允许女人再睡在我的屋顶下。"这指的是未来。毫无疑问，他将天棚粉刷过，天棚下的记忆抹掉了。或许该说是重漆过，因为那是一块很美观的木天棚。总之，假如天棚有眼，就像墙有耳朵，那么罗登使他的天棚焕然一新了，漆了一层新漆，有关任何女人在下面睡过的所有记忆——不过,在正常情况下大家毕竟是睡在天棚下,而不是屋顶下——都永远被抹掉了。

"那你也绝不睡在任何女人的屋顶下吗?"

这句话给了他一个突然袭击。他没有准备好如何使他那句话反过来也适用于这句话。我甚至可以感到他在飞快地思索,实际上他最愉悦的一些假期都是靠女主人的魅力而度过的。甚至一些最好的旅馆也是由女人管理的。

"啊!嘿!那可不是一回事,你明白。常言道,出门在外就得随遇而安了。不过,尽最大可能吧,我定了规矩,不明目张胆、冒冒失失地睡在女人的屋顶下!"

"的确如此!"我说,心头一颤。"我也如此!"

现在我对他的风流韵事更迷惑不解了。从未听说他谈起过这桩风流韵事:他甚至在与妻子的通信中也从未谈及此事。那位女士——她既是女主妇又是情妇——她家离罗登家只有步行五分钟的路程。她有丈夫,但她丈夫在外交部门工作,或类似的工作,使他在离家足够远的地方忙碌。是的,足够远了。而作为丈夫,他是个彻头彻尾的外交家。这是个力量平衡的问题。如果说他肩负着忙于大千世界的事务,她作为另一端相对照的力量,则集中于巩固好自己在家里的地位。

她还是一位可爱的女子,甚至算得上容貌姣好。她有两个孩子,长得长腿儿,细高挑,像粉丁香花含苞欲放的样子。不过真的很可爱。而且她还是一位神秘莫测的女子。她从不说闲话。她从不谈论自己。也许她受过苦,也许她特幸福,也许这就是使她缄默的原因。也许她睿智有余,对自己的幸福也都保持优雅、缄默的态度。当然,她从未提及过自己的痛苦,甚或困难:当然后者她一定会有不少,因为她丈夫亚历克·德拉蒙德有时会逃回家躲避突发的债务。他轻易地花光自己的钱、他妻子的钱,还有那更要命的一步,也花光别人的钱。这时就得想办法处理这事儿。于是珍妮特,可怜的人儿,就得带上帽子一次次外出。但她从不谈及这件事。至少,她只是暗示亚历克挣的钱不太足以满足他的花销。可是尽管如此,大家也都没闭着眼走路,亚历克·德拉蒙德,不管他做什么,并没有秘密地藏起他的威力。

罗登和他都很友好,确实如此!他俩从不说闲话。德拉蒙德不说闲话,他只是天马行空,独往独来。而罗登虽然会聊天到后半夜,他也从不"说闲话"。对他最近的男友,他也从不谈及珍妮特,只说她是位非常可爱的女子,是他的邻居:他承认喜爱她的孩子。他们常来看他。

我琢磨起罗登来,他这是在故弄玄虚。这可真叫人受不了。他每天去看珍妮特,当然是我们亲眼看到的:来来回回地。这谁还能看不见吗?不过他总是早上

11点钟左右去，不在那儿吃午饭；或者他下午去，回家吃晚饭。显然，他晚上从不在那儿。可怜的珍妮特，她活得真像个寡妇。

好吧，假如罗登就要大吹大擂地证明这事儿显而易见是柏拉图式的，纯粹柏拉图式的，为何他不自自然然地说？为何他不干脆地说"我很喜欢珍妮特·德拉蒙德，她是我非常亲密的朋友"？为何一提起她的名字他就有点儿局促不安，然后就吓得沉默不语，不然就非常勉强地说："是啊，她是个蛮可爱的女子。我常见她，但主要是由于孩子的缘故。我倾心于她的孩子们！" 然后他就会以异样的眼光看我，好像掩藏什么似的。可是，有什么可藏的呢？假如他是那位女子的朋友，那又有什么？那不是蛮有趣的友谊嘛。再假如他是她的情夫，谢天谢地，他早该以此为荣并有所流露，开诚布公地流露。

但是，不，在他们的关系上，他绝没有流露出一丝自豪感或者愉悦感。相反，有的只是这番做作的矜持。事实上，珍妮特也是同样的矜持。她也尽可能避免提及他的名字。但是我知道，非常确信地知道，她有所感觉。我怀疑她比从前爱亚历克更爱罗登。而且我还感到这一切都有秘而不宣的味道。她受人秘而不宣。受之于谁呢？受之于两个男人？或者只受之于罗登？或者受之于德拉蒙德？是为了她丈夫的缘故吗？不可能！为了孩子的缘故？可是为何呢？孩子们都喜爱罗登。

现在孩子们每周去三次他那儿学音乐，这已成习惯。我不是说他教孩子们钢琴之类的事。罗登是个素养很高的业余音乐家。他教孩子们唱歌，孩子们用纤细、少女气的嗓音唱精巧、短小的歌儿，而且他的确获得了孩子们的欢心；他使孩子们在音乐中感受到真正的自己，而且纯净无比、毫不费力，就像小小的火焰光芒四射，这一点孩子们自己很难做到。他做得确实漂亮、惹人喜欢。他教孩子们的是音乐，那种对音乐的微妙感觉。孩子们另有教师负责常规练习。

甚至连小女孩们，以自己稚嫩的方式，都爱上罗登了！因此，假如其母亲也爱上了，以自己成熟女人的方式爱上了，那又何妨呢？

可怜的珍妮特！她太沉默寡言、太难以琢磨：对她有秘而不宣之咒啊！她很像一朵半开放的玫瑰，有人在上面绑了一圈线，结果就开放不了了。可是为何呢？到底为何呢？在她身上的确有神秘之处。我绝不能问她，因为我知道她敏感的心陷得太深：或者说是她的自尊心。

与此同时，罗登的确没有什么神秘之处，他一贯举止文雅、相貌堂堂，又老于世故。他无神秘之处：至少对男人来说如此。他所热衷的只是某种故弄玄虚的把戏。

月复一月，他每天都去拜访一位孤独、非常迷人的女子——不，近来是一天两次，尽管总是在日落之前——见此情形之后，再听这家伙啜一口中度波尔图红酒，撇起嘴说："我已经发誓绝不允许女人再在我屋顶下睡觉了！"谁会不恼羞成怒，还听他那一套！

我几乎疾言厉色地说："哦，见鬼去吧！那你那个珍妮特呢？"但我还是及时止住，那毕竟不是我的事，假如他就要故弄玄虚，随他去吧。

假如他的意思是不允许他的妻子再在他屋顶下睡觉的话，那我可以理解。他和她，他们俩彼此确实很微妙，但是命中注定不幸地结婚了。

而谁也不想离婚。并且谁也不对对方的行为强加任何干预。他说："女人生活在月球上，男人生活在地球上。"而她却说："我一点儿也不会在意，假如他爱珍妮特·德拉蒙德，她真可怜。这对他是一种变化，使他不过于自恋。而且对她也是个变化，假如有人爱她——"

可怜的珍妮特！但是他不允许她睡在他的屋顶下，不，给钱也不允许。而且显然他从未在她的屋顶下睡过——假如可以说她有个屋顶。因此这算怎么回事儿？

当然，假如他们是朋友，只是朋友，也无妨！但是那样的话，为何要大谈不允许女人睡在他的屋顶下？纯粹是故弄玄虚！

成语说得好，绝不可让猫从袋子里出来，也就是天机不可泄漏。但是有一天晚上我清楚地听见袋子里有喵喵的叫声，而且我甚至相信自己看见一只爪子穿破了帆布袋。

那是在九月份——一切如同往常——我竖起耳朵听雨是否停止，这样我就可以回家了，因为我对"风笛"音乐有点儿厌倦了。我在与罗登共进晚餐，一直在听他讲他最喜欢的话题：当然不是女人，也不是她们为何不应该睡在他的屋顶下，而是14世纪曲调和风囊乐器伴奏的问题。

天色未晚——还没到十点钟——但我坐不住了，想回家。雨声不再有了。这时罗登似乎打算在唱完独角戏之后停一会儿。

突然有敲门声，罗登的男仆霍肯侧身进来。战争期间罗登曾在某个稀奇古怪的职位上担任过少校，他退役后把霍肯一同带了回来。霍肯看起来容光焕发，年纪有35岁。他出现在门口，脸上露出极为茫然、惊恐的表情。他可真是个绝好的演员。

"有一位女士，先生！"霍肯说，一脸绝对的茫然。

"什么？"罗登厉声问道。

"有一位女士！"——霍肯的嗓音小心翼翼地降了下来："是德拉蒙德夫人，先生！"此时他谦卑地低着头，眼睛只看自己的脚。

罗登脸色变得煞白，嘴唇颤动。

"德拉蒙德夫人！在哪儿？"

霍肯抬头迅速瞥了主人一眼。

"我带她进了餐厅，客厅没点火。"

罗登突然站起身，焦躁不安地走了两三步。他拿不定主意。最后他说，唇齿间充满焦虑不安：

"带她到这儿来。"

然后他以戏剧性的动作转向我。

"这都是怎么一回事儿，我真的不知道，"他说。

"我得赶紧走，"我说着，直奔门口。

他抓住我的胳膊。

"不行，看在上帝的份上！看在上帝的份上，别走，帮我一把！"

他紧紧抓住我的胳膊，直到抓痛我，他的双眼狂躁不安。我还从未见识过罗登威严的一面。

我急忙退回到炉边——我们在罗登的房间里，那儿放着书和钢琴——这时德拉蒙德夫人出现在门口。她属于肤色红润的那种女人，此时可比平常苍白得多了；她瞥了我一下，一双大眼睛似乎在责备我：你这个不速之客！你这个爱管闲事之人！我无言以对，只能干瞪眼。她身着黑色披巾，这我很熟悉，罩在黑色晚礼服之上。

"罗登！"她说着转向罗登，从其意识中抹去了我的存在。霍肯轻轻带上门，我能感觉到他就在门外，像鹰一样警觉地听着。

"坐下，珍妮特，"罗登说，脸上露出苦笑，而他一旦露出这副表情就摆脱不掉，因此他的这副嘴脸实在是太古怪了，就像一副面具，他既不能戴好也不能摘下。他有几种互相冲突的表情集于一脸，而且都凝固在那儿。

德拉蒙德夫人让披巾在肩膀上向后随意滑动，白皙的手指交叉着顶着裙子，双臂向下使劲，双眼可怕地瞪着罗登。我开始溜向房门。

罗登也开始紧随其后。

"别，别走！别走！你千万别走，"他极为恐慌地说。

我看了一眼德拉蒙德夫人。她用沉重、阴郁的眼神瞪着罗登。至于我，她则完全不予理睬。她对于我在地球上存在一秒钟都不可饶恕。我溜回到皮扶手椅子后面的位置，就像要藏起来。

"快坐下，珍妮特，"罗登又对她说。"抽根儿烟。喝点什么？"

"不，谢了！"她说，就好像把两个词儿合在一起含糊地发出来。"不，谢了。"

然后她又继续用沉重、不祥的眼光瞪着罗登。

罗登递给她烟，他递过去银烟盒时，手在颤抖。

"不，谢了！"她又含糊地说道，都没看那盒子一眼，而是一直用阴郁、沉重的眼光瞪着罗登。

罗登转过脸，点烟耽搁了好长时间，他背对着德拉蒙德夫人，以便逃避不停地盯着他的眼光。他小心翼翼地去取烟缸，然后小心翼翼地将烟缸放在可及之处——此间他一直试图不被那瞪着他的眼光一扫而空。她站在那儿，手指扣在一起，平直、丰满、美观的手臂向下压着，紧靠裙子，她还在盯着罗登。

罗登心不在焉地将胳膊肘靠在壁炉架上——不一会儿他突然惊起，叫铃。德拉蒙德夫人的眼光从他身上移走了一会儿，去注视他用中指按铃的按钮。这时一阵紧张的等待，打断了以往那种紧张。我们等待着。没人过来。罗登又叫铃。

"真怪了！"他自言自语道。霍肯通常都是很及时的。霍肯不是女人，他睡在罗登的屋顶下，因此他没有理由不应铃。现在房间里的紧张气氛骤变，那都是因为这场新的悬念。可以说，可怜的珍妮特阴郁的眼光现在变得慢慢地松弛下来。人们的注意力分散了。霍肯在哪儿？罗登第三次叫铃，这次又长又响。现在珍妮特不再是悬念的中心。霍肯在哪儿？这个问题突显，超过任何其他问题。

"我去厨房看看，"我说着朝房门走去。

"不，不。我去，"罗登说。

可我已经到了通道——罗登紧随其后。厨房很整洁，令人愉快，但空无一人；桌上只有一瓶啤酒和两个玻璃杯。罗登对这个厨房同我对这个厨房一样陌生——他从不进仆人的地方。但使我感到奇怪的是，啤酒瓶是空的，而且两个玻璃杯都用过。我知道罗登注意不到这些。

"真怪了！"罗登说，指的是他的男仆不在。

就在这时，我们听见仆人所住阁楼上的脚步声，罗登打开门，发现霍肯抱着床单和用品下来。

"你在干什么？"

"什么！——"片刻停顿。"我在晾晒洗净的用品，晚上睡觉前别浪费了炉火。"

霍肯下到厨房，满脸通红，双眼放光，头发乱蓬蓬的，他接着将亚麻用品平搭在炉火前的椅子上。

"希望我没做错什么事，先生，"他以最讨人欢心的方式说。"你在按铃吗？"

"三遍！把亚麻布放一边，拿一瓶啤酒来。"

"对不起，先生。从前面听不见铃声，先生。"

千真万确。这所房子虽然不大，但它是为一个神经高度敏感的作家而建造的，仆人的生活区与主人的是断开的，是后填补在房子的其他部分的。

罗登不再说床单与用品之事，但他看起来脸色更苍白了。

我们回到了音乐室。珍妮特挪到了壁炉边，她站在那儿，手放在炉台上。她环顾四周，看着我们，迷惑不解。

"咱们来一瓶酒，"罗登说，"就让我拿下你的披巾吧。"

"那霍肯在哪儿？"她挖苦地问。

"哦，楼上忙着呐。"

"他是个忙碌的年轻人，真忙！"她讥讽地说。她不舒服地坐在我才坐过的那把椅子的一角。

当霍肯端着盘子过来，她说：

"我不想喝。"

罗登请我喝，于是我拿了一杯。珍妮特怀疑地看着满脸通红、两眼放光的霍肯，好像明白点儿了什么。

男仆离开了房间。我们喝起酒来，这时尴尬的情形又回来了。

"罗登！"珍妮特突然说，就好像用左轮手枪向他开火。"亚历克今晚回家来了，情形比以前更糟，他要同我做爱，以此来摆脱烦恼的纠缠。我无法再忍受。我爱的是你，我实在无法忍受亚历克同我太近。一旦他的要求受阻——当他激动起来，他会很危险。所以我只好来这儿。我别无选择。"

她突然停下来，就像机关枪突然停止射击。我们都感到迷惑不解。

"你做得对，"罗登开口说，语调含糊、不定……

"我对，不对吗？"她急切地说。

"我来告诉你我的做法，"罗登说。"我今晚去找个旅店，你就待在这儿。"

"就在霍肯的亲切保护之下，这是你的意思？"她冷嘲热讽地说。

"怎么！——我可以叫贝茨夫人来吗，"他说。

贝茨夫人是罗登的女管家。

"你自己不能待在这儿保护我吗？"她平静地说。

"我！我！那怎么行，我发过誓——不是吗，乔？"——他转向我——"不许任何女人再睡在我屋顶下。"——他满脸苦笑。

珍妮特向上瞧了天棚一会儿，随后沉默不语。过了一会儿她又说：

"就像所谓的修道院！"

这时珍妮特起身去拿披巾，补充说：

"那么，我还是走吧。"

"乔送你回家，"罗登说。

她脸转向我。

"不要你送我回家,你不介意吧,布拉德利先生?"她瞪着我说。

"不,如果你不要我送的话,"我说。

"霍肯驾车送你,"罗登说。

"噢,不,不要他送!"她说。"我自己走。晚安。"

"我拿帽子,"罗登结结巴巴地说,愤愤不平。"等着!等着!大门锁上了。"

"我来时门开着,"她说。

罗登按铃叫霍肯打开短车道尽头的铁门,他自己急忙穿上大衣戴上围巾,摸索着找电筒。

"你等我回来再走,好吗?"他向我请求道。"假如今晚你能不走,那我就太高兴了。床单会烘干的。"

我只能答应——随后他带了把雨伞就出门了,同时叫霍肯拿着手电筒在前面照路。他们就这样出了门,一行人沿着小路,穿过空地,走向德拉蒙德夫人家,霍肯在前拿着手电筒和雨伞,弯曲着转过身照亮德拉蒙德夫人的前方,德拉蒙德夫人只拿着雨伞,形单影只地走在两道光线之间,罗登从雨伞下用手电筒照在德拉蒙德夫人的后面。我进了屋。

终于结束了!至少,眼下是结束了!

在罗登家过夜之前,我想上楼看一看客卧室里的床铺潮湿到什么程度。罗登从不邀请客人来家——他情愿自己出门拜访。

客卧房间不错,隔着走廊离罗登的卧室不远——房门就在后加的仆人房对面。仆人房的门开着,有一束灯光射出。我走进空房间,打开灯。

使我吃惊的是,房里的床看起来好像有人睡过——床单动过、枕头压过。我将手伸进被窝,还热着呢。真怪了!

我站在那儿环顾四周,正感到有些惊奇,忽然听见有人轻声地叫:"乔!"

"哎!"我本能地答应着,虽然感到惊讶,还是立即大步走出房间,穿过仆人的房门,直奔那声音。灯光从一间开着的仆人房间里照出来。

房间里传出憋回去的轻轻尖叫声,于是我站着朝一间像是霍肯的房间看,看见一条柔软、漂亮、白皙的大腿和女性漂亮的臀部,在很短的女睡衣里忽隐忽现,正在爬上一张窄小的床,之后那漂亮臀部的主人突然停下来,将脸蒙在被里,无迹可寻,就像沙地里的鸵鸟。

我小心地退出去,下楼给自己倒了一杯酒。很快罗登回来了,看起来就像最后一幕里的哈姆雷特。

他没说话,我也没说。我们坐着只是抽烟。只是当他送我上楼睡觉时,在已经收拾得洁净无瑕的卧室里,他感伤地说:

"为什么女人们都不满足于男人要她们做的那样？"

"为什么她们不呢！"我厌烦地说。

"我觉得我把一切都交代清楚了，"他说。

"你开头就开错了，"我说。

我这么说着，霍肯房间里漂亮女人臀部的图景又出现在我的头脑中。对了，霍肯的头儿开得好，无论他在哪儿结束，他都开得好。

早上霍肯给我拿来茶点的时候，很温顺，就像一只猫。我问他天气如何，他问我晚上睡得如何，我是否舒服？

"非常舒服！"我说。"不过，恐怕是我赶你出去了。"

"我，先生？"他回敬我一脸的惊慌。

但我还是瞪了他一眼。

"你的名字叫乔？"我问他。

"你说的对，先生。"

"我也叫乔，"我说。"不过，我没看见她的脸，因此也就没关系了。我觉得你当时会有点儿挤，床有点儿小！"

"哟，先生！"他回我以微笑，表现出惊人的厚颜无耻，然后降下嗓音显示出绝对的自信。"这可是宅子里最好的床，这确实是。"他又轻轻地加上一句。

"你没有都试吧，肯定！"

他脸上显出又恨又怕的表情！

"没有，先生，我的确没有。"

那一天，罗登在去突尼斯的路上，先去了伦敦，霍肯也跟他去了。罗登的屋顶依然如故。

德拉蒙德一家也离开了——他们去了某个地方，他们的离去使当地许多好事的商人及其家眷们颇不满足。

D. H. Lawrence

❧ The Rocking-Horse Winner ❧

The story tells about a family tragedy employing devices of the modern fairy tale and a mockingly detached tone to moralize on the value of human love and the dangers of money. Hester, a woman full of greed and having a fixation with luck and money, realizes she is incapable of fully loving her children and being a good mother only when her own greed and misguiding teachings has finally killed her son Paul. The story emphasizes the dysfunctional relationship between a mother and her child. In the story, greed is depicted as an evil that replaces love in the human heart and can obscure truth. Like Lawrence's other works, "The Rocking-Horse Winner" is known for its explorations of human nature and its illustration of the nature of materialism.

There was a woman who was beautiful, who started with all the advantages, yet she had no luck. She married for love, and the love turned to dust. She had bonny children, yet she felt they had been thrust upon her, and she could not love them. They looked at her coldly, as if they were finding fault with her. And hurriedly she felt she must cover up some fault in herself. Yet what it was that she must cover up she never knew. Nevertheless, when her children were present, she always felt the centre of her heart go hard. This troubled her, and in her manner she was all the more gentle and anxious for her children, as if she loved them very much. Only she herself knew that at the centre of her heart was a hard little place that could not feel love, no, not for anybody. Everybody else said of her: "She is such a good mother. She adores her children." Only she herself, and her children themselves, knew it was not so. They read it in each other's eyes.

There were a boy and two little girls. They lived in a pleasant house, with a garden, and they had discreet servants, and felt themselves superior to anyone in the neighborhood.

Although they lived in style, they felt always an anxiety in the house. There was never enough money. The mother had a small income, and the father had a small income, but not nearly enough for the social position which they had to keep up. The father went into town to some office. But though he had good prospects, these prospects never materialized. There was always the grinding sense of the shortage of money, though the style was always kept up.

At last the mother said: "I will see if *I* can't make something." But she did not know where to begin. She racked her brains, and tried this thing and the other, but could not find anything successful. The failure made deep lines come into her face. Her children were growing up, they would have to go to school. There must be more money, there must be more money. The father, who was always very handsome and expensive in his tastes, seemed as if he never *would* be able to do anything worth doing. And the mother, who had a great belief in herself, did not succeed any better, and her tastes were just as expensive.

And so the house came to be haunted by the unspoken phrase: *There must be more money! There must be more money!* The children could hear it all the time though nobody said it aloud. They heard it at Christmas, when the expensive and splendid toys filled the nursery. Behind the shining modern rocking-horse, behind the smart doll's house, a voice would start whispering: "There *must* be more money! There *must* be more money!" And the children would stop playing, to listen for a moment. They would look into each other's eyes, to see if they had all heard. And each one saw in the eyes of the other two that they too had heard. "There *must* be more money! There *must* be more money!"

It came whispering from the springs of the still-swaying rocking-horse, and even the horse, bending his wooden, champing head, heard it. The big doll, sitting so pink and smirking in her new pram, could hear it quite plainly, and seemed to be smirking all the more self-consciously because of it. The foolish puppy, too, that took the place of the teddy-bear, he was looking so extraordinarily foolish for no other reason but that he heard the secret whisper all over the house: "There *must* be more money!"

Yet nobody ever said it aloud. The whisper was everywhere, and therefore no one spoke it. Just as no one ever says: "We are breathing!" in spite of the fact that breath is coming and going all the time.

"Mother," said the boy Paul one day, "why don't we keep a car of our own? Why do we always use uncle's, or else a taxi?"

"Because we're the poor members of the family," said the mother.

"But why *are* we, mother?"

"Well—I suppose," she said slowly and bitterly, "it's because your father has no luck."

The boy was silent for some time.

"Is luck money, mother?" he asked, rather timidly.

"No, Paul. Not quite. It's what causes you to have money."

"Oh!" said Paul vaguely, "I thought when Uncle Oscar said *filthy lucker*, it meant money."

"*Filthy lucre* does mean money," said the mother, "But it's lucre, not luck."

"Oh!" said the boy, "Then what is luck, mother?"

"It's what causes you to have money. If you're lucky you have money. That's why it's better to be born lucky than rich. If you're rich, you may lose your money. But if you're lucky, you will always get more money."

"Oh! Will you? And is father not lucky?"

"Very unlucky, I should say," she said bitterly.

The boy watched her with unsure eyes.

"Why?" he asked.

"I don't know. Nobody ever knows why one person is lucky and another unlucky."

"Don't they? Nobody at all? Does nobody know?"

"Perhaps God. But He never tells."

"He ought to, then. And aren't you lucky either, mother?"

"I can't be, if I married an unlucky husband."

"But by yourself, aren't you?"

"I used to think I was, before I married. Now I think I am very unlucky indeed."

"Why?"

"Well—never mind! Perhaps I'm not really," she said.

The child looked at her to see if she meant it. But he saw, by the lines of her mouth, that she was only trying to hide something from him.

"Well, anyhow," he said stoutly, "I'm a lucky person."

"Why?" said his mother, with a sudden laugh.

He stared at her. He didn't even know why he had said it.

"God told me," he asserted, brazening it out.

"I hope He did, dear!" she said, again with a laugh, but rather bitter.

"He did, mother!"

"Excellent!" said the mother, using one of her husband's exclamations.

The boy saw she did not believe him; or rather, that she paid no attention to his assertion. This angered him somewhere, and made him want to compel her attention.

He went off by himself, vaguely, in a childish way, seeking for the clue to "luck".

Absorbed, taking no heed of other people, he went about with a sort of stealth, seeking inwardly for luck. He wanted luck, he wanted it, he wanted it. When the two girls were playing dolls in the nursery, he would sit on his big rocking-horse, charging madly into space, with a frenzy that made the little girls peer at him uneasily. Wildly the horse careered, the waving dark hair of the boy tossed, his eyes had a strange glare in them. The little girls dared not speak to him.

When he had ridden to the end of his mad little journey, he climbed down and stood in front of his rocking-horse, staring fixedly into its lowered face. Its red mouth was slightly open, its big eye was wide and glassy-bright.

"Now!" he would silently command the snorting steed. "Now take me to where there is luck! Now take me!"

And he would slash the horse on the neck with the little whip he had asked Uncle Oscar for. He knew the horse could take him to where there was luck, if only he forced it. So he would mount again and start on his furious ride, hoping at last to get there.

"You'll break your horse, Paul!" said the nurse.

"He's always riding like that! I wish he'd leave off!" said his elder sister Joan.

But he only glared down on them in silence. Nurse gave him up. She could make nothing of him. Anyhow, he was growing beyond her.

One day his mother and his Uncle Oscar came in when he was on one of his furious rides. He did not speak to them.

"Hallo, you young jockey! Riding a winner?" said his uncle.

"Aren't you growing too big for a rocking-horse? You're not a very little boy any longer, you know," said his mother.

But Paul only gave a blue glare from his big, rather close-set eyes. He would speak to nobody when he was in full tilt. His mother watched him with an anxious expression on her face.

At last he suddenly stopped forcing his horse into the mechanical gallop and slid down.

"Well, I got there!" he announced fiercely, his blue eyes still flaring, and his sturdy long legs straddling apart.

"Where did you get to?" asked his mother.

"Where I wanted to go," he flared back at her.

"That's right, son!" said Uncle Oscar. "Don't you stop till you get there. What's the horse's name?"

"He doesn't have a name," said the boy.

"Gets on without all right?" asked the uncle.

"Well, he has different names. He was called Sansovino last week."

"Sansovino, eh? Won the Ascot. How did you know this name?"

"He always talks about horse-races with Bassett," said Joan.

The uncle was delighted to find that his small nephew was posted with all the racing news. Bassett, the young gardener, who had been wounded in the left foot in the war and had got his present job through Oscar Cresswell, whose batman he had been, was a perfect blade of the 'turf'. He lived in the racing events, and the small boy lived with him.

Oscar Cresswell got it all from Bassett.

"Master Paul comes and asks me, so I can't do more than tell him, sir," said Bassett, his face terribly serious, as if he were speaking of religious matters.

"And does he ever put anything on a horse he fancies?"

"Well—I don't want to give him away—he's a young sport, a fine sport, sir. Would you mind asking him himself? He sort of takes a pleasure in it, and perhaps he'd feel I was giving him away, sir, if you don't mind."

Bassett was serious as a church.

The uncle went back to his nephew and took him off for a ride in the car.

"Say, Paul, old man, do you ever put anything on a horse?" the uncle asked.

The boy watched the handsome man closely.

"Why, do you think I oughtn't to?" he parried.

"Not a bit of it! I thought perhaps you might give me a tip for the Lincoln."

The car sped on into the country, going down to Uncle Oscar's place in Hampshire.

"Honor bright?" said the nephew.

"Honor bright, son!" said the uncle.

"Well, then, Daffodil."

"Daffodil! I doubt it, sonny. What about Mirza?"

"I only know the winner," said the boy, "That's Daffodil."

"Daffodil, eh?"

There was a pause. Daffodil was an obscure horse comparatively.

"Uncle!"

"Yes, son?"

"You won't let it go any further, will you? I promised Bassett."

"Bassett be damned, old man! What's he got to do with it?"

"We're partners. We've been partners from the first. Uncle, he lent me my first five shillings, which I lost. I promised him, honour bright, it was only between me and him; only you gave me that ten-shilling note I started winning with, so I thought you were lucky. You won't let it go any further, will you?"

The boy gazed at his uncle from those big, hot, blue eyes, set rather close together. The uncle stirred and laughed uneasily.

"Right you are, son! I'll keep your tip private. How much are you putting on him?"

"All except twenty pounds," said the boy. "I keep that in reserve."

The uncle thought it a good joke.

"You keep twenty pounds in reserve, do you, you young romancer? What are you betting, then?"

"I'm betting three hundred," said the boy gravely. "But it's between you and me, Uncle Oscar! Honor bright?"

"It's between you and me all right, you young Nat Gould," he said, laughing. "But where's your three hundred?"

"Bassett keeps it for me. We're partners."

"You are, are you! And what is Bassett putting on Daffodil?"

"He won't go quite as high as I do, I expect. Perhaps he'll go a hundred and fifty."

"What, pennies?" laughed the uncle.

"Pounds," said the child, with a surprised look at his uncle. "Bassett keeps a bigger reserve than I do."

Between wonder and amusement Uncle Oscar was silent. He pursued the matter no further, but he determined to take his nephew with him to the Lincoln races.

"Now, son," he said, "I'm putting twenty on Mirza, and I'll put five on for you on any horse you fancy. What's your pick?"

"Daffodil, uncle."

"No, not the fiver on Daffodil!"

"I should if it was my own fiver," said the child.

"Good! Good! Right you are! A fiver for me and a fiver for you on Daffodil."

The child had never been to a race-meeting before, and his eyes were blue fire. He pursed his mouth tight and watched. A Frenchman just in front had put his money on Lancelot. Wild with excitement, he flayed his arms up and down, yelling "*Lancelot! Lancelot!*" in his French accent.

Daffodil came in first, Lancelot second, Mirza third. The child, flushed and with eyes blazing, was curiously serene. His uncle brought him four five-pound notes, four to one.

"What am I to do with these?" he cried, waving them before the boys eyes.

"I suppose we'll talk to Bassett," said the boy. "I expect I have fifteen hundred now; and twenty in reserve; and this twenty."

His uncle studied him for some moments.

"Look here, son!" he said. "You're not serious about Bassett and that fifteen hundred, are you?"

"Yes, I am. But it's between you and me, uncle. Honour bright?"

"Honour bright all right, son! But I must talk to Bassett."

"If you'd like to be a partner, uncle, with Bassett and me, we could all be partners. Only, you'd have to promise, honor bright, uncle, not to let it go beyond us three. Bassett and I are lucky, and you must be lucky, because it was your ten shillings I started winning with …"

Uncle Oscar took both Bassett and Paul into Richmond Park for an afternoon, and there they talked.

"It's like this, you see, sir," Bassett said. "Master Paul would get me talking about racing events, spinning yarns, you know, sir. And he was always keen on knowing if I'd made or if I'd lost. It's about a year since, now, that I put five shillings on Blush of Dawn for him: and we lost. Then the luck turned, with that ten shillings he had from you: that we put on Singhalese. And since that time, it's been pretty steady, all things considering. What do you say, Master Paul?"

"We're all right when we're sure," said Paul. "It's when we're not quite sure that we go down."

"Oh, but we're careful then," said Bassett.

"But when are you *sure*?" Uncle Oscar smiled.

"It's Master Paul, sir," said Bassett in a secret, religious voice. "It's as if he had it from heaven. Like Daffodil, now, for the Lincoln. That was as sure as eggs."

"Did you put anything on Daffodil?" asked Oscar Cresswell.

"Yes, sir, I made my bit."

"And my nephew?"

Bassett was obstinately silent, looking at Paul.

"I made twelve hundred, didn't I, Bassett? I told uncle I was putting three hundred on Daffodil."

"That's right," said Bassett, nodding.

"But where's the money?" asked the uncle.

"I keep it safe locked up, sir. Master Paul he can have it any minute he likes to ask for it."

"What, fifteen hundred pounds?"

"And twenty! And *forty*, that is, with the twenty he made on the course."

"It's amazing!" said the uncle.

"If Master Paul offers you to be partners, sir, I would, if I were you: if you'll excuse me," said Bassett.

Oscar Cresswell thought about it.

"I'll see the money," he said.

They drove home again, and, sure enough, Bassett came round to the garden-house with fifteen hundred pounds in notes. The twenty pounds reserve was left with Joe Glee, in the Turf Commission deposit.

"You see, it's all right, uncle, when I'm sure! Then we go strong, for all we're worth, don't we, Bassett?"

"We do that, Master Paul."

"And when are you sure?" said the uncle, laughing.

"Oh, well, sometimes I'm *absolutely* sure, like about Daffodil," said the boy, "and sometimes I have an idea; and sometimes I haven't even an idea, have I, Bassett? Then we're careful, because we mostly go down."

"You do, do you! And when you're sure, like about Daffodil, what makes you sure, sonny?"

"Oh, well, I don't know," said the boy uneasily. "I'm sure, you know, uncle; that's all."

"It's as if he had it from heaven, sir," Bassett reiterated.

"I should say so!" said the uncle.

But he became a partner. And when the Leger was coming on Paul was "sure" about Lively Spark, which was a quite inconsiderable horse. The boy insisted on putting a thousand on the horse, Bassett went for five hundred, and Oscar Cresswell two hundred. Lively Spark came in first, and the betting had been ten to one against him. Paul had made ten thousand.

"You see," he said. "I was absolutely sure of him."

Even Oscar Cresswell had cleared two thousand.

"Look here, son," he said, "this sort of thing makes me nervous."

"It needn't, uncle! Perhaps I shan't be sure again for a long time."

"But what are you going to do with your money?" asked the uncle.

"Of course," said the boy, "I started it for mother. She said she had no luck, because father is unlucky, so I thought if I was lucky, it might stop whispering."

"What might stop whispering?"

"Our house. I *hate* our house for whispering."

"What does it whisper?"

"Why—why"—the boy fidgeted—"why, I don't know. But it's always short of money, you know, uncle."

"I know it, son, I know it."

"You know people send mother writs, don't you, uncle?"

"I'm afraid I do," said the uncle.

"And then the house whispers, like people laughing at you behind your back. It's awful, that is! I thought if I was lucky—"

"You might stop it," added the uncle.

The boy watched him with big blue eyes, that had an uncanny cold fire in them, and he said never a word.

"Well, then!" said the uncle. "What are we doing?"

"I shouldn't like mother to know I was lucky," said the boy.

"Why not, son?"

"She'd stop me."

"I don't think she would."

"Oh!"—and the boy writhed in an odd way—"I don't want her to know, uncle."

"All right, son! We'll manage it without her knowing."

They managed it very easily. Paul, at the other's suggestion, handed over five thousand pounds to his uncle, who deposited it with the family lawyer, who was then to inform Paul's mother that a relative had put five thousand pounds into his hands, which sum was to be paid out a thousand pounds at a time, on the mother's birthday, for the next five years.

"So she'll have a birthday present of a thousand pounds for five successive years," said Uncle Oscar. "I hope it won't make it all the harder for her later."

Paul's mother had her birthday in November. The house had been "whispering" worse than ever lately, and, even in spite of his luck, Paul could not bear up against it. He was very anxious to see the effect of the birthday letter, telling his mother about the thousand pounds.

When there were no visitors, Paul now took his meals with his parents, as he was beyond the nursery control. His mother went into town nearly every day. She had discovered that she had an odd knack of sketching furs and dress materials, so she worked secretly in the studio of a friend who was the chief "artist" for the leading drapers. She drew the figures of ladies in furs and ladies in silk and sequins for the newspaper advertisements. This young woman artist earned several thousand pounds a year, but Paul's mother only made several hundreds, and she was again dissatisfied. She so wanted to be first in something, and she did not succeed, even in making sketches for drapery advertisements.

She was down to breakfast on the morning of her birthday. Paul watched her face as she read her letters. He knew the lawyer's letter. As his mother read it, her face hardened and became more expressionless. Then a cold, determined look came on her mouth. She hid the letter under the pile of others, and said not a word about it.

"Didn't you have anything nice in the post for your birthday, mother?" said Paul.

"Quite moderately nice," she said, her voice cold and hard and absent.

She went away to town without saying more.

But in the afternoon Uncle Oscar appeared. He said Paul's mother had had a long interview with the lawyer, asking if the whole five thousand could not be advanced at once, as she was in debt.

"What do you think, uncle?" said the boy.

"I leave it to you, son."

"Oh, let her have it, then! We can get some more with the other," said the boy.

"A bird in the hand is worth two in the bush, laddie!" said Uncle Oscar.

"But I'm sure to *know* for the Grand National; or the Lincolnshire; or else the Derby. I'm sure to know for *one* of them," said Paul.

So Uncle Oscar signed the agreement, and Paul's mother touched the whole five thousand. Then something very curious happened. The voices in the house suddenly went mad, like a chorus of frogs on a spring evening. There were certain new furnishings, and Paul had a tutor. He was *really* going to Eton, his father's school, in the following autumn. There were flowers in the winter, and a blossoming of the luxury Paul's mother had been used to. And yet the voices in the house, behind the sprays of mimosa and almond-blossom, and from under the piles of iridescent cushions, simply trilled and screamed in a sort of ecstasy: "There *must* be more money! Oh-h-h; there *must* be more money. Oh, now, now-w! Now-w-w-there *must* be more money! —more than ever! More than ever!"

It frightened Paul terribly. He studied away at his Latin and Greek with his tutor. But his intense hours were spent with Bassett. The Grand National had gone by: he had not "known", and had lost a hundred pounds. Summer was at hand. He was in agony for the Lincoln. But even for the Lincoln he didn't "know", and he lost fifty pounds. He became wild-eyed and strange, as if something were going to explode in him.

"Let it alone, son! Don't you bother about it!" urged Uncle Oscar. But it was as if the boy couldn't really hear what his uncle was saying.

"I've got to know for the Derby! I've got to know for the Derby!" the child reiterated, his big blue eyes blazing with a sort of madness.

His mother noticed how overwrought he was.

"You'd better go to the seaside. Wouldn't you like to go now to the seaside, instead of waiting? I think you'd better," she said, looking down at him anxiously, her heart curiously heavy because of him.

But the child lifted his uncanny blue eyes.

"I couldn't possibly go before the Derby, mother!" he said. "I couldn't possibly!"

"Why not?" she said, her voice becoming heavy when she was opposed. "Why not? You can still go from the seaside to see the Derby with your Uncle Oscar, if that that's what you wish. No need for you to wait here. Besides, I think you care too much about these races. It's a bad sign. My family has been a gambling family, and you won't know till you grow up how much damage it has done. But it has done damage. I shall have to send Bassett away, and ask Uncle Oscar not to talk racing to you, unless you promise to be reasonable about it: go away to the seaside and forget it. You're all nerves!"

"I'll do what you like, mother, so long as you don't send me away till after the Derby," the boy said.

"Send you away from where? Just from this house?"

"Yes," he said, gazing at her.

"Why, you curious child, what makes you care about this house so much, suddenly? I never knew you loved it."

He gazed at her without speaking. He had a secret within a secret, something he had not divulged, even to Bassett or to his Uncle Oscar.

But his mother, after standing undecided and a little bit sullen for some moments, said: "Very well, then! Don't go to the seaside till after the Derby, if you don't wish it. But promise me you won't think so much about horse-racing and *events*, as you call them!"

"Oh no," said the boy casually. "I won't think much about them, mother. You needn't worry. I wouldn't worry, mother, if I were you."

"If you were me and I were you," said his mother, "I wonder what we should do!"

"But you know you needn't worry, mother, don't you?" the boy repeated.

"I should be awfully glad to know it," she said wearily.

"Oh, well, you *can*, you know. I mean, you *ought* to know you needn't worry," he insisted.

"Ought I? Then I'll see about it," she said.

Paul's secret of secrets was his wooden horse, that which had no name. Since he was emancipated from a nurse and a nursery-governess, he had had his rocking-horse removed to his own bedroom at the top of the house.

"Surely you're too big for a rocking-horse!" his mother had remonstrated.

"Well, you see, mother, till I can have a *real* horse, I like to have *some* sort of animal about," had been his quaint answer.

"Do you feel he keeps you company?" she laughed.

"Oh yes! He's very good, he always keeps me company, when I'm there," said Paul.

So the horse, rather shabby, stood in an arrested prance in the boy's bedroom.

The Derby was drawing near, and the boy grew more and more tense. He hardly heard what was spoken to him, he was very frail, and his eyes were really uncanny. His mother had sudden strange seizures of uneasiness about him. Sometimes, for half an hour, she would feel a sudden anxiety about him that was almost anguish. She wanted to rush to him at once, and know he was safe.

Two nights before the Derby, she was at a big party in town, when one of her rushes of anxiety about her boy, her first-born, gripped her heart till she could hardly speak. She fought with the feeling, might and main, for she believed in common sense. But it was too strong. She had to leave the dance and go downstairs to telephone to the country. The children's nursery-governess was terribly surprised and startled at being rung up in the night.

"Are the children all right, Miss Wilmot?"

"Oh yes, they are quite all right."

"Master Paul? Is he all right?"

"He went to bed as right as a trivet. Shall I run up and look at him?"

"No," said Paul's mother reluctantly. "No! Don't trouble. It's all right. Don't sit up. We shall be home fairly soon." She did not want her son's privacy intruded upon.

"Very good," said the governess.

It was about one o'clock when Paul's mother and father drove up to their house. All was still. Paul's mother went to her room and slipped off her white fur cloak. She had told her maid not to wait up for her. She heard her husband downstairs, mixing a whisky and soda.

And then, because of the strange anxiety at her heart, she stole upstairs to her son's room. Noiselessly she went along the upper corridor. Was there a faint noise? What was it?

She stood, with arrested muscles, outside his door, listening. There was a strange, heavy, and yet not loud noise. Her heart stood still. It was a soundless noise, yet rushing and powerful. Something huge, in violent, hushed motion. What was it? What in God's name was it? She ought to know. She felt that she knew the noise. She knew what it was.

Yet she could not place it. She couldn't say what it was. And on and on it went, like a madness.

Softly, frozen with anxiety and fear, she turned the door-handle.

The room was dark. Yet in the space near the window, she heard and saw something plunging to and fro. She gazed in fear and amazement.

Then suddenly she switched on the light, and saw her son, in his green pyjamas, madly surging on the rocking-horse. The blaze of light suddenly lit him up, as he urged the wooden horse, and lit her up, as she stood, blonde, in her dress of pale green and crystal, in the doorway.

"Paul!" she cried. "Whatever are you doing?"

"It's Malabar!" he screamed in a powerful, strange voice. "It's Malabar!"

His eyes blazed at her for one strange and senseless second, as he ceased urging his wooden horse. Then he fell with a crash to the ground, and she, all her tormented motherhood flooding upon her, rushed to gather him up.

But he was unconscious, and unconscious he remained, with some brain-fever. He talked and tossed, and his mother sat stonily by his side.

"Malabar! It's Malabar! Bassett, Bassett, I *know*! It's Malabar!"

So the child cried, trying to get up and urge the rocking-horse that gave him his inspiration.

"What does he mean by Malabar?" asked the heart-frozen mother.

"I don't know," said the father stonily.

"What does he mean by Malabar?" she asked her brother Oscar.

"It's one of the horses running for the Derby," was the answer.

And, in spite of himself, Oscar Cresswell spoke to Bassett, and himself put a thousand on Malabar: at fourteen to one.

The third day of the illness was critical: they were waiting for a change. The boy, with his rather long, curly hair, was tossing ceaselessly on the pillow. He neither slept nor regained consciousness, and his eyes were like blue stones. His mother sat, feeling her heart had gone, turned actually into a stone.

In the evening Oscar Cresswell did not come, but Bassett sent a message, saying could he come up for one moment, just one moment? Paul's mother was very angry at the intrusion, but on second thoughts she agreed. The boy was the same. Perhaps Bassett might bring him to consciousness.

The gardener, a shortish fellow with a little brown moustache and sharp little brown eyes, tiptoed into the room, touched his imaginary cap to Paul's mother, and stole to the bedside, staring with glittering, smallish eyes at the tossing, dying child.

"Master Paul!" he whispered. "Master Paul! Malabar came in first all right, a clean win. I did as you told me. You've made over seventy thousand pounds, you have; you've got over eighty thousand. Malabar came in all right, Master Paul."

"Malabar! Malabar! Did I say Malabar, mother? Did I say Malabar? Do you think I'm lucky, mother? I knew Malabar, didn't I? Over eighty thousand pounds! I call that lucky, don't you, mother? Over eighty thousand pounds! I knew, didn't I know I knew? Malabar came in all right. If I ride my horse till I'm sure, then I tell you, Bassett, you can go as high as you like. Did you go for all you were worth, Bassett?"

"I went a thousand on it, Master Paul."

"I never told you, mother, that if I can ride my horse, and get there, then I'm absolutely sure—oh, absolutely! Mother, did I ever tell you? I am lucky!"

"No, you never did," said his mother.

But the boy died in the night.

And even as he lay dead, his mother heard her brother's voice saying to her, "My God, Hester, you're eighty-odd thousand to the good, and a poor devil of a son to the bad. But, poor devil, poor devil, he's best gone out of a life where he rides his rocking-horse to find a winner."

Questions

1. What is the source of the alienation and what tragedy is caused by the alienation in the story?
2. Like D. H. Lawrence's other works, "The Rocking-Horse Winner" carries the theme of criticizing the destructive influence of modern industrial civilization on human nature. Demonstrate the role of irony in it.
3. What are the basic elements in a fable? "The Rocking-Horse Winner" is a modern fable, highlighting some modern devices employed in the short story. What do you think of their functions in terms of style and thematic significance?
4. Comment on the relationship between people distorted by money and the materialized relation among family members under the industrial civilization.
5. What is the thematic significance of the story to our contemporary life?

木马赢家

这个短篇小说讲述了一个家庭悲剧,它运用现代寓言的形式和反讽的表现手法充分展现了人性亲情的价值和金钱带给人类的种种危险。海斯特,一个充满了贪欲、无休止地追求好运和金钱的女人,在她自己的贪婪和误导性说教最终杀死了她的儿子保罗之后,才意识到她无法完全爱她的孩子,无法做一个好母亲。该故事侧重描写了一种被扭曲的母子关系。在小说中,贪婪被描绘成一种荼毒人类心灵之爱,是掩盖真相的恶魔。正如劳伦斯的其他作品一样,《木马赢家》对人类的本性和物质主义的本质进行了深刻的探索和揭示。

有一位貌美的妇人,她本来具有各种优势,然而运气却不佳。她为了爱情而结了婚,但这爱却化成了灰烬。她有健康活泼的孩子,然而她却觉得这些孩子是有人强加给她的,她无法去爱他们。他们用冰冷的目光看着她,似乎总是在找她的碴儿。于是她很快就感觉到她必须要掩饰住自己身上的某种缺点。然而,她必须要掩饰的究竟是什么,她自己也不知道。不过,当她的孩子们在场的时候,她总感觉到自己的内心深处会变得僵硬起来。这给她带来了不少麻烦。在言谈举止方面,她比以前越发温柔,更加关心她的孩子们,好像她非常爱他们。只有她自己明白,在她内心深处,有一个体会不到爱,不,体会不到对任何人的爱的旮旯。外人在谈及她的时候总会说:"她是个非常好的母亲。她深爱着自己的孩子们。"只有她自己,还有她的孩子们,知道事实并非如此。他们从彼此的目光中看出了这一点。

她有一个男孩和两个小女孩,他们住在一幢有花园的舒适房子里,身边有体贴入微的仆人,这让他们觉得自己比住在周围的任何人都高出一等。

虽然他们生活入时,但在家中他们总会感到有一种焦虑。钱总是不够用。母亲有一份微薄的收入,父亲也有一份微薄的收入,但这几乎不足以维持他们不得不维持的社会地位。父亲在城里任职。尽管他的前景还不错,但这些前景都形同虚设,从未真正实现过。他们总是痛苦地感到钱不够用,尽管这种入时的生活方式还一直在维持着。

终于,母亲说:"我要看看我是否能干点什么。"但她并不知道从何干起。她绞尽脑汁,尝试着做了一件又一件的事情,但她没有在任何一件事情上取得成功。失败使她脸上爬满了皱纹。孩子们在一天天长大,他们得上学。必须要有更多的钱,必须要有更多的钱。父亲总是那么风度翩翩,出手大方,他似乎从来没有能力去做任何值得一做的事情。而这位总是充满自信的母亲也没有取得什么更大的成功，但在花钱的兴趣上与丈夫相比毫不逊色。

于是，这座房子里便会时常萦绕着一句从未被说出的话：必须要有更多的钱！必须要有更多的钱！尽管没有人将它大声地说出来，但孩子们却时时都能听到。在圣诞节，当精美昂贵的玩具摆满儿童房的时候，他们听到了这句话。从那匹光亮耀人的新式木马后面，从那个漂亮的木偶房子后面，时常会传来一种微弱的声音："必须要有更多的钱！必须要有更多的钱！"孩子们在玩耍时总会停下来去听一会儿这种声音。他们常常会互相对视着，看看大家是否都听到了。每个人都从另外两个人的眼神中看出他们都听到了。"必须要有更多的钱！必须要有更多的钱！"

这声音从那匹不停摇晃的木马的弹簧那里发出来，甚至连那匹正低着头咯咯作响的木马也听到了这种声音。那只大洋娃娃，眯着眼睛坐在她的新童车里得意地傻笑着，她听清楚了这声音，因为这声音，她似乎有意识地比以前笑得越发得意了。那只蠢笨的小狗，占据着玩具熊的位置，也显得格外的蠢笨，不为别的，而是因为听到了房间里萦绕着这秘密的低语："必须要有更多的钱！"

然而没有人曾大声说过这句话。这句低语随处都可以听到，因此没有人大声将它说出来。正如没有人会去说"我们在呼吸！"一样，即便呼吸无时无刻都在进行。

"妈妈，"有一天保罗说，"我们为什么不能有辆属于自己的车呢？我们为什么总是用叔叔的车，要不就是用出租车？"

"因为我们是这个家族中的穷人，"母亲说。

"妈妈，那我们为什么穷呢？"

"哦——我想，"她慢慢地，抱怨地说，"那是因为你父亲运气不佳。"

小男孩沉思了一会儿。

"运气就是钱吗，妈妈？"他很羞怯地问道。

"不，保罗，不完全是。运气可以让你有钱。"

"哦！"保罗含糊地说道，"我以为奥斯卡叔叔说的不义之财就是钱哪。"

"不义之财的确是钱，"母亲说，"但那是财，不是运气。"

"哦！"男孩说，"那什么是运气，妈妈？"

"运气可以让你有钱。如果你运气好，你就有钱。那就是为什么出生时运气好要比出生时富裕要好。如果你富裕，你可能会失去你的钱。但如果你运气好，你总是会得到更多的钱。"

"哦！你会吗？父亲运气不好吗？"

"应该说他运气很不好，"她心酸地说。

男孩用迟疑的眼神看着她。

"为什么？"他问道。

"我不知道。没人知道为什么有的人运气好，而有的人运气不好。"

"人们不知道？根本没有人知道？没人知道？"

"也许只有上帝知道。但他不会说出来。"

"那么他应当说出来。你也运气不好吗，妈妈？"

"如果我嫁给一个运气不好的丈夫，我不可能运气好。"

"那如果是你一个人，你会运气好吗？"

"在我结婚以前，我常认为我的运气不错，可现在我认为我的运气的确很不好。"

"为什么？"

"好了——不说了！也许我不是真的运气不好，"她说。

孩子看着她，想看她是否真的那么想。但从她的口形看，他看得出她只是想尽力对他隐瞒些什么。

"好了，不管怎样，"他勇敢地说，"我是个运气好的人。"

"为什么？"母亲说道，突然一笑。

他凝视着母亲，甚至不知道为什么说了这句话。

"上帝告诉我了，"他大胆地说了出来。

"真希望他告诉你了，亲爱的！"她又一次带着一丝苦笑说。

"他的确告诉我了，妈妈！"

"好极了！"母亲用丈夫常使用的一句感叹语说道。

男孩看出她并不相信他；或者，她根本没有注意到他的断言。这使男孩有些生气，使他想迫使母亲注意他。

他独自离开了。茫然中，他以幼稚的方法寻找"运气"的线索。他全神贯注，完全忘记了他人的存在，悄悄地在心中寻找着"运气"。他需要运气，需要它，太需要它了。当两个女孩在儿童房玩布娃娃的时候，他便骑在大木马上，向空中狂冲，那疯狂劲儿使两个小女孩用不安的眼神直盯着他。木马在疾驰，小男孩波浪式的黑发在飘扬，眼中露出了奇异的光芒。小女孩们不敢同他说话。

当这一疯狂的短暂旅程一结束，他便从木马身上爬下来，然后站在他的木马前，凝视着木马的面部下方。木马那红色的嘴微微张开，大大的眼睛圆睁着，晶莹透亮。

"驾！"他轻声地命令正在吐鼻息的骏马。"驾，把我带到有好运的地方去！驾，带我去。"

接着，他便用从奥斯卡叔叔那儿要来的小皮鞭抽打木马的颈部。他知道，只要他逼迫木马，木马便能够把他带到有好运的地方去。于是，他又爬上木马，开始了疯狂的旅程，希望能到达好运所在的地方。他知道自己一定能到达那儿。

"你会把木马弄坏的，保罗！"保姆说。

"他老是那样骑马！真希望他能停下来！"他的姐姐琼说道。

但男孩只是默默地凝视着她们。保姆也只好由他去。她拿他无可奈何。他已经长大了，保姆管不了了。

一天，当他还像以往那样疯狂地骑着马时，母亲和奥斯卡叔叔进来了。他没有同大人说话。

"喂，小骑手！骑马冠军吗？"他叔叔说。

"你都这么大了，怎么还玩木马？你知道自己已不再是小小孩了，"母亲说道。

但是，保罗只是用他那双紧蹙的大眼睛愤愤地看了他们一眼。他全身伏在马背上，谁也不想理睬。母亲看着他，脸上带着焦虑的表情。

终于，他突然不再逼迫木马机械地奔驰，他从木马上滑下来。

"好了，我到那儿了！"他激动地宣称，眼中仍在闪光，坚实的双腿分开站立着。

"你到哪儿了？"母亲问道。

"我想去的地方，"他目光炯炯地回过头来看了她一眼。

"对了，小家伙！"奥斯卡叔叔说，"不到那儿不罢休。那匹马叫什么名字？"

"他没有名字，"男孩说。

"没有名字也行？"叔叔问道。

"哦，它有不同的名字。它上周叫作桑索维诺"。

"桑索维诺，噢？在阿斯科特马赛上得胜的，你怎么知道它的名字的？"

"他总是和巴塞特一起谈论马赛，"琼说。

叔叔发现小侄儿对赛马的新闻了如指掌，感到很高兴。年轻的园丁巴塞特在战争中左脚受了伤，通过奥斯卡·克斯韦尔他找到了现在这份工作。他曾经是克斯韦尔的勤务兵，是赛马场上的老手。他生活在赛马比赛中，小男孩和他生活在一起。

奥斯卡·克斯韦尔从巴塞特那儿知道了这一切。

"保罗少爷来问我，所以我只能告诉他，先生，"巴塞特说，脸色十分严肃，就好像在谈论宗教事务。

"他是否给他看中的马下过注？"

"哦——我不想出卖他——他是个年轻的玩家，好玩家，先生，您还是问他本人吧。他对马赛有点儿兴趣，也许他会觉得我出卖了他，先生，请你别介意。"

巴塞特的表情像教堂般严肃。

叔叔回到侄儿那儿，带他坐车去兜风。

"嗨，保罗，老伙计，你在马身上下过注吗？"叔叔问道。

男孩仔细地看了一眼这位英俊的男人。

"嗨，您是不是认为我不该这么做？"他回避道。

"一点儿也没有。我认为，关于林肯赛马会，也许你可以给我一点儿提示。"

车疾速驶进了乡村，朝奥斯卡叔叔在汉普夏郡的住处开去。

"说真的？"侄儿说。

"说真的，小家伙！"叔叔说。

"好了，那么，就水仙了。"

"水仙！我怀疑，乖小子，米尔泽如何？"

"我只知道赢马，"男孩说，"就是水仙。"

"水仙，嗯？"

他们停了一会儿。相比之下，水仙其貌不扬。

"叔叔！"

"什么，小家伙？"

"你不会把这提示再往外传吧？我答应过巴塞特。"

"该死的巴塞特，那老家伙，这与他有什么关系？"

"我们是合伙人。我们一开始就是合伙人。叔叔，他借给我5先令，我输掉了。我答应过他，说真的，这只是我和他之间的秘密；只是在你给我那张10先令的票子后我才开始赢的，因此，我认为你运气不错。你不会把这事再往外传，对吧？"

男孩一双热切、紧蹙的蓝色大眼睛凝视着叔叔。叔叔感到一阵颤动，不安地笑了。

"好了，小子！我一定保密。你在它身上下了多少赌注？"

"除了20英镑外所有的钱，"男孩说。"我留着那20英镑。"

叔叔认为这很可笑。"你留下20英镑，是不是，你这个小家伙真能编？那你下了多少注呢？"

"我赌300英镑，"男孩严肃地说。"但这是你我之间的秘密，奥斯卡叔叔！说真的？"

叔叔哈哈大笑。"是你我之间的秘密，行了，你这小纳特·古尔德，"他笑道："但你的300英镑在哪儿？"

"巴塞特替我保存着。我们是合伙人。"

"你们是合伙人！那么巴塞特在水仙身上下了多少赌注？"

"我想他不会下我这么多。也许他会下150。"

"什么？便士吗？"叔叔笑道。

"英镑，"这孩子用惊讶的目光看着叔叔说："巴塞特留的备用钱比我多。"

奥斯卡叔叔感到惊讶和有趣，他沉默下来。他不再进一步追问此事，但决定带侄儿去参加林肯赛马会。

"好了，小子，"他说，"我打算在米尔泽身上赌20英镑，并且给你5英镑赌你想投注的马。你选什么？"

"水仙，叔叔。"

"不，不要把这张5元的钞票投在水仙身上。"

"如果这5元的英镑是我自己的，我就要投在水仙身上，"孩子说。

"好的，好的！我投一张5英镑的钞票在水仙身上，你也投一张5英镑的钞票在水仙身上。"

这孩子从来没有去过赛马场，他的眼中充满蓝色的火焰。他嘴唇紧闭，观看着。前面有个法国人刚刚把钱投在兰斯洛特身上。他激动万分，上下舞动着手臂，用法国口音大叫着："兰斯洛特！兰斯洛特！"

水仙获得了第一名，兰斯洛特第二名，米尔泽第三名。孩子充满着喜悦，眼中闪耀着光芒，显得好奇而宁静。叔叔给他领来了四张5元的钞票。赌注比率是四比一。

"我拿这些钱干点什么？"他叫道，拿着钱在男孩眼前晃动着。

"我想咱们得和巴塞特谈谈，"男孩说。"我想自己有1500英镑了；存20元备用；这是20元。"

叔叔仔细端详了他一会儿。

"看这儿，小子。"他说。"关于巴塞特和那1500元你不是认真的，对吧？"

"不，我是认真的。但这是你我之间的秘密。发誓！"

"好吧，发誓，小子！但我必须同巴塞特谈谈。"

"叔叔，如果你愿意与巴塞特做我合伙人，那我们都是合伙人。只是您必须答应，发誓，叔叔，除了我们三人不能让其他人知道这个秘密。巴塞特和我运气好，你也一定运气好，因为是用你给的10先令我才开始赢的……"

奥斯卡叔叔同时把巴塞特和保罗带到里士满公园度过了一个下午。他们在那儿谈了话。

"事情是这样的,您知道,先生,"巴塞特说:"保罗少爷让我谈赛马的事,讲故事,您知道,先生。他总是对我的输赢感兴趣。自从我为他把5先令投在'破晓红霞'身上——我们输了,到现在已经有一年了。后来我们时来运转,我们把您给他的10先令投在僧伽罗身上。自那一次以后,总的来讲,一直都相当稳定。你说呢,保罗少爷?"

"当我们有把握时,我们就一切都很好,"保罗说。"当我们不太有把握时,便会失利。"

"哦,但我们自那以后便小心翼翼,"巴塞特说。

"但你们什么时候才有把握呢?"奥斯卡叔叔笑着说。

"是保罗少爷,先生,"巴塞特用神秘、宗教式的声音说道。"好像他是从天堂获得的信息。比如现在水仙在林肯赛马会上获胜。那是笃定的事情。"

"你在水仙身上下过注吗?"奥斯卡·克斯韦尔问。

"下过,先生。我下过。"

"我侄儿呢?"

巴塞特固执地不说话,看着保罗。

"我挣了1200英镑,对吧,巴塞特?我告诉过叔叔我在水仙身上下注300英镑。"

"对,"巴塞特点头说道。

"但钱在哪儿?"叔叔问道。

"我把它安全地锁起来了,先生。保罗少爷想什么时候要,什么时候就可以拿到。"

"什么,1500镑?"

"还有20!是40,那20是他在赛马场上赢的。"

"真是太神奇了!"叔叔说。

"我要是您的话,如果保罗少爷让您入伙,先生,我一定会愿意的;请原谅我,"巴塞特说。

奥斯卡·克斯韦尔想了想。

"我得看看那些钱,"他说。

他们又驱车回到家里。真是千真万确。巴塞特来到花园小屋,拿出1500英镑的钞票。那20镑的备用钱留在乔·格里那儿,作为赛马佣金储备。

"你看,叔叔,当我有把握的时候,就一切都很好!我们全力出击。是吧,巴塞特?"

"我们正是这样做的,保罗少爷。"

"你什么时候有把握呢?"叔叔笑着说。

"哦，这么说吧，有时我绝对有把握，比如水仙，"男孩说，"有时我有想法，有时候甚至想法也没有，是吧，巴塞特？那样我们就小心翼翼，因为这种情况下我们多半是输。"

"啊，是这样！当你有把握时，比如水仙，是什么让你有把握的，乖小子？"

"哦，我不知道，"男孩不安地说。"我有把握，你知道，叔叔，就这么简单。"

"就好像他是从上天得到提示，先生，"巴塞特强调说。

"我想是吧！"叔叔说。

叔叔也成了合伙人。当莱吉尔赛马会开始的时候，保罗对"活力火花"确信无疑，这是一匹很不显眼的马。男孩坚持在这匹马身上下注1000英镑。巴塞特下了500英镑。奥斯卡·克斯韦尔下了200英镑。

"活力火花"获得第一名，赌注的比率是十比一。保罗赢了10000英镑。

"你瞧，"他说，"我对他绝对有把握。"

甚至奥斯卡·克斯韦尔也净得了2000英镑。

"听着，小子，"他说，"这种事使我神经紧张。"

"不必紧张，叔叔！也许我要很长时间才能再有把握。"

"但是你拿这些钱做什么用呢？"叔叔问道。

"当然，"男孩说，"我是为了妈妈才干这个的。她说她没有运气，是因为爸爸运气不好，因此，我想，如果我运气好，也许它会停止低语。"

"什么东西会停止低语？"

"我们的房子。我讨厌我们的房子里萦绕着的那种低语声。"

"低语些什么？"

"呃——呃"——男孩有点坐立不安——"呃，我不知道。但我们总是缺钱，您知道，叔叔。"

"我知道，小子，我知道。"

"你知道人们总是给妈妈送来催账的单子，对吧，叔叔？"

"我知道，"叔叔说。

"然后房子里就开始萦绕那种低语声，就像人们在你身后耻笑你一样。真是糟透了！我想如果我运气好的话——"

"你可以阻止它，"叔叔说。

男孩用蓝色的大眼睛看着他，眼中发出一道奇怪的冷光，一言不发。

"好了，就这样！"叔叔说。"我们怎么办呢？"

"我不想让母亲知道我运气好，"男孩说。

"为什么不呢,小子?"

"她会阻止我的。"

"我想她不会阻止。"

"噢!"——男孩奇怪地扭动了一下身体——"我不想让她知道,叔叔。"

"行,小子!我们做这件事不让她知道。"

他们的事做得很轻松。在别人的建议下,保罗把5000英镑交给叔叔放在家庭律师那儿,然后由家庭律师通知保罗的母亲,说有一位亲戚在他那儿放了5000英镑,钱必须在以后的五年内每年母亲生日那天按一次1000英镑的数目付给。

"这样,她就可以连续五年得到一份1000英镑的礼物,"奥斯卡·叔叔说:"我希望以后日子不会使她更为难。"

保罗的妈妈在11月过生日。近来房子里萦绕着的那种低语声比以前更为严重了,尽管保罗运气很好,但他还是难以忍受这声音。他特别急于想知道告诉母亲有关1000英镑的那封生日贺信会产生的效果。

没有客人的时候,保罗同父母一起吃饭,因为他不再由保姆照看。母亲几乎天天都进城。她发现自己有一种奇怪的爱好,喜欢画皮装和衣料。因此,她偷偷地在一个朋友的画室里工作。这位朋友是大布商们的主要"艺术家"。她为报纸广告画穿皮装的女士以及穿带闪光装饰片丝绸衣服的女士。这位年轻的女艺术家一年挣几千英镑,但保罗的母亲只挣了几百英镑,她又不满足了。她想在某些方面争第一,但是她并没有成功,甚至在画布商广告方面也是如此。

生日那天早晨,她在楼下吃早饭。她读信时,保罗看着她的脸。他知道是律师写的信。母亲读信时,脸沉了下来,变得更加没有表情。然后,她的嘴角显露出了一种冷淡而又坚定的神情。她把信藏在一堆信的下面,只字不提关于信的事情。

"您的邮件中有祝贺您生日的好东西吧,妈妈?"保罗说。

"马马虎虎还说得过去吧,"她用冷漠而漫不经心的声调说道。

她没有多说,到城里去了。

但是,奥斯卡叔叔下午露面了。他说保罗的母亲与律师有过长谈,问是否可以将所有5000英镑一次提前付给,因为她欠有债务。

"你说呢?叔叔,"男孩说。

"由你来决定,孩子。"

"唉,那么让她拿走吧!我们可以用另外的钱再去挣一些,"男孩说。

"双鸟在林不如一鸟在手,小伙子!"奥斯卡叔叔说。

"但有关全国大赛我肯定会搞清楚的,或者林肯赛马会,或者德比赛马会。我肯定能弄清楚其中之一,"保罗说。

就这样，奥斯卡叔叔签了协议，保罗的妈妈拿到了所有的5000英镑。接着，发生了一件奇怪的事情。房子里的声音突然疯狂起来，像春天夜里青蛙一齐发出呱呱声。房子里有了一些新家具，保罗有了一位家庭教师。秋天，他真的要去父亲上过的伊顿学校念书了。家里冬天也有了鲜花盛开，保罗母亲从前就习惯于这种奢侈。然而，房子里萦绕的那种声音，从含羞草花和杏仁树枝后，从彩虹色坐垫堆下，房子里的声音简直是在疯狂地尖叫："必须要有更多的钱！噢……；必须要有更多的钱。噢，噢，噢……必须要有更多的钱……比任何时刻都要多！比任何时刻都要多！"

这把保罗吓坏了。他一直在跟家庭教师学习拉丁语和希腊语，回避此事。但他最紧张的时刻是与巴塞特一起度过的。全国马会大赛已经过去，他没有弄"清楚"，并且输了100英镑。夏天已到。他痛苦地等待林肯赛马会。但其至在林肯赛马会中，他也没有弄"清楚"，并且输了50英镑。他两眼发直，行为古怪，好像有什么东西将在他体内爆炸一样。

"甭管它，小子！不要为此烦恼！"奥斯卡叔叔恳求道。但男孩好像根本听不见叔叔在说些什么。

"我一定能弄清楚德比赛马会！我一定能弄清楚德比赛马会！"男孩反复说道，蓝色的大眼睛里疯狂的火焰在燃烧。

母亲注意到他太紧张了。

"你最好去海滨待一些时间。你去海滨待些时间，不要再等了！我认为你最好去海滨，"她焦虑地看着他说，心情因为他而有些沉重。

然而，男孩抬起了他那双神秘的蓝眼睛。

"我不可能在德比赛马会之前去，妈妈！"他说。"我不可能去！"

"为什么不呢？"她说，遭到反对时她的声音有些沉重。"为什么不呢？如果你愿意的话，你仍然可以从海滨同奥斯卡叔叔一道去参加德比赛马会。没有必要在这儿等。另外，我认为你对这些比赛过于关心了。这是个不好的预兆。我的家庭是个好赌的家庭，等你长大了才会了解它的坏处有多大。但是它已经带来了坏处。我要打发巴塞特走，要奥斯卡叔叔不跟你谈论赛马的事，除非你以理智的态度看待它。去海滨把它忘掉。你整个儿神经分分的！"

"您愿意怎么着我都行，妈妈，只要你在德比赛马会过后再把我送走，"男孩说。

"把你从哪儿送走？就从这房子？"

"是的，"他凝视着她说道。

"呃，你这怪孩子，是什么东西突然使你这么在乎这房子？我知道你从来没有喜欢过它。"

他凝视着她，一言不发。他的秘密之中有秘密，甚至对巴塞特和奥斯卡叔叔也未曾透露过。

然而，母亲站在那儿犹豫不决，一阵愠怒之后说，"好吧，就这样！只要你愿意，在德比马赛之前不去海滨。但是，答应我不要过多地关心你所说的那些赛马会或赛事！"

"哦，不会，"他漫不经心地说道。"我不会过多地关心它们，妈妈。您不必担心。妈妈，如果我是您的话，我不会担心的。"

"如果你是我，而我是你，"母亲说，"我不知道我们会做什么！"

"但您知道您不必担心，妈妈，对吧？"男孩重复道。

"我非常高兴我知道，"她厌倦地说。

"哦，行了，您能知道，您知道。我的意思是，您应当知道您不必担心，"他坚持道。

"我应当知道吗？那么，我得看一看，"她说。

保罗秘密中的秘密是他那没有名字的木马。自从他不再受保姆和家庭女教师的照管以来，他把木马搬到了顶楼卧室。

"的确，你已长大了，不再适合玩木马了！"母亲告诫道。

"啊，您知道，妈妈，在我有一匹真正的马之前，我喜欢周围有某种动物，"这是他巧妙的回答。

"你觉得它会跟你做伴？"她笑了。

"噢，对了！它真好，当我在那儿时，他总是跟我做伴，"保罗说。

因此，这一破旧不堪的木马，就以一种固定的腾跃姿态立在了保罗的卧室里。

德比马赛即将来临。男孩感到越来越紧张。他几乎什么也听不进，他很脆弱，他的眼神简直叫人不可思议。他的母亲，突然对他有一种奇怪而不安的感觉。有时，整整半个小时，她会突然对他感到不安，这不安几乎是极度的痛苦。她想立即赶到他那儿去，看看他是否安全。

离德比马赛还有两个晚上，她正在城里参加一个大型舞会，突然对儿子，即第一胎孩子的担心掠过了她的心头，直到她几乎说不出话来。她尽力控制住自己的感情，因为她相信常理。但这种感觉实在是太强烈了。她不得不离开舞会，来到楼下给乡下打电话。家庭女教师在深夜里听到电话铃声大为吃惊。

"孩子们都好吗？威尔莫特小姐。"

"噢，好，他们都很好。"

"保罗少爷呢？他没事吧？"

"他准时上床睡觉。要不要我跑上楼去看看他？"

"不了，"保罗母亲不情愿地说。"不！不用麻烦了。没事。别熬夜了。我们很快就回来。"她不想让儿子的隐私受到打扰。

"那好吧，"家庭女教师说。

保罗的父母驾车回到房子时大约是一点钟。夜很静。保罗的母亲来到房间，脱下白色的皮外套。她告诉过女仆不要熬夜等她。她听见丈夫在楼下调制威士忌苏打。

然后，由于心中奇怪的焦虑，她偷偷上楼来到了儿子的房间。她轻轻地顺着楼上走廊走。有一种微弱的声音？是什么声音？

她肌肉紧张，站在儿子的门外，聆听着。有一种奇怪、沉重，但不太响的声音。她的心静了下来。是一种无声的噪音，急促而有力。是一种巨大、强烈而又宁静的运动。这是什么？这到底是什么？她应当知道。她感觉到自己知道这是什么声音。她知道这是什么。

然而她不能确定这是什么，她说不出这是什么，但那声音发疯似的一直在继续。

她出于担心和惧怕，轻轻地转动了房门的手柄。

房子里一片漆黑。然而窗边的空地上，她听见并看到有东西在来回摇动。她用恐惧和惊诧的眼光凝视着。

然后，她突然把灯打开，看见儿子穿着绿色的睡衣，发疯似的在木马背上摇动。灯光突然照亮了他，他正在催促木马。灯光也照亮了她，她站在那儿，披着金发，身穿浅绿透明的衣裳，站在门口。

"保罗！"她叫道，"你在干什么？"

"是马拉巴尔！"他用有力而古怪的声音尖叫道。"是马拉巴尔！"

在他停止催促木马时，瞪眼看了她一秒钟，目光古怪而漠然。接着，他啪的一声跌落到地上，而她，她那饱受折磨的母性涌了上来，她冲上前去将他扶起。

但他失去了知觉，而且一直昏迷不醒，头有些热。他边说话边摇头，母亲像石块一样坐在他身旁。

"马拉巴尔！是马拉巴尔！巴塞特，巴塞特，我清楚！就是马拉巴尔！"

就这样，孩子叫着，挣扎着爬起来，催促带给他灵感的木马。

"他说的马拉巴尔是什么意思？"母亲心如冰冻般地问。

"不知道，"父亲毫无表情地说。

"他说的马拉巴尔是什么意思？"她问奥斯卡兄弟。

"是德比马赛中的一匹马，"他这样答道。

奥斯卡忍不住，对巴塞特说了，他自己在马拉巴尔身上下了1000英镑赌注，是十四比一。

保罗得病的第三天情况变得严重起来：他们期待着能有所好转。男孩留着长长的卷发，头在枕头上不停地摆动。他既没有入睡，也没有恢复知觉。他的双眼像蓝色的宝石。他的母亲坐在那儿感到魂不守舍，实际上变成了一块石头。

傍晚，奥斯卡·克斯韦尔没有来，但巴塞特带来口信，问他能不能来待一会儿，就一会儿？保罗的母亲对这种打扰十分恼怒，但回头一想又同意了。男孩依然如故。也许巴塞特能让他醒过来。

园丁个头矮小、留着棕色小胡须，长着一双棕色小眼睛，他踮着脚走进了房间，朝保罗母亲做了一个想象中的脱帽礼，轻轻地来到床边，用发亮的小眼睛注视着翻来覆去、生命垂危的孩子。

"保罗少爷！"他轻声地说道："保罗少爷！马拉巴尔真的得了第一名，大获全胜。我照你说的去做了。你挣了70000英镑，你有，你有80000多英镑。马拉巴尔真的赢了，保罗少爷。"

"马拉巴尔！马拉巴尔！我说的是马拉巴尔吗，妈妈？我说的是马拉巴尔，对吧？我认为这就是运气，对吧？妈妈。80000多英镑！我认为这就叫运气，对吧，妈妈？80000多英镑！我清楚，难道我不清楚我是清楚的吗？马拉巴尔真的赢了。如果我骑着我的木马一直骑到我有把握，我就可以告诉你，巴塞特，你可以想下多少赌注就下多少赌注。你是不是所有钱全下了注，巴塞特？"

"我下了1000英镑，保罗少爷。"

"妈妈，我从来没有告诉您，我能骑木马，并且到那儿，然后，感到有绝对的把握——啊，绝对把握！妈妈，我不是告诉过您吗？我的运气好！"

"不，你从来没有说过，"母亲说。

然而，男孩在夜里死了。

甚至就是在他死的时候，母亲听到了她兄弟的声音："我的上帝。海斯特，你净赢80000多英镑，却输了可怜的儿子。但是可怜的家伙，可怜的家伙，他走得好，不用过骑木马去寻找赢家的生活了。"

D. H. Lawrence

The Shadow in the Rose Garden

This story tells about a young honeymoon couple. The husband is a laboring electrician in the mines. Considering him socially inferior, the wife keeps a cool and aloof attitude towards him, which makes him hateful and angry. On the first morning of her honeymoon, the young wife visits the familiar rose garden, which reminds her of the time spent there with a young soldier whom she believes to be dead. Before leaving the garden, however, she discovers that he is still alive but now a lunatic. She confesses her secret to her husband. Shocked not only by her last love affair but also by the fact of her past lover's madness, he can't help her stop her self-dissolution. It is considered a very symbolic story of high quality with super skills of constructing plots and depicting characters.

A rather small young man sat by the window of a pretty seaside cottage trying to persuade himself that he was reading the newspaper. It was about half-past eight in the morning. Outside, the glory roses hung in the morning sunshine like little bowls of fire tipped up. The young man looked at the table, then at the clock, then at his own big silver watch. An expression of stiff endurance came on to his face. Then he rose and reflected on the oil-paintings that hung on the walls of the room, giving careful but hostile attention to "The Stag at Bay". He tried the lid of the piano, and found it locked. He caught sight of his own face in a little mirror, pulled his brown moustache, and an alert interest sprang into his eyes. He was not ill-favoured. He twisted his moustache. His figure was rather small, but alert and vigorous. As he turned from the mirror a look of self-commiseration mingled with his appreciation of his own physiognomy.

In a state of self-suppression, he went through into the garden. His jacket, however, did not look dejected. It was new, and had a smart and self-confident air, sitting upon a confident body. He contemplated the Tree of Heaven that flourished by the lawn, then sauntered on to the next plant. There was more promise in a crooked apple tree covered with brown-red fruit. Glancing round, he broke off an apple and, with his back to the house, took a clean, sharp bite. To his surprise the fruit was sweet. He took another. Then again he turned to survey the bedroom windows overlooking the garden. He started, seeing a woman's figure; but it was only his wife. She was gazing across to the sea, apparently ignorant of him.

For a moment or two he looked at her, watching her. She was a good-looking woman, who seemed older than he, rather pale, but healthy, her face yearning. Her rich auburn hair was heaped in folds on her forehead. She looked apart from him and his world, gazing away to the sea. It irked her husband that she should continue abstracted and in ignorance of him; he pulled poppy fruits and threw them at the window. She started, glanced at him with a wild smile, and looked away again. Then almost immediately she left the window. He went indoors to meet her. She had a fine carriage, very proud, and wore a dress of soft white muslin.

"I've been waiting long enough," he said.

"For me or for breakfast?" she said lightly. "You know we said nine o'clock. I should have thought you could have slept after the journey."

"You know I'm always up at five, and I couldn't stop in bed after six. You might as well be in pit as in bed, on a morning like this."

"I shouldn't have thought the pit would occur to you, here."

She moved about examining the room, looking at the ornaments under glass covers. He, planted on the hearthrug, watched her rather uneasily, and grudgingly indulgent. She shrugged her shoulders at the apartment.

"Come," she said, taking his arm, "let us go into the garden till Mrs Coates brings the tray."

"I hope she'll be quick," he said, pulling his moustache. She gave a short laugh, and leaned on his arm as they went. He had lighted a pipe.

Mrs Coates entered the room as they went down the steps. The delightful, erect old lady hastened to the window for a good view of her visitors. Her china-blue eyes were bright as she watched the young couple go down the path, he walking in an easy, confident fashion, with his wife, on his arm. The landlady began talking to herself in a soft, Yorkshire accent.

"Just of a height they are. She wouldn't ha' married a man less than herself in stature, I think, though he's not her equal otherwise." Here her granddaughter came in, setting a tray on the table. The girl went to the old woman's side.

"He's been eating the apples, gran'," she said.

"Has he, my pet? Well, if he's happy, why not?"

Outside, the young, well-favoured man listened with impatience to the chink of the teacups. At last, with a sigh of relief, the couple came in to breakfast. After he had eaten for some time, he rested a moment and said:

"Do you think it's any better place than Bridlington?"

"I do," she said, "infinitely! Besides, I am at home here—it's not like a strange sea-side place to me."

"How long were you here?"

"Two years."

He ate reflectively.

"I should ha' thought you'd rather go to a fresh place," he said at length.

She sat very silent, and then, delicately, put out a feeler.

"Why?" she said. "Do you think I shan't enjoy myself?"

He laughed comfortably, putting the marmalade thick on his bread.

"I hope so," he said.

She again took no notice of him.

"But don't say anything about it in the village, Frank," she said casually. "Don't say who I am, or that I used to live here. There's nobody I want to meet, particularly, and we should never feel free if they knew me again."

"Why did you come, then?"

"'Why?' Can't you understand why?"

"Not if you don't want to know anybody."

"I came to see the place, not the people."

He did not say any more.

"Women," she said, "are different from men. I don't know why I wanted to come—but I did."

She helped him to another cup of coffee, solicitously.

"Only," she resumed, "don't talk about me in the village." She laughed shakily. "I don't want my past brought up against me, you know." And she moved the crumbs on the cloth with her finger-tip.

He looked at her as he drank his coffee; he sucked his moustache, and putting down his cup, said phlegmatically:

"I'll bet you've had a lot of past."

She looked with a little guiltiness, that flattered him, down at the tablecloth.

"Well," she said, caressive, "you won't give me away, who I am, will you?"

"No," he said, comforting, laughing, "I won't give you away."

He was pleased.

She remained silent. After a moment or two she lifted her head, saying:

"I've got to arrange with Mrs Coates, and do various things. So you'd better go out by yourself this morning—and we'll be in to dinner at one."

"But you can't be arranging with Mrs Coates all morning," he said.

"Oh, well—then I've some letters to write, and I must get that mark out of my skirt. I've got plenty of little things to do this morning. You'd better go out by yourself."

He perceived that she wanted to be rid of him, so that when she went upstairs, he took his hat and lounged out on to the cliffs, suppressedly angry.

Presently she too came out. She wore a hat with roses, and a long lace scarf hung over her white dress. Rather nervously, she put up her sunshade, and her face was half-hidden in its coloured shadow. She went along the narrow track of flag-stones that were worn hollow by the feet of the fishermen. She seemed to be avoiding her surroundings, as if she remained safe in the little obscurity of her parasol.

She passed the church, and went down the lane till she came to a high wall by the wayside. Under this she went slowly, stopping at length by an open doorway, which shone like a picture of light in the dark wall. There in the magic beyond the doorway, patterns of shadow lay on the sunny court, on the blue and white sea-pebbles of its paving, while a green lawn glowed beyond, where a bay tree glittered at the edges. She tiptoed nervously into the courtyard, glancing at the house that stood in shadow. The uncurtained windows looked black and soulless, the kitchen door stood open. Irresolutely she took a step forward, and again forward, leaning, yearning, towards the garden beyond.

She had almost gained the corner of the house when a heavy step came crunching through the trees. A gardener appeared before her. He held a wicker tray on which were rolling great, dark red gooseberries, overripe. He moved slowly.

"The garden isn't open today," he said quietly to the attractive woman, who was poised for retreat.

For a moment she was silent with surprise. How should it be public at all?

"When is it open?" she asked, quick-witted.

"The rector lets visitors in on Fridays and Tuesdays."

She stood still, reflecting. How strange to think of the rector opening his garden to the public!

"But everybody will be at church," she said coaxingly to the man. "There'll be nobody here, will there?"

He moved, and the big gooseberries rolled.

"The rector lives at the new rectory," he said.

The two stood still. He did not like to ask her to go. At last she turned to him with a winning smile.

"Might I have ONE peep at the roses?" she coaxed, with pretty wilfulness.

"I don't suppose it would matter," he said, moving aside: "you won't stop long—"

She went forward, forgetting the gardener in a moment. Her face became strained, her movements eager. Glancing round, she saw all the windows giving on to the lawn were curtainless and dark. The house had a sterile appearance, as if it were still used, but not inhabited. A shadow seemed to go over her. She went across the lawn towards the garden, through an arch of crimson ramblers, a gate of colour. There beyond lay the soft blue sea with the bay, misty with morning, and the farthest headland of black rock jutting dimly out between blue and blue of the sky and water. Her face began to shine, transfigured with pain and joy. At her feet the garden fell steeply, all a confusion of flowers, and away below was the darkness of tree-tops covering the beck.

She turned to the garden that shone with sunny flowers around her. She knew the little corner where was the seat beneath the yew tree. Then there was the terrace where a great host of flowers shone, and from this, two paths went down, one at each side of the garden. She closed her sunshade and walked slowly among the many flowers. All round were rose bushes, big banks of roses, then roses hanging and tumbling from pillars, or roses balanced on the standard bushes. By the open earth were many other flowers. If she lifted her head, the sea was upraised beyond, and the Cape.

Slowly she went down one path, lingering, like one who has gone back into the past. Suddenly she was touching some heavy crimson roses that were soft as velvet, touching them thoughtfully, without knowing, as a mother sometimes fondles the hand of her child. She leaned slightly forward to catch the scent. Then she wandered on in abstraction. Sometimes a flame-coloured, scentless rose would hold her arrested. She stood gazing at it as if she could not understand it. Again the same softness of intimacy came over her, as she stood before a tumbling heap of pink petals. Then she wondered over the white rose, that was greenish, like ice, in the centre. So, slowly, like a white, pathetic butterfly, she drifted down the path, coming at last to a tiny terrace all full of roses. They seemed to fill the place, a sunny, gay throng. She was shy of them, they were so many and so bright. They seemed to be conversing and laughing. She felt herself in a strange crowd. It exhilarated her, carried her out of herself. She flushed with excitement. The air was pure scent.

Hastily, she went to a little seat among the white roses, and sat down. Her scarlet sunshade made a hard blot of colour. She sat quite still, feeling her own existence lapse. She was no more than a rose, a rose that could not quite come into blossom, but remained tense. A little fly dropped on her knee, on her white dress. She watched it, as if it had fallen on a rose. She was not herself.

Then she started cruelly as a shadow crossed her and a figure moved into her sight. It was a man who had come in slippers, unheard. He wore a linen coat. The morning was shattered, the spell vanished away. She was only afraid of being questioned. He came forward. She rose. Then, seeing him, the strength went from her and she sank on the seat again.

He was a young man, military in appearance, growing slightly stout. His black hair was brushed smooth and bright, his moustache was waxed. But there was something rambling in his gait. She looked up, blanched to the lips, and saw his eyes. They were black, and stared without seeing. They were not a man's eyes. He was coming towards her.

He stared at her fixedly, made unconscious salute, and sat down beside her on the seat. He moved on the bench, shifted his feet, saying, in a gentlemanly, military voice:

"I don't disturb you—do I?"

She was mute and helpless. He was scrupulously dressed in dark clothes and a linen coat. She could not move. Seeing his hands, with the ring she knew so well upon the little finger, she felt as if she were going dazed. The whole world was deranged. She sat unavailing. For his hands, her symbols of passionate love, filled her with horror as they rested now on his strong thighs.

"May I smoke?" he asked intimately, almost secretly, his hand going to his pocket.

She could not answer, but it did not matter, he was in another world. She wondered, craving, if he recognized her—if he could recognize her. She sat pale with anguish. But she had to go through it.

"I haven't got any tobacco," he said thoughtfully.

But she paid no heed to his words, only she attended to him. Could he recognize her, or was it all gone? She sat still in a frozen kind of suspense.

"I smoke John Cotton," he said, "and I must economize with it, it is expensive. You know, I'm not very well off while these lawsuits are going on."

"No," she said, and her heart was cold, her soul kept rigid.

He moved, made a loose salute, rose, and went away. She sat motionless. She could see his shape, the shape she had loved, with all her passion: his compact, soldier's head, his fine figure now slackened. And it was not he. It only filled her with horror too difficult to know.

Suddenly he came again, his hand in his jacket pocket.

"Do you mind if I smoke?" he said. "Perhaps I shall be able to see things more clearly."

He sat down beside her again, filling a pipe. She watched his hands with the fine strong fingers. They had always inclined to tremble slightly. It had surprised her, long ago, in such a healthy man. Now they moved inaccurately, and the tobacco hung raggedly out of the pipe.

"I have legal business to attend to. Legal affairs are always so uncertain. I tell my solicitor exactly, precisely what I want, but I can never get it done."

She sat and heard him talking. But it was not he. Yet those were the hands she had kissed, there were the glistening, strange black eyes that she had loved. Yet it was not he. She sat motionless with horror and silence. He dropped his tobacco pouch, and groped for it on the ground. Yet she must wait if he would recognize her. Why could she not go! In a moment he rose.

"I must go at once," he said. "The owl is coming." Then he added confidentially: "His name isn't really the owl, but I call him that. I must go and see if he has come."

She rose too. He stood before her, uncertain. He was a handsome, soldierly fellow, and a lunatic. Her eyes searched him, and searched him, to see if he would recognize her, if she could discover him.

"You don't know me?" she asked, from the terror of her soul, standing alone.

He looked back at her quizzically. She had to bear his eyes. They gleamed on her, but with no intelligence. He was drawing nearer to her.

"Yes, I do know you," he said, fixed, intent, but mad, drawing his face nearer hers. Her horror was too great. The powerful lunatic was coming too near to her.

A man approached, hastening.

"The garden isn't open this morning," he said.

The deranged man stopped and looked at him. The keeper went to the seat and picked up the tobacco pouch left lying there.

"Don't leave your tobacco, sir," he said, taking it to the gentleman in the linen coat.

"I was just asking this lady to stay to lunch," the latter said politely. "She is a friend of mine."

The woman turned and walked swiftly, blindly, between the sunny roses, out of the garden, past the house with the blank, dark windows, through the sea-pebbled courtyard to the street. Hastening and blind, she went forward without hesitating, not knowing whither. Directly she came to the house she went upstairs, took off her hat, and sat down on the bed. It was as if some membrane had been torn in two in her, so that she was not an entity that could think and feel. She sat staring across at the window, where an ivy spray waved slowly up and down in the sea wind. There was some of the uncanny luminousness of the sunlit sea in the air. She sat perfectly still, without any being. She only felt she might be sick, and it might be blood that was loose in her torn entrails. She sat perfectly still and passive.

After a time she heard the hard tread of her husband on the floor below, and, without herself changing, she registered his movement. She heard his rather disconsolate footsteps go out again, then his voice speaking, answering, growing cheery, and his solid tread drawing near.

He entered, ruddy, rather pleased, an air of complacency about his alert figure. She moved stiffly. He faltered in his approach.

"What's the matter?" he asked, a tinge of impatience in his voice. "Aren't you feeling well?"

This was torture to her.

"Quite," she replied.

His brown eyes became puzzled and angry.

"What is the matter?" he said.

"Nothing."

He took a few strides, and stood obstinately, looking out of the window.

"Have you run up against anybody?" he asked.

"Nobody who knows me," she said.

His hands began to twitch. It exasperated him, that she was no more sensible of him than if he did not exist. Turning on her at length, driven, he asked:

"Something has upset you, hasn't it?"

"No, why?" she said neutral. He did not exist for her, except as an irritant.

His anger rose, filling the veins in his throat.

"It seems like it," he said, making an effort not to show his anger, because there seemed no reason for it. He went away downstairs. She sat still on the bed, and with the residue of feeling left to her, she disliked him because he tormented her. The time went by. She could smell the dinner being served, the smoke of her husband's pipe from the garden. But she could not move. She had no being. There was a tinkle of the bell. She heard him come indoors. And then he mounted the stairs again. At every step her heart grew tight in her. He opened the door.

"Dinner is on the table," he said.

It was difficult for her to endure his presence, for he would interfere with her. She could not recover her life. She rose stiffly and went down. She could neither eat nor talk during the meal. She sat absent, torn, without any being of her own. He tried to go on as if nothing were the matter. But at last he became silent with fury. As soon as it was possible, she went upstairs again, and locked the bedroom door. She must be alone. He went with his pipe into the garden. All his suppressed anger against her who held herself superior to him filled and blackened his heart. Though he had not known it, yet he had never really won her, she had never loved him. She had taken him on sufferance. This had foiled him. He was only a labouring electrician in the mine, she was superior to him. He had always given way to her. But all the while, the injury and ignominy had been working in his soul because she did not hold him seriously. And now all his rage came up against her.

He turned and went indoors. The third time, she heard him mounting the stairs. Her heart stood still. He turned the catch and pushed the door—it was locked. He tried it again, harder. Her heart was standing still.

"Have you fastened the door?" he asked quietly, because of the landlady.

"Yes. Wait a minute."

She rose and turned the lock, afraid he would burst it. She felt hatred towards him, because he did not leave her free. He entered, his pipe between his teeth, and she returned to her old position on the bed. He closed the door and stood with his back to it.

"What's the matter?" he asked determinedly.

She was sick with him. She could not look at him.

"Can't you leave me alone?" she replied, averting her face from him.

He looked at her quickly, fully, wincing with ignominy. Then he seemed to consider for a moment.

"There's something up with you, isn't there?" he asked definitely.

"Yes," she said, "but that's no reason why you should torment me."

"I don't torment you. What's the matter?"

"Why should you know?" she cried, in hate and desperation.

Something snapped. He started and caught his pipe as it fell from his mouth. Then he pushed forward the bitten-off mouth-piece with his tongue, took it from off his lips, and looked at it. Then he put out his pipe, and brushed the ash from his waistcoat. After which he raised his head.

"I want to know," he said. His face was greyish pale, and set uglily.

Neither looked at the other. She knew he was fired now. His heart was pounding heavily. She hated him, but she could not withstand him. Suddenly she lifted her head and turned on him.

"What right have you to know?" she asked.

He looked at her. She felt a pang of surprise for his tortured eyes and his fixed face. But her heart hardened swiftly. She had never loved him. She did not love him now.

But suddenly she lifted her head again swiftly, like a thing that tries to get free. She wanted to be free of it. It was not him so much, but it, something she had put on herself, that bound her so horribly. And having put the bond on herself, it was hardest to take it off. But now she hated everything and felt destructive. He stood with his back to the door, fixed, as if he would oppose her eternally, till she was extinguished. She looked at him. Her eyes were cold and hostile. His workman's hands spread on the panels of the door behind him.

"You know I used to live here?" she began, in a hard voice, as if wilfully to wound him. He braced himself against her, and nodded.

"Well, I was companion to Miss Birch of Torril Hall—she and the rector were friends, and Archie was the rector's son." There was a pause. He listened without knowing what was happening. He stared at his wife. She was squatted in her white dress on the bed, carefully folding and re-folding the hem of her skirt. Her voice was full of hostility.

"He was an officer—a sub-lieutenant—then he quarrelled with his colonel and came out of the army. At any rate"—she plucked at her skirt hem, her husband stood motionless, watching her movements which filled his veins with madness—"he was awfully fond of me, and I was of him—awfully."

"How old was he?" asked the husband.

"When—when I first knew him? Or when he went away?—"

"When you first knew him."

"When I first knew him, he was twenty-six—now—he's thirty-one— nearly thirty-two—because I'm twenty-nine, and he is nearly three years older—"

She lifted her head and looked at the opposite wall.

"And what then?" said her husband.

She hardened herself, and said callously:

"We were as good as engaged for nearly a year, though nobody knew—at least—they talked—but—it wasn't open. Then he went away—"

"He chucked you?" said the husband brutally, wanting to hurt her into contact with himself. Her heart rose wildly with rage. Then "Yes", she said, to anger him. He shifted from one foot to the other, giving a "Ph!" of rage. There was silence for a time.

"Then," she resumed, her pain giving a mocking note to her words, "he suddenly went out to fight in Africa, and almost the very day I first met you, I heard from Miss Birch he'd got sunstroke—and two months after, that he was dead—"

"That was before you took on with me?" said the husband.

There was no answer. Neither spoke for a time. He had not understood. His eyes were contracted uglily.

"So you've been looking at your old courting places!" he said. "That was what you wanted to go out by yourself for this morning."

Still she did not answer him anything. He went away from the door to the window. He stood with his hands behind him, his back to her. She looked at him. His hands seemed gross to her, the back of his head paltry.

At length, almost against his will, he turned round, asking:

"How long were you carrying on with him?"

"What do you mean?" she replied coldly.

"I mean how long were you carrying on with him?"

She lifted her head, averting her face from him. She refused to answer. Then she said:

"I don't know what you mean, by carrying on. I loved him from the first days I met him—two months after I went to stay with Miss Birch."

"And do you reckon he loved you?" he jeered.

"I know he did."

"How do you know, if he'd have no more to do with you?"

There was a long silence of hate and suffering.

"And how far did it go between you?" he asked at length, in a frightened, stiff voice.

"I hate your not-straightforward questions," she cried, beside herself with his baiting. "We loved each other, and we WERE lovers—we were. I don't care what YOU think: what have you got to do with it? We were lovers before ever I knew you—"

"Lovers—lovers," he said, white with fury. "You mean you had your fling with an army man, and then came to me to marry you when you'd done—"

She sat swallowing her bitterness. There was a long pause.

"Do you mean to say you used to go—the whole hogger?" he asked, still incredulous.

"Why, what else do you think I mean?" she cried brutally.

He shrank, and became white, impersonal. There was a long, paralysed silence. He seemed to have gone small.

"You never thought to tell me all this before I married you," he said, with bitter irony, at last.

"You never asked me," she replied.

"I never thought there was any need."

"Well, then, you SHOULD think."

He stood with expressionless, almost childlike set face, revolving many thoughts, whilst his heart was mad with anguish.

Suddenly she added:

"And I saw him today," she said. "He is not dead, he's mad."

Her husband looked at her, startled.

"Mad!" he said involuntarily.

"A lunatic," she said. It almost cost her her reason to utter the word. There was a pause.

"Did he know you?" asked the husband in a small voice.

"No," she said.

He stood and looked at her. At last he had learned the width of the breach between them. She still squatted on the bed. He could not go near her. It would be violation to each of them to be brought into contact with the other. The thing must work itself out. They were both shocked so much, they were impersonal, and no longer hated each other. After some minutes he left her and went out.

Questions

1. Explain the metaphorical meaning of the story's title. How do you understand the word "shadow" in the title?
2. The author described the rose garden in great detail. Why did he do this?
3. What does "the crooked apple tree" symbolize? Is this novel a symbolic one?
4. The husband was very angry and shocked when he learned the secret. Comment on the husband's reflection.
5. What do you think of the wife? Does she deserve readers' sympathy or condemnation?

玫瑰园中的影子

　　以下的短篇小说讲述了一对度蜜月的年轻夫妇的故事。丈夫是煤矿电工。妻子认为丈夫的地位低微，因此对他的态度冷漠、高傲，这使得丈夫十分恼火。在蜜月第一天的早上，妻子来到了熟悉的玫瑰园，回想起以前同一位年轻的士兵在此度过的美好时光。她一直都以为自己的情人已经死了。当她要离开时却发现以前的情人还活着，但现已变成了疯子。她向丈夫坦白了自己的秘密。丈夫为此感到十分的震惊，却又无法使妻子释怀。该短篇小说被认为是一篇充满象征主义手法的上乘之作，展示了劳伦斯在设计情节和刻画人物方面的高超技艺。

　　海边一座漂亮的别墅窗边，坐着一位身材相当瘦小的年轻人，他正耐着性子看报纸。这时大约是早上八点半。窗外，绚丽的玫瑰沐浴在晨光之中，犹如一只只碗状小火球翘立枝头。年轻人看看桌子，又看看钟，再看看自己的大银表，脸上显出越来越不耐烦的表情。接着，他站起来，开始打量墙上挂着的油画，对那幅名为《走投无路的牡鹿》的画特别感兴趣，但充满了挑剔的神情。他想把钢琴盖打开，却发现是锁着的。他无意中在一面小镜子里看见了自己的面孔，便捋了一下棕色的胡须，人也立刻来了精神。他长得不难看。他又整了整胡子。他的身材相当矮小，人却机敏、有活力。他从镜子前转过身去，对自己的相貌感到既自怜又欣赏。

　　他克制着自己的情绪走进了花园。不过，他的外套看上去可够精神的。衣服是新的，穿在他那充满自信的身上，显得既帅气又神气十足。他仔细打量了一会儿草地旁边一棵繁茂的臭椿树，然后漫步走向另一棵树。枝条弯曲的苹果树上结满了深红色的果实。他向四周望了望，摘下一个苹果，背对着房子，很干脆地咬了一口。令他惊讶的是苹果很甜。于是他又咬了一口。然后他转过身去，打量起花园对面的卧室窗户来。他突然看到一个女人的身影，不觉吃了一惊。但那只不过是他的妻子。她正向大海的方向眺望，但很显然并没有注意到他。

　　有好一会儿，他看着她，观察着她。她是个美貌女子，看起来年龄比他大，面色很苍白，但很健康。脸上露出渴望的神情。她一头浓密、红褐色的头发蓬松、卷曲着堆在额头。她凝视着大海，没有理会他和他的世界。她是如此的忘我，全然没有理会自己丈夫的存在。这使他十分恼怒。他摘下几个深红色的果子，朝窗户那边扔过去。她吃了一惊，满脸微笑地扫了他一眼，随后又把目光移开了。随后她几乎是马上离开了窗口。他走进屋子里去见她。她身材匀称，神态高傲，穿着一身柔软的白色细布衣裙。

"我已经等很久了，"他说。

"是等我，还是等吃早餐？"她轻声地问道。"我们说好了九点钟碰头的。我本以为旅行之后你该多睡一会儿的。"

"你知道我一直是五点钟起床，过了六点，我就再也睡不着了。像今天这样的早晨，懒在床上还不如下井呢。"

"想不到在这个地方你也竟然会想到矿坑。"

她在房间里来回走动，到处察看着，看着玻璃罩下面的小摆设。他站在壁炉前的地毯上注视着她，相当不自在，流露出勉强的宽容。她对着房间耸了耸肩膀。

"走吧，"她说着，挽起他的手臂。"我们先到花园里去，等科茨太太准备好早餐再进来。"

"希望她能快一点儿。"他整理了下胡须，说道。她短促地笑了一声，便依偎在他的手臂上一起走了出去。他已点燃了烟斗。

他们刚走下台阶，科茨太太就走进了房间。这个老太太，腰板挺直，讨人喜欢。她快步走到窗前，好更仔细地打量她的房客。瞧着这对年轻夫妇沿着小道走过去，她那青瓷色的眼睛亮了起来。那个男人挽着妻子，神态轻松而又自信。女房东用她那约克郡口音轻声地自言自语道：

"他们俩儿刚好一般高。我就知道她是不会嫁给一个比她矮的男人的，不过，其他方面他可配不上她。"这时，她的孙女儿走了进来，把一个托盘放在桌子上。女孩走到老太太身边。

"奶奶，他吃我们的苹果了，"她说。

"是吗？宝贝，是这样，要是他高兴，就让他吃好了。"

屋子外面，那位一表人才的年轻人不耐烦地倾听着屋里茶杯的叮当声。最后，长舒一口气，二人一起进屋吃早饭了。吃了一会儿，他停下来，说道：

"你觉得这个地方就是比布赖德林顿好？"

"当然好了，"她说，"绝对是个好地方！而且，我在这里感到亲切、自在——对我来说这里不像是海边某个陌生的地方。"

"你过去在这里住了多久？"

"两年。"

他吃着饭，若有所思。

"我还以为你更愿意去个新地方呢，"他终于说道。

她坐在那儿，沉默不语，然后，小心翼翼地试探着。

"为什么这么说？"她说。"你认为我在这里会不开心？"

他满意地笑起来，在面包上抹了厚厚一层果酱。

"希望你开心，"他说。

她又不大注意他了。

"不过，你在村子里什么都别说，弗兰克，"她漫不经心地说道，"别说我是谁，或者我曾经在这里住过。我没有特别想要见的人。要是那些人认出了我，我们就不再那么自在了。"

"既然这样，那你为什么还要到这里来呢？"

"为什么？难道你不明白为什么？"

"不明白，如果你谁都不想见。"

"我来是为了看看这个地方，不是来看人。"

他没再说话。

"女人，"她说，"跟男人不一样。我也不知道自己为什么要来——可我还是来了。"

她周到地又给他倒了一杯咖啡。

"只是，"她接着说，"在村子里别说起我，"她不安地笑了笑。"你知道，我可不愿意听别人提起过去令人不快的事。"说着，她用指尖收拾着桌布上的面包屑。

他边喝咖啡边望着她，然后捋了捋小胡子，放下杯子，冷冷地说：

"我敢说你有好多事瞒着我。"

她有点内疚地低头盯着桌布，这使他感到很受用。

"那么，"她轻柔地说，"你不会说出我是谁，是吧？"

"不会，"他说道，边安慰她，边笑了起来，"我不会说的。"

他感到高兴。

她一直沉默不语。过了好一会儿，她抬起头说：

"我要跟科茨太太安排一下，好多事儿要做。所以今天早晨你就一个人出去吧——我们一点钟回到这里吃午饭。"

"可是，你跟科茨太太不会用一个上午做安排吧？"他说。

"噢，还有——我还得写几封信，把裙子上的那块污迹洗掉。上午我有一大堆琐事要做。你还是自个儿出去吧。"

他看出来她是一心要摆脱他。于是，等她上楼后，他便拿起帽子，克制着内心的恼怒，朝着悬崖那边慢慢溜达过去。

不一会儿，她也出门了。她戴着一顶插满玫瑰花的帽子，还在白裙上围了一条蕾丝纱巾。她有些紧张地打开了一把阳伞，把她的脸半遮在阳伞的彩色阴影下。她沿着一条狭窄的石板路走着，那些石板已经被渔民们踩得凹下去了。她像是在逃避着周围的一切，仿佛只有躲在阳伞的阴影下她才感到安全。

她走过教堂，穿过小巷，径直走到路边的一堵高墙前。她在墙下慢慢地移动着脚步，最后在一扇敞开的大门前停下来。在黑色墙的衬托下，那个门洞就像是色彩鲜艳的一幅画。门洞里是一片奇妙的景象，形状各异的阴影印在洒满阳光的院子里和蓝白两色卵石铺砌的地面上，再过去是一片绿意盎然的草坪，长在草坪边上的一株月桂树，枝叶闪闪发光。她踮脚紧张地走进院子，瞥了一眼树荫里的那幢房子。窗子都没有挂窗帘，看上去黑漆漆的，没有生气。厨房的门敞开着。她犹犹豫豫地向前迈了一步，然后又迈了一步，身体前倾，满怀渴望，走向那边的花园。

　　当她几乎就要走到屋子的拐角时，听到一阵沉重的脚步声从树丛中传来。一个园丁出现在她面前。他托着一只柳条编成的托盘，盘里滚动着一些大个的、熟透了的紫红色醋栗。他走得很慢。

　　"今天花园不开放。"他静静地对着这位迷人的妇人说。这时，她正犹豫着准备退回去。

　　好半天她惊讶得沉默不语。这座花园怎么会对外开放呢？

　　"它什么时候开放？"她灵机一动，开口问道。

　　"教区长允许人们在星期五和星期二时参观。"

　　她站着没动，考虑着园丁的话。教区长向公众开放他的花园，这是多么奇怪的事啊！

　　"不过，所有人都会到教堂去。"她故意对那个男人说，"这里就没人了，是不是？"

　　他动了一下，那些大醋栗也跟着滚动着。

　　"教区长搬到新房子去住了，"他说。

　　两个人都原地站着。他不想开口请她离开。最后，她转身给他一个迷人的微笑。

　　"可以让我看看那些玫瑰吗，就一眼？"她央求着，口气动人而任性。

　　"我想那该没什么问题，"他说着，身子闪到一边。"你不会待太久——"

　　她向前走过去，转眼便把园丁忘在脑后。她的脸色变得紧张，动作也急促起来。她向四周看去，注意到所有面向草坪的窗户都没有挂窗帘，黑漆漆的。房子呈现出一派荒凉的景象，好像人们还在使用它，却又无人居住。一丝阴影好像掠过她的心头。她穿过草坪向花园走去，穿过一道爬满了紫红色蔷薇的拱门，这是一道彩色的大门。海湾就在最尽头处，蒙蒙晨雾中，海水轻柔地荡漾着，最远处的海峡满是黑色岩石，在蓝天碧海的相交之处，凸现出模糊的轮廓。她的脸开始泛出光辉，痛苦和欢乐交织在一起。花园在她的脚下变得陡峭起来，向下倾斜，斜坡上到处是五颜六色的鲜花，远处，在黑压压一片树木的遮盖之下，一条小溪流淌而过。

她向花园转过身去，她的四周满是在阳光下盛开的鲜花。她还记得花园的某个角落里，一棵紫杉树下有一个座位。那边还有一个长满鲜花的花圃。从这个地方开始，有两条小路通向花园的两侧。她合起阳伞，漫步在花丛中间。周围全是玫瑰花丛，有大片的玫瑰，还有从柱子上垂挂下来的玫瑰，以及种植得整整齐齐、花枝漂亮的玫瑰花丛。园里的空地上还栽种着其他的鲜花。如果她抬起头，就能望见远处突起的大海，还有海角。

她沿着一条小路慢慢地走过去，在那里徘徊着，像是回到了过去。突然，她伸手触摸着一些深红的玫瑰花，感觉花儿柔软得就像丝绒一样。她抚摸着花朵，犹如母亲在不知不觉中亲抚孩子的小手一般。她向前微微弯下身子去嗅花香。然后，她又慢慢地、随意地继续前行。有时，她会被一株没有香气、颜色火红的玫瑰所吸引。于是她就站在那里，盯着它看，仿佛她从不认识似的。而有时，当她站在一大丛粉红色的花朵前面时，同样温柔的亲切感也会涌上心头。接着她又惊叹于那株洁白的玫瑰，它的中间部分像冰一般晶莹剔透，还带点浅绿色。就这样，慢慢地，她像一只多愁善感的蝴蝶，在小路上飞着，最后飞到一个长满玫瑰的露台前面。鲜艳、明快的花朵，似乎把露台挤得满满的。这使她感到羞怯，玫瑰花是这么茂盛，这么绚丽。花儿仿佛在相互倾谈、嬉笑。她感觉自己好像置身于陌生人群中。同时，玫瑰花又令她欢欣鼓舞，心花怒放。她兴奋得脸色绯红。这儿的空气清新宜人。

她快步来到白玫瑰花丛中的一把小椅子前，坐了下来。她那把大红色的阳伞在花丛中显得格外惹人注目。她一动不动地坐着，觉得自己的生命在流逝。她只不过是一朵玫瑰，一朵充满期待却又无法开放的玫瑰。一只小苍蝇飞落在她的膝上，又停在她的白裙上。她看着苍蝇，仿佛它落在了一朵玫瑰花上。她完全忘却了自己。

这时一个影子从她的身前晃过，吓了她一跳。一个人走进她的视线。那人穿着拖鞋，走路悄无声息。他穿着一件亚麻布做的外套。早晨的气氛顷刻瓦解，其魔力荡然无存。她害怕别人盘问她。他走上前来，她站起身来。可是一看见他，她顿时全身无力，又跌坐在椅子上。

来者是个年轻人，外表像军人，身材稍微有些发胖。他乌黑的头发梳理得光滑而整齐，胡子上涂了蜡。但是他的步伐却显得不太灵活。她嘴唇发白，向上望，看见了他的眼睛。那双眼睛黑黑的，直瞪瞪的，却没有神采，不像男子汉的眼神。他朝她走来。

他直勾勾地盯着她，下意识地打了个招呼，就在她旁边坐下。他在长椅上动来动去，两只脚不停地挪动着，用一种既绅士又不失军人风度的口吻说道：

"我没打扰你吧?"

她说不出话,浑身瘫软。他的衣着相当讲究,穿一件黑色衣服和亚麻外套。她动弹不得。她看见了他的手,小指上戴着那只她非常熟悉的戒指,她觉得自己简直要晕过去了。整个世界都混乱了。她无奈地坐在那里。那象征着她狂热爱情的双手,现在正放在他健壮的大腿上,令她内心充满了恐惧。

"我可以吸烟吗?"他用亲热的、几乎是神神秘秘的口吻问道,同时把手伸进了口袋。

她无法回答,但那没关系,他生活在另一个世界里。她满心疑虑,又充满渴望,不知他是否认出了她——是否还能认出她。她痛苦地坐在那里,脸色苍白。可是,她又不得不忍受这一切。

"我没有烟丝了,"他若有所思地说。

但是她没有注意他说的话,只是仔细地打量着他。他还能认出她来吗?还是什么都忘了?她一动不动,不安地期待着。

"我吸的是约翰·科顿牌烟丝,"他说道,"这种烟丝很贵,所以我不得不省着点。你知道,这些诉讼案子不结束,我的生活就不能好过。"

"是啊,"她说。她的心都凉了,魂儿僵硬。

他动了动,随意做了个敬礼的姿势,就走开了。她坐着,一动不动。她仍看得出他的身型,那副她曾经痴心热恋过的身躯:结实、军人般的头颅,那曾经匀称的身材现在已经走形了。可这并不是他。她内心充满恐惧,无法理解。

他突然又走了回来,手插在外套口袋里。

"你不介意我吸烟吧?"他说,"这样也许我就能把事情看得更清楚一些。"

他重新在她身边坐下,装满烟斗。她注视着他那双手,手指匀称而有力。那双手过去就一直容易微微地发抖。很久以前她就曾对此感到惊讶,不懂为什么这么健康的人手会抖。而现在,那双手移动着,不听使唤,烟丝散乱地挂到了烟斗外面。

"我有些官司要打,但法律官司是谁也说不准的。我把我的要求完全、清楚地告诉律师了,可就是办不成事。"

她坐在那里听他说着。但这并不是他。可是,这双手就是她曾亲吻过的,这双发亮、奇特的黑眼睛也是她曾爱过的。然而,这并不是他。她静静地坐在那里,充满恐惧,默默无语。他把烟口袋弄掉了,便在地上摸索着。可她还是想等一等,看看他是否还认得她。她为什么就不走呢!过了片刻,他站起身来。

"我得马上走了,"他说,"猫头鹰要来了。"随后,他又悄悄地说:"他的真名并不叫猫头鹰,那是我给他起的外号。我得去看看他是不是已经来了。"

她也站了起来。他站在她面前,犹豫不决。他帅气、有军人气质,却是个疯子。她用眼睛盯着他,一遍一遍地盯着他,想看看他还能否认得她,想知道自己是否还能发现原来的他。

"你不认识我?"她站在一边,从心底里感到害怕。

他回过头来疑惑地看着她。她只得直视投来的目光。他两眼闪亮,使劲儿盯着她,可目光里却没有灵性。他向她靠近。

"对,我认识你。"他目不转睛地盯着她,专注而又疯狂,把自己的脸凑过来,离她更近了。她吓坏了。这个强壮的疯子离她实在太近了。

一个男人急匆匆走了过来。

"今天早上花园不对外开放,"他说。

那个精神病人停了下来,看着他。管理员走到椅子跟前,拾起掉在那儿的烟口袋。

"先生,别把你的烟丝掉在这儿,"他说着把烟口袋交给了这位穿亚麻布外套的先生。

"我正要请这位女士留下来一起吃午饭呢,"这位先生彬彬有礼地说,"她是我的一位朋友。"

这位女子转身飞快地离开了,她盲目地穿过鲜艳的玫瑰花丛,走出花园,走过那幢没挂窗帘、窗户黑洞洞的房屋,穿过铺着鹅卵石的院子,直走到大街上。她匆忙而盲目地朝前走着,没有犹豫,也不知道自己要到哪里去。她一回到别墅,便走上楼,摘下帽子,一下子坐到床上。她觉得仿佛自己身上的一些内膜组织被撕成了两半,感觉自己就像个没有思想、没有感觉的人。她坐在那里呆呆地望着窗口,那里有条常青藤的枝蔓正在海风的吹拂下慢慢地上下摇摆。天空中是从阳光照耀的海水中反射出来的奇异的光芒。她静静地坐在那里,好像灵魂出窍一般。她只觉得自己要生病了,鲜血从被撕裂的五脏六腑中流出。她静静地坐在那里,什么都不想做。

过了一会儿,她听见丈夫在楼下走动,脚步声很重;她依旧坐着不动,注意着丈夫的动静。她听见他那相当沮丧的脚步声又出去了,然后是他说话的声音和回答别人的声音,后来又是变得开心起来的声音,接着那踏实的脚步声又走近了。

他走了进来,面色红润,相当高兴,敏捷的身躯透露出一种自得的神态。她呆板地动了一下。他走过来,略显迟疑。

"你怎么了?"他问道,口气中略微有一丝不耐烦。"你不舒服?"

这话对她来说无异于一种折磨。

"很不舒服。"

他的棕色眼睛现出困惑和愤怒的神情。

"发生了什么事？"他说。

"没事。"

他向前走了几步，固执地站在那里，眼睛望着窗外。

"你见到什么人了吗？"他问。

"没遇到认识我的人，"她说。

他的手抽搐起来。她对他根本不理不睬，就好像他不存在一样，这使他异常愤怒。终于迫不得已，他对她发火了：

"你遇到了烦心事，是不是？"

"没有。怎么可能？"她无动于衷地答道。在她心里，他除了令人生厌外，根本就不存在。

他怒火中烧，脖子上青筋暴起。

"看起来像是有事，"他说着，努力克制自己不露出怒气，因为他好像没有理由发脾气。他离开，下了楼。而她仍坐在床上，心情还没有完全恢复平静。她讨厌他，因为他老是折磨她。时间就这样过去了。她闻到午餐开始了，还闻到丈夫在花园里吸烟。但是她动弹不得，像是没了魂儿。铃声叮咚响起来。她听见丈夫进了屋。接着他又一次走上楼来。他每走一步，她的心便跟着紧一下。他打开了房门。

"该吃饭了，"他说。

她真受不了丈夫在眼前，因为他老在打扰她。她不能恢复正常的生活。她僵硬地站了起来，走下楼去。吃午餐时，她既没胃口吃饭，也没心情讲话。她坐在那里，心绪不宁、痛苦万分，像是丢了魂儿。他则竭力装出若无其事的样子。然而，到后来，他也变得沉默了，一肚子火气。她很快就借机离开，又回到楼上，还锁上了卧室的门。她必须独自待一会儿。他叼着烟斗去了花园。她对他那种高人一等的态度使他异常愤怒。他克制住怒火，但内心却灰暗沉重。他这一刻才认识到自己从来没有真的得到她，她也从来没有爱过他。她只是勉强嫁给他而已。这使他很受打击。他只不过是矿上出苦力的电工，她条件比他优越。他一直都依着她。但她一直没把他当回事，那种受伤害和受羞辱的感觉越来越强烈。现在，他满腔的怒火都涌上心头。

他回身走进屋子。她第三次听见他上楼的脚步声。她的心跳好像都停了。他扭动门把手，推门——门锁着。他又试了一下，更用力地推门。她的心跳都停了。

"你锁门了吗？"他怕房东太太听见，便轻声问道。

"锁着，等一会儿。"

她害怕他会硬闯进来，于是起身把门锁打开。她心里恨他，因为他老是缠着她。他走了进来，嘴里叼着烟斗。她又回到床上像刚才那样坐着。他把门关上，背对着门站着。

"到底发生了什么事？"他毅然决然地问。

他是那么令人生厌，她一眼都不想看他。

"你就不能让我一个人待会儿？"她把脸扭向一旁。

他飞快地正面看了她一眼，觉得羞愧，马上没了气势。接着他看起来好像思索了一会儿。

"你有事瞒着我，是不是？"他很有把握地问。

"是的，"她说道，"可你不能因为这事就来折磨我。"

"我没折磨你。到底怎么回事儿？"

"你干嘛要知道？"她愤恨而绝望地喊道。

啪的一声，什么东西断了。他吃了一惊，烟斗从嘴里掉了下来，他赶紧接住。接着他用舌头把咬断的烟嘴推了出来，用手从嘴里拿下来，看了一眼。他把烟斗熄灭，又掸了掸背心上的灰，然后抬起头。

"我想知道，"他说道，脸色灰白，面目丑陋。

他们谁都不看对方。她知道他现在是真的动怒了。他的心重重地跳着。她恨他，可又无法抵制。突然，她抬起头对他大声说。

"你有什么权力要知道我的事？"她问道。

他看着她。看着他痛苦的眼神和呆滞的脸，她感到一阵惊讶。但她的心很快又硬起来。她从来就没有爱过他，现在仍然不爱他。

可是突然她又飞快地昂起头，像是要获得自由。她想摆脱某种束缚。这个束缚不是因为他，而是她强加给自己的，可怕地束缚着她。自己强加的束缚是最难摆脱的。她现在仇恨一切，又想毁灭一切。他背对着房门，立在那里，好像要和她一直抗争到底，直到她消亡。她看着他，目光冷漠，充满敌意。他那双做工的手平放在身后的门板上。

"你知道我过去在这儿住过？"她用生硬的口气说道，仿佛故意要伤害他。

他点了点头，打起精神准备对付她。

"我那时在托里尔庄园给伯奇小姐当女伴——她和教区长是朋友，阿奇是教区长的儿子。"她停顿了一下。他倾听着，不知所措，只是瞪着妻子。妻子穿着白裙，蹲坐在床上，小心地把裙边折来折去。她的嗓音充满了敌意。

"他是个军官——一个陆军少尉——后来跟上校发生了争吵，便离开了陆军。不管怎么说，"——她摆弄着裙边，丈夫站在那里，一动不动，注视着她，她的这些举动令他发疯——"他非常爱我，我也爱他——非常爱他。"

"他当时多大？"丈夫问道。

"是——是我刚认识他的时候？还是他离开的时候？"

"你刚认识他的时候。"

"刚认识他时，他26岁——现在——该有31岁——差不多32岁吧——我现在29岁，他差不多比我大3岁。"

她抬起了头，看着对面的墙壁。

"那后来呢？"丈夫问道。

她硬起心肠，冷冰冰地说道：

"差不多一年，我们几乎算是订了婚，尽管别人都不知道——至少——人们在背地里议论过——可是——没有公开过。后来他走掉了——"

"他抛弃了你？"丈夫冷酷地说，故意伤她的心，想让她和自己大吵大闹。怒火在她心底升起。为了激怒他，她说"是的"。他把身体重心从一只脚移到另一只，盛怒中"呸"了一声。有一会儿他们谁都不说话。

"后来，"她接着说道，痛苦使她的话里有了点嘲讽的味道。"他突然到非洲去打仗了。几乎正是在那一天我第一次遇到你。后来伯奇小姐告诉我，他在非洲中了暑——两个月后，他死了——"

"那都是在你跟我要好以前发生的事吧？"丈夫说道。

没有回答。有好一会儿两人都没说话。他感到茫然，双眼紧缩，面目可憎。

"这么说，你今天是去故地重游、重温旧情啰！"他说，"难怪你今天早上想自己出去。"

她还是没回答任何问话。他从门口走到窗边，站在那里，手放在背后，身子背对着她。她看着他，他的手看起来丑陋不堪，后脑勺也令人生厌。

最后，他极不情愿地转过身问道：

"你和他在一块儿调情有多长时间？"

"你什么意思？"她冷冷地回答。

"我的意思是，你和他调情有多长的时间？"

她抬起头，把脸转过去不去看他。她拒绝回答。后来她说道：

"我不明白你说的'调情'是什么意思。但我可以告诉你，从最初遇见他的日子里我就爱上了他——就是我和伯奇小姐在一起两个月以后。"

"你肯定他爱你吗？"他讥讽道。

"我知道他爱我。"

"他已经和你分开了，你怎么知道？"

接下来是一段长时间的沉默，充满了仇恨和痛苦。

"你们两人的关系发展到什么程度？"他终于问道，语气胆怯而生硬。

"我讨厌你这些转弯抹角的问题，"她喊道，对他的试探忍无可忍。"我们曾彼此相爱，我们曾是情人——是的。我不在乎你是怎么想的：这事和你没关系，在认识你之前我们就是情人——"

"情人——情人，"他说道，脸色煞白。"你是说，你跟那个当兵的有过一腿，做出那种事以后才来找我娶你——"

她坐在那里，吞咽着内心的苦楚。长时间的沉默。

"你是说，你们过去经常——经常干那事儿？"他仍然有些怀疑地问道。

"当然了，你以为我还会有别的意思？"她冷酷地嚷道。

他泄气了，脸色苍白，表情也变得冷漠起来。一阵长久的、令人窒息的沉默。他的身材似乎显得更小了。

"在我娶你之前你从来就没想过要把这一切告诉我，"终于，他用辛辣的嘲讽口吻说道。

"你也没问过我。"她回答道。

"我从来没想过有这个必要。"

"是吗？那么，你应该想到的。"

他站在那里，面孔如孩子似的无助，毫无表情，头脑里却思绪纷杂，一腔怒火令他要发狂。

突然她又加了一句。

"我今天看见他了，"她说。"他没死，不过疯了。"

丈夫看着她，感到震惊。

"疯了！"他不由自主地说道。

"是个精神病，"她说。她好不容易才说出这句话，这几乎令她崩溃。又一阵沉默。

"他认出你了？"丈夫小声问道。

"没有。"她说。

他站在那里，看着她。终于，他弄清楚他们之间的裂痕有多深了。她仍然蹲坐在床上。他没法走近她。他们之间任何争吵对彼此都是伤害。这事只能顺其自然了。他们两人都受到强烈的震撼，此时都冷静下来，不再怨恨对方。过了几分钟，他丢下她走了出去。

Katherine Mansfield
(1888—1923)

Katherine Mansfield, originally named Kathleen Mansfield Beauchamp, is a prominent modern short story writer noted for her distinctive prose style with poetic overtones. She was born and brought up in colonial New Zealand, and then left for England at the age of 19, where she encountered Modernist writers such as D. H. Lawrence and Virginia Woolf with whom she became close friends. During the First World War Mansfield contracted extrapulmonary tuberculosis which made her return to New Zealand impossible and led to her death at the age of 34.

Mansfield's early stories are collected in *In a German Pension* (1911) which reflects her initial disillusion with human relationship in modern times. *Prelude* (1918) includes a series of beautifully evocative stories of her family memories of New Zealand. *Bliss* (1920) secured her reputation as a short story writer with her typical art. Mansfield achieved the height of her artistic power in *The Garden, and Other Stories* (1922), which includes the stories such as "Her First Ball," "The Garden Party, " "At the Bay," "The Voyage," "The Stranger," and the short story classic "Daughters of the Late Colonel," a subtle account of the genteel frustration. Her delicate stories focus on the psychological conflicts in the characters. Under certain influence of Chekhov, her stories are often characterized by the obliqueness of narration and subtlety of observation, which in turn much influenced the development of the short story as an independent literary form.

Her First Ball

The following is a story about Leila, a country girl who first attends a ball in the city. She is fascinated by all the hustle and bustle of the city, and the Sheridan girls' fashion and fad equally attract her. The ball is even more dazzling with all the decorations, furnishing, music and dancers. Excitedly, eagerly and a little self-contemptuously, she waits for her dance partners. Her young dance partners do not seem very interesting, and then comes along the old fat man. The old man is very skilful in dance and experienced in life.

Everything seems fine till the old man mentions how time passes and soon all the youth and attraction will be gone, and then Leila suddenly gets depressed. But very soon she resumes her gaiety and radiance. The story reveals a thrilling truth of the sensational passage of time, and yet youth triumphs temporarily.

Exactly when the ball began Leila would have found it hard to say. Perhaps her first real partner was the cab. It did not matter that she shared the cab with the Sheridan girls and their brother. She sat back in her own little corner of it, and the bolster on which her hand rested felt like the sleeve of an unknown young man's dress suit; and away they bowled, past waltzing lamp-posts and houses and fences and trees.

"Have you really never been to a ball before, Leila? But, my child, how too weird—" cried the Sheridan girls.

"Our nearest neighbour was fifteen miles," said Leila softly, gently opening and shutting her fan.

Oh dear, how hard it was to be indifferent like the others! She tried not to smile too much; she tried not to care. But every single thing was so new and exciting... Meg's tuberoses, Jose's long loop of amber, Laura's little dark head, pushing above her white fur like a flower through snow. She would remember for ever. It even gave her a pang to see her cousin Laurie throw away the wisps of tissue paper he pulled from the fastenings of his new gloves. She would like to have kept those wisps as a keepsake, as a remembrance. Laurie leaned forward and put his hand on Laura's knee.

"Look here, darling," he said. "The third and the ninth as usual. Twig?"

Oh, how marvellous to have a brother! In her excitement Leila felt that if there had been time, if it hadn't been impossible, she couldn't have helped crying because she was an only child and no brother had ever said "Twig?" to her; no sister would ever say, as Meg said to Jose that moment, "I've never known your hair go up more successfully than it has to-night!"

But, of course, there was no time. They were at the drill hall already; there were cabs in front of them and cabs behind. The road was bright on either side with moving fan-like lights, and on the pavement gay couples seemed to float through the air; little satin shoes chased each other like birds.

"Hold on to me, Leila; you'll get lost," said Laura.

"Come on, girls, let's make a dash for it," said Laurie.

Leila put two fingers on Laura's pink velvet cloak, and they were somehow lifted past the big golden lantern, carried along the passage, and pushed into the little room marked "Ladies." Here the crowd was so great there was hardly space to take off their things; the noise was deafening. Two benches on either side were stacked high with wraps. Two old women in white aprons ran up and down tossing fresh armfuls. And everybody was pressing forward trying to get at the little dressing-table and mirror at the far end.

A great quivering jet of gas lighted the ladies' room. It couldn't wait; it was dancing already. When the door opened again and there came a burst of tuning from the drill hall, it leaped almost to the ceiling.

Dark girls, fair girls were patting their hair, tying ribbons again, tucking handkerchiefs down the fronts of their bodices, smoothing marble-white gloves. And because they were all laughing it seemed to Leila that they were all lovely.

"Aren't there any invisible hair-pins?" cried a voice. "How most extraordinary! I can't see a single invisible hair-pin."

"Powder my back, there's a darling," cried some one else.

"But I must have a needle and cotton. I've torn simply miles and miles of the frill," wailed a third.

Then, "Pass them along, pass them along!" The straw basket of programmes was tossed from arm to arm. Darling little pink-and-silver programmes, with pink pencils and fluffy tassels. Leila's fingers shook as she took one out of the basket. She wanted to ask someone, "Am I meant to have one too?" but she had just time to read: "Waltz 3. *Two, Two in a Canoe*. Polka 4. *Making the Feathers Fly*," when Meg cried, "Ready, Leila?" and they pressed their way through the crush in the passage towards the big double doors of the drill hall.

Dancing had not begun yet, but the band had stopped tuning, and the noise was so great it seemed that when it did begin to play it would never be heard. Leila, pressing close to Meg, looking over Meg's shoulder, felt that even the little quivering coloured flags strung across the ceiling were talking. She quite forgot to be shy; she forgot how in the middle of dressing she had sat down on the bed with one shoe off and one shoe on and begged her mother to ring up her cousins and say she couldn't go after all. And the rush of longing she had had to be sitting on the veranda of their forsaken up-country home, listening to the baby owls crying "More pork" in the moonlight, was changed to a rush of joy so sweet that it was hard to bear alone. She clutched her fan, and, gazing at the gleaming, golden floor, the azaleas, the lanterns, the stage at one end with its red carpet and gilt chairs and the band in a corner, she thought breathlessly, "How heavenly; how simply heavenly!"

All the girls stood grouped together at one side of the doors, the men at the other, and the chaperones in dark dresses, smiling rather foolishly, walked with little careful steps over the polished floor towards the stage.

"This is my little country cousin Leila. Be nice to her. Find her partners; she's under my wing," said Meg, going up to one girl after another.

Strange faces smiled at Leila—sweetly, vaguely. Strange voices answered, "Of course, my dear." But Leila felt the girls didn't really see her. They were looking towards the men. Why didn't the men begin? What were they waiting for? There they stood, smoothing their gloves, patting their glossy hair and smiling among themselves. Then, quite suddenly, as if they had only just made up their minds that that was what they had to do, the men came gliding over the parquet. There was a joyful flutter among the girls. A tall, fair man flew up to Meg, seized her programme, scribbled something; Meg passed him on to Leila. "May I have the pleasure?" He ducked and smiled. There came a dark man wearing an eyeglass, then cousin Laurie with a friend, and Laura with a little freckled fellow whose tie was crooked. Then quite an old man—fat, with a big bald patch on his head—took her programme and murmured, "Let me see, let me see!" And he was a long time comparing his programme, which looked black with names, with hers. It seemed to give him so much trouble that Leila was ashamed. "Oh, please don't bother," she said eagerly. But instead of replying the fat man wrote something, glanced at her again. "Do I remember this bright little face?" he said softly. "Is it known to me of yore?" At that moment the band began playing; the fat man disappeared. He was tossed away on a great wave of music that came flying over the gleaming floor, breaking the groups up into couples, scattering them, sending them spinning....

Leila had learned to dance at boarding school. Every Saturday afternoon the boarders were hurried off to a little corrugated iron mission hall where Miss Eccles (of London) held her "select" classes. But the difference between that dusty-smelling hall—with calico texts on the walls, the poor, terrified little woman in a brown velvet toque with rabbit's ears thumping the cold piano, Miss Eccles poking the girls' feet with her long white wand—and this was so tremendous that Leila was sure if her partner didn't come and she had to listen to that marvellous music and to watch the others sliding, gliding over the golden floor, she would die at least, or faint, or lift her arms and fly out of one of those dark windows that showed the stars.

"Ours, I think—" Someone bowed, smiled, and offered her his arm; she hadn't to die after all. Someone's hand pressed her waist, and she floated away like a flower that is tossed into a pool.

"Quite a good floor, isn't it?" drawled a faint voice close to her ear.

"I think it's most beautifully slippery," said Leila.

"Pardon!" The faint voice sounded surprised. Leila said it again. And there was a tiny pause before the voice echoed, "Oh, quite!" and she was swung round again.

He steered so beautifully. That was the great difference between dancing with girls and men, Leila decided. Girls banged into each other and stamped on each other's feet; the girl who was gentleman always clutched you so.

The azaleas were separate flowers no longer; they were pink and white flags streaming by.

"Were you at the Bells' last week?" the voice came again. It sounded tired. Leila wondered whether she ought to ask him if he would like to stop.

"No, this is my first dance," said she.

Her partner gave a little gasping laugh. "Oh, I say," he protested.

"Yes, it is really the first dance I've ever been to." Leila was most fervent. It was such a relief to be able to tell somebody. "You see, I've lived in the country all my life up till now...."

At that moment the music stopped and they went to sit on two chairs against the wall. Leila tucked her pink satin feet under and fanned herself, while she blissfully watched the other couples passing and disappearing through the swing doors.

"Enjoying yourself, Leila?" asked Jose, nodding her golden head.

Laura passed and gave her the faintest little wink; it made Leila wonder for a moment whether she was quite grown up after all. Certainly her partner did not say very much. He coughed, tucked his handkerchief away, pulled down his waistcoat, took a minute thread off his sleeve. But it didn't matter. Almost immediately the band started and her second partner seemed to spring from the ceiling.

"Floor's not bad," said the new voice. Did one always begin with the floor? And then, "Were you at the Neaves' on Tuesday?" And again Leila explained. Perhaps it was a little strange that her partners were not more interested. For it was thrilling. Her first ball! She was only at the beginning of everything. It seemed to her that she had never known what the night was like before. Up till now it had been dark, silent, beautiful very often—oh yes—but mournful somehow. Solemn. And now it would never be like that again—it had opened dazzling bright.

"Care for an ice?" said her partner. And they went through the swing doors, down the passage, to the supper-room. Her cheeks burned, she was fearfully thirsty. How sweet the ices looked on little glass plates and how cold the frosted spoon was, iced too! And when they came back to the hall there was the fat man waiting for her by the door. It gave her quite a shock again to see how old he was; he ought to have been on the stage with the fathers and mothers. And when Leila compared him with her other partners he looked shabby. His waistcoat was creased, there was a button off his glove, his coat looked as if it was dusty with French chalk.

"Come along, little lady," said the fat man. He scarcely troubled to clasp her, and they moved away so gently, it was more like walking than dancing. But he said not a word about the floor. "Your first dance, isn't it?" he murmured.

"How did you know?"

"Ah," said the fat man, "that's what it is to be old!" He wheezed faintly as he steered her past an awkward couple. "You see, I've been doing this kind of thing for the last thirty years."

"Thirty years?" cried Leila. Twelve years before she was born!

"It hardly bears thinking about, does it?" said the fat man gloomily. Leila looked at his bald head, and she felt quite sorry for him.

"I think it's marvellous to be still going on," she said kindly.

"Kind little lady," said the fat man, and he pressed her a little closer and hummed a bar of the waltz. "Of course," he said, "you can't hope to last anything like as long as that. No-o," said the fat man, "long before that you'll be sitting up there on the stage, looking on, in your nice black velvet. And these pretty arms will have turned into little short fat ones, and you'll beat time with such a different kind of fan—a black bony one." The fat man seemed to shudder. "And you'll smile away like the poor old dears up there, and point to your daughter, and tell the elderly lady next to you how some dreadful man tried to kiss her at the club ball. And your heart will ache, ache"—the fat man squeezed her closer still, as if he really was sorry for that poor heart—"because no one wants to kiss you now. And you'll say how unpleasant these polished floors are to walk on, how dangerous they are. Eh, Mademoiselle Twinkletoes?" said the fat man softly.

Leila gave a light little laugh, but she did not feel like laughing. Was it—could it all be true? It sounded terribly true. Was this first ball only the beginning of her last ball, after all? At that the music seemed to change; it sounded sad, sad; it rose upon a great sigh. Oh, how quickly things changed! Why didn't happiness last for ever? For ever wasn't a bit too long.

"I want to stop," she said in a breathless voice. The fat man led her to the door.

"No," she said, "I won't go outside. I won't sit down. I'll just stand here, thank you." She leaned against the wall, tapping with her foot, pulling up her gloves and trying to smile. But deep inside her a little girl threw her pinafore over her head and sobbed. Why had he spoiled it all?

"I say, you know," said the fat man, "you mustn't take me seriously, little lady."

"As if I should!" said Leila, tossing her small dark head and sucking her underlip....

Again the couples paraded. The swing doors opened and shut. Now new music was given out by the bandmaster. But Leila didn't want to dance any more. She wanted to be home, or sitting on the veranda listening to those baby owls. When she looked through the dark windows at the stars they had long beams like wings....

But presently a soft, melting, ravishing tune began, and a young man with curly hair bowed before her. She would have to dance, out of politeness, until she could find Meg. Very stiffly she walked into the middle; very haughtily she put her hand on his sleeve. But in one minute, in one turn, her feet glided, glided. The lights, the azaleas, the dresses, the pink faces, the velvet chairs, all became one beautiful flying wheel. And when her next partner bumped her into the fat man and he said, "Pardon," she smiled at him more radiantly than ever. She didn't even recognise him again.

Questions

1. What sensation did Leila have on her way to the ball and in the hall?
2. How did Leila's living environment differ from her present situation?
3. What did Leila think of her young partners?
4. What happened when the old and fat man danced and talked with Leila?
5. Why didn't Leila even recognise the old man when her partner bumped her into him?

凯瑟琳·曼斯菲尔德
（1888—1923）

凯瑟琳·曼斯菲尔德，原名凯思林·曼斯菲尔德·比彻姆，是杰出的现代短篇小说家，以其独特的散文风格和诗意的内涵著称于世。她出生并成长于当时仍属英国殖民地的新西兰。她19岁赴英国，在那里结识了现代派作家劳伦斯和伍尔夫，并彼此成为密友。第一次世界大战期间，曼斯菲尔德感染肺外器官结核病，因而她不能再回新西兰，并于34岁去世。

曼斯菲尔德的早期短篇小说收录于《在德国疗养院》（1911），反映出她最初对现代人际关系的幻灭。《序曲》（1918）中的一组小说讲述了她对新西兰家庭生活真情美好的回忆。《至福》（1920）确立了她短篇小说家的地位，代表了她的艺术风格。曼斯菲尔德的最高艺术成就体现在《花园及其他故事》小说集中，其中包括《第一次舞会》《花园晚会》《在海湾》《航程》《陌生人》，还有堪称经典、描写上流社会苦闷的《已故上校的女儿们》。曼斯菲尔德的小说技巧精致，着重于人物心理冲突的刻画。她的创作在一定程度上受到契诃夫的影响，以叙事的曲委与观察的精细为突出特点，继而又极大地影响了短篇小说作为独立文学形式的发展。

第一次舞会

下面的故事讲述了一个叫莱拉的乡下姑娘第一次参加城里舞会的感受。她迷恋于城市的喧嚣与热闹，谢里丹家的姑娘们的时尚同样吸引着她。舞会里的装饰、陈设、音乐以及舞伴更是令人眼花缭乱。她兴奋、焦急，同时有点儿自卑地等待着自己的舞伴。年轻的舞伴们都显得有些乏味，后来终于来了一个胖老头。老头舞艺精湛、阅历丰富。一切似乎都很惬意，直到老头提及时光易逝，一切青春美貌很快就会一去不复返，这时莱拉突然陷入沮丧。可不一会儿她就恢复了快乐与光彩。故事揭示出时光易逝这一冷酷的现实，而青春只是暂时占了上风。

究竟舞会是何时开始的，莱拉已经觉得难以说清楚了。也许她的第一个舞伴就是出租马车了。虽然她与谢里丹家的小姐、公子同坐一辆马车，但那并不妨碍她的这一想法。她坐在后排窄小的角落里，手放在车的软垫上，就像触摸到一位陌生小伙子礼服上的袖子；他们翩翩起舞，跳着华尔兹，转过两旁的灯柱、房屋、栅栏、树木。

"你以前真的没参加过舞会吗，莱拉？可怜蛋儿，这也太离谱啦——"谢里丹家的小姐们嚷嚷着。

"我们家最近的邻居也有15英里远，"莱拉低声说，轻轻地开合着扇子。

嗨，要像其他人那样不为所动真难啊！莱拉克制着笑容，尽量别大惊小怪，可是眼前的一切太新奇、太刺激了……梅格的夜来香、乔斯的琥珀长链、劳拉精美的黑头发就像雪中冒出的花儿，从她的白裘皮里直往外窜。她会永久记住这些。就连表哥劳里从新手套扣上扯下片片棉纸扔掉，她都感到心疼。她很想留下那些棉纸，作为纪念品，作为念想。劳里前倾着身子，将手放在劳拉的膝盖上。

"瞧这儿，亲爱的，"劳里说。"像往常一样，还是第三、第九，明白？"

嗨，有个兄弟该多好！激动中的莱拉感到，如果时间允许、如果场合允许，她真想哭出来，因为她是独生女，从没有兄弟对她说过"明白？"一词；也没有姐妹会像当下梅格对乔斯说这样的话："我从没见你的头发梳得像今晚这么利索！"

但眼下根本没时间。他们已经到了演练厅，前后都是出租马车。马路两侧移动着扇状的灯光，一片通明；人行道上兴高采烈的伴侣们步履飘然；精巧的绣鞋就像鸟儿般紧追不舍。

"抓紧我，莱拉，别丢啦，"劳拉说。

"快点，小姐们，咱们快冲过去，"劳里说。

莱拉双指触在劳拉粉红色天鹅绒大衣上，他们在人群的簇拥下抬脚穿过头顶上金色的大灯笼，顺着走廊前行，然后被推进了标有"女士"的小房间。房间里人实在太多，根本就没地方放东西，噪音简直震耳欲聋。两边的长凳堆满了外套。两个带白围裙的老妇人来回忙着，抖动着怀里新接过来的衣物。人人都往前挤，去抢远处对面的小梳妆台和镜子。

剧烈颤抖的汽灯光亮照着女化妆室。小姐们急不可待，已经跳动起来。门再次打开，演练厅传来一阵乐声，大家都跳起来，几乎顶了到天花板。

黑发、金发的小姐们在整理头发，再次扎紧缎带，将手绢塞进紧身的胸衣前，抚平大理石似的白颜色的手套。大家都笑逐颜开，莱拉觉得每个人似乎都很动人。

"有隐形发卡吗？"有人喊。"真怪了！一个隐形发卡都找不到。"

"往我后背扑点粉，谢了，亲爱的，"另一个喊。

"我要针线。我的褶边都破了几里地啦，"第三个叫嚷着。

然后，"传一下，传一下！"装舞会曲目单的草篮传过每个人的手臂。篮子里粉红银边的节目单小巧玲珑，还有粉红色的铅笔和毛茸茸的穗子。莱拉手指颤抖着从篮子里拿出一份节目单。她本来想问问，"我也该拿一份吗？"但等她刚看完节目单中"华尔兹3：俩俩人一轻舟。波尔卡4：让羽毛纷飞"，梅格就喊起来，"好了吗，莱拉？"于是她们穿过走廊里拥挤的人群奔向演练厅。

跳舞还未开始，但乐队已经调音完毕。大厅里人声鼎沸，恐怕就是乐队开始演奏也听不见乐曲。莱拉紧靠着梅格，目光越过梅格的肩膀朝前张望，她感到甚至是横挂在天花板上颤动的小彩旗都在喧哗。莱拉完全忘却了羞怯，她忘却了自己之前还坐在床上的情形。当时她刚打扮到一半，一只鞋在地上，另一只穿在脚上，求母亲打电话给表姊妹，告诉她们自己还是不去了。之前她有一阵子向往着自己就坐在乡下老宅的阳台上，在月光下听猫头鹰幼仔"呱啊，呱啊"地叫，而眼下这种向往却变成了一阵喜悦，她急切地想与人分享这种美妙的感受。莱拉紧握着扇子，眼睛盯着闪烁不停的金色地板、杜鹃花、灯笼，在另一头的舞台上有红地毯、金粉色椅子，还有角落里的乐队。她屏住呼吸激动地想，"多优美啊，简直优美极了！"

少女们都成群结队地站在门的一边，男士站在另一边；少女的年长女伴们身穿黑裙，傻傻地笑着，穿过磨亮的地板小心翼翼地迈着碎步走向舞台。

"这是我乡下来的小表妹莱拉，对她好点哦。给她找几个舞伴，我得照应她，"梅格上前对一个个少女说。

一个个陌生的脸庞对莱拉笑着——笑得甜美、含糊。一句句陌生的话语应答着："当然喽，亲爱的。"可莱拉感到少女们并没正眼瞧她，个个都盯着男士们。男士们怎么还不开始？他们在等什么？男士们聚在一起站在那里，面带微笑，他们平整着手套，轻拍着自己油亮的头发。忽然间，就好像才打定主意要做什么，他们轻轻滑过镶花地板，在少女间顿时响起一阵欢娱的骚动。一位高个儿、金发白肤的男士飞快地来到梅格跟前，抓过节目单，迅速在上面划拉了几笔；梅格将那位男士传给莱拉。"我可以有此殊荣吗？"男士弯腰示意，面带微笑。然后过来一位皮肤黝黑戴眼镜的男士，随后劳里带一位朋友到来，劳拉带来一位面部略有雀斑、领带歪歪斜斜的小伙儿。再后来，一位年迈老者——体态肥胖，头顶秃了一大块——拿过莱拉的节目单，嘀咕着，"我看看，我看看！"他长时间地将自己黑压压写满名字的节目单与莱拉的节目单比照着。莱拉有些害臊，这似乎使老人很不安。"嗨，请别介意，"莱拉急切地说。那胖子并没回答，只是在节目单上写了写，又瞧了她一眼。"我还记得这张快乐、可爱的脸？"他柔和地说。"这不是往日熟悉不过的吗？"就在此时乐队开始奏曲，胖子随即就消失了。一阵响亮的音乐划过闪烁发亮的地板，将老人席卷而去，音乐声将人群劈成一队队舞伴，将他们分散开去，使他们旋转起来⋯⋯

莱拉在寄宿学校学过跳舞。每个星期六下午，寄宿生都被赶到一座波纹铁皮建筑的礼堂。在那里来自伦敦的埃克尔斯小姐上她的"精选"课。礼堂里充满尘土味,墙上有印在棉布上的经文。一位可怜巴巴、惊恐万状的小妇人戴着棕色天鹅绒无边女帽,帽子上还带着两只兔耳朵,她重重地弹奏着冰冷的钢琴。埃克尔斯小姐还用长长的白棍子时不时捅女孩们的脚。那教堂里的情形与眼下这舞厅比起来真是天壤之别。莱拉确信地感到,如果她的舞伴不来,她只能听这美妙的音乐,看别人在金色的地板上来回滑动,翩翩起舞,那么她会必死无疑,也可能会昏过去,或者抬起胳膊飞出那扇黑洞洞的窗户,窗外星光闪烁。

"该我们了吧——"有人弯腰,微笑,将手臂伸向莱拉。结果她活下来了。有人将手托在了她的腰际,她就像被抛向池塘里的花儿一样摇摆起来。

"舞池的地板不错嘛?"她的耳边响起慢条斯理、有气无力的声音。

"我觉得滑溜极了,太美了,"莱拉说。

"什么!"那有气无力的声音表现出很惊讶的样子。莱拉又说了一遍。过了一小会儿,那声音回应道:"哦,是啊!"她又被转了过去。

那位男士掌控得很漂亮。莱拉确信,同女士与同男士跳舞就是大不一样。女士总是撞到你,还互相踩脚,作为男舞伴的女士总是使劲抓着你。

这时的杜鹃花已不再是形单影只,粉色、白色的花儿像一面面小旗不停地流动。

"上个星期你去贝尔斯舞会了吗?"那话音又传过来,听起来很懈怠。莱拉不知是否应该问他是不是想停下来。

"没有,这是我第一次舞会,"她回答道。

莱拉的舞伴略带喘息地笑了一下。"嗨,是吗,"他表示不解。

"真的,这真是我第一次参加舞会。"莱拉激动地说。能把这事说出去真是一种解脱。"你知道,我之前一直生活在乡下……"

就在说话这当儿,音乐停止了,他们两人过去坐在靠墙的两张椅子上。莱拉将她那粉红色如缎面一般光滑的双脚收拢起来,扇着风;她欣喜地看着其他舞伴出入于转门。

"开心吧,莱拉?"满头金发的乔斯问,频频点头。

劳拉打身边过,快速向莱拉眨了眨眼;这使得莱拉不禁问自己到底长大没有。当然,莱拉的舞伴并没多说什么。他咳嗽着,揣起手绢,向下拽了拽马甲,从衣袖上拽掉一条细线。不过一切都无关紧要。几乎没有间歇,舞乐又奏响,莱拉的第二个舞伴就好像从天棚上蹦到了她跟前。

"舞池地板不错,"新舞伴说。难道这儿人人都以舞池地板开始交谈吗?随后就是"星期二你去尼弗兹舞会了吗?"于是莱拉又解释了一遍。说来也许有点儿怪,莱拉后来的舞伴对此并没有显出更大的兴趣。这可是她的第一次舞会,真令人惊诧！一切对她还只是开始。在此之前，她似乎从来都不知舞会之夜是什么样。此前，她脑海中的舞会之夜一直是昏暗、寂静，常常是很美的——哦，是啊——还有点儿哀婉，严肃而隆重。可现在一切不复从前了——展现在眼前的是一片耀眼的光芒。

"要冰点吗？"莱拉的舞伴说。于是他们穿过转门，沿着走廊来到晚餐厅。莱拉脸颊火热，她渴坏了。冰点在小玻璃盘子上看起来好吃极了，霜冻的匙儿冷极了，也冰冻过！待他们回到舞厅，那位胖老头在门边等她。看到他老态龙钟的样子，莱拉又吃惊不小；他本该与老爹老娘们在乐台上才是。莱拉将他与其他舞伴相比，他越发显得寒酸。老头的马甲皱皱巴巴，手套的纽扣也掉了一颗，外衣看起来就像沾满滑石粉。

"过来，小淑女，"胖老头说。他几乎无须搂住莱拉的腰，就轻柔地跳起来，看起来更像是走路而不是跳舞。但他对舞池的地板只字未提。"第一次跳舞吧？"他小声说。

"你怎么知道的？"

"嘿，"胖老头说，"这就是老年人阅历的作用！"他微微喘息着，带着她掠过一对笨拙的舞伴。"你看，30年了，我就没停止过跳舞。"

"30年？"莱拉叫出声来。也就是她出生前老头就跳了12年了！

"是啊，难以想象啊！"胖老头闷闷不乐地说。莱拉看了看他的秃顶，为他感到难过。

"我觉得一切都还在继续就很好，"她亲切地说。

"好心的小淑女，"胖老头说，他把莱拉搂得更近了点儿，哼了一节华尔兹。"当然，"他接着说，"谁也不能指望一件事能延续那么长时间，做不到。"胖老头说，"在那很早之前，你就会坐在那乐台上，身着黑天鹅绒外衣，成为旁观者。你这漂亮的胳膊就会变得又短又粗，打起拍子来所用的扇子也会大不一样——变成一副黑色骨扇。"胖老头说话间似乎战栗起来。"接着你会远远地在那儿微笑，就像那些可怜、可爱的老妇人们，指向自己的女儿，告诉旁边的老妇人，某个讨厌的男人在俱乐部舞会上如何试图亲吻自己的女儿。这时你的心会隐隐作痛，作痛，"——胖老头搂得更紧了，就好像真的为那颗可怜的心感到惋惜——"因为现在再也没人想亲吻你了。你会说这光亮的地板走上去太不舒服了，太危险了。嗯，舞会皇后？"胖老头轻声地说。

莱拉轻轻笑了一声，但她并不想笑。这——这一切是真的吗？听起来可是真真切切，可怕极了。难道这第一次舞会就是她最后一次舞会的开始吗？这时舞乐似乎变了调，听起来悲伤、忧愁，随后上升为一声叹息。嗨，一切变得真快啊！幸福怎么就不能天长地久呢？天长地久有什么不行呢？

"我想停下来,"莱拉气喘吁吁地说。胖老头引她到门边。

"不,"莱拉说,"我不出去。我不坐下。我只想在这儿站一会儿,谢谢。"她靠着墙,脚点着节拍,摘下手套,努力露出笑容。可在她心灵深处,一个小女孩将无袖连衣裙蒙在头上,啜泣着。老头干嘛要这么扫兴?

"我说,你该明白,"胖老头说,"我说的不必当真,小淑女。"

"就好像我真当真似的!"莱拉说,摇晃着满头黑发的小脑袋,吸吮着下唇……

舞伴们又列队开始。转门开开关关。这时在乐队指挥的调动下奏起了新舞曲。但是莱拉不想再跳了。她想回家,或是坐在阳台上听小猫头鹰的叫声。她望着黑洞洞的窗户,外面星光闪烁,长长的光束就像翅膀……

但很快轻柔、甜美、令人销魂的舞曲奏响,一位卷发小伙子向她弯腰请她跳舞。出于礼貌,她还得跳舞,直到找到梅格。她很不自然地走到中间,很傲慢地将手搭在小伙子的袖子上。但只过了一分钟,转了一圈,她的脚步就轻快地滑动起来。周围的灯光、杜鹃花、裙子、红扑扑的脸庞、丝绒的椅子,一切都变成了一个美妙飞转的轮盘。而当她的下一个舞伴带着她撞到了那位胖老头,老头说"对不起"之时,她的笑容比以往更加灿烂。她甚至根本就没认出那老头儿。

Bliss

The following is a powerful story with the profound ironic twist and vivid subjective experience in Bertha Young's life. It is an exploration of her ecstasy to the extreme of euphoria and the unraveling of an incident beyond her imagination. Beneath the surface of the perfect satisfaction in her life lies certain danger of mental and psychological insecurity and isolation. The pear tree and the two cats serve as strong contrasting symbols and the omen is finally proved by her husband's affair with her friend Miss Fulton in the end of the story when her bliss is completely shattered.

Although Bertha Young was thirty she still had moments like this when she wanted to run instead of walk, to take dancing steps on and off the pavement, to bowl a hoop, to throw something up in the air and catch it again, or to stand still and laugh at—nothing—at nothing, simply.

What can you do if you are thirty and, turning the corner of your own street, you are overcome, suddenly by a feeling of bliss—absolute bliss!—as though you'd suddenly swallowed a bright piece of that late afternoon sun and it burned in your bosom, sending out a little shower of sparks into every particle, into every finger and toe? ...

Oh, is there no way you can express it without being "drunk and disorderly"? How idiotic civilisation is! Why be given a body if you have to keep it shut up in a case like a rare, rare fiddle?

"No, that about the fiddle is not quite what I mean," she thought, running up the steps and feeling in her bag for the key—she'd forgotten it, as usual—and rattling the letter-box. "It's not what I mean, because—Thank you, Mary"—she went into the hall. "Is nurse back?"

"Yes, M'm."

"And has the fruit come?"

"Yes, M'm. Everything's come."

"Bring the fruit up to the dining-room, will you? I'll arrange it before I go upstairs."

It was dusky in the dining-room and quite chilly. But all the same Bertha threw off her coat; she could not bear the tight clasp of it another moment, and the cold air fell on her arms.

But in her bosom there was still that bright glowing place—that shower of little sparks coming from it. It was almost unbearable. She hardly dared to breathe for fear of fanning it higher, and yet she breathed deeply, deeply. She hardly dared to look into the cold mirror —but she did look, and it gave her back a woman, radiant, with smiling, trembling lips, with big, dark eyes and an air of listening, waiting for something... divine to happen... that she knew must happen... infallibly.

Mary brought in the fruit on a tray and with it a glass bowl, and a blue dish, very lovely, with a strange sheen on it as though it had been dipped in milk.

"Shall I turn on the light, M'm?"

"No, thank you. I can see quite well."

There were tangerines and apples stained with strawberry pink. Some yellow pears, smooth as silk, some white grapes covered with a silver bloom and a big cluster of purple ones. These last she had bought to tone in with the new dining-room carpet. Yes, that did sound rather far-fetched and absurd, but it was really why she had bought them. She had thought in the shop: "I must have some purple ones to bring the carpet up to the table." And it had seemed quite sense at the time.

When she had finished with them and had made two pyramids of these bright round shapes, she stood away from the table to get the effect—and it really was most curious. For the dark table seemed to melt into the dusky light and the glass dish and the blue bowl to float in the air. This, of course, in her present mood, was so incredibly beautiful.... She began to laugh.

"No, no. I'm getting hysterical." And she seized her bag and coat and ran upstairs to the nursery.

Nurse sat at a low table giving Little B her supper after her bath. The baby had on a white flannel gown and a blue woollen jacket, and her dark, fine hair was brushed up into a funny little peak. She looked up when she saw her mother and began to jump.

"Now, my lovey, eat it up like a good girl," said nurse, setting her lips in a way that Bertha knew, and that meant she had come into the nursery at another wrong moment.

"Has she been good, Nanny?"

"She's been a little sweet all the afternoon," whispered Nanny. "We went to the park and I sat down on a chair and took her out of the pram and a big dog came along and put its head on my knee and she clutched its ear, tugged it. Oh, you should have seen her."

Bertha wanted to ask if it wasn't rather dangerous to let her clutch at a strange dog's ear. But she did not dare to. She stood watching them, her hands by her side, like the poor little girl in front of the rich girl with the doll.

The baby looked up at her again, stared, and then smiled so charmingly that Bertha couldn't help crying:

"Oh, Nanny, do let me finish giving her her supper while you put the bath things away."

"Well, M'm, she oughtn't to be changed hands while she's eating," said Nanny, still whispering. "It unsettles her; it's very likely to upset her."

How absurd it was. Why have a baby if it has to be kept—not in a case like a rare, rare fiddle—but in another woman's arms?

"Oh, I must!" said she.

Very offended, Nanny handed her over.

"Now, don't excite her after her supper. You know you do, M'm. And I have such a time with her after!"

Thank heaven! Nanny went out of the room with the bath towels.

"Now I've got you to myself, my little precious," said Bertha, as the baby leaned against her.

She ate delightfully, holding up her lips for the spoon and then waving her hands. Sometimes she wouldn't let the spoon go; and sometimes, just as Bertha had filled it, she waved it away to the four winds.

When the soup was finished Bertha turned round to the fire. "You're nice—you're very nice!" said she, kissing her warm baby. "I'm fond of you. I like you."

And indeed, she loved Little B so much—her neck as she bent forward, her exquisite toes as they shone transparent in the firelight—that all her feeling of bliss came back again, and again she didn't know how to express it—what to do with it.

"You're wanted on the telephone," said Nanny, coming back in triumph and seizing *her* Little B.

Down she flew. It was Harry.

"Oh, is that you, Ber? Look here. I'll be late. I'll take a taxi and come along as quickly as I can, but get dinner put back ten minutes—will you? All right?"

"Yes, perfectly. Oh, Harry!"

"Yes?"

What had she to say? She'd nothing to say. She only wanted to get in touch with him for a moment. She couldn't absurdly cry: "Hasn't it been a divine day!"

"What is it?" rapped out the little voice.

"Nothing. *Entendu*," said Bertha, and hung up the receiver, thinking how much more than idiotic civilisation was.

They had people coming to dinner. The Norman Knights—a very sound couple—he was about to start a theatre, and she was awfully keen on interior decoration, a young man, Eddie Warren, who had just published a little book of poems and whom everybody was asking to dine, and a "find" of Bertha's called Pearl Fulton. What Miss Fulton did, Bertha didn't know. They had met at the club and Bertha had fallen in love with her, as she always did fall in love with beautiful women who had something strange about them.

The provoking thing was that, though they had been about together and met a number of times and really talked, Bertha couldn't make her out. Up to a certain point Miss Fulton was rarely, wonderfully frank, but the certain point was there, and beyond that she would not go.

Was there anything beyond it? Harry said "No." Voted her dullish, and "cold like all blonde women, with a touch, perhaps, of anaemia of the brain." But Bertha wouldn't agree with him; not yet, at any rate.

"No, the way she has of sitting with her head a little on one side, and smiling, has something behind it, Harry, and I must find out what that something is."

"Most likely it's a good stomach," answered Harry.

He made a point of catching Bertha's heels with replies of that kind... "liver frozen, my dear girl," or "pure flatulence," or "kidney disease,"... and so on. For some strange reason Bertha liked this, and almost admired it in him very much.

She went into the drawing-room and lighted the fire; then, picking up the cushions, one by one, that Mary had disposed so carefully, she threw them back on to the chairs and the couches. That made all the difference; the room came alive at once. As she was about to throw the last one she surprised herself by suddenly hugging it to her, passionately, passionately. But it did not put out the fire in her bosom. Oh, on the contrary!

The windows of the drawing-room opened on to a balcony overlooking the garden.

At the far end, against the wall, there was a tall, slender pear tree in fullest, richest bloom; it stood perfect, as though becalmed against the jade-green sky. Bertha couldn't help feeling, even from this distance, that it had not a single bud or a faded petal. Down below, in the garden beds, the red and yellow tulips, heavy with flowers, seemed to lean upon the dusk. A grey cat, dragging its belly, crept across the lawn, and a black one, its shadow, trailed after. The sight of them, so intent and so quick, gave Bertha a curious shiver.

"What creepy things cats are!" she stammered, and she turned away from the window and began walking up and down....

How strong the jonquils smelled in the warm room. Too strong? Oh, no. And yet, as though overcome, she flung down on a couch and pressed her hands to her eyes.

"I'm too happy — too happy!" she murmured.

And she seemed to see on her eyelids the lovely pear tree with its wide open blossoms as a symbol of her own life.

Really—really—she had everything. She was young. Harry and she were as much in love as ever, and they got on together splendidly and were really good pals. She had an adorable baby. They didn't have to worry about money. They had this absolutely satisfactory house and garden. And friends—modern, thrilling friends, writers and painters and poets or people keen on social questions—just the kind of friends they wanted. And then there were books, and there was music, and she had found a wonderful little dressmaker, and they were going abroad in the summer, and their new cook made the most superb omelettes....

"I'm absurd. Absurd!" She sat up; but she felt quite dizzy, quite drunk. It must have been the spring.

Yes, it was the spring. Now she was so tired she could not drag herself upstairs to dress.

A white dress, a string of jade beads, green shoes and stockings. It wasn't intentional. She had thought of this scheme hours before she stood at the drawing-room window.

Her petals rustled softly into the hall, and she kissed Mrs. Norman Knight, who was taking off the most amusing orange coat with a procession of black monkeys round the hem and up the fronts.

"... Why! Why! Why is the middle-class so stodgy—so utterly without a sense of humour! My dear, it's only by a fluke that I am here at all—Norman being the protective fluke. For my darling monkeys so upset the train that it rose to a man and simply ate me with its eyes. Didn't laugh—wasn't amused—that I should have loved. No, just stared—and bored me through and through."

"But the cream of it was," said Norman, pressing a large tortoiseshell-rimmed monocle into his eye, "you don't mind me telling this, Face, do you?" (In their home and among their friends they called each other Face and Mug.) "The cream of it was when she, being full fed, turned to the woman beside her and said: 'Haven't you ever seen a monkey before?'"

"Oh, yes!" Mrs. Norman Knight joined in the laughter. "Wasn't that too absolutely creamy?"

And a funnier thing still was that now her coat was off she did look like a very intelligent monkey—who had even made that yellow silk dress out of scraped banana skins. And her amber ear-rings: they were like little dangling nuts.

"This is a sad, sad fall!" said Mug, pausing in front of Little B's perambulator. "When the perambulator comes into the hall—" and he waved the rest of the quotation away.

The bell rang. It was lean, pale Eddie Warren (as usual) in a state of acute distress.

"It is the right house, isn't it?" he pleaded.

"Oh, I think so—I hope so," said Bertha brightly.

"I have had such a *dreadful* experience with a taxi-man; he was *most* sinister. I couldn't get him to stop. The *more* I knocked and called the *faster* he went. And *in* the moonlight this *bizarre* figure with the *flattened* head *crouching* over the *lit-tle* wheel..."

He shuddered, taking off an immense white silk scarf. Bertha noticed that his socks were white, too—most charming.

"But how dreadful!" she cried.

"Yes, it really was," said Eddie, following her into the drawing-room. "I saw myself *driving* through Eternity in a *timeless* taxi."

He knew the Norman Knights. In fact, he was going to write a play for N.K. when the theatre scheme came off.

"Well, Warren, how's the play?" said Norman Knight, dropping his monocle and giving his eye a moment in which to rise to the surface before it was screwed down again.

And Mrs. Norman Knight: "Oh, Mr. Warren, what happy socks?"

"I *am* so glad you like them," said he, staring at his feet. "They seem to have got so *much* whiter since the moon rose." And he turned his lean sorrowful young face to Bertha. "There is a moon, you know."

She wanted to cry: "I am sure there is—often—often!"

He really was a most attractive person. But so was Face, crouched before the fire in her banana skins, and so was Mug, smoking a cigarette and saying as he flicked the ash: "Why doth the bridegroom tarry?"

"There he is, now."

Bang went the front door open and shut. Harry shouted: "Hullo, you people. Down in five minutes." And they heard him swarm up the stairs. Bertha couldn't help smiling; she knew how he loved doing things at high pressure. What, after all, did an extra five minutes matter? But he would pretend to himself that they mattered beyond measure. And then he would make a great point of coming into the drawing-room, extravagantly cool and collected.

Harry had such a zest for life. Oh, how she appreciated it in him. And his passion for fighting—for seeking in everything that came up against him another test of his power and of his courage—that, too, she understood. Even when it made him just occasionally, to other people, who didn't know him well, a little ridiculous perhaps.... For there were moments when he rushed into battle where no battle was.... She talked and laughed and positively forgot until he had come in (just as she had imagined) that Pearl Fulton had not turned up.

"I wonder if Miss Fulton has forgotten?"

"I expect so," said Harry. "Is she on the phone?"

"Ah! There's a taxi, now." And Bertha smiled with that little air of proprietorship that she always assumed while her women finds were new and mysterious. "She lives in taxis."

"She'll run to fat if she does," said Harry coolly, ringing the bell for dinner. "Frightful danger for blonde women."

"Harry—don't!" warned Bertha, laughing up at him.

Came another tiny moment, while they waited, laughing and talking, just a trifle too much at their ease, a trifle too unaware. And then Miss Fulton, all in silver, with a silver fillet binding her pale blonde hair, came in smiling, her head a little on one side.

"Am I late?"

"No, not at all," said Bertha. "Come along." And she took her arm and they moved into the dining-room.

What was there in the touch of that cool arm that could fan—fan—start blazing—blazing—the fire of bliss that Bertha did not know what to do with?

Miss Fulton did not look at her; but then she seldom did look at people directly. Her heavy eyelids lay upon her eyes and the strange half-smile came and went upon her lips as though she lived by listening rather than seeing. But Bertha knew, suddenly, as if the longest, most intimate look had passed between them—as if they had said to each other: "You too?"—that Pearl Fulton, stirring the beautiful red soup in the grey plate, was feeling just what she was feeling.

And the others? Face and Mug, Eddie and Harry, their spoons rising and falling—dabbing their lips with their napkins, crumbling bread, fiddling with the forks and glasses and talking.

"I met her at the Alpha show—the weirdest little person. She'd not only cut off her hair, but she seemed to have taken a dreadfully good snip off her legs and arms and her neck and her poor little nose as well."

"Isn't she very *liée* with Michael Oat?"

"The man who wrote *Love in False Teeth*?"

"He wants to write a play for me. One act. One man. Decides to commit suicide. Gives all the reasons why he should and why he shouldn't. And just as he has made up his mind either to do it or not to do it—curtain. Not half a bad idea."

"What's he going to call it—'Stomach Trouble'?"

"I *think* I've come across the *same* idea in a little French review, *quite* unknown in England."

No, they didn't share it. They were dears—dears—and she loved having them there, at her table, and giving them delicious food and wine. In fact, she longed to tell them how delightful they were, and what a decorative group they made, how they seemed to set one another off and how they reminded her of a play by Chekhov!

Harry was enjoying his dinner. It was part of his—well, not his nature, exactly, and certainly not his pose—his—something or other —to talk about food and to glory in his "shameless passion for the white flesh of the lobster" and "the green of pistachio ices—green and cold like the eyelids of Egyptian dancers."

When he looked up at her and said: "Bertha, this is a very admirable *soufflée!*" she almost could have wept with child-like pleasure.

Oh, why did she feel so tender towards the whole world tonight? Everything was good—was right. All that happened seemed to fill again her brimming cup of bliss.

And still, in the back of her mind, there was the pear tree. It would be silver now, in the light of poor dear Eddie's moon, silver as Miss Fulton, who sat there turning a tangerine in her slender fingers that were so pale a light seemed to come from them.

What she simply couldn't make out—what was miraculous—was how she should have guessed Miss Fulton's mood so exactly and so instantly. For she never doubted for a moment that she was right, and yet what had she to go on? Less than nothing.

"I believe this does happen very, very rarely between women. Never between men," thought Bertha. "But while I am making the coffee in the drawing-room perhaps she will 'give a sign'."

What she meant by that she did not know, and what would happen after that she could not imagine.

While she thought like this she saw herself talking and laughing. She had to talk because of her desire to laugh.

"I must laugh or die."

But when she noticed Face's funny little habit of tucking something down the front of her bodice—as if she kept a tiny, secret hoard of nuts there, too—Bertha had to dig her nails into her hands—so as not to laugh too much.

It was over at last. And: "Come and see my new coffee machine," said Bertha.

"We only have a new coffee machine once a fortnight," said Harry. Face took her arm this time; Miss Fulton bent her head and followed after.

The fire had died down in the drawing-room to a red, flickering "nest of baby phoenixes," said Face.

"Don't turn up the light for a moment. It is so lovely." And down she crouched by the fire again. She was always cold . . . "without her little red flannel jacket, of course," thought Bertha.

At that moment Miss Fulton "gave the sign."

"Have you a garden?" said the cool, sleepy voice.

This was so exquisite on her part that all Bertha could do was to obey. She crossed the room, pulled the curtains apart, and opened those long windows.

"There!" she breathed.

And the two women stood side by side looking at the slender, flowering tree. Although it was so still it seemed, like the flame of a candle, to stretch up, to point, to quiver in the bright air, to grow taller and taller as they gazed—almost to touch the rim of the round, silver moon.

How long did they stand there? Both, as it were, caught in that circle of unearthly light, understanding each other perfectly, creatures of another world, and wondering what they were to do in this one with all this blissful treasure that burned in their bosoms and dropped, in silver flowers, from their hair and hands?

For ever—for a moment? And did Miss Fulton murmur: "Yes. Just *that*." Or did Bertha dream it?

Then the light was snapped on and Face made the coffee and Harry said: "My dear Mrs. Knight, don't ask me about my baby. I never see her. I shan't feel the slightest interest in her until she has a lover," and Mug took his eye out of the conservatory for a moment and then put it under glass again and Eddie Warren drank his coffee and set down the cup with a face of anguish as though he had drunk and seen the spider.

"What I want to do is to give the young men a show. I believe London is simply teeming with first-chop, unwritten plays. What I want to say to 'em is: 'Here's the theatre. Fire ahead.'"

"You know, my dear, I am going to decorate a room for the Jacob Nathans. Oh, I am so tempted to do a fried-fish scheme, with the backs of the chairs shaped like frying-pans and lovely chip potatoes embroidered all over the curtains."

"The trouble with our young writing men is that they are still too romantic. You can't put out to sea without being seasick and wanting a basin. Well, why won't they have the courage of those basins?"

"A *dreadful* poem about a *girl* who was *violated* by a beggar *without* a nose in a lit-tle wood...."

Miss Fulton sank into the lowest, deepest chair and Harry handed round the cigarettes.

From the way he stood in front of her shaking the silver box and saying abruptly: "Egyptian? Turkish? Virginian? They're all mixed up," Bertha realised that she not only bored him; he really disliked her. And she decided from the way Miss Fulton said: "No, thank you, I won't smoke," that she felt it, too, and was hurt.

"Oh, Harry, don't dislike her. You are quite wrong about her. She's wonderful, wonderful. And, besides, how can you feel so differently about someone who means so much to me. I shall try to tell you when we are in bed tonight what has been happening. What she and I have shared."

At those last words something strange and almost terrifying darted into Bertha's mind. And this something blind and smiling whispered to her: "Soon these people will go. The house will be quiet —quiet. The lights will be out. And you and he will be alone together in the dark room—the warm bed...."

She jumped up from her chair and ran over to the piano.

"What a pity someone does not play!" she cried. "What a pity somebody does not play."

For the first time in her life Bertha Young desired her husband. Oh, she'd loved him—she'd been in love with him, of course, in every other way, but just not in that way. And equally, of course, she'd understood that he was different. They'd discussed it so often. It had worried her dreadfully at first to find that she was so cold, but after a time it had not seemed to matter. They were so frank with each other —such good pals. That was the best of being modern.

But now—ardently! ardently! The word ached in her ardent body! Was this what that feeling of bliss had been leading up to? But then, then—"My dear," said Mrs. Norman Knight, "you know our shame. We are the victims of time and train. We live in Hampstead. It's been so nice."

"I'll come with you into the hall," said Bertha. "I loved having you. But you must not miss the last train. That's so awful, isn't it?"

"Have a whisky, Knight, before you go?" called Harry.

"No, thanks, old chap."

Bertha squeezed his hand for that as she shook it.

"Good night, good-bye," she cried from the top step, feeling that this self of hers was taking leave of them for ever.

When she got back into the drawing-room the others were on the move.

"... Then you can come part of the way in my taxi."

"I shall be so thankful *not* to have to face *another* drive *alone* after my *dreadful* experience."

"You can get a taxi at the rank just at the end of the street. You won't have to walk more than a few yards."

"That's a comfort. I'll go and put on my coat."

Miss Fulton moved towards the hall and Bertha was following when Harry almost pushed past.

"Let me help you."

Bertha knew that he was repenting his rudeness—she let him go. What a boy he was in some ways—so impulsive—so—simple.

And Eddie and she were left by the fire.

"I *wonder* if you have seen Bilks' *new* poem called *Table d'Hôte*," said Eddie softly. "It's *so* wonderful. In the last Anthology. Have you got a copy? I'd *so* like to *show* it to you. It begins with an *incredibly* beautiful line: 'Why Must it Always be Tomato Soup?'"

"Yes," said Bertha. And she moved noiselessly to a table opposite the drawing-room door and Eddie glided noiselessly after her. She picked up the little book and gave it to him; they had not made a sound.

While he looked it up she turned her head towards the hall. And she saw... Harry with Miss Fulton's coat in his arms and Miss Fulton with her back turned to him and her head bent. He tossed the coat away, put his hands on her shoulders and turned her violently to him. His lips said: "I adore you," and Miss Fulton laid her moonbeam fingers on his cheeks and smiled her sleepy smile. Harry's nostrils quivered; his lips curled back in a hideous grin while he whispered: "Tomorrow," and with her eyelids Miss Fulton said: "Yes."

"Here it is," said Eddie. "'Why Must it Always be Tomato Soup?' It's so *deeply* true, don't you feel? Tomato soup is so *dreadfully* eternal."

"If you prefer," said Harry's voice, very loud, from the hall, "I can phone you a cab to come to the door."

"Oh, no. It's not necessary," said Miss Fulton, and she came up to Bertha and gave her the slender fingers to hold.

"Good-bye. Thank you so much."

"Good-bye," said Bertha.

Miss Fulton held her hand a moment longer.

"Your lovely pear tree!" she murmured.

And then she was gone, with Eddie following, like the black cat following the grey cat.

"I'll shut up shop," said Harry, extravagantly cool and collected.

"Your lovely pear tree—pear tree—pear tree!"

Bertha simply ran over to the long windows.

"Oh, what is going to happen now?" she cried.

But the pear tree was as lovely as ever and as full of flower and as still.

Questions

1. How was Bertha Young feeling at the beginning of the story? And why?
2. Why did she hate civilisation?
3. How were her dinner guests different or similar in their behavior and taste?
4. What are the main symbols in the story and what do they symbolize?
5. Why did she suddenly feel something strange and almost terrifying in her mind near the end of the story?

至 福

　　下面的故事叙述了女主人公伯莎·杨的人生中某种意味深长、充满反讽的突转，生动地描述了她的主观体验。故事探究了她因极端自我陶醉所产生的幸福感的根由，揭露了一桩超乎她想象的事件的发生。其实，在她心满意足的人生表象之下，隐藏着某种精神与心理上的不安与孤独。故事运用梨树和两只猫作为鲜明的对比象征。这种不祥之兆最终被伯莎的丈夫与她的朋友富尔顿小姐的外遇所证明，女主人公的幸福也随之被彻底打碎。

　　虽然伯莎·杨都30岁了，但她仍然有时会走着走着就想跑，想在马路牙子上蹦上蹦下，滚铁环，把东西抛到空中再用手去接，或是想静静地站着大笑——没有任何原因——就那样毫无理由地大笑。

　　假如你30岁了，转过街角，突然被一种幸福感——彻头彻尾的幸福感！——所折服，就好像是突然之间吞下了黄昏时的一片明媚的阳光，而那片阳光在你的胸中燃烧起来，迸发出串串火花，射入每一个细胞，每一根手指和脚趾，你该怎么办呢？……

　　哦，除了在"喝醉酒和神志不清时"，再没有能说清这种感情的时候了吗？教养是多么的愚蠢！如果只能将身体像稀有小提琴般封闭在琴盒里的话，拥有它还有何用？

　　"不，小提琴之类的东西不能表达我的意思，"她边想边快步跑上台阶，一只手在包里摸钥匙——她又忘带了，她总是忘——另一只手胡乱地掏着信箱。"那不能表达我的意思，因为——谢谢，玛丽"——她走进大厅。"奶妈回来了吗？"

　　"是的，夫人。"

　　"水果送来了吗？"

　　"是的，夫人。都送来了。"

　　"把水果送到餐厅来，好吗？我上楼之前会把它们都摆好的。"

　　餐厅里很昏暗，也很冷。但是伯莎还是把外衣脱了；她受不了大衣紧裹的感觉，多一分钟也受不了，她的双臂感到阵阵凉气。

　　但是在她的胸中，那片明亮发光的地方还在——那一串串火花就是从那里迸射出来的。那简直让人无法承受。她几乎都不敢喘气，因为她怕火焰会被撩拨得更高，不过她还是深深地、深深地喘了口气。她几乎不敢去看那冰冷的镜子——但她还是看了，镜子里映出一个女人，容光焕发，颤抖的嘴唇微带笑容，一双乌黑的大眼睛，一副倾听的神情，在等待着某种事情……某种神圣事情的发生……她知道那件事一定会发生……必定无疑。

玛丽用盘子把水果端了进来，还拿来一个玻璃碗和一个蓝碟子，非常可爱的一个碟子，它的色泽有些奇怪，好像被放在牛奶里泡过了似的。

"我把灯打开好吗，夫人？"

"不用，我看得很清楚。"

橘子和草莓般粉嘟嘟的苹果。一些黄色的梨如丝般光滑，一些带有银色光泽的白葡萄和一大串紫葡萄。她刚买来的这些水果是为了装点餐厅里的新地毯用的。是啊，这的确听起来别扭，令人不可思议，但这的确是她买这些水果的原因。她在商店里就想："我必须得买点紫葡萄，那样才能让地毯和桌子看起来浑然一体。"当时这理由好像很充分。

她把水果都摆上了，用这些明亮浑圆的形状堆起了两座金字塔，她站到离桌子远些的地方看看摆放的效果——真是太妙了，因为深色的桌子好像融入了昏暗的光线里，那个玻璃碟和蓝色的碗仿佛飘在了空中一般。这一切，当然，以她现在的心情来衡量，是那么的美丽，令人难以置信的美丽……她开始大笑起来。

"不，不。我有些兴奋过了头。"她抓起包和大衣向楼上的婴儿房跑去。

奶妈坐在一张矮桌旁给洗完澡的小宝宝喂晚饭。宝宝穿着一件白色的法兰绒长袍，一件蓝色的羊毛上衣，她那乌黑纤细的头发被梳成了一个滑稽可笑的小山峰形状。宝宝抬起头看见妈妈进来，开始蹦跳起来。

"来吧，宝贝，像个乖女孩，把饭吃光光，"奶妈边说，边努了努嘴唇，伯莎明白她的意思，她又在错误的时间来婴儿房了。

"她表现好吗，奶妈？"

"她一下午都是个小乖乖，"奶妈小声说。"我们去公园了，我坐在一张椅子上，把她从童车里抱出来，一只大狗走过来把头放在我的膝盖上，她一把抓住狗的耳朵，使劲拽。哦，你该看看那场面。"

伯莎想问她，让孩子抓一只陌生的狗的耳朵会不会很危险。但是她没敢问。她站在那里看着奶妈和小宝宝，两只手放在一侧，就像一个穷苦的小女孩站在一个拿着洋娃娃的富有的小女孩身边一样。

小宝宝又抬起头来看着她，目不转睛，然后非常可人地笑起来，伯莎再也忍不住了，她大声地说：

"哦，奶妈，就让我给她把饭喂完吧，你去把洗澡的东西收拾一下。"

"嗯，夫人，她吃东西的时候不应该换人喂，"奶妈说，接着又嘟嘟囔囔道："这样会扰乱她的心情，很可能会让她感到不高兴的。"

多么不可思议呀。如果生了孩子就得把她放到——不是像一把极其罕见的小提琴的匣子里——而是另一个女人的臂弯里的话，我为什么要生她？

"哦，我一定要喂她！"她说。

奶妈非常不高兴地把孩子送到她怀里。

"既然这样，那么不要让她吃完饭后太兴奋了。你知道，夫人，你让她兴奋了，之后我可有罪受了。"

谢天谢地！奶妈拿着浴巾走出了房间。

"现在你只属于我了，我的小宝贝儿，"伯莎说着，此时孩子依偎在她怀里。

她兴高采烈地吃着饭，一边撅起嘴唇够勺子，一边舞动着小手。一会儿，她咬住勺子不放；一会儿，伯莎刚舀好一勺饭，她就把勺子扒拉到一边儿去了。

给孩子喂完汤后，伯莎转向炉火。"你真可爱——你真太可爱了！"她边说，边亲吻着孩子暖暖的身体。"我喜欢你，太喜欢你了。"

的确，她太爱小宝宝了——宝宝向前欠身时露出的脖子，在火光的映衬下仿佛透明一般精致的脚趾头——她所有的幸福感又一次袭来，她再一次不知该如何表达这种感受——不知该如何是好。

"您的电话，"奶妈得意扬扬地回来，边说边一把抱回她的小宝宝。

她飞奔下楼。是哈里的电话。

"哦，是你吗，伯莎？是这样，我得晚会儿到。我会搭个出租车尽可能快点回去，晚饭推迟十分钟——好吗？行吗？"

"好，没问题。哎，哈里！"

"啊？"

她要说什么？她没什么要说的。她只想和他多说一会儿话。她不能莫名其妙地大喊："今天难道不是一个神圣的日子吗！"

"什么事？"对方小声地责问道。

"没什么。就这么定了，"伯莎说道，然后放下了话筒，心想，教养何止是愚蠢。

他们请了人来吃饭。诺曼爵士夫妇——非常值得信任的一对——他很快会开一家剧院，而她则痴迷于室内装潢。还有一位年轻人，名叫埃迪·沃伦，他刚刚出版了一本小诗集，人人都想和他共进晚餐。另外一位是伯莎的"发现"，名叫珀尔·富尔顿。富尔顿小姐是干什么的，伯莎一无所知。她们在俱乐部相识，伯莎爱上了她，她总是会爱上那些有点儿不同寻常的漂亮女人。

挑起她兴趣的是，尽管她们曾一起去过几个地方，见过好多次面，也确实谈过话，但是伯莎还是搞不清她是怎样一个人。她只知道富尔顿小姐真诚至极，世间少有，但除此之外她就一无所知了，仅此而已。

她还隐藏些什么吗？哈里说"没有"。他说她是个反应迟钝的人，而且"像所有金发碧眼的女人一样冷冰冰的，也许有点儿大脑缺血"。但是伯莎不同意他的说法，至少现在她绝对不同意。

"不对，看她坐着时头微微偏向一侧，还面带微笑那样子，背后一定有点什么，哈里，我必须搞清楚那背后到底是什么。"

"很可能说明她的胃口好，"哈里回答说。

他特意用那样的回答接伯莎的话茬……再不然就是"肝冷，亲爱的"，或者"纯粹是肠胃气胀"，或是"肾病"，等等。出于某种特殊的缘故，伯莎喜欢他这样说，而且达到了青睐有加的程度。

她走进客厅点燃炉火，然后把玛丽精心摆放的垫子一个接一个地捡起来，又把它们重新扔回到椅子和沙发上。这样一弄使房间看起来大不相同，立刻有了些生气。她正要扔最后一个垫子，却惊奇地发现自己突然间搂着垫子不放了，分外冲动。但这还是没能熄灭她胸中的火焰。哦，正相反！

客厅的窗户外面是一个阳台，从那里可以俯瞰花园。在花园的最远处，靠墙的地方，有一棵修长、纤细的梨树，树上满是盛开的鲜花；它亭亭玉立，在浅绿色的天空的映衬下，显得那么平静安详。就是站在这么远的地方看，伯莎还是会禁不住感到树上没有一个花蕾，也没有一片凋谢的花瓣。树下面，花坛里，红黄相间的郁金香，繁花紧簇，仿佛是在依偎着薄暮。一只灰猫，拖着肚子悄悄地爬过草坪，还有一只黑猫，它的影子，尾随其后。看到它们——那么专注又那么迅速，伯莎莫名其妙地打了个寒战。

"猫是多么让人毛骨悚然的动物啊！"她不连贯地说，转过身背朝窗户，开始走来走去……

在温暖的房间里长寿花真香啊。太香了吗？哦，不。她猛地倒在沙发上，像是被征服了一般，双手按在眼睛上。

"我太幸福了——太幸福了！"她低语着。

她仿佛在眼前看到了那棵可爱的梨树和它那盛开的花朵，那是她自己生命的象征。

千真万确——千真万确——她拥有一切。她年轻。哈里和她像以往一样深爱着对方，他们彼此相处得非常好，绝对是一对好伴侣。她有一个可爱的宝宝。他们不必为钱发愁。他们拥有这座相当令人满意的花园洋房。他们的那些既时尚又令人兴奋的朋友们——要么是作家、画家或诗人，要么是对社会问题有敏锐洞察力的人——都是他们乐于交往的。他们一起读书，一起听音乐，她还找了一个可爱的小裁缝为她做衣服，他们夫妇夏天出国去度假，他们的新厨子能做最美味的煎蛋……

"我真是想入非非，莫名其妙！"她直起腰来，但是觉得很眩晕，很沉醉。那一定是春天的缘故吧。

是啊，是春天。现在她感到太累了，无力上楼去换衣服。

白色礼服，一串玉珠链，绿色的鞋和长丝袜。这不是有意设计的。她站在客厅窗边的几个小时之前才想到这身装束。

她走进门厅，裙摆发出轻柔的沙沙声。诺曼爵士夫人正在那里脱她那件十分滑稽的橘黄色外套，外套的皱边和前襟有一排黑猴子图案。她吻了诺曼爵士夫人一下，表示欢迎。

"哎呀！哎呀！中产阶级怎么那么古板——没有丝毫幽默感。亲爱的，怎么说都是出于侥幸我才能来到这儿——有诺曼在，我才得以侥幸来到这儿。我心爱的猴子们把火车上的人惹烦了，他们都瞪起眼珠子，简直要把我吃了。谁也不笑——没觉得好笑——我本想看到他们会觉得好玩。但并非如此，他们只是盯着看——简直烦透了。"

"但是精彩的是，"诺曼边说，边把单边眼镜的龟甲镜框靠眼睛里推了推，"你不介意我提这事，对吧，'脸儿'？"（在他们家里以及朋友圈儿里，他们彼此称呼对方为"脸儿"和"缸子"。）"精彩的是，她吃饱喝足后，扭头对她旁边的女士说：'你以前没见过猴子吗？'"

"啊，是啊！"诺曼爵士夫人一起笑起来。"是不是太过精彩了？"

更为滑稽的是，她现在脱了大衣，看起来真像一只十分聪明伶俐的猴子——一只甚至能用扒开的香蕉皮做件黄色丝绸礼服的猴子。还有她那对儿琥珀色的耳环：就像两颗小坚果一样，摇来摆去。

"这真叫人大跌眼镜！""缸子"说着停在了小宝宝的婴儿车前。"当婴儿车推进厅里时——"他摆了摆手，没有把这句套用来的话说完。

门铃响了。是瘦削、面色苍白的埃迪·沃伦，（和以往一样）一副受苦受难的样子。

"是这家儿，对吧？"他一本正经地问。

"哦，我想是的——希望如此，"伯莎说，声音明快响亮。

"出租车司机真是太可恶了，他也太恶毒了。我叫他停，他偏不停。我越敲呀、喊呀，他就开得越快。月光下，这个蜷缩在小——小方向盘上，长着扁脑袋瓜的古怪家伙……"

他打了个哆嗦，摘下一个宽大的白色丝巾。伯莎注意到他的袜子也是白色的——非常扎眼。

"真是够讨厌的!"她大声说。

"可不是吗,"埃迪边说,边跟着她走进客厅。"我看见自己正坐着一辆永无休止的出租车穿越永恒。"

他认识诺曼爵士夫妇。事实上,等诺曼爵士夫妇的剧院建成,他就要为他们写一部剧。

"哎,沃伦,剧写得怎么样了?"诺曼爵士一边说,一边摘下眼镜,让他的眼睛能够在重新戴镜前露出来一会儿。

诺曼爵士夫人说:"哎哟,沃伦先生,多可爱的袜子呀?"

"真高兴您喜欢,"他盯着脚说道。"自打月亮升起来,我的袜子看起来白得多了。"他那张瘦削、可怜、年轻的脸转向伯莎。"你知道吗,月亮出来了。"

她真想大叫:"千真万确——常出来——常出来!"

他真是一个非常有魅力的人。"脸儿"也是,她穿着香蕉皮色的晚礼服蹲在火炉前,"缸子"也挺有魅力,他正在抽着烟,一边弹着烟灰,一边说:"新郎官儿为何踯躅在后?"

"他到了。"

砰的一声,前门开了又关上。哈里嚷道:"喂,你们好啊。五分钟就下来。"大家听到他爬上楼梯。伯莎忍不住笑了起来;她知道丈夫非常喜欢带着压力做事。其实,五分钟算得了什么呢?但是他愿意让自己相信五分钟要紧很。然后,他就能在走进客厅时显得那么潇洒冷静,让在座的人都注意他。

哈里对生活就是有这样一种强烈的爱。啊,她是多么欣赏丈夫这一点。他那种坚决抗争的激情——在所有与他作对的事情中,他都试图证明自己抗争的力量、勇气和激情——这,她也心领神会。即便在个别情况下,在别人——那些不熟悉他的人——的眼里,他可能会显得有些不可理喻……因为有时他会匆忙投入一场战斗,而其实根本就没仗好打……她说呀,笑呀,完全没有想起珀尔·富尔顿还没有来,直到他走进来(就像她所想象中的那样走进来)时,她才想起来。

"不知道是不是富尔顿小姐忘了?"

"我觉得是,"哈里说。"她能接到电话吗?"

"啊!来了辆出租车。"伯莎笑着,一副主人得意的模样。当她找来的女性没人认识,还很神秘的时候,她总会是这副样子。"她简直就住在出租车里。"

"真那样的话,她很快就会发胖,"哈里一边泰然自若地说,一边按铃示意开饭。"这对金发女郎来说特别危险。"

"哈里——别这样!"伯莎笑着提醒他说。

又过了一小会儿,他们一边等着,一边笑呀,说呀,那么无拘无束,那么不经意。随后,富尔顿小姐笑着走进来,一身银装,浅黄色的头发用一条银色的发带扎着,头微微偏向一侧。

"我迟到了吗?"

"没有,一点儿也没有,"伯莎说道。"来吧。"她挽着富尔顿小姐的胳膊走进餐厅。

碰触着她清凉的胳膊,伯莎感到有东西正在扇呀——扇呀——开始燃烧起来——燃烧起来——她不知如何处理那团幸福的火焰。

富尔顿小姐没看她,那只是因为她几乎从来不正面看人。她的眼睑厚厚的,奇怪而似笑非笑的表情浮现出来,掠过双唇,仿佛她是靠听活着,而不是靠看。但是她们彼此之间好像已经完成了那长长的、非常亲密的一瞥——就好像是她们已经对彼此说过:"你也是这个感觉?"——珀尔·富尔顿正在搅动盛在灰色盘子里诱人的红色汤汁,伯莎突然觉得富尔顿小姐脑子里想着的正是她自己所想的。

其他人呢?"脸儿"和"缸子",埃迪和哈里,他们的勺子抬起来又放下去——用餐巾纸轻轻擦拭着嘴唇,把面包掰碎,无意识地摆弄着叉子和玻璃杯,一边还说着话。

"我是在阿尔法展演会上遇到的她——一个最最神秘、小巧的人物。她不仅剪了头发,而且还好像对她的腿、胳膊、脖子和她那可怜的小鼻子也都进行过非常恰如其分的修剪。"

"她是不是和迈克尔·奥特关系很密切?"

"那个写《假牙之恋》的人?"

"他想为我写一部剧。独幕剧。一个人,决定自杀。说他为什么要自杀和为什么不能自杀的所有原因。而就当他下定决心要么自杀,要么不自杀时——落幕。真是个不错的主意。"

"他要给剧本起个什么名儿——'胃的烦恼'?"

"我觉得我在一本不起眼儿的法国评论里见过同样的构思,在英国根本没有人知道那本杂志。"

他们在一起却各谈各的。他们是顶可爱——顶可爱的人——她喜欢让他们来这儿吃饭,为他们准备可口的食物和酒。事实上,她想告诉他们,他们是多么令人愉快,他们聚在一起叫她多有面子,他们彼此互相凸显个性,她不禁想起了契诃夫的一部剧!

哈里正吃着饭。他谈论起食物,对"龙虾的白肉和开心果味冰淇淋中的绿色——那绿、那冷就像埃及舞女的眼皮一样——所产生的毫无掩饰的热情"颇为自豪。这些是他的——唔，确切地说，不是他的本性，当然也不是他的一种姿态——是他的——某种属性或是其他什么。

他抬起头来看着妻子说："伯莎，这奶酥的味道真是棒极了！"伯莎简直就要像个孩子一样喜极而泣了。

啊，今晚她为何会对整个世界都那么温情脉脉？一切都很好——都很适宜。所发生的一切似乎再一次充满了她那本来已满溢的幸福之杯。

尽管如此，在她的脑海深处还有那棵梨树。现在它该是银色的了吧，在可怜又可爱的埃迪的月光下，就像富尔顿小姐一样的银色，她坐在那里，用那双纤细的手指摆弄着一个橘子，她的手指那么的白，仿佛发出了一丝光亮。

她怎么也弄不明白——想不通——的是，她怎么能这么准确、这么迅速地就能猜出富尔顿小姐的心情。因为她从来就没有对她的正确判断有过一丝怀疑，然而，她还得继续做些什么呢？什么都不用做了。

"我相信这种事在两个女人间是很少、很少发生的。在两个男人间从来就没有过，"伯莎心想。"但当我在客厅准备咖啡时，她可能会'显现某些迹象'。"

她怎么会那样想，她不知道，之后又会发生些什么，她也无法想象。

这样想着，她看到自己一边聊天，一边笑。她不得不聊个不停，因为她太想笑了。

"我必须得笑，要么就得死掉。"

但当她注意到"脸儿"把她紧身胸衣前面的什么东西往下压的那个滑稽小动作时——就好像是她也在那儿秘密地藏了一小堆坚果似的——伯莎不得不用指甲戳手——为的是别笑得太厉害了。

最后晚餐总算结束了。"来看看我的新咖啡机，"伯莎说。

"我们只是两星期才换一次新咖啡机，"哈里说。"脸儿"这次挽着她的胳膊，富尔顿小姐低着头跟在后面。

客厅里的火已经熄灭，变成了一个红色摇曳不定的"凤雏的巢穴，""脸儿"形容说。

"先别点灯。太美了。"她又蜷缩在火炉旁边。她总是觉得冷……"当然，这是因为她没穿那件红色的小法兰绒半大衣的缘故，"伯莎心想。

就在这时，富尔顿小姐"显露了迹象"。

"你家有花园吗？"她的声音镇定、倦怠。

这声音对伯莎来说太优美了，她能做的只有顺从。她穿过房间，把窗帘拉开，推开那扇长长的窗户。

"在那儿！"她吸了一口气。

两个女人肩并肩地站在一起，看着那棵纤细、开满鲜花的树。尽管它看起来是那样的沉寂，就像是蜡烛的火焰一般，在鲜亮的空气中向上伸展着，指向着，战栗着，在她们盯着它看时越长越高——几乎要够到那盘浑圆的银月亮的边缘了。

她们在那儿站了多久呢？可以说，她俩都被那超灵的光环裹住了，彼此甚为相知，都是另一个世界里的生灵，都在思索着她们将要在这个世界里干些什么，用在她们胸中燃烧着的、从她们的头发和手中如银花般掉落的福佑宝物去干些什么？

是永远——还是瞬间？是富尔顿小姐在小声说"是的，就是它"，还是伯莎在做梦？

猛然间，灯被点亮了，"脸儿"煮了咖啡，哈里说："我亲爱的爵士夫人，别问我关于我孩子的事。我从不瞧她。等到她有了情人，我才会对她有点儿兴趣。""缸子"把他那温暖的单片眼镜摘下来一会儿，然后重新戴上；埃迪·沃伦喝了口咖啡后把杯子放下，一脸苦相，好像是他喝下了一只蜘蛛，还看到了。

"我想做的就是给年轻人们一次表现的机会。我相信伦敦到处都是一流尚未成文的剧本。我想对他们说的是：'剧院在这儿呢。向前冲吧。'"

"要知道，亲爱的，我要为雅各布·内森夫妇装修一个房间。哦，我十分有兴趣做一个炸鱼的图案，把椅子的后背做成平底锅的形状，窗帘的四周都绣上可爱的土豆片。"

"咱们的文学青年的问题是他们仍旧太过于浪漫了。在海上你不可能不晕船，不要盆子接着。唔，他们怎么就没有盆子的勇气呢？"

"这首讨厌的诗讲述了一个被没鼻子的乞丐在一个小——小树林里非礼的女孩的故事……"

富尔顿小姐深深地陷在一把最矮的椅子里，哈里向所有在座的人递烟。

他站在富尔顿小姐前面，边晃动那个银盒子边唐突地说："埃及的？土耳其的？弗吉尼亚的？都混在一起了。"从他的姿势，伯莎可以看出富尔顿小姐不仅让他觉得烦，他是真讨厌她。富尔顿小姐说："不，谢谢，我不抽烟。"从她说话的方式，伯莎可以断定富尔顿小姐也觉察出了他的想法，而且为此颇感伤心。

"嘿，哈里，别不喜欢她。你对她很不公平。她人非常、非常好。再说，一个对我来说很重要的人，你怎么会有如此不同的感觉呢？今晚睡觉前我会试着告诉你所发生的一切，我和她有什么相同之处。"

在伯莎琢磨这些时，某种奇怪得近乎可怕的东西突然闯入了她的脑海。这看不见的东西带着微笑小声地对她说："很快这些人就要走了。这房子将安静下来——安静下来。灯会熄灭。你和他会单独待在那间漆黑的屋子里——温暖的床上……"

她从椅子上跳起来快步走到钢琴边。

"没人弹琴多可惜呀！"她大声说。"没人弹琴多可惜呀。"

伯莎·杨有生以来第一次渴望与丈夫做爱。是啊，她爱过他——当然，她以其他任何方式爱过他，唯独没有那种方式。当然，同样地，她明白他与众不同。他们经常谈论这事。最初发现她自己那么冷淡时，她曾备感焦虑，但是过了一段时间以后，好像就没事儿了。他们彼此那么坦诚——那么好的一对儿。现代人就是这点最好。

但是现在——热血沸腾啊！热血沸腾啊！这个字眼在她热血沸腾的身体里隐隐作痛！这是那种幸福感导致的吗？但是然后呢，然后呢——"亲爱的，"诺曼爵士夫人说，"你知道我们的不便之处。我们受制于时间和火车。我们住在哈姆斯特德。今晚真好。"

"我送你到门厅，"伯莎说。"我喜欢你们待在这儿。但是你们千万不能错过末趟火车。那样就太糟糕了，对吧？"

"走前喝杯威士忌吧，爵士？"哈里招呼道。

"不啦，谢谢，老朋友。"

伯莎为此和他握手时捏了一下他的手。

"晚安，再见，"她站在最上面的台阶大声说道，她感到自己的这个自我在和他们永别。

等她再回到客厅的时候，其他人也在起身告别。

"……那么你可以坐我的出租车走一段。"

"你太好了，有了那段可怕的经历以后，我再也不想独自搭出租车了。"

"这条街走到头儿，有出租车搭乘站，你可以在那里搭出租车。用不着走多少路。"

"那挺方便。我去穿大衣。"

富尔顿小姐朝门厅走去，伯莎跟随其后。就在这时，哈里差不多是从她身边挤了过去。

"我来帮你吧。"

伯莎知道他这是为他的粗鲁行为赎罪呢——她就由他去了。他在某些方面真像个孩子似的——那么冲动——那么——单纯。

只剩下她和埃迪两个人待在火炉旁边。

"我不知道你看没看过比尔克斯的新诗，叫《套餐》，"埃迪轻声说。"好极了。在最后一卷里。你有吗？我非常乐意指给你看。诗的第一行格外的美：'为什么总是番茄汤？'"

"我有，"伯莎说。她轻轻地走到客厅门对面的一张桌子旁，埃迪悄悄地跟在她后面。她拿起那本小书递给他，他们都轻手轻脚。

他找那首诗时，她把头转向门厅。她看见……哈里手里拿着富尔顿小姐的大衣，富尔顿小姐转过身背朝着他，低着头。他把大衣扔到一边，把手放到她的肩膀上，猛地将她转过来。从口形上看，他好像在说："我喜欢你。"富尔顿小姐则把她月光般的手指放在他的脸颊上，脸上挂着她那倦怠的笑容。哈里的鼻孔颤动着，他的嘴唇向后缩，咧开嘴，一副令人讨厌的笑容，他小声地说："明天。"富尔顿小姐眨眨眼睛示意："好。"

"在这儿呢，"埃迪说。"'为什么总是番茄汤？'这真是千真万确，你觉得呢？永远是讨厌的番茄汤。"

"如果你愿意，"是哈里的声音，声音很大，从门厅里传过来，"我可以打电话叫个车到门口来接你。"

"哦，不了。没有必要，"富尔顿小姐说，她朝伯莎走过来，纤细的手指朝她伸过来，让她握着。

"再见。非常感谢。"

"再见，"伯莎说。

富尔顿小姐的手又擎了一会儿。

"你家的梨树真可爱！"她咕哝着。

随后她就走了，埃迪跟在后面，就像是一只黑猫跟在灰猫的后面。

"我要休息了，"哈里说，声音极为冷淡镇定。

"你家的梨树真可爱——梨树——梨树！"

伯莎只是跑到那扇长窗旁边。

"哦，现在又会发生什么呢？"她哭泣道。

但是那棵梨树还是和往常一样可爱，开满了鲜花，仍旧那样寂静无声。

Joyce Cary
(1888—1957)

Joyce Cary was born in Londonderry, Ireland. His father, from a declining Anglo-Irish family, was a civil engineer in England. At seventeen, with an inherited income of £300, Cary studied art in Edinburgh and Paris, and then he decided that he could better express himself as a writer.

After the First World War, he settled in Oxford to write. Despite his publication of some short stories under a pseudonym, Cary struggled for ten years to translate his view of life into a novel. Once *Aissa Saved* (1932) was completed, he wrote with great fluency. It drew on his African years, as did *An American Visitor* (1933), *The African Witch* (1936) and *Mister Johnson* (1939), the last a memorable portrait of a native clerk. Ireland inspired *Castle Corner* (1938) and *A House of Children* (1941), an evocation of summers in his childhood which won the James Tait Black Prize.

Cary next drew on the art world for a complex trilogy, in which each book is narrated by one of three main characters. *Herself Surprised* (1941), *To Be a Pilgrim* (1942) and *The Horse's Mouth* (1944) are notable for the anarchic painter Gulley Jimpson. A second, more somber trilogy dealt with politics: *Prisoner of Grace* (1952), *Except the Lord* (1954) and *Not Honor More* (1955). A trilogy on religion was to follow, but Cary was dying; a single, uncompleted novel, *The Captive and the Free*, was published in 1959.

Cary's concern for artistic and political liberty also found an outlet in treatises such as *The Case for African Freedom* (1941) and *Art and Reality* (1956). He returned to Africa in 1943 to script the film *Men of Two Worlds* and films were also made of *The Horse's Mouth* and *Mister Johnson*.

New Women

The story "New Women" is a reflection of the New Women movement, which was a reaction to the gender role. Advocates of the New Women ideal were found among novelists, playwrights, journalists and political thinkers. The supporters' aim was to encourage women to liberate themselves from male domination, manage their lives and leave behind anything that might restrict their pursuit of happiness and self-realization. Joyce Cary's sympathy with women went happily along with his generous approval of emancipation of women and his indignation at the discrimination against women.

Samuel Thompson, civil servant, was the only child of Athenia Battersby, the famous feminist leader. She is said to have been the original inventor of the plan for burning letter-boxes. She designed the suffrage hat, and wrote a book proving that Shakespeare was Queen Elizabeth. But it is a shame for the modem generation of women to laugh at Athenia. They owe her a big debt. She had courage and character, she really did a great deal to get them votes and sacrificed much of herself in the process—her sense of humor, for instance.

She forbade marriage to her followers, as a degradation, but after women's votes were granted, she married Sandy Thompson, a feminist as enthusiastic as herself, and taught him to cook; in fact, made him a modern husband thirty years before his time. He would do the washing-up while she dashed out to meetings.

Not that Sandy was put upon. He himself proposed to do the washing-up and learned how to sew. He was a man of pugnacious temperament who loved any excuse for a fight. If he had not been brought up a Christian pacifist, he would have made a first-class thug. As an organizer of suffrage demonstrations, he loved to bash policemen, and he hemmed dusters to show how much he considered women a superior sex.

Their marriage was very happy in its own way. But dedicated parents are bad for children, whose imaginations, like their bodies, cannot bear to remain fixed in any one position. Samuel had an austere upbringing—both parents taught him from his earliest years that boys were little better than brutes. But, as friends later pointed out to him, he had no right to complain of anything, he was lucky to exist at all, and had almost certainly been an accident. Athenia was even more against motherhood, at least for feminist pioneers, than marriage. She held that responsible educated women should devote themselves to the professions, in order to take a commanding place in the life of the country.

Samuel took the point and was humbly grateful for life, such as it was. He grew up a modest and retiring character. Even in his office in the Ministry of Energy, he was hardly known, except as a signature, by anyone outside his own staff. He belonged to no clubs and played no games except Patience. His bobby was collecting stamps, but he also took an absorbed interest in the latest scientific developments, as recorded in his morning paper, an old Liberal daily which, by tradition, gave at least half a column a week to general culture. The theory of the expanding universe occupied him for months and drove his acquaintances distracted. He was also extremely concerned in nuclear physics and the possibility of the disappearance of the world one morning owing to an accident at Harwell.

He especially avoided the company of women; he appeared a confirmed old bachelor. But at forty-six, to everyone's astonishment, he fell in love with one of the secretaries at the office and married her. Aminta was a very smart young woman direct from college and right up to date. She condescended to Picasso and was completely bored with the subject of homosexuality. She wore a Victorian cameo in her hat and had two fine drawings by Millais in her flat.

The wedding was in church. Aminta was a keen churchwoman. This was slightly embarrassing to Samuel, who had never even been baptised. Athenia Battersby had strong views about religion. As a scientist, she called it nonsense; as a feminist, a man-made device for the subjection of women. But Aminta pushed him through the service and he did not disgrace himself.

They settled in a charming little villa at Kew, Ruskin Gothic, and furnished it with some good mid-Victorian mahogany. Aminta was lucky enough to find a Clarkson Stansfield sea picture in a junk shop and to get it for ten pounds. This fine work gave great distinction to their sitting-room. Aminta's treasure was a gilt clock under an original glass dome, which required and received a draped mantelpiece.

Aminta now proposes to entertain Samuel's friends and is surprised to find he hasn't any. She has dozens of both sexes and all ages, especially friends from college. All these young women are in jobs or just married or both. They arrive every day to see Aminta, bringing small babies or bottles of claret. All of them want to see Samuel, and gaze curiously at him, tell him that Aminta will make a very good wife in spite of her intelligence, and, when they go away, say to each other, like all friends of a new-married person, "But how extraordinary—how on earth did it happen—can it last?"

They suspect that their dear but reckless Aminta has acquired Samuel as a collector's piece.

Samuel is embarrassed by all these young people, especially the girls. They shock him by their conversation about the most intimate details of their love affairs and the complexes of their lovers; they startle him by their strong views on the subject of marriage, and especially the duties of a wife and mother. They have no patience with a girl who can't cook, clean, wash, drive any make of car, mend linen, put in a fuse, do running repairs on household gadgets, choose, store and decant a respectable wine, and pick a smokable cigar at a smokable price.

As for children, they all want six apiece and take the view that if any child does not turn out a perfectly integrated and responsible member of society, the mother will be entirely to blame.

When Samuel dares to murmur that there can be bad fathers, they gaze at him for a moment and then say that no doubt mothers sometimes make that excuse, but it's not really an excuse. They obviously think that any woman ought to be able to cope with any kind of man, including the worst of fathers. Cope is their great word. Though polite to Samuel, they don't take him very seriously. When he raises the question of the expanding universe one evening, he is assured by two girls at once, of whom one has taken a first-class in mathematics and is a Fellow of her college, that it is a stunt for the tabloids. The universe, they say, can be made to dance the polka with a suitable equation; it depends only on which system you use. The mathematician, who is in the eighth month of her second child, then returns to the subject of lyings-in. Is it better to have a monthly nurse at home or go to hospital? Either way things can go wrong, and then the party discusses some cases that have gone wrong, with the technical elaboration of experts. It is, for instance, quite wrong to suppose that the widest hips are a guarantee of safety. Samuel listens with horror, and breaks into cold sweats. Aminta is small, with an eighteen-inch waist and hips of that rare type that look slim even in jeans.

Aminta, after two months of marriage, is already expecting. She has been decided on six children from the age of ten. She, too, has had a feminist mother.

Samuel mutters in his sleep and wakes up with a moan. Next day he begins to flutter about Aminta like a nervous hen. She must not lift that chair, she must not use her arms, she must not run on the stairs, she must not go out this morning, it is too hot or too cold. Aminta laughs at him and obeys till he has gone to the office. Luckily, at this time his newspaper brings out some articles on painless childbirth, and Samuel rushes out at once to buy all the books. Aminta is commanded to do exercise, to learn how to relax. And she obeys. For Aminta herself has been a little apprehensive, even if she says nothing about it. What girl doesn't have some anxiety in her first pregnancy?

Aminta has lost her parents young, and her family was small and scattered—Service people. A naval cousin dropped in from Hong Kong one day with a real Chinese jar of the genuine ginger. An elder sister, an Anglican nun, brought her an original Negro carving from Central Africa. A great-aunt from the Midlands, who had sent her, for wedding present, a plated muffineer dating from her own wedding, asked herself for a week because she could stand anything except modern hotels.

She was a little thin woman of seventy-six with the complexion of a sea captain. Her nose was Atlantic blue, a dark fierce blue like the middle of a storm cloud. Her mahogany cheeks were as dark as a cabin door. Her forehead, a sharp line above her eyebrows, was dead white, like that of an old sailor. But she had not the suave and ingratiating manner of the liner captain; she was bluff and gruff. She had got her complexion from sixty years in the hunting field where she had made a distinguished career as the first woman M.F.H., at least of a smart pack.

Even in town she wore the mannish dress affected by pioneer women of the late eighties; a Tyrol felt, a double-breasted reefer, a man's hard collar and four-in-hand tie.

She was amazed and disgusted by the furniture, especially the gilt clock and the draped chimney board. "Good God," she said, "Just like my granny's, and she was a stuffy old relic even for Dawlish. All that dusty rubbish went out with moustache cups."

She thought the Stansfield equally out of date. She herself possessed a seascape, a Boudin: "But of course, I know this modern French stuff doesn't appeal to everyone."

She brought a brace of pheasants and two bottles of port, Croft '26. She instructed Aminta to cook the pheasants, an anxious job for so particular a gourmet, but she allowed no one but herself to decant the port.

And over a second glass that evening, she unbent so far as to say she could forgive Samuel everything but his mother.

"My God," she said, "what a disaster—that vote. When I was young, women ran the civilized world, let's say, France down to Longchamp and England up to Newmarket, but they don't run anything now, except those ridiculous nylons. My generation were people; we made ourselves respected, but you girls are just a sex. Look at the advertisements."

When she heard of Aminta's relaxing exercises, she snorted, "There you are—just what I said—as if women were all the same size and shape, just lumps of sex stamped out from the same batch of cake mixture and served up in the same frills."

She poured and savored her third glass, accepted a cigar, glanced at the name on the box, said, "How do you afford Havanas? You young ones today spoil yourselves."

"They were for you," said Aminta.

"I thought so," said she with the grim smile of an M.F.H. "Getting round the old fool on her weak side."

Suddenly she became extraordinarily genial, in the way of so many gruff old people who seemed astonished and overwhelmed at the least mark of affection. Probably the old woman paid for her local glory in loneliness. All at once she couldn't do too much for her dear Aminta and Sammy. She would send them game every week and her own recipe for bread sauce. She would order a dozen of burgundy at once—that was the stuff for breeding gals, nothing like it to make blood. As for the lying-in, there was only one man in England—one that a woman could trust—her own man, Dr McMurdo.

"He's delivered all the Hunt children for forty years, and he's set my collar-bone five times. He's been retired since the war, but he'd do anything for me. I'll bring him up at once to look over the ground."

And she wired the next morning. She belonged to the generation before phones.

Samuel swore that no Blankshire bone-setter should come near his Aminta. But Dr McMurdo came the next day. It was apparently true that he would do anything for a lady so distinguished in history as Aminta's aunt. He was also in his seventies, an enormous man with a huge, round purple face and a great swag belly. He was dressed in a shaggy yellow tweed with four-inch blue check and a duster-pattern white flannel waistcoat. He ate and drank with all the gusto of a Falstaff. To see him at table would have been an inspiration to Stratford. He, too, was an expert on port. His manner with the patient was less fatherly than familiar. He did not exactly slap her on the behind after his examination, but it was more than a pat.

When she talked about her relaxing exercises and painless childbirth, he grinned like a satyr and answered with more affectionate pats, "Leave it to me, dear. That's what I'm here for. Just you relax."

And he winked at Thompson—a wink combining all the genial villainy of a Falstaff with all the cynicism, as Thompson put it, of an abortionist. And, as soon as Aminta had her first real pain, out came the chloroform mask. She knew nothing more till she woke up feeling beautifully flat and heard, as in the far distance, a baby crying somewhere, and gradually realized that this was her baby.

After that, it somehow came about that McMurdo attended also for the other two children. They are brought up in the new style, to mind their manners, and to get up when their papa comes to table—just as Aminta promised to obey, so she says a house must have its head and supports the authority of the father. The result is that when she threatens them, "I'll tell Papa," they become instantly as good as gold and amenable as lambs. They are happy, lively, and reasonable; they have no moral problems and always know the right thing to do even when they don't mean to do it.

The Thompson family, in short, is a very happy one—Aminta's friends, who assured Samuel that her intelligence would not prevent her from making a success of marriage, were night, Samuel adores her. Their only subject of occasional difference is the vote. As a son of his mother he thinks Aminta takes the vote too lightly.

Not that she despises it. "Of course, it's a thing one has to have," she says, "like mumps. But why do they always have elections on wet days and put the polling booths in back-yards among municipal dustbins? What do votes do after all?"

Though Aminta makes a great deal of Samuel's authority as master of the house, it is noticed that she runs everything; looks after all the money, pays all the bills, even at Samuel's new croquet club, drives the car and chooses the family holiday. What's more, when in that frantic fortnight before Budget Day, Samuel, like all senior Government clerk, brings back memos in the evenings and even for the Sunday, she will sit down and knock up a quite masterly report on the Calorific Value of Brick Dust, or the Profitable Utilization of Factory Smoke.

In this happiness, Samuel has bloomed in a late florescence. He has given up stamps and collects glass paperweights. He wears a bowler and fancy waistcoat. His trousers grow narrower and narrower. He says that nowadays there is so little difference between political parties that old Liberals like himself might as well vote blindfold. And last election he very nearly did vote Conservative. The only reason why he refrained at the last moment was because he discovered that the Liberal candidate was a strong supporter of Sunday observance, and he has become a devoted churchman with a leaning to evangelism. In short, he is nearly a new man.

Questions

1. What is the author's point of view? Discuss its appropriateness.
2. Who are the new women as referred to in the story? What are the common features assigned to the new women?
3. Is Aminta one of the new women? How does she leave behind the things that might restrict her pursuit of happiness and self-realization?
4. What has transformed Samuel into a new man at last? What does his final attitude towards the vote indicate?
5. Discuss the role of Aminta's great aunt. Is she one of the new women? Why or why not?

乔伊斯·卡里
（1888—1957）

乔伊斯·卡里出生于爱尔兰的伦敦德里。他的父亲是一个土木工程师，出生于破落的英裔爱尔兰家庭。17岁时，卡里继承了300英镑，在爱丁堡和巴黎学习美术。之后，他决定当作家以便更好地抒发自己的情感。

第一次世界大战以后，他定居牛津开始写作。虽然他已经用笔名发表了几篇短篇小说，在此后的十年里，他努力将自己对生活的感悟写进长篇小说。《被拯救的阿伊萨》（1932）完成之后，他的写作变得更加流畅顺利。这部小说的灵感来自于他在非洲的经历，后来的三部作品《一位美国客人》（1933）、《非洲女巫》（1936）和《约翰逊先生》（1939）也同样取材于非洲的生活，其中最后一部令人难忘地描绘了一位当地的职员。爱尔兰同样给他灵感，他写就了《城堡一隅》（1938）和《孩子们的房屋》（1941），在其中回忆了他儿时夏季度假的经历，并且因此赢得了詹姆斯·泰特·布莱克奖。

卡里也从艺术世界获得灵感，写就了复杂的三部曲，其中每一本小说都是由一位主人公担当叙述者。《她自己大吃一惊》（1941）、《成为朝圣者》（1942）和《马嘴》（1944）中都出现了那位无法无天的画家古利·吉姆逊。卡里的第二个三部曲是关于政治的，包括《优雅的囚徒》（1952）、《除了上帝之外》（1954）和《没有更多荣誉》（1955），书中的笔调更加忧郁。之后，卡里又计划写作一个宗教三部曲，但是生命垂危的他已无法完成。最后一部小说《被俘的和自由的》没有完成，但还是在1959年发表了。

卡里对艺术和政治自由的关心还体现在很多论文中，例如《非洲自由的案例》（1941）和《艺术和现实》（1956）。为了撰写电影剧本《两个世界的男人》，他在1943年又回到非洲，后来他的小说《马嘴》和《约翰逊先生》也先后被拍成电影。

新女性

短篇小说《新女性》的创作灵感来自于新女性运动。这个运动是对性别角色的反应。很多小说家、戏剧家、记者和思想家都非常同情和赞成新女性运动，这些支持者的目的是鼓励女性解放自己、摆脱束缚，从而获得幸福以及实现自己的人生价值。在这部短篇小说里，卡里表达了对女性的同情、对妇女解放运动的支持以及对各种歧视的愤慨。

塞缪尔·汤普森是一个小公务员，是艾瑟尼娅·巴特斯比的独生子。艾瑟尼娅是著名的女权运动的领袖，据说是她首创了焚烧信箱的计划。她设计了选举帽子，并且写书证明莎士比亚就是伊丽莎白女王。嘲笑艾瑟尼娅的新时代女性应该感到羞愧，因为她们都亏欠于她。她有勇气、有个性，费尽苦心帮助她们取得了选举权。在这个过程中，她自我牺牲了很多，例如她的幽默感。

她禁止自己的追随者结婚，认为那是堕落。但是在女性取得选举权之后，她嫁给了同样热衷于女权运动的桑迪·汤普森。她教会他烹饪，并且将他培养成了一个现代丈夫，让他领先于自己的时代三十年。每当她匆忙出去参加会议的时候，他都会洗洗涮涮。

桑迪并非被迫做这一切，他自己主动要求刷盘子洗碗，还开始学习缝纫。他生性好斗，总喜欢借机打架。如果他没有自幼被培养成为一个信奉基督教的和平主义者，他一定会成为一流的暴徒。作为争取选举权示威游行的组织者，他喜欢痛打警察，还给抹布镶边以显示他确信女性的优越性。

他们享受着与众不同的幸福婚姻。但是事业型的父母对孩子们无益，他们的想象力和身体都没法固定于某处。塞缪尔的家教非常严，父母从小就告诉他男孩子比野兽也好不到哪儿去。后来朋友们又指出，他没有权利抱怨，他能够生存就已经很幸运了，因为他的出生根本就是一个意外。相对于婚姻来说，艾瑟尼娅更加反对女权运动者做母亲，至少她认为作为女权先驱者应该如此。她坚信那些受过良好教育、负有责任心的女性应该献身于事业，这样才能在本国的生活中处于主导地位。

塞缪尔明白了这些，他对现有的生活充满了谦卑的感恩之情。长大后的他谦虚谨慎、离群索居。甚至在能源部他本人的办公室，他也很少为人知晓；除了他的助手们之外，别人只知道他的签名。他没有参加任何俱乐部，单人纸牌是他唯一的游戏。他的爱好是收集邮票，然而他对晨报上登载的科学研究的最新发展也颇为关注。这是一份很老的自由主义者晨报，按照传统，每周都用至少半个版面刊登大众文化的内容。宇宙扩张的理论占据他的头脑长达数月之久，并且让所有认识他的人都心烦意乱。他对核物理也非常关注，生怕哈维尔实验室的一个事故会使得整个世界在某个早上突然消失。

他小心回避和女士们在一起，看起来像个坚定不移的老单身汉。让所有人震惊的是，在46岁的时候，他居然爱上了办公室里的一名秘书，并且和她结婚了。阿明塔年轻、聪明，刚刚大学毕业，非常时尚。她对毕加索不屑一顾，对同性恋已经彻底厌倦了。她的帽子上镶有一块维多利亚时期的宝石，家里珍藏了两幅米莱的画作。

婚礼是在教堂举行的，阿明塔是位虔诚的女信徒。塞缪尔觉得稍有尴尬，因为他都没有经历过浸礼。艾瑟尼娅·巴特斯比强烈反对宗教。作为一个科学家，她认为宗教是胡言乱语；作为一个女权主义者，她认为宗教是男人臣服女人的工具。但是阿明塔还是帮助他完成了典礼，他也并没有失态。

他们居住在哥特拉斯金丘区的一个迷人的小别墅，家具是用上等的维多利亚中期的桃花心木制作的。阿明塔幸运地在旧货店发现了克拉克森·斯坦斯菲尔德一幅海洋的绘画，花10英镑买了下来。这幅作品让他们的卧室别具一格。阿明塔的宝贝是一个镀金的钟表，被放置在一个别致的玻璃圆顶下面，与之相配的是一个被围帘遮住的壁炉架。

阿明塔建议要招待一下塞缪尔的朋友，却惊讶地发现他一个朋友也没有。她的朋友男男女女、老老少少，共有十几个，特别是那些大学里的同学。所有这些年轻的女朋友有的工作了，有的结婚了，或者二者俱全。她们每天都来看望阿明塔，带上自己的小孩，或者是红葡萄酒。她们都想看看塞缪尔，她们好奇地瞧他，告诉他虽然阿明塔很聪明，但是她会是一个好妻子。但当她们离开时，就会像所有新婚夫妇的朋友那样，互相议论。"多么离奇啊——这究竟是怎么回事——这会持续多久？"

她们怀疑可爱却又草率的阿明塔会把塞缪尔当作一件藏品。

这些年轻人让塞缪尔感到尴尬，特别是那些年轻的女孩子。让他震惊的是，她们竟然谈论自己风流韵事中最隐私的细节，谈论她们情人的癖好。她们对于婚姻的强硬态度也让他很吃惊，特别是关于妻子和母亲的责任。对于那些不会煮饭，打扫，洗衣服，开车，缝补亚麻制品，上保险丝，修理家用电器，选择、贮藏和倒高档葡萄酒以及选择物美价廉的雪茄的女孩，她们不屑一顾。

至于孩子，她们每人想要6个，并且认为，如果某个孩子没有成为一个全面发展的、有责任心的公民，那完全是妈妈的责任。

当塞缪尔冒险嘟囔一句，也可能有坏爸爸，她们瞪着他，然后说，妈妈们无疑会以此为借口，但这不是理由。她们显然认为，每一个女人都应该有能力对付任何男人，包括那些最糟糕的父亲。"对付"是她们最喜欢的词汇。虽然她们对塞缪尔很礼貌，但是并不拿他当回事。一天晚上，当他提起宇宙扩张的问题，立刻得到了两名女孩子的附和，说那一定是小报的头条新闻。其中一个是数学方面的顶尖高手，并且是大学学会中的特别会员。她们说，找到合适的方程式可以让宇宙跳波尔卡舞，这完全取决于你使用哪个系统。那个数学家的第二个孩子已经八个月了，她又回到了分娩的话题。是请个护士在家好呢，还是去医院好呢？这两种方式都可能出问题，然后她们又讨论了一些反面的例子以及专家们的技术指导。例如，认为臀部肥大就能够保证安全的想法是错误的。塞缪尔恐惧地听着，出了一身冷汗。阿明塔身材娇小，十八英寸的腰围，即使穿着牛仔裤，臀部也显得非常小。

结婚两个月之后，阿明塔就怀孕了。她从10岁的时候就决定要生6个孩子，她的妈妈也是个女权运动者。

塞缪尔在睡梦中嘀咕着，醒来的时候也呻吟着。第二天，他就像一只焦虑的母鸡一样围着阿明塔转来转去。她不能搬椅子，不能挥动手臂，不能在台阶上跑，早上太冷或太热的时候都不能出去。阿明塔嘲笑他，服从他的命令，直到他去上班。幸运的是，这时他在报纸上看到了几篇无痛生产的文章，塞缪尔立刻冲了出去，买回了所有这方面的书籍。阿明塔被勒令锻炼身体，学习如何放松，她服从了。因为她自己也有些担忧，虽然她并没有说出来。哪个女孩子能在第一次怀孕的时候就一点也不担心呢？

阿明塔年幼的时候父母就不在了，她的家人不多，并且居住得很分散——都是现役军人。一天，一个海军的堂兄从香港来探望她，给她带来一坛纯正的中国生姜。她的一个姐姐是英国国教的修女，送给她一个来自中部非洲新颖别致的黑人雕刻。一位生活在中部地区的姑姥姥送给她一个镀金的细孔瓶作为结婚礼物，这个细孔瓶是她自己结婚时候的。她姑姥姥犹豫了整整一周，因为她哪儿都能住，就是住不了现代化的宾馆。

她是一个身材矮小的女人，已经76岁了，脸上的皮肤粗糙得像一个船长。她的鼻子像大西洋一样蓝，那种黑暗而猛烈的蓝色就像是暴风雨中的乌云。她桃花心木一般的面颊就像舱门一样颜色深暗。她的额头在眉毛以上的部分颜色惨白，看起来像一个老兵一样，但是她却没有船长那样温和而迷人的举止，而是直率而生硬。60年的狩猎生涯让她的皮肤变成了那样，而她却开创了辉煌的事业，成为第一位猎狐犬主人，虽然只是一小群。

即使在城里，她的着装还是十分男性化：一顶蒂罗尔毡帽，一件双排扣水手上衣，男式的坚硬的衣领和打活结的领带。这样的装束是受了80年代末女权运动先驱们的影响。

她对那些家具感到震惊和厌恶，特别是那个镀金的钟表和被围帘遮住的壁炉台。"上帝啊，"她说，"这就像我祖母的家具，连德力士人都会觉得那是个乏味而老旧的古董。所有这些积满灰尘的垃圾都应该和那些胡子茶杯一起扔掉。"

她认为斯坦斯菲尔德也是非常过时，她自己也收藏了一幅海景图，是布丹的。"我当然明白，这种法国现代派的东西没有人会喜欢。"

她买了一对野鸡和两瓶波尔图葡萄酒，克罗夫特26牌子的。她教阿明塔怎样烹饪野鸡，这对于一位特别挑剔的美食家来说是个令人焦躁不安的工作，但是除了自己之外，她不允许任何人倒酒。

那天晚上，第二杯酒下肚之后，她彻底放松下来，竟然说出她可以原谅塞缪尔的一切，只是他妈妈除外。

"我的上帝，"她说，"多么大的灾难啊——那个选举。当我年轻的时候，女人经营着这个文明的世界，比如，法国的珑骧包和英国的纽马克特外套，但是现在她们不再经营任何东西，除了那些可笑的尼龙。我们那一代人得到了别人的尊重，但是你们这些女孩子就只有性了。看看那些广告吧。"

当她听说阿明塔的放松运动时，轻蔑地说："你们就是这样——就像我说的那样——就好像女人都是同样的尺寸和形状，就像从同一块大蛋糕上切割下来的性块团，然后添加同样的装饰来出售。"

她给自己倒上了第三杯，慢慢品尝着，点燃了一支雪茄。她的眼睛扫过盒子上的商标，说："你们怎么买得起哈瓦那雪茄？你们现在的年轻人真是太奢侈了。"

"那是给你准备的，"阿明塔说。

"怪不得呢，"她的脸上浮现出猎狐犬主人的那种令人生畏的微笑，"利用我这个老傻瓜的弱点来讨好我。"

突然，她变得无比亲切，就像很多坏脾气的老人，得到一点点关爱就感到惊讶，为之动容。也许这个老妇人付出了孤独的代价才取得了在当地的名声。一时间，她觉得不论为亲爱的阿明塔和山姆做多少事都不够。她会每周都给他们送自己的战利品，告诉他们面包沙司的配方。她会立刻订购十几瓶勃艮第红葡萄酒——那东西对怀孕的女孩子最有好处，没有什么比它更补血。至于分娩，全英国只有一个人——只有一个人值得女人们信任——她自己的男人，马克默多医生。

"四十多年里，他接生了亨特家所有的孩子，他曾经五次给我接合了锁骨。他战后就退休了，但是他愿意为我做任何事情。我会立刻让他过来熟悉一下环境。"

第二天早上，她就来了电报，她们那一代人是不习惯使用电话的。

塞缪尔发誓说，他绝不会让布兰克郡的接骨医生靠近他的阿明塔。但是第二天，马克默多医生来了。很显然，他愿意为阿明塔姑姥姥那样杰出的女性做任何事情。他也70多岁了，身材高大，长着一张巨大的、紫色的圆脸和一个巨大的、下垂的肚子。他穿了一件粗糙的花呢黄色外套，上面印有四英寸大的蓝色方格，外着宽松的白色法兰绒马甲。他像福斯塔夫一样兴致勃勃地吃饭喝酒，应该就是他的吃相给斯特拉福德镇的莎士比亚带来了灵感。他也同样是波尔图葡萄酒的专家。他对待病人的态度与其说是慈爱，倒不如说是亲近。检查结束后，他倒没抽她屁股一下，但也绝不是普通的一拍。

当她说起放松运动和无痛生产的时候，他笑得像个好色之徒，更加充满深情地拍着她说："亲爱的，这就交给我吧。这就是我来的目的，你尽管放松就好了。"

然后他冲着汤普森挤了挤眼睛——如汤普森所说，这个举止包含了福斯塔夫那种温和的邪恶和施堕胎术者的愤世嫉俗。阿明塔刚开始阵痛，他就拿出了氯仿麻醉面罩，于是她就什么也不知道了，直到醒来后感觉自己那么的平坦，并且听见远处一个婴儿在啼哭，接着才慢慢地意识到那是她的孩子。

在那之后，听说另外两个孩子也是马克默多医生接生的。他们接受的是新式的家教——要注意自己的举止，并且爸爸出现在餐桌边时应该起立——阿明塔也曾保证过会遵守这些规矩。她说每个家庭都应该有个"头儿"，因此应该维护爸爸的权威。结果，当她威胁孩子们，"我去告诉爸爸"，他们立刻就会改正错误，变得乖巧无比。他们没有道德问题，并且总会下意识做出正确的事情。

也就是说，汤普森一家非常幸福——阿明塔的朋友们曾经告诉塞缪尔她的智慧绝不会影响他们的婚姻幸福，看来她们是对的。塞缪尔非常喜欢她，他们之间唯一的分歧就是选举权的问题。作为一位女权运动先驱的儿子，他认为阿明塔对待选举过分冷淡。

她也并不是蔑视选举。"当然，选举权是每个人必须都拥有的，"她说，"就像腮腺炎一样。但是，他们为什么总在雨天投票，为什么总把投票站设在市政府后院的垃圾堆附近？选举是为了什么？"

虽然阿明塔努力营造塞缪尔一家之主的权威，但是人们还是注意到，她经营着家里的一切，掌管着所有的收入，付各种账单，甚至是塞缪尔槌球俱乐部的费用，开车，决定家庭休假的日期。并且，在预算日之前的疯狂的两周，塞缪尔和所有的资深政府公务员一样，都会在晚上，甚至星期天将备忘录带回家中。阿明塔就会静下心来，赶制一篇精湛的工作报告，谈论一下砖厂粉尘的生热价值或者工厂烟尘的有效利用。

在幸福的滋润下，塞缪尔迎来了迟到的花季。他放弃了集邮，改为收集玻璃镇纸。他戴着硬圆顶礼帽，穿着精美的马甲，他的裤腿也变得越来越窄。他说，现如今政党之间已经没有什么差别，像他这样的自由党人也可以闭着眼睛投票了。上次竞选，他就险些投给了保守党。他没有这样做的唯一原因就是，他突然发现自由党的候选人极力支持周日礼拜。他现在已经成为一个虔诚的教会成员，倾向于福音教派。简单地说，他几乎变成了另外一个人。

Dylan Thomas
(1914—1953)

Dylan Thomas, Welsh poet, storyteller and playwright, is well known for his works of comic exuberance, rhapsodic rhythm, and pathos. Thomas performed poorly at school but learned a lot in English poetry through his own efforts. At 16 he left school to work as a journalist, and at 21 he moved to London and developed his highly original verse style. He married Caitlin Macnamara who was to bear him three children. Thomas greatly enjoyed his success but drank excessively. His 1953 US tour ended in his death brought up by alcoholism. He is regarded as one of the 20th century's most influential poets.

The main themes of Dylan Thomas' poetry are nostalgia, death, sex and lost innocence. He adopted a bardic tone and claimed a priestlike function for the poet, well combining complex technical discipline with verbal harmonies. Many of his best-known poems are included in such collections as *Death and Entrance* (1946), *In Country Sleep* (1952) and *Collected Poems* (1952), among which is "Do Not Go Gentle into That Good Night". In addition to poetry, Thomas also wrote short stories and scripts for film and radio. His first stories included in *The Map of Love* (1955) and *A Prospect of the Sea* (1955) are much linked with his development as a poet. However, *Portrait of the Artist as a Young Dog* (1940) presents distinctively realistic and humourous scenes. The characteristic blend of humour and pathos is given lively expression in his play *Under Milk Wood* (1954). *A Child's Christmas in Wales* (1955), including his best-known prose, celebrates the characters, events, and presents in a child's experience of holiday.

The True Story

The following story is a grisly murder, the girl and her plan to do away with the woman upstairs for her money. Despite its compactness and simplicity, the story has tremendous impact. It reflects the dreamy girl's individual struggle from darkness towards some measure of light. Though the murder is committed, the girl has fulfilled certain repentance by her "flying".

The old woman upstairs had been dying since Helen could remember. She had lain like a wax woman in her sheets since Helen was a child coming with her mother to bring fresh fruit and vegetables to the dying. And now Helen was a woman under her apron and print frock and her pale hair was bound in a bunch behind her head. Each morning she got up with the sun, lit the fire, let in the red-eyed cat. She made a pot of tea and, going up to the bedroom at the back of the cottage, bent over the old woman whose unseeing eyes were never closed. Each morning she looked into the hollows of the eyes and passed her hands over them. But the lids did not move, and she could not tell if the old woman breathed. "Eight o'clock, eight o'clock now," she said. And at once the eyes smiled. A ragged hand came out from the sheets and stayed there until Helen took it in her padded hand and closed it round her cup. When the cup was empty Helen filled it, and when the pot was dry she pulled back the white sheets from the bed. There the old woman was, stretched out in her nightdress, and the colour of her flesh was grey as her hair. Helen tidied the sheets and attended to the old woman's wants. Then she took the pot away.

Each morning she made breakfast for the boy who worked in the garden. She went to the back of the door, opened it, and saw him in the distance with his spade. "Half past eight now," she said. He was an ugly boy and his eyes were redder than the cat's, two crafty cuts in his head forever spying on the first shadows of her breast. She put his food in front of him. When he stood up he always said, "Is there anything you want me to do?" She had never said, "Yes." The boy went back to dig potatoes out of the patch or to count the hens' eggs, and if there were berries to be picked off the garden bushes she joined him before noon. Seeing the red currants pile up in the palm of her hand, she would think of the stain of the money under the old woman's mattress. If there were hens to be killed she could cut the throats far more cleanly than the boy who let his knife stay in the wound and wiped the blood on the knife along his sleeves. She caught a hen and killed it, felt its warm blood, and saw it run headless up the path. Then she went in to wash her hands.

It was in the first weeks of spring that she made up her mind to kill the woman upstairs. She was twenty years old. There was so much that she wanted. She wanted a man of her own and a black dress for Sundays and a hat with a flower. She had no money at all. On the days that the boy took the eggs and vegetables to market she gave him sixpence that the old woman gave her, and the money the boy brought back in his handkerchief she put into the old woman's hand. She worked for her food and shelter as the boy worked for his, though she slept in a room upstairs and he slept in a straw bed over the empty sheds.

On a market morning she walked into the garden so that the plan might be cooled in her head. It was a fine May day with no more than two clouds in the sky, two unshapely hands closing round the head of the sun. "If I could fly," she thought, "I could fly in at the open window and fix my teeth in her throat." But the cool wind blew the thought away. She knew that she was no common girl, for she had read books in the winter evenings when the boy was dreaming in the straw and the old woman was alone in the dark. She had read of a god who came down like money, of snakes with the voices of men, and of a man who stood on the top of a hill talking with a piece of fire.

At the end of the garden where the fence kept out the wild, green fields she came to a mound of earth. There she had buried the dog she had killed for catching and killing the hens. On a rough cross the date of the death was written backwards so that the dog had not died yet. "I could bury her here," said Helen to herself, "by the side of the grave, so that nobody could find her." And she patted her hands and reached the back door of the cottage before the two clouds got round the sun.

Inside there was a meal to be prepared for the old woman, potatoes to be mashed up in the tea. With the knife in her hand and skins in her lap, she thought of the murder she was about to do. The knife made the only sound, the wind had dropped down, her heart was as quiet as though she had wrapped it up. Nothing moved in the cottage; her hand was dead on her lap; she could not think that smoke went up the chimney and out into the still sky. Her mind, alone in the world, was ticking away. Then, when all things were dead, a cock crew, and she remembered the boy who would soon be back from market. She had made up her mind to kill before he returned, but the grave must be dug and the hole filled up. Helen felt her hand die again in her lap. And in the middle of death she heard the boy's hand lift the latch. He came into the kitchen, saw that she was cleaning potatoes, and dropped his handkerchief on the table. Hearing the rattle of money, she looked up at him and smiled. He had never seen her smile before.

Soon she put his meal in front of him, and sat sideways by the fire. As he raised the knife to his mouth, he felt full glance of her eyes on the sides of his eyes. "Have you taken up her dinner?" he asked. She did not answer. When he had finished he stood up from the table and asked, "Is there anything you want me to do?" as he had asked a thousand times. "Yes," said Helen.

She had never said "Yes" to him before. He had never heard a woman speak as she did then. The first shadow of her breast had never been so dark. He stumbled across the kitchen to her and she lifted her hands to her shoulders. "What will you do for me?" she said, and loosened the straps of her frock so that it fell about her and left her breast bare. She took his hand and placed it on her flash. He stared at her nakedness, then said her name and caught hold of her. She held him close. "What will you do for me?" She let her frock fall on the floor and tore the rest of her clothes away. "You will do what I want," she said as his hands dropped on her.

After a minute she struggled out of his arms and ran softly across the room. With her naked back to the door that led upstairs, she beckoned him and told him what he was to do. "You help me, we shall be rich," she said. He smiled and nodded. He tried to finger her again but she caught his fingers and opened the door and led him upstairs. "You stay here quiet," she said. In the old woman's room she looked around her as if for the last time, at the cracked jug, the half-open window, the bed and the text on the wall. "One o'clock now," she said into the old woman's ear, and the blind eyes smiled. Helen put her fingers round the old woman's throat. "One o'clock now," she said, and with a sudden movement knocked the old woman's head against the wall. It needed but three little knocks, and the head burst like an egg.

"What have you done?" cried the boy. Helen called for him to come in. He stared at the naked woman who cleaned her hands on the bed and at the blood that made a round, red stain on the wall, and screamed out in horror. "Be quiet," said Helen, but he screamed again at her quiet voice and scurried downstairs.

"So Helen must fly," she said to herself, "fly out of the old woman's room." She opened the window wider and stepped out. "I am flying," she said.

But she was not flying.

Questions

1. What is striking about the story?
2. Pick out sentences where figures of speech are used and discuss their literary effect.
3. Do you wish to write like Dylan? Do you think the writing style is straightforward? Why?
4. What is the implication of the word "fly" under the writer's pen?
5. Analyse the characteristics of the characters in the story.

迪伦·托马斯
(1914—1953)

爱尔兰诗人、小说家和剧作家迪伦·托马斯以其作品丰富的喜剧色彩、恣意的韵律和悲悯的情调而闻名。托马斯学业平平,但他自学英国诗歌收获颇丰。他16岁辍学做了记者,21岁搬到伦敦,形成自己风格迥异的诗风。他与凯特琳·麦克那马拉结婚,并育有三个孩子。托马斯生前即享有巨大成功,但他酗酒无度。1953年的美国之旅使他因酒精中毒猝死。他被誉为20世纪最有影响的诗人之一。

他的诗歌主要围绕着怀旧、死亡、性以及失去的童真。他采用吟游诗人的音调,认为诗人拥有牧师的功能,将复杂的创作技巧与和谐的语言表达完美地结合在一起。他的许多名诗收在《死亡与入口》(1946)、《乡村睡眠》(1952)、《诗选》(1952)等诗集中,其中最著名的一首是《不要悄悄走进那温柔之夜》。除此之外,托马斯还写短篇小说、电影脚本和广播剧。他早期的小说收入《爱之图》(1955)和《海景》(1955)中,与其诗人生涯密切相关。而《一个小狗艺术家的肖像》(1940)则显示出鲜明的现实主义和幽默诙谐的特点。幽默与悲悯的独特结合充分表现在剧本《牛奶树下》(1954)中。《威尔士孩子的圣诞节》(1955)收录了他写的最精美的散文,这些散文赞美了孩子过节时遇到过的人物、事件及收到的礼物。

真实的故事

下面的故事讲述的是一个可怕的谋杀案,一个女孩为金钱而谋杀了楼上的老妇人。尽管故事情节紧凑、简洁,但却具有很强的感染力。故事反映了一个充满梦想的女孩独自在黑暗中向光明奋争的过程。虽然女孩犯了谋杀罪,但她最终的"飞翔"也从某种程度上实现了自己的救赎。

自打海伦记事以来,住在楼上的那个老妇人就已经与死去无二了。她躺在那里如同一个蜡人。在海伦很小的时候,她就随着做女佣的母亲来到这里,为奄奄一息的老妇人带水果和蔬菜。现在,小女孩海伦已长大成人,她系着围裙,穿着印花上衣,浅色的头发在脑后束成一个马尾辫。每天清晨她都起得很早,先生火,然后开门放进那只红眼猫。她沏上一壶茶,来到村舍后方的卧室,俯身贴近老妇人,她那双眼睛看不见但却总是睁着。每天早上,海伦都要直对着这双深陷的眼窝，用手贴近她眼前晃动，但是老妇人的眼皮从来没有任何反应，她甚至怀疑她是否还在呼吸。"八点了，已经八点了，"她说。随着话音，那双眼睛突然笑了。从被子里伸出一双干枯的手，就一直那么伸着，直到海伦那双丰满的手握住它，并让它握住杯子。一杯水喝完了，海伦为她续上，一壶水喝干了，海伦把白色被褥从床上掀起来。老妇人就穿着睡衣四肢伸展着躺在那里，肤色就像她自己的头发一样灰白。海伦为她整理好被褥，伺候她方便，然后才拎着便壶离开房间。

每天早上，她还要给在园子里干活的男孩做饭。她走到后门，打开门就望见远处手提铁锹的男孩。"八点半了，"她说。那男孩长得很丑，一双眼睛比那只猫的还要红，脑袋前面两只贼眼总在窥视着她胸前乳房突出处。她把饭菜放在他的面前。每当站起来的时候，他都会问："你需要我做些什么吗？"但她从来没说过"好"。之后那男孩回菜地挖土豆，或是数鸡蛋；如果园子里的树丛上有浆果要摘，她就在中午前一起帮他摘。每当看见掌心里红红的果实越积越多，海伦总会想到老妇人床垫下钱的印记。每当杀鸡的时候，海伦总能干净利落地割断鸡的脖子，比那个男孩强得多；而那个男孩总会将刀滞留在刀口里，用衣袖抹去刀上的血迹。她则抓住鸡，一刀毙命，用手摸摸温热的鸡血，瞧着那无头鸡在小路上乱蹦，随后便进屋洗手去了。

那是在春天的前几周，她下定决心要杀掉楼上那个老妇人。她20岁，她想要的太多了。她要属于自己的男人、一件做礼拜的黑礼服、一顶带有缀饰的帽子，但她却身无分文。每当男孩去集市出售鸡蛋和蔬菜时，她就把老妇人给自己的六便士交给男孩，再把男孩包在手绢里卖东西换回的钱全部交到老妇人手里。她为了自己的吃住而干活，那男孩也为他自己的而干，只是她每晚睡在楼上的卧室里，而那个男孩只能睡在空工棚上层铺满麦秆的床上。

赶集的那天早上，她走进园子以使自己可以冷静地思考一下那个计划。那是五月晴朗的一天，天上不超过两朵云彩，像是两只不匀称的大手合拢在太阳的头上。"假如我会飞，"她思忖着，"我就能从敞开的窗户飞进去，用牙咬断她的喉咙。"但一阵凉风刮走了这一想法。她知道自己不是一个寻常的女孩，因为在无数个冬夜里，当那个男孩在麦秆床上进入梦乡时，老妇人独自躺在黑暗中时，她却在读书。她读到了财神爷下凡的故事、会说话的蛇的故事，还有一个汉子站在山顶上带着火演讲的故事。

在园子的尽头有栅栏将一片荒野绿地隔开，她走到那里的一个小土堆旁。土堆里埋的是她杀掉的狗，因为那只狗追赶并咬死过母鸡。在一个粗糙的十字架上倒刻着狗死去的日期，就算是这条狗还活着。"我可以把她埋在这儿，"她自言自语,"埋在这个坟墓旁边,这样就不会有人发现她了。"她轻轻地拍了拍手,在那两片云彩飘过太阳前,回到了村舍的后门。

在屋里,她要为老妇人准备晚饭,土豆泥和在茶水里。她手里握着刀,大腿上还粘着土豆皮,算计着自己行将实施的谋杀。屋里静得只能听到刀的声响,风声落下了,她的心跳声是那么的微弱,就好像被包裹起来一样。村舍里无丝毫动静,她的手在大腿上僵直不动,炊烟顺着烟筒冒出去,飘向寂静的天空,此时的她竟浑然不觉。她的思绪在孤寂中一分一秒地溜过。突然,在一片死一般的寂静中,公鸡鸣叫起来,她这才意识到那男孩就快从集市回来了。她决心已定,在男孩回来之前杀掉那个老妇人,但还要先挖好坟坑,然后再把墓穴填上。海伦又觉得自己的手在大腿上僵直不动。就在死神即将向老妇人逼近时,突然传来男孩开门的声音。那男孩来到厨房,看见海伦正在洗土豆,他把包着钱的手绢放到了桌子上。听见钱的响声,海伦抬起头冲着他笑了笑。他从未见她以前笑过。

很快她就把饭菜摆在他面前,然后坐到火炉旁。男孩举起刀往嘴里送吃的,这时他从眼角感到她一直在盯着他。"老妇人的饭送去了吗?"他问道。她却没有回答。吃完饭后,他从饭桌旁站起身随后又问道:"你需要我做些什么吗?"这是男孩重复过上千次的问话。"好啊,"海伦说。

海伦以前从来没对他说过"好"。他也从未听见女人像她这么说过。她的乳房突出部位的影子也从来没有映衬得这深。他笨手笨脚地穿过厨房向她走去,海伦两手抬向肩膀。"想为我做点什么吗?"她边说边松开了衣带,上衣顺着肩膀滑落下来,裸露出乳房。她将男孩的手抓过来,放了自己最吸引人处。男孩直盯着海伦裸露的胴体,然后喊着她的名字,一把将她抱了过来。她也抱紧了男孩。"想为我做点什么吗?"海伦让外衣滑落在地,然后褪下剩余的衣裙。"叫你做什么就做什么,"她说,男孩的手落在她身上。

海伦很快从他的怀里挣脱出来,轻轻地跑过房间。她将裸背对着上楼的门,召唤他过去,告诉他该做什么。"你帮我,我们就发了,"她说。那男孩笑了笑,点了点头。他又想伸指头摸她,但她抓住他的手指,随即开门,带他上楼。"你悄悄等着,"她说。在老妇人的房间,她像是最后一次环顾一遍屋里的一切,有那裂缝的茶壶、半掩着的窗户、床以及挂在墙上的经文。"现在是一点钟,"她冲着老妇人的耳朵说。那双瞎眼笑了。海伦用手指掐住老妇人的脖子。"现在是一点钟,"她说着,突然用力把老妇人的头向墙撞去。只稍微撞了三下,老妇人的头就像鸡蛋似的崩裂了。

"你干什么了?"男孩大喊起来。海伦招呼他进去。他惊恐地看着这个赤裸的女人正在床单上擦手上的血迹，墙面上也有一团鲜红的血迹。他惊叫起来。

"住嘴，"海伦冷静地说，但他还是狂叫着冲下楼去。

"好了，海伦也要飞了，"她自言自语，"从老妇人的房间飞出去。"她将窗户开大，然后一步跨了出去。"我飞了，"她说。

可她飞不起来。